PLAYING
& FOR KEEPS
A TEMPTING STRANGER

LORI COPELAND

LEISURE BOOKS   NEW YORK CITY

A LEISURE BOOK®

January 1993

Published by

Dorchester Publishing Co., Inc.
276 Fifth Avenue
New York, NY 10001

PLAYING
FOR KEEPS

CHAPTER ONE

The sound of a lone rooster loudly crowing its good morning to the world filtered slowly into the bedroom of the old two-story farmhouse as Jessica Cole nestled between the light sheets on the bed that had been hers through all her childhood years. She drowsily opened her eyes to see the faint streaks of dawn breaking gently over the horizon. Her eyes moved languidly around the old familiar room, stopping to rest lovingly on the small photograph sitting on her dressing table. The clear images of Uncle Fred, Aunt Rainey, and herself as a child laughed happily back at her. Tears filled Jessica's eyes as she allowed herself to think about why she had been summoned home once again.

It was still hard for Jessica to realize that Aunt Rainey had followed Uncle Fred so swiftly in death. Just six months ago Jessica had come home to help Aunt Rainey bury Uncle Fred under that same old spreading oak where they had laid Aunt Rainey to rest just two short days ago. Jessica sighed softly as she turned on her side, the faint light in the room growing ever brighter.

Uncle Fred and Aunt Rainey had been well loved in this small Texas town. Of that Jessica had been assured the morning of Aunt Rainey's funeral. Jessica had sat at the small grave site, her eyes roaming slowly over the old familiar faces that had been so much a part of Jessica's life ever since Uncle Fred and Aunt Rainey had taken her into their home as the child they were never able to have, following the death of her own parents in an automobile accident when she was only four years old.

She could still hear Aunt Rainey's weak voice, two days before her death, saying to her, "You were ours as surely as if I had given birth to you myself. Fred and I were never blessed with the children we always wanted," she whispered in a tired voice. "Not that the Lord hasn't been real good to us," she hastened to add. Her eyes took on a soft misty look as she continued. "We had each other, and I've thanked the good Lord every day for that, but there's just something special about a child in a man's life. It just kinda completes things. So when God seen fit to send you to us, well . . . You've been a good girl, Jessie, and we loved you," she finished.

"Oh, Aunt Rainey," Jessica murmured. "I loved both of you so much!" A tear slid silently down her cheek as the old rooster crowed once again. Was it only a few days ago that they had talked and held each other's hands, trying to give some small measure of comfort to each other?

Jessica shifted restlessly as she recalled the group of mourners, her mind unwillingly focusing on the tall man who had stood just to the left of the old tree, his hat in his hand, his head bowed. The sun glistened brightly on his thick golden-brown hair, causing Jessica to catch her breath momentarily. He was just a little over six feet tall, his tanned skin gleaming a dark bronze against the pale green of his western-cut suit. His shoulders were straight and broad. His massive chest tapered down to a lean waist and slim hips, where his perfectly tailored trousers were molded to his muscular legs and thighs. *There should be a law against anyone looking that good,* Jessica thought resentfully. Why was it her rotten luck to see him, on top of all the other painful old memories? Her eyes traveled slowly back up his perfectly proportioned body, and she blushed deeply as his brilliant jade-green eyes locked with her soft violet ones. She lowered her eyes quickly back to the grave.

Her attention snapped back to the comforting voice of the minister. As she heard his voice saying the amen she lifted her head once again and encountered the unwavering gaze of Jason Rawlings. The moment passed fleetingly as the mourners began moving away from the grave. Several stopped by the chair Jessica was sitting in to offer soft condolences, a gentle pat on the arm, words of sympathy. Pastor Franklin stepped to her side, taking her arm as they started slowly toward the long black limousine waiting at the side of the road. Her good-byes had been said the night before at the funeral home. Now it was simply a matter of getting to the car and driving away. Somehow it didn't seem to be enough. Her misty eyes rested on the light-gray casket one final time as the long black car pulled out of the cemetery onto the dusty road.

Now, in her bedroom, she closed her eyes for a moment, letting her thoughts drift lazily back to Jason Rawlings. Of course, he would have been there in spite of that one mad, crazy night eight years ago. He hadn't been at Uncle Fred's funeral because he had been out of town on business. Jason had been like a son to Fred and Rainey. Their property had adjoined his parents', and they had been good neighbors for many years.

Jessica smiled ironically as she pushed the covers back and got out of bed. Heading for the shower, she thought back to all the years she had had a crush on Jason. She had tagged after him, constantly under his feet, when she was growing up. All through high school her heart had leaped in her throat every time he had ridden over to do business with Uncle Fred or just to pay a visit to Aunt Rainey's kitchen, where there always seemed to be his favorite pie or cake.

There were three Rawlings boys, although you couldn't have proven it by Jessica. Her eyes never went beyond Jason. Being the eldest, he always seemed so much more mature, even though he teased her just as badly as Eric and Randall did.

As she stepped into the shower the clear, refreshing water cooled her burning skin. She remembered how as she developed into a lovely young woman Jason had continued to look on her as an annoying child until that one hot summer night when he had stopped by to ask Uncle Fred's opinion of a piece of new machinery he wanted to buy.

At seventeen Jessica had turned into a real beauty, able to hold her own with any rival. She had always been a thin child, but almost unnoticeably her young body had been taking on the softly feminine curves of womanhood. Her slim yet shapely body was a golden brown that summer from all the hours she had spent swimming in the local swimming hole.

Now she smiled with satisfaction as she soaped her body in gentle strokes. She smugly recalled how her high, firm breasts, tiny waist, and shapely sun-darkened legs had turned most of the local boys' heads. Her thick, lustrous raven hair was usually worn loose, which made her eyes, an unusual shade of violet framed by spiky, long lashes, appear larger than they really were. People who knew Jessica could safely judge her moods by the color of those eyes—a soft, seductive violet most of the time, turning to an angry, churning dark purple when she was upset. The inability to fully control her temper was really the only flaw in Jessica's otherwise sunny nature. She couldn't help it—it just got the best of her sometimes.

She turned in the shower to rinse off and thought back to that particular evening, when she had had a date with Jim Weston, one of the local boys. She had just stepped out of the house while waiting for him to pick her up when she saw Jason ride up on his horse and stop in the barnyard. Her heart jumped into her throat as the tall, lean figure dismounted agilely from his brown and white Appaloosa and shook hands with Uncle Fred. Jessica's eyes lingered on his form, involuntarily drinking in the sight of his handsome face as he talked quietly with her uncle. He glanced up momentarily, catching Jessica's hungry gaze. She blushed hotly as he bestowed one of those cute, sexy winks on her before going on with his conversation. Jessica was embarrassed that he had caught her so openly drooling over him. She slipped inside the small shed where Uncle Fred kept a small calf that had taken ill shortly after birth. Jessica had been giving it special care for the last few weeks, and the calf had shown rapid improvement. Kneeling down to pat the silky head, Jessica talked softly to the animal, marveling at the large brown eyes staring up so innocently into her own compassionate ones.

Shaking her head violently under the water, as if she could rid herself of the memory, Jessica leaned over to turn off the taps. She grabbed a towel and briskly dried herself, then hurried into her bedroom and put on the robe that she had left draped across the foot of the bed.

As Jessica came out of the bedroom she was met by Aunt Rainey's old tabby cat. Rubbing against her leg, Tabby turned sorrowful eyes up to Jessica.

"Poor baby," Jessica said comfortingly, reaching down

15

to scratch behind the soft furry ears. "You miss her, too, don't you?"

Picking the cat up in her arms, she continued on to the big airy kitchen that used to be so alive with the smell of breads and cakes baking or some other delectable aroma drifting from the old stove that sat in the corner. She put the cat down and headed for the coffeepot and plugged it in. Then she set a small saucer of cream down on the floor for Tabby and waited for the pot to perk.

Taking her coffee to the oak table sitting in front of the open window that looked out onto Aunt Rainey's backyard, she sat down. All her aunt's flowers were there to see, blooming in rare profusion, almost as if in silent tribute to her. Two lilac bushes were spilling their fragrance into the yard as Jessica's gaze found the big old "snowball bush" she had played under as a child for so many hours in the late summer evenings. As she drank in the fragrance her mind jumped back to that night Jason had come to her in the shed.

Jason had stepped into the dimly lit shed, his eyes squinting to adjust to the near darkness. "Are you in here, Angel?" He called her by the pet name he had always used when they were kids.

"Yes, Jason," she murmured, wishing desperately he would call her sweetheart or darling or something romantic just once instead of Angel. Angel sounded so—so young!

Jessica's pulse began to race as he knelt down beside her, the faint aroma of his aftershave washing over her. His large hand reached out to stroke the calf's side gently before his eyes roamed slowly over the low cut of her beige sundress, his emerald gaze boldly fastening on her voluptuous breasts. Jessica met his blatant stare, her eyes beginning to sparkle dangerously.

"Mercy!" Jason seemed at a loss for words. A cocky little grin spread rapidly across his face. "When did you, 'er . . . grow up, little girl?"

16

Jessica flushed a bright crimson as she tried to pull the top of her dress up a little farther. "What's the matter, Jason? Isn't Marcy—grown-up?" she retorted snidely. Marcy Evans was a *gorgeous* redhead Jason had been dating for the last few months.

Jason shook his head longingly, that little grin still on his handsome face. "Not as—uh—grown-up as you are, Jessie."

Jessica stood up, totally disgusted with the whole conversation. "Excuse me, Jason, but I have a date." She tossed her head regally and started around him.

Jason stuck his muscled arm out on the rafter directly behind her, blocking her exit. "What's your hurry, Angel? I didn't hear a car drive up."

Jessica felt as if someone had suddenly shut off the supply of air to her lungs. Jason's face was dangerously close to hers now, his beautiful green eyes languidly running over her slightly flushed face. Jessica began to tremble as he brought one large hand up to cup her face gently.

"Damn, little Jessie!" he whispered huskily. "I think you've turned into a woman while I wasn't looking."

Jessica smiled weakly, her eyes locked hypnotically with his. "You *definitely* have not been looking. I can testify to that!" She laughed shakily.

"How old are you now, anyway?" Jason ran the tip of his finger around the creamy perfection of her jawline, turning Jessica's knees to water.

"Seventeen."

"Is that a fact? Seventeen," he mused lightly, his soft breath fanning her face. Jessica moistened her lips with the tip of her tongue, the feeling of light-headed giddiness assailing her now. "I wonder what it's like to kiss a girl of seventeen," Jason teased softly, his fingers tracing soft patterns along her face.

"I'm sure if anyone would know, you would," Jessica breathed unsteadily, her hands working their way up shyly around his neck. This had to be some glorious,

17

wonderful dream, and Jessica prayed she'd never waken from it.

Jason's arm dropped from the rafter to encircle her waist, tenderly drawing her closer to his lean, taut thighs, his breathing quickening. "No, you're wrong there, Angel. My women are usually a little older than seventeen"—he grinned—"but I have a feeling I'm about to establish a new record—even for me." He brought his mouth down to brush gently across Jessica's quivering lips. At first contact with Jason's mouth Jessica grew even weaker, and she leaned feebly against his granite frame.

"What's the matter, Angel, haven't you ever been kissed before?" He drew back hesitantly, his face seriously scanning Jessica's.

"Of course I've been kissed before," Jessica whispered raggedly. "Just never—by you."

Jason's mouth turned up in just a hint of a smile as he brought his mouth close to hers. "And you *still* haven't been kissed by me, but I plan on taking care of that . . ." His mouth came down gently, then opened more fully over hers, his tongue reaching out to search demandingly for hers. Jessica had been wrong! She had only thought she had been kissed. *Never* had she been so totally caught up in a man's arms, so completely powerless over her own body. She surged against Jason, her arms wrapped tightly around his neck, her body straining for closer contact with his. The kiss deepened as Jason's hands came up to cup one of her breasts tenderly, the soft white mound fitting perfectly in his large hand . . . almost as if it had been made for his hand only.

"Jessie! Where are you, girl?" The booming voice of Uncle Fred rang out as Jessica and Jason broke apart, breathing in quick, short spurts.

"Jim's here, Jessie."

Jason dropped his arms from around Jessica's waist reluctantly. "Your date's here."

"I know," she whispered.

"Well, old woman of seventeen," he said, drawing her back for one last long kiss, "I'll be seeing you around. Thanks for my lesson on kissing—uh—younger women!"

Jessica was still having difficulty in catching her breath as she gulped, "You're welcome. And thank *you*," she finished timidly.

Jason pushed his Stetson back on his head, eyeing her seductively, his mouth forming a wicked grin. "My pleasure, Angel."

Jessica stepped out of the shed, her pulse still pounding. She had just experienced one of the most wonderful events of her life, but she really wished it had not happened. Although it was something that she had daydreamed and fantasized about over and over again, she knew it would only be harder now. There would never be a future for her and Jason. He was ten years older than she, and no matter what had taken place a few minutes ago, she was still "little Jessie Cole" to him.

The next few days dragged by slowly for Jessica, her mind unwillingly reliving the moments in Jason's arms that hot evening in the old shed. She would wake in the middle of the night from a fitful sleep and lie in her dark room remembering the feel of his persuasive mouth on hers, and tears would rise swiftly to her eyes as a sense of total helplessness engulfed her. In a few weeks she would leave for college and never have the opportunity to see him except on occasional visits home. Sighing softly, she would toss restlessly and stare out the large window beside her bed. The quiet sounds of the night would fill the room as Jessica's eyes drooped sleepily. Her last coherent thoughts before sinking back down into soft gray mist would be of golden-brown hair, kissed by the sun, and the most beautiful jade-green eyes God had ever put on this earth.

Jessica came back to the present with a sense of deep loss and took her empty cup to the sink, rinsed it out, and put it in the side drainer. She'd better finish packing away some of Aunt Rainey's personal possessions, she decided reluctantly.

She had worked steadily through the hot morning, removing old memories, when it suddenly occurred to her that she wanted to stay here in the old house that held so much of her past. *Well, why not,* she reasoned. She had no real ties in Austin. She could easily inform the school that she would not be back this fall. For the last four years she had taught home economics in the local school system there, living in her small garage apartment, not far from the school.

Yes, she pondered, *why not move back here?* Maybe with the inheritance she would receive from the estate she could start her own little catering business, something that had been on her mind now for quite awhile. Even though the town was small, she thought that it could accommodate such a business. Nothing elaborate, just something big enough to support her and give her the opportunity to do what she loved best—cook (or "create," as her professor in college always said).

For a brief moment Jessica let her mind teasingly play around with the idea of what her life would have been like if Aunt Rainey and Uncle Fred had not intervened in her marriage to Jason. Right now she would probably have a home of her own to care for. That's what she really wanted more than anything in the whole world. She couldn't wait for the day when she would have her *own* yard full of flowers and children to care for and a husband to cuddle close to every night and share the wild, joyful union she had experienced with Jason that one wonderful night eight long years ago.

Jessica sighed wistfully, taking another one of Aunt Rainey's dresses and folding it. Here she was, twenty-five years old, and she still didn't have any of those things. Not that she hadn't received plenty of opportunities, because she had. In fact she had been very seriously involved with a professor two years ago, but somehow there always seemed to be a large void in her life in the area of love. So she broke off that relationship and since then had kept all her suitors at a distance. After every brief courtship she came away with the distinct feeling that Russell or Mark or whoever was not who she wanted in her dream house. No, only one face kept recurring to her—one with lazy green eyes, a golden-haired chest, and a warm caressing mouth—but he was lost to her forever.

She felt guilty that she had not been back home more often in the last few years. Every letter she had received from Aunt Rainey had the same theme: Come home for good, Jessica. Toward the end, when their health was failing rapidly, Aunt Rainey had apologized for her and Fred's interference in her marriage and begged Jessica's forgiveness. She pleaded that they had done what they thought best at the time but had been plagued by doubts over the years.

Jessica had written to assure her that she loved them and forgave them, although the hurt was still deeply entrenched in her heart. She could never come home again to stay, and she hoped they understood. *It honestly wasn't all their fault,* she thought resentfully. If Jason had *really* loved her, he would have fought harder to keep the marriage. Instead he had walked away that morning eight years ago, and she hadn't seen him since.

Well, she was ready to change her life now—to come back home. She was adult enough to live in the same town with Jason. After all, he was just a man—granted, an exceptional man, but a man nonetheless. And she *certainly* wasn't the same love-sick girl she had been eight years ago. There were *plenty* more fish in the sea where he came from. She was just going to have to look a little harder for the one she wanted, that was all.

She packed away the rest of her aunt's belongings and went into the bedroom to dress. Standing in her bikini bra and panties, she searched through her closet for something to wear, letting the tiny bit of breeze coming through the open window cool her sticky body.

Boy, how I wish I could put on a pair of shorts and a cool halter top, she thought, giggling out loud as she imagined the look on Judge Baker's face had she really had the nerve to show up like that. *He must be a least seventy years old by now, or maybe older,* she thought. He had been not only Uncle Fred's lawyer but a very close friend of the family's all the years she was growing up.

Discarding the idea of the shorts, she reached for a cotton wraparound skirt instead, adding a matching light-weight top with tiny threads of lavender running through it. The trim on the blouse brought out the violet of her eyes. She always managed to have a fairly decent tan, she mused as she twisted around in front of the mirror hanging on her closet door, so she wouldn't need any hose. It was at times like this that she really appreciated the dark coloring she had inherited from her Spanish mother and grandmother. Even in the dead of winter she always had a golden-brown glow about her. In the summer it turned to a deep bronze shade.

Deciding she would pass inspection, she reached for her brown strap sandals and bounded back down the stairs, pausing in front of the hall mirror to check her hair. She ran a brush through the long, thick dark tresses and thought back to that night when Jason had come to take her out.

Jessica, Uncle Fred, and Aunt Rainey had been sitting on the large front porch of the old farmhouse after supper that Saturday night, hoping to catch a cool breeze in the hot early evening. Aunt Rainey sat fanning herself with a paper fan, her crisp cotton housedress beginning to wilt in the stifling heat.

"I don't know what we're going to do without you, Jessie, when you're gone," Aunt Rainey said with a sigh, "but I'm as excited as if I was going to college myself." She beamed.

Jessica smiled tenderly, patting her aunt's wrinkled hand. "I'll be home often, Aunt Rainey. Besides, now you and Uncle Fred will have all the time in the world to be alone and do things together for a change," she teased lightly.

"Fiddle," Aunt Rainey scoffed blushingly, "we had all those years alone before we got you. We'll probably wander around this old house like chickens with their heads cut off after you leave!"

The sound of a car pulling into the drive caught their attention, and Jessica's heart leaped into her throat as she saw Jason emerge from the driver's side. His eyes held hers briefly as he walked up onto the porch.

"Jason! How are you, boy," Uncle Fred greeted him exuberantly, pulling up an extra chair. "Sit down and tell us what brings you over here on a hot night like tonight?"

"Let me get you a glass of lemonade," Aunt Rainey offered, springing to her feet.

Jason's laughter filled the soft night's air as he waved away the suggested cold drink with his hand. "Sit still, Rainey. I just stopped by to see if I could borrow your pretty niece for the evening."

Jessica had been standing spellbound, her eyes greedily devouring the handsome man standing before her. Her heart thudded against her ribs as Jason's words penetrated her scrambled thoughts.

"You want to borrow me?" she asked unbelievingly, her knees turning to liquid jelly. *Borrow me,* she thought wildly. *He could* have *me if he wanted me!*

Jason grinned, giving her a cocky wink. "If you're not busy tonight, Angel."

"Busy tonight? Why you can see for yourself she's not busy tonight," Uncle Fred boomed out happily. "She's just been sitting here getting on Rainey and my nerves," he teased with a twinkle in his blue eyes.

"Good, I'll have her back early, sir," Jason promised, reaching for Jessica's arm.

The smell of wildly blooming honeysuckle hung heavy in the air as Jessica stepped shakily off the porch, still holding Jason's arm. She fought the urge to stop and pinch herself to see if she was dreaming. Helping her into the passenger side of the car, he quickly slid into the driver's side and backed the car smoothly out onto the dusty farm road.

As they sped down the road in the early twilight Jessica finally managed to find her voice and asked meekly, "Where are we going?"

Glancing over at her, Jason gave her a devastating smile. "It's such a nice night I thought we'd take a ride," he said simply. "Anywhere in particular you'd like to go?"

"No, anywhere's fine with me," Jessica said lamely.

As they drove through the warm night Jessica began to loosen up, and before long they were talking and laughing like the friends they had always been. Jason drove for an hour, covering all the familiar places of the small town, finally ending up at a restaurant where they could get hamburgers and Cokes. After placing their orders Jason leaned back in the small booth, stretching out his long legs under the table.

"I heard you were leaving for Austin in a few weeks," he said casually, his hands toying with the flatware on the table.

"Yes," Jessica replied, wishing desperately she had something to do with her own hands.

Jason grinned. "I don't know what I'll do. It'll be almost like losing my shadow," he teased. Jessica felt a hot blush rising to her cheeks as his twinkling green eyes continued to silently torment her. "I'm sorry I embarrassed you, Angel," Jason relented, reaching out to take her small hand in his large one. "It just suddenly occurred to me, when I heard you were leaving, that I was going to miss having a little violet-eyed pixie trailing after me everytime I looked up."

"I don't imagine it will take you long to get over it,"

Jessica replied softly. "By the time I come back from college, you and Marcy will probably be married and have two kids," she finished miserably, folding her napkin into a neat square.

"Think so, huh?" he said. "You could be right. She's quite a lady," he admitted.

Jessica snorted disgustedly. "I wouldn't go so far as to call her a lady!"

Jason rolled his eyes upward toward the ceiling. "Maybe you're right," he agreed wickedly. "Let's just class her as a very delightful—uh—woman."

The waitress brought their hamburgers and Cokes, placing them on the table in front of them. Jessica's eyes fell on the large slice of onion lying serenely on her plate. Indecision flickered briefly across her face as she sheepishly stole a quick glance to see if Jason was eating his. Her eyes came into contact with his laughing green ones. Quickly averting her gaze, she slapped the onion on her bun, dousing it liberally with catsup.

Jason heaved a dramatic sigh, then placed his onion ceremoniously on his hamburger.

"Are you coming back here after you finish college?" he asked, taking a large bite out of the bun.

"Mmmmm . . ." Jessica said, her mouth full. Managing to swallow the bite she had in her mouth, she addressed his question. "I really don't know. It will depend on where I find a job." Grabbing a napkin, she wiped the hamburger juice from her mouth. She *hated* to eat in front of a date.

"What are you going to be when you grow up?" he sparred, reaching for his Coke.

"A teacher," she remarked idly, picking up her hamburger again.

"Damn! The kids nowadays have all the luck," Jason said, his gaze skipping boldly over her snug light-blue knit top. "I never remember having a teacher that looked like you!"

Jessica lifted her eyes to grin at him saucily. "Isn't that

a coincidence. I'll just bet that few of my male students will look like you, either!"

They finished their meal in happy camaraderie, lightly bantering back and forth with each other. Jessica wished the night would never end, but all too soon Jason got up to pay the check, and they were back out in the car, on the way to the farm.

Walking her to the door, Jason kept his arm draped casually around her narrow waist. When they reached the bottom of the steps, he pulled her lightly into the circle of his arms. Tipping her face up, he studied her in the pale moonlight. "I've had a nice time tonight, Angel," he told her softly.

"Oh, I have too. Thank you for asking me, Jason." Jessica's hands felt cold and clammy, and that strange weakness began to invade her knees again.

"Can I see you again before you leave for school, Jessie?" he asked, his hands tenderly exploring up and down her bare arms.

"I thought you were dating Marcy," Jessica whispered.

"I am, but that doesn't mean I can't date anyone else. There's no kind of commitment between us yet." His mouth began to search her neck playfully, sending cold chills down her spine.

"Well, in that case I'd be most happy to see you again, Mr. Rawlings," she told him.

Jessica lifted her face expectantly, waiting for his kiss, but no kiss came. Just a light, playful peck on the end of her nose. As he turned her firmly toward the front door, talking as he walked, he said casually, "I'll be by tomorrow night. We can eat first, then take in that new movie playing at the Tower—if that's all right with you."

"Fine," Jessica mumbled, surprised she would be seeing him again so soon. Surprised but estatic.

Numbly Jessica caught the dreamy expression in her eyes as her hand paused holding the brush in midair. She looked at herself steadily in the mirror and flinched at the memory of how that night had set the pattern for the next three weeks. Jason was with Jessica every minute he could spare away from his family's farm. They took long drives, went to movies, had late-night swims, went on picnics, or just sat on Uncle Fred and Aunt Rainey's big porch in the old swing, curled contentedly in each other's arms—the days of eating onions on their hamburgers long past.

Uncle Fred and Aunt Rainey grew more disturbed every day, cautioning Jessica that she still had four years of college ahead of her before she could ever think of settling down—not to mention the fact that Jason was ten years older than she. Because of Uncle Fred's heart condition Jessica would always smile and assure them they had nothing to be concerned about. It was just a last-minute summer romance that would soon be forgotten by both Jason and her when she left for Austin. Jessica might have been successful in fooling Uncle Fred and Aunt Rainey, but she couldn't fool herself. She knew that even though Jason might very well forget this summer, she never would. She was hopelessly in love with him—but, Jessica thought, smiling to herself, what's new about that? She had been in love with him all her life.

The clock had ticked down to the last three days before Jessica was to leave, and her heart was heavy as she got ready for her date with Jason that Thursday night. Taking extreme care with her appearance, she slipped on a white eyelet sundress, which made her dark tan look creamy and smooth in the soft light of her bedroom. After she left, he would go back to dating Marcy and she would be the one in his arms every night. A sharp, stabbing pain sliced through Jessica's mind as she brushed her long black hair angrily back from her face. Oh, why did she have to leave now, of all times? Maybe if she stayed around just a little longer, Jason would ask her to marry him and she would gladly stay here forever, locked in his strong arms. *Snap out of it, Jessica!* she sternly warned herself. Uncle Fred and Aunt Rainey would never allow her to marry at her age. Jessica felt she owed them such a large debt of gratitude for taking her in and providing a loving home for her when her parents were killed that she could never intentionally break their hearts by not following their wishes. With a pall of gloom hanging over her head she went downstairs to meet Jason.

They spent the evening in good spirits, with Jason being attentive as usual. Jessica continually tried to shove the thought of her leaving back in to the far recesses of her mind.

After the movie and a bite to eat they found themselves at a loss for words, and Jason regretfully pointed out that it was nearly time for her to be home. Driving along in the soft summer night, Jason suddenly turned the car in the direction of Potter's swimming hole. Jessica looked over at him in surprise. "Where are we going?"

"I thought we might spend a few minutes down here—just for ol' times' sake." He grinned devilishly. "Any objections?"

"Only one," Jessica said.

"What's that, Angel?" Jason turned to face her in the soft moonlight streaming through the car window, puzzlement written on his handsome face.

"Does it have to be just a few minutes?" she whispered seductively, winding her arms around his neck.

Jason pulled the car up under a large spreading oak tree and turned off the ignition, trying unsuccessfully to avoid Jessica's teasing love play as she ran her tongue lightly over and around his ear, down his neck, then around to capture his warm, sweet lips.

"Damn, Jessica," he mumbled, reaching to pull her softly rounded curves closer to his lean, taut body. "Hasn't anyone ever told you there's a limit to what a man can take, sweetheart?" His mouth began to search hungrily down her neck, his hands intimately exploring her young, firm body. The peaceful sounds of the night, a lone whippoorwill calling, the tiny tree frogs singing in harmony, the katydids and jarflies blended in a sweet melodious background as Jessica became lost in Jason's arms in a world of fiery kisses, his hands and mouth awakening new feelings in her innocent body, feelings that were confusing yet unbearably exciting.

Jason moved to lay her down on the car seat, settling his warm body over hers as he continued to assault her with slow, sensuous, languid kisses. She could feel his body responding to hers as they quickly reached the point where they were both beyond coherent thought. With a strangled groan Jason tore his mouth away from Jessica's, cupping her face between his two large hands. Jessica's soft violet eyes met lazy green desire-filled ones.

"Marry me, Jessie."

"What . . ." Jessica's mind was reeling, the night taking on an unreal, dreamlike quality.

"I said, marry me—tonight. We'll drive up to Dennison and be married in a couple of hours. Please, sweetheart. I'm going crazy wanting you." His mouth took hers in a demanding, possessive kiss once again. "I want you so bad, Angel, I can taste it!" Jason whispered tightly.

"But what about school—Aunt Rainey—Uncle Fred . . ." Jessica murmured between heated kisses.

"I don't know. What about them?" Jason whispered. "All I know is I'm going out of my mind wanting you."

"Oh, Jason, darling, I want you too." Jessica held him tighter to her trembling body. This was like some wild, wonderful dream. Jason here in her arms telling her he loved her and wanted her. He *had* said he loved her, hadn't he? Oh, well, it didn't matter. The only thing that really mattered was that he was asking her to marry him. If he didn't love her now, she'd *make* him love her later. With a sigh of blissful content she pulled his mouth back down to hers. "Oh, yes, Jason, I'll marry you!" She could recall saying the words as clearly as if it been yesterday.

She quickly pulled all her hair straight back from her

face, securing part of it with a large barrette on the top, letting the rest hang freely down her back, trying bravely to forget the night she had become Jason's wife. Adding a light natural-color lip gloss to her soft lips, she snapped her purse closed.

"Well, cat," she remarked to Tabby, "I'll see you after a while." When he heard his name, he walked courteously to the front door with her.

Jessica stepped out into the mounting heat of the afternoon, her eyes falling on the old pickup Uncle Fred had kept all these years. "Good grief!" she agonized. She had completely forgotten—that was the only means of transportation she had at the moment. She hadn't brought her own sporty little Datsun with her. After receiving the call from Doc Perkins that Aunt Rainey didn't have much longer, she had simply thrown her things in a suitcase and had a friend drive her to the airport.

That truck has to be at least thirty years old, she thought with distress as she looked at the old gray jalopy sitting in the driveway. It looked like an accident on its way to happen, she observed as she walked around the truck, her eyes taking in the faded paint and dented fender on the right-hand side. The old running boards were beginning to rust away from the sides of the truck. As she peered into the stifling hot interior her heart sank—it certainly didn't have air conditioning. She could almost hear Uncle Fred's booming voice on that hot summer day fifteen years ago when she had complained of the heat as he was driving her home from church one morning.

"You hot, punkin?" he had joked. "Well, why didn't you say something sooner? I'll just turn on the air-conditioner and cool you right down!"

Jessica looked up at him with skepticism and replied rather agitatedly, "We don't have any air-conditioner in this old truck."

"Why, we do, too, punkin," he assured her. "I've got that old reliable two-sixty kind."

30

Still not ready to believe him, she asked suspiciously, "What's that?"

"Why, I just roll down two windows and go sixty miles an hour," his voice boomed. Then he and Aunt Rainey both laughed uproariously. Jessica gave him a blank look and could not for the life of her see what was so funny. Grown-ups could be so dumb sometimes!

Opening the door on the driver's side, she got in and turned the key in the ignition. After a series of groaning protests the old engine came to life.

"Well, it's been awhile," she reminded it, "but I think I remember how. Now, if you'll just cooperate with me, you and I will get along fine."

After thinking it over for a minute the truck gave her its answer. It promptly died.

"Horseflies!" she muttered and began the tedious grinding again, trying to breathe life back into the engine. Sweat was beginning to trickle down her back and thoughts of a salvage yard were dancing merrily through her mind when it backfired once and then sprang instantly to life.

"That was wise," she assured it and ground the old gears into reverse.

Now it was trying too hard to please her. The gas pedal seemed to want to go a lot faster than she wanted to, and the engine was revving so, she had to keep a foot on the brake as well as the gas pedal. She shot out of the farmyard at an alarming speed. Luckily the road was very lightly traveled, so she had it more or less to herself as she headed for town. As she bumped along the dirt road her eyes swept across the unchanging countryside, until the scenery seemed to fade away, replaced by memories of her wedding night, which surfaced unbidden to burn vividly in her mind.

Deciding that it was best not to tell Uncle Fred or Aunt Rainey until after they were married, Jessica called home, explaining that she had decided to spend the night with a

31

girl friend in town. She hated to deceive her aunt and uncle, but she wasn't sure how they would react to the marriage. No, it would be far better to face them already married.

It took them a couple of hours to drive to the border town of Denison, Texas. They were married quietly by a twenty-four-hour justice of the peace. Promising her a ring as soon as they got back, Jason took her tenderly into his arms, sealing their marriage vows with a kiss of love.

Leaving the small wedding chapel, Jessica clung to Jason's arm, her love and happiness shining in her luminous eyes. On the way back home they found a small out-of-the-way motel nestled in a large grove of pine trees where they could spend the night. Opening the door, Jason scooped his young bride up in his strong arms and carried her across the threshold, his mouth covering hers in a kiss of total possession.

It suddenly dawned on Jessica she knew absolutely nothing about being a wife to Jason. A look of indecision crossed her radiant face as Jason let her slide seductively down the length of his body to the floor.

"Is there any particular reason for that frown on your beautiful face, Mrs. Rawlings?" Jason asked, his mouth nibbling on the sensitive part of her earlobe and making Jessica shudder deliciously. Bringing her slender fingers up to his golden-brown hair, she wrapped them snugly in the thick, wiry texture before drawing his searching mouth down to hers for a long, exquisite kiss. It was several minutes before Jessica could sanely answer Jason's question.

"No. I just suddenly realized I know nothing about— being a wife to you," she whispered shyly. "I don't know the things that please you, the things that make you happy, the things that are important in your life."

With a tolerant grin Jason brought her face close to his. In the dim light of the room she could see his tender eyes grow serious. "We have the rest of our lives to find out

32

those things about each other," he told her lovingly, stroking the side of her smooth face tenderly. "As for being a wife to me—I have a feeling you'll catch on quick," he added wickedly. "You certainly have all the right equipment for the job." His hand rested lightly and possessively on one of her soft, firm breasts. Jessica could feel her knees begin to tremble as Jason's hands reached for the zipper running down the back of her dress, sliding it down slowly until it reached the bottom. His mouth began a slow search of her neck, exploring the hollows, nibbling hotly around her ear, grasping its lobe between his strong white teeth. Jessica drew her breath in sharply, her legs nearly buckling from weakness. With gentle hands he let the soft fabric slip quietly to the floor. The only sound was the uneven breathing of the man and woman standing in the middle of the small intimate room and the rustling of her dress as it hit the floor.

"There's no need to be afraid, Angel," Jason promised huskily, his mouth lightly toying with hers. "We'll take it nice and slow. I'll show you the beauty of becoming a woman." His mouth became firmer as it opened over hers, his tongue searching for hers in the moist recesses. He continued to draw her nearer, his hands effortlessly unsnapping the clasp on her bra, letting it join the white eyelet dress on the floor. He stood back to get a better view of the magnificent form before him, resting his hands on her hips. "Beautiful—simply beautiful." His deep voice was barely above a whisper. Jessica gloried in the fact that her new husband was pleased with her—she wanted to spend her whole life pleasing him. She loved him so much she thought she would burst with happiness. Overwhelmed with emotion, she reached for his face to pull it to hers, her lips longing to taste his kisses once again. He complied willingly, his hand gently caressing the smooth, taut curve of her belly, his thumbs crooking under the rim of her lace panties, sliding them over her hips, eliminating the last remaining article. A tiny quiver washed over her as his hands surveyed the curve of her hips, the soft delicacy of her buttocks. He whispered soothing words of love against her lips, calming her fears and heightening her passion. "You're mine to have and to hold from this day forward, Angel. I'll never, never hurt you," he breathed just before he brought his mouth down to sweetly partake of the feast before him.

As Jason moaned softly against her throat Jessica swooned toward his comforting body, unable to find the words to tell him of her feelings at this moment. Her love for him expanded and overflowed as he gently lifted his young timid bride and laid her on the bed. She trembled as he pulled away to remove his clothes. He smiled reassuringly, bringing his mouth back down to capture hers for a brief kiss. "Angel," he whispered, "my clothes are going to have to come off if we are going to have a wedding night."

Her eyes searched his longingly. "I know, my darling Jason," she murmured softly. "I'm not afraid."

He lovingly stroked her hair back from her face and kissed each eyelid. "I love your eyes." Then he kissed the tip of her nose. "I love your nose." Then each cheek. "I love your lovely face." Her lips parted slightly as she opened them in a silent pleading. "Yes, Angel, I love those, too," he assured her, his mouth descending to hers in a long, passionate, mind-drugging embrace, her hands clutching wildly at his shirt. He raised his face from hers, reluctant to leave her for even a second. "Would you like to do the honors of undressing me?" he asked in a husky passion-laden tone.

Jessica felt her cheeks warm at the suggestion, but at the same time it stirred a secret longing in her to discover the delights of Jason's body, to feel every inch of his manliness. She smiled tenderly, her hands reaching for the buttons on his shirt. "Since this is my first day on the job, you'll have to be patient with me."

Jason covered her tiny hands with his, clutching them

to his chest. "Take your time, Angel. As I told you before, we've got a lifetime." He brought her hands to his mouth and kissed each fingertip before releasing them to continue their pleasurable task. Her slender fingers tried desperately to release the buttons, fumbling with agonizing slowness, shaking so hard she cried out in frustration, "Please, you do it, Jason."

A deep chuckle emanated from his throat as he stood up to strip his clothing, letting his join hers on the floor in wild array. Jessica watched in awe. The sight of his nakedness sent surges of hot liquid through her veins. He was more than a dream—he was real—he was hers. As he reached to enfold her in his arms once again he rasped hoarsely, "Come here, Angel. It's time for lesson number two."

It was as if a slow burning ember caught a sudden wild gust of wind as they clung hungrily to each other. Jason seemed to lose the last precarious hold he had on sanity as the soft curves of Jessica's body blended intimately with the hard, granite strength of his.

Jessica's hands began a slow search of Jason's body, gliding over his back, his strong thighs, his firm buttocks. As she became familiar with every part of her love she elicited tortured groans from him. She writhed in agonizing desire as he took her exploring hands in his and directed them to a new and different place, his groans turning into sweet tormented moans as she shyly began to gently caress him. The feel of her slender fingers fluttering over his skin kindled an urgency in him that had a will of its own.

"Angel," he moaned, "I don't think I can wait any longer."

Her body moved closer in response to his urgent plea. Her mouth searched for his in the darkness, her kiss transmitting a message loud and clear. She was ready—eager—to become his wife.

The wall of control completely burst as Jason moved to

35

let his body possess hers in a way it never had before. Jessica became lost in a white sphere of fire and delight, demanding to know the full joy of her body's new awakening. Rising to unbelievable heights, Jason and Jessica hung suspended in air, soaring together on a swelling tide of rapture, before drifting back gently, lightly, to earth.

As they lay in the afterglow she clung weakly to him, her face buried in his moist chest, tears of joy falling like soft summer rain against his skin. A low throaty chuckle rumbled in Jason's chest as he held her, lovingly stroking her damp, raven hair.

"See, I told you, Mrs. Rawlings," he teased softly.

"Told me what?" Jessica whispered shakily.

Bringing his mouth back down to hers, he whispered softly against her lips. "I just had a hunch you'd learn fast!"

"Oh, Jason," she murmured tenderly. "Never in my wildest dreams did I think it would be like this."

"Then I gather you have no complaints, Mrs. Rawlings?" Jason pulled her close, the sweet languidness of their lovemaking still holding them prisoners.

"No complaints, Mr. Rawlings."

They drifted off into a contented slumber, only to awaken toward early morning to search hungrily again for each other, their young bodies eager and ready for each other, the newness of their love overriding all else. They watched the sun come up together, lying in each other's arms, happy, secure, and content in their new life together.

At the sound of a horn honking sharply behind her Jessica abruptly forced her attention back to her driving. The truck seemed to have taken on a life of its own, and by the time she came screeching into town, mothers were frantically gathering their children in off the street. She came roaring up the drive of old Judge Baker's house in a cloud of dust, the engine dying a jerky death as she reached down to turn off the key. The elderly man standing on the other side of a hedge watering his flowers and trees looked up quite calmly.

"Afternoon, Jessica," he greeted her. "Goin' to a fire?"

"No." She smiled timidly. "Just having a little trouble with my gas pedal," she told him sweetly. She got out and in retaliation slammed the truck door with a forceful blow. "That was very funny," she told the truck sarcastically.

Coming around to the front of the house, she heard a voice calling her name.

"Jessica! Jessica, is that you?" She saw Maureen Winters running toward her excitedly.

"Maureen?" she cried and ran over to meet her halfway. They threw their arms around each other and dissolved in a fit of giggles.

"I haven't seen you in ages," Maureen was scolding. "Why have you stayed away from home so long!"

"Oh, I've really been tied to my job," she answered vaguely. They had been best friends all during high school, and Jessica had flown back to be maid of honor when Maureen had married Pete Winters four years ago.

"I'm sorry that I didn't get to talk to you the other day at the graveyard," Maureen apologized, "but Pete had to go straight back to work. You know how sorry we both are." She reached over to hug Jessica again.

"I know, and thank you," Jessica murmured, precariously close to tears in this good friend's comforting arms. "My goodness, Jamie is growing so, I hardly recognize him," she said, bending down to talk to the little boy who had just skidded up on his Big Wheels.

"Hi, Jesseeka," he called, giving her a radiant smile.

"Hi, Jamie," she said. "Are you being a good boy?"

Large solemn brown eyes met her gaze as he nodded his head in an earnest affirmation. "You got any puppies I can play with today?" he asked hopefully. The last time Jessica had seen him, Uncle Fred's beagle had just given birth to a new litter. Jamie had played happily with them all afternoon and left screaming his protests in the arms of his mother.

"No," she said sorrowfully for the benefit of the small boy, "they've all gone to live somewhere else now."

"Oh," he said as his face fell. Trying once again, he asked, "Do you got a kid I can play with?"

"No," she said sorrowfully, for herself this time, "I don't have one of those either, but I wish I did."

He turned his head in the direction of the gray relic sitting in the driveway. "Is that your truck?"

"Yes," she said smiling. "Do you like it?"

"Yuk, no!" he said adamantly. "It's ugly."

"Jamie!" His mother sounded shocked. "That isn't a nice thing to say to Jessica!"

Jessica laughed, "No, but very truthful!"

"Well, listen, I have to be running on," Maureen was saying. "Call me sometime and let's have lunch together. I'll fill you in on all the local gossip, and you can fill me in on what's been keeping you in Austin."

"Fine," she agreed readily. "As soon as I get things under control, I'll give you a call."

"Great! Come on, Jamie, let's get going," she ordered.

" 'Bye, Jesseeka," he called as he went pedaling loudly on down the street.

CHAPTER TWO

The clock in the steeple of the old Methodist church sitting on the corner was just tolling two when Jessica stepped onto the porch. The mouth-watering aroma of someone's pot roast cooking for their evening meal assailed her nostrils as she reached down and rang the doorbell. The door was opened immediately by a pleasant pudgy-faced woman whose mouth broke into a large smile when she saw Jessica standing there. Judge Baker's wife was a roly-poly little woman who made you feel good just to be around her. Uncle Fred used to tease Aunt Rainey about her weight sometimes, telling her if she didn't lay off the sweets, she'd soon be as big as Edna Baker. He'd laugh and say that when she walked down the aisle for

Sunday morning services, her fanny looked like two wild-cats wrestling in a gunnysack. "Yessir"—he'd grin—"if being fat was a crime, ol' Edna would be in for a life sentence."

"Jessica Cole, come in here, girl, and let me look at you." Mrs. Baker beamed. "My goodness gracious, you're prettier than ever! I told the judge just this morning, why you hadn't run off to Hollywood to be one of them big movie stars is beyond me," she rattled on. "Mercy sakes, Fred and Rainey was proud of you!"

Jessica blushed at the outlandish praise, and hoping to steer the conversation into another channel, she asked, "I'm not too early?"

"Heavens to Betsy, child, not if you don't mind waiting until the judge finishes his lunch. He won't be long now. Come on, sweetie, you can wait for the judge in his study."

She proceeded to lead the way through the comfortable old living room. The clock on the mantle was chiming, and Jessica heard Edna's birds singing in their cages in front of the window. They moved on down the hall and stopped in front of a large oak door. She poked her head in the open door and motioned for Jessica to enter. "Now, you just make yourself at home. The judge will be right with you in a little bit." Mrs. Baker patted Jessica's shoulder as Jessica sank into the overstuffed chair in front of the judge's desk. Mrs. Baker quietly closed the door behind her, leaving Jessica to gaze around the room distractedly. As she sat with her hands in her lap waiting to hear the will Jessica couldn't help but think back to how her aunt and uncle had reacted to the news of her marriage to Jason.

"Married!" Aunt Rainey had sunk weakly into the chair at the kitchen table.

"Well, I won't hear of it," Uncle Fred boomed out, his loud, deep voice echoing around the room.

Jessica sought the comfort of Jason's arm, panic filling her. She had never dreamed they would take it this badly.

"Merciful heavens, boy! What in the world were you thinking of? She's nothing but a baby yet!" Uncle Fred's face was red and his breathing growing heavy and raspy. "She's not ready to take on the responsibility of a marriage!"

"She's seventeen, sir," Jason respectfully reminded him, holding tight to Jessica's trembling hand.

"Jessica, dear, what about school?" Aunt Rainey pleaded, tears filling her pale eyes. "What about all the plans we made?"

Jessica had never felt so low or guilty. She was fully aware of their dream for her. They had never had an education, and for years they had talked of nothing else for Jessica. It was as if they wanted to relive their life through her.

Jason shifted around uncomfortably, his eyes searching for Jessica's.

"It will just have to be annulled," Uncle Fred said, sitting down wearily in his chair. The late-morning sunshine shown on his face, which had grown pale and ashen since they had entered the room only minutes earlier.

"Fred, take your medicine," Aunt Rainey pleaded between tears, getting up to get the amber-colored bottle from the shelf.

"I'm sorry, sir, but we love each other, and I can't let you annul the marriage," Jason said firmly.

"You don't have a damn thing to say about it, son. She's under age," he said bluntly, popping one of the tiny white pills under his tongue. "I can't let *you* destroy something we dreamed of and worked for all our life. You're a fine man, Jason. I have no qualms about you as a person. I've known you all your life, but I'll move heaven and earth to get this marriage set aside—annulled—whatever it takes. You can trust my word on that, son. Jessica!"

Jessica snapped to attention, her heart feeling as though it were being torn in two. "What, Uncle Fred?"

"Go to your room, girl. I'll handle things from here on out!"

Jessica looked wildly at Jason, tears flooding her violet eyes. "But, Uncle Fred, I love him . . ."

"*I said go to your room, girl!*" he roared.

"Jessica." Jason's helpless voice came to her. "Stay here. Don't leave me. Somehow we'll work this thing out together." His beautiful green eyes were pools of living torment.

"I'm sorry, Jason. It's out of your hands," Fred told him grimly.

"Come with me, dear. Let me take you to your room." Aunt Rainey reached for Jessica's hand. "Let the men settle this alone."

"No," she screamed, her nerves finally breaking. "Just leave me alone—all of you. Just leave me alone!" Tears were running in rivulets down her cheeks.

Suddenly Uncle Fred gasped sharply, and all eyes in the room focused on him.

"Fred!" Rainey ran over, clutching his arm, turning back pleadingly to Jason and Jessica. "Please," she begged, "do as he says." Her tired old face was filled with pain and worry.

"Are you coming with me, Jessica?" Jason asked tensely. "I don't want to do anything to jeopardize Fred's health, honey, but don't let them ruin your life," he pleaded. "Don't let them do this to us, Angel."

"Oh, Jason, don't make me choose between you and them." How could she choose between breaking Uncle Fred and Aunt Rainey's hearts, maybe bringing on a fatal heart attack in the process—and giving up the man she loved more than her own life. It was an impossible decision.

Jason started slowly for the door, defeat showing plainly on his handsome face.

"All right, Jessica. I'll try to make the choice for you. Maybe they are right. Apparently you *are* too young for marriage. But when I walk out that door, there'll be no turning back. Either you come with me now, or we'll both forget this marriage ever took place."

Jessica looked around at the faces in the room, Aunt Rainey's tear-streaked one, Uncle Fred's sickly gray one, her beloved Jason's. Death would be an easier choice for her at this moment.

Recognizing the torn look of anguish on her face, Jason slowly opened the door, his eyes growing misty. "Goodbye, Jessie," he said softly and walked quietly out of her life.

Tears welled up in Jessica's eyes at the painful memory of her lost love, and she hoped the judge would hurry. She sat drumming her fingertips on the arm of the old chair as she stared at the wall in front of her, rapidly blinking back her tears. Resignedly she realized she had no control over the memories or the emotions that seemed to flood through her, and if she was ever going to get through the reading of the will, she decided, she would have to give them full rein. She thought back to the two days before she had left for college. They were the blackest in Jessica's life. She went to the phone a hundred times, her hand hovering over the receiver, aching to call Jason to come after her, but always walking away crying. Her heart filled with a deep resentment toward her aunt and uncle, and she began to look forward to the day when she would board the bus for Austin.

That day finally dawned, dark and rainy, suiting Jessica's mood. As the bus pulled slowly out of town she closed her eyes, tears cascading silently down her cheeks. She would fulfill her obligation to her aunt and uncle, and then she would come back and somehow, someway she would make Jason Rawlings notice her again. Right now all she had to concentrate on was getting through the next four years. "God help me," she prayed as she dropped into a heartbroken, exhausted sleep.

The next few years passed slowly, Jessica never forgetting that one summer night in Jason's arms. She came home only when necessary, her heart never able to totally forgive Uncle Fred and Aunt Rainey. Jessica would avoid all mention of Jason on her brief visits home. After college she had secured the teaching job in Austin, staying on to live there permanently in her small three-room garage apartment. Her life had settled down into a normal pattern, from which the only thing missing was love.

Jessica's mind shifted back to the present. There was simply no reason to cry over spilt milk. She had grieved for Jason for eight years. It was time she started to build a new life for herself. Although Aunt Rainey had never said so, Jason was probably married again by now with two or three little golden-haired, emerald-eyed children running around somewhere.

At that moment the door opened behind her and the booming voice of Judge Baker exploded into the room. "Well, well, if it isn't little Jessie Cole," he blared as he came around her chair and bent down to peck her on the cheek. Mrs. Baker stood beside him, smiling down at Jessica. He straightened and moved to stand behind his massive oak desk. "My, my," he teased with a twinkle in his eye, "what I wouldn't give to be thirty years younger right now. Why, Mama would be a fool to turn around and walk out of this room, leaving me alone with a pretty little thing like you." Looking at her, he gave "Mama" a big licentious grin.

"Oh, go on with you, Daddy. If you were thirty years younger, you'd still be too old for her. But," she added to assure him, "I'd still be here," and beamed happily back at him.

He let out a deep hooting laugh and patted her ample bottom. "No need to get worried, Mama. I've had you for fifty years, my eyes are blind . . . Well, almost!" he added, turning his gaze back to Jessica.

"Horsefeathers! You old goat." She laughed. "Go on

with you. You'll scare this little thing to death. Now, you behave yourself. I've got a cake in the oven and haven't got time to stand around listening to your foolishness." She turned and gave him a saucy grin, along with some sound, parting advice: "Just remember your age, Daddy, and your heart!"

He roared with laughter as she shut the door with a resounding bang.

He sat in the large leather chair behind his desk and looked benignly at Jessica.

"Jessie, dear"—his voice was so kind—"we're so sorry about your loss of Fred and Rainey so close together. There wasn't a finer pair of people as far as Mama and I were concerned." He stood and walked over to the window, looking out at the street. "You know, when you live to be Mama's and my age, it seems you spend half your time burying the people you love and have spent most of your life with."

He stood for a moment with a faraway look in his eyes—eyes that didn't quite have the brightness they used to have. With a slight shrug of his stooped shoulders he turned back to the business of living. He cleared his throat, shuffled through some papers lying before him, and began.

"My dear, this should basically be very simple. As you know, all that Fred and Rainey had will naturally be yours." He sat back down at his desk. For the first time Jessica could ever recall, he had a rather sheepish look on his face.

"Uh—there is only one small stipulation to the will that Fred and Rainey added about a year ago." He glanced up at Jessica and continued. "I don't imagine you're going to like it."

Not like it. Jessica couldn't imagine what the judge meant but mentally braced herself for what was to come.

Judge Baker began to explain the details of the will. "Land, house, material possessions, etc., etc., all to go to you with the stipulation that you return to run the farm for six months. If you insist on remaining in Austin, then the entire estate will be left to Manor Methodist Church, where, as you know, Fred and Rainey had been members for over fifty years."

Jessica sat with a stunned expression on her face, rage simmering within her. How *dare* they play God with her life again! She was an adult—perfectly capable of controlling her own destiny. She jumped to her feet and stormed over to the large window which looked out on the main street. "How could they do it?" she exclaimed. "*Why* did they do it?"

"Why?" the judge said gently. "Because they loved you, Jessie. They simply could not stand the thought of you never coming back to the home and land they had loved. They have waited patiently all these years, hoping you'd return"—the judge cleared his throat before continuing—"and that you had forgiven them. It weighed heavily on their minds, Jessica—what they had done to you and Jason."

"It should have," Jessica replied in a rare show of hurt feelings, "but they knew I had forgiven them. How in the world am I going to run that farm? I know very little about it now. I've been gone all these years!"

The judge began to shuffle through a stack of papers on his desk, seeming to search for the right words. Finally, tossing the papers aside in agitation, he blurted out, "Fred suggested you hire Jason to do it."

"*What?*" Jessica's mouth gaped in shock.

"Now think about it for a minute, Jessica. It could make a whole lot of sense. He's one of the biggest ranchers around right now. His property adjoins yours, plus he's got the manpower to run both ranches. And—to tell you the truth, I don't know of another man around I would trust or even recommend to do the job for you."

Jessica stood in front of his wooden desk, speechless. Finally, able to find her tongue, she said in a determined voice, "Even if *I* would think about anything that preposterous, Judge Baker, I'm sure Jason would *never* have anything to do with such an asinine suggestion. My gosh, you *do* realize we didn't exactly part the best of friends. I seriously doubt that he would cross the road to pull my fanny out of a fire."

"Oh, now, Jessica," the judge admonished laughingly, "that was a long time ago. You are two reasonable adults now, more than able to conduct a simple business agreement—which is all this would be."

Jessica snorted in a very unladylike way.

"I suggest you take a few days to think this over, dear. As soon as you calm down, I'm sure you'll view things differently."

As Jessica let herself out into the hot afternoon air her mind was spinning in a thousand directions. What in the world was she going to do now? Even though she had wanted to come back home, it was the principle of the thing! She had to have that inheritance to start her business, but she sure in the devil hated to think she was being forced to claim it.

Well, her hands seemed to be tied. No money, no business. She couldn't see much of a choice. It was either crawling to Mr. High and Mighty Rawlings or going back to eking out a living for the rest of her life in a schoolroom. Jessica literally stomped her foot in a fit of anger.

Storming back out to the old truck, she remembered the words of Judge Baker as she had angrily complained about the unfairness of the will. "Ah, Jessica, my child," he had answered wearily as he took off his glasses and began to massage his tired old eyes with his wrinkled hands, "few things in life *are* fair, my dear. That's a sad lesson I'm afraid we all have to learn."

So where did that leave her? she asked herself as she climbed back behind the wheel of the truck, tears welling up in her violet eyes like pools of shimmering water. Why did everything have to be so complicated?

Wiping her eyes with the backs of her hands, she reached down to turn the key in the ignition, issuing a stern warning to the old truck. "Don't *you* give me any trouble. I'm definitely not in the mood for it!" It groaned into life reluctantly. She threw it into reverse and shot out of the driveway like a missile. *That damn gas pedal again,* she thought as she struggled wildly to get the truck under control. To her mounting horror it gave one long backfire, and with a surge of speed that left her breathless, it careened out onto the street backward, heading straight toward one of the late-model pickups sitting idling in front of the feedstore.

Jessica closed her eyes tight and jammed her foot on the brake, but to no avail. She felt the bone-jarring jolt as the truck finally came to a sudden halt, sitting halfway through the side of the dark-blue pickup. She opened her eyes slowly and let out a shaky breath. Not a sound could be heard for a few moments as she sat there trying to gather her wits about her. Suddenly, as if just coming out of a paralyzed state, people around her started moving.

"My lordy, are you hurt, little lady?" cried Luther, one of the men who worked at the feed store, adding in an excited voice, "Boy, we can sure thank our lucky stars there was no one around this here truck just now. Why, when I looked up and saw you a flyin' out of that driveway like a bat out of hell—oh, pardon me, ma'am, but as I was saying, I looked up, and then I sez to ol' Jason, 'Man, someone's just bought you a new truck!' "

"Jason?" Oh, good heavens, that was *all* she needed now! *Please, God,* she pleaded, *don't let this be his truck!* But the thought had barely left her mind when her eyes caught the figure of a tall, dark, ridiculously good-looking man striding toward her. He stopped directly in front of her old truck, placing the small cheroot he was holding, between his strong, white teeth and putting his hands on his slim hips. Taking one despairing look at his truck, he turned back around slowly and fixed his brilliant jade-green gaze on her.

Jessica smiled beguilingly at him as her words of long ago came back home to her. She had always vowed that someday she would make Jason Rawlings notice her again. Well, this was the day.

She tumbled out of the truck, her face feeling as red as a beet. How in the world could she have hit *his* truck when there were so many others sitting around to choose from? By this time Jason was squatting on the ground, trying to see the damage beneath his truck. Jessica could see clearly underneath his truck from where she stood, and she was sure he would not like what he saw. There seemed to be all kinds of odds and ends hanging down.

Jason straightened up and looked over at Jessica, who stood there silently. The humidity of the hot afternoon had plastered her thin blouse to her voluptuous breasts, and his eyes seemed to lock boldly on that part of her anatomy as he said in a dry tone, "I sure as hell hope you don't teach driver's ed up there in Austin!"

"Of course not," she snapped indignantly, looking around sheepishly to see who was listening to this obnoxious conversation.

"Well," Jason said in a bored tone as he turned his attention back to the truck, "I hope your insurance is good." He looked at her again. "You do have insurance, don't you?"

"Certainly I have insurance, uh—I mean, I think I do."

He gave her an exasperated look and said, "Well, when do you think you might know—for sure, Jessica?"

Jessica took a deep breath and started over. "What I mean is, I'm sure I do on my other car. I'll call my agent as soon as I get home and check to be sure. I assure you your truck will be taken care of, Jason," she said in her school-teacher-chastising-a-naughty-child voice. *Heavens! He must think I'm an idiot!* "Look, I'm really sorry about this. It's that darn gas pedal on my truck. It keeps sticking on me. I certainly didn't single your truck out personally, you know! I made every effort to avoid hitting it—well, for heaven's sake, *I* could have been hurt, you know," she added, her face flushed from the heat, her lavender eyes snapping.

Jason turned his direct, clear gaze back to roam suggestively over her slightly agitated form, looking rather forlorn beside the wrecked truck. "Well, were you?" he asked.

"Was I what?" she shot back, slightly unnerved by his bold appraisal.

"Were you hurt, Jessica?" He was getting a little perturbed now.

She gave an exasperated sigh. "Do I look like I'm hurt?"

A tiny, infuriating grin appeared unwillingly as he observed, "No, little Jessie, you certainly don't look like you've been hurt."

There it was again, that "little Jessie" bit.

"Look," he said brusquely, pulling his eyes away from her, his mind returning to business, "I haven't got all day to stand here. I'm late for an appointment right now."

Jessica's knees felt rubbery and weak now that his gaze had left her. She eyed his truck warily and turned back to him.

"What will you do? You can't drive it like that, can you?"

He looked at her as if he were having to deal with someone who was slightly crazy. "Right," he affirmed.

"You don't have to be sarcastic," she blazed indignantly.

"I didn't mean to be, Jessica," he assured her. "Why don't *you* drive it home for me?"

She felt the color flooding to her cheeks again.

"I was due at the bank ten minutes ago. When I'm through, I'll have one of my men pick me up." He reached up to take his large Stetson hat off, wiping the sweat from his dusty brow. Jessica's heart caught in her throat as her eyes fell involuntarily on the mass of thick, golden-brown hair, which by now was nearly blond from endless hours in the hot Texas sun. Her eyes traveled slowly down the cut of the blue western shirt that was moistly molded to his broad, thick chest and the tight-fitting jeans, which made Jessica only too aware of an older, leaner, harder man than the one she had loved so fiercely eight years ago. The familiar weak longing crept silently over her as she forced her attention back to what he was saying. She blushed hotly as she encountered a pair of lazy green eyes mockingly aware of her less than ladylike assessment of him.

"I'll have one of my men check with you tomorrow about the insurance," he stated briskly, then turned and started to walk hurriedly toward the bank.

"Uh . . . Jason." Jessica swallowed hard.

Jason turned momentarily, a scowl of irritation lining his brow. "What now?" he snapped.

"Do you think you might have a few minutes to stop by the house tonight?" Jessica asked meekly, biting her tongue to overcome the feeling of humiliation that flooded her.

Surprise flickered briefly across Jason's face as he came to a dead halt. Turning to face her, he asked cautiously, "Come by your house tonight? Why?"

Jessica felt like the temperature had risen ten degrees, and perspiration began to trickle down her back in rivulets. "I, ah—have something I need to discuss with you, if you could spare a few minutes," she added lamely. This was *awful!* He was looking at her as if she had just escaped from the looney bin.

Jason continued to study her flustered, hot face for a moment before asking discreetly, "Isn't this something we could settle right now?"

Jessica's spunk returned swiftly. "No, I would need more than fifteen seconds to say what I have to say!"

Jason turned back toward the bank, his long strides moving rapidly away from Jessica. "I'll be by around seven," he tossed indifferently over his shoulder as he crossed the street.

Indecision flickered lightly over her face, and then she rushed to catch up with his long, manly gait. "Jason, one more thing." She was nearly out of breath trying to match his pace. You would think he could be enough of a gentleman to at least slow down while she was talking to him, she fumed—but no, if anything, he only increased his strides. Moving faster, she finally caught up with him and, taking hold of his arm, jerked him to an abrupt stop. "Will Marcy be coming with you?" she blurted.

"Who?"

"Marcy. Marcy Evans."

His face had a blank expression. "Why in the hell would Marcy Evans be coming with me?" he asked in amazement.

"Well"—Jessica shrugged—"I just thought maybe you and she might be married by now . . ."

Jason threw his head back and laughed hilariously.

"Me and Marcy Mercy!"

"Marcy Mercy?" she answered with a frown of confusion on her face. She wasn't quite sure where this conversation had gone wrong.

"Yeah," he grinned, his strong white teeth flashing in his bronze face, "she married Willis Mercy. You surely remember him. His old man owns the bank."

"Marcy Evans *married* Willis 'Bo Bo' Mercy?" she shrieked in surprise. "My gosh! He's as dull as a brown shoe!"

Jessica could feel her heart lighten considerably. At least Jason hadn't married that redheaded witch!

"Sure, they got married several years ago," he said, beginning to laugh grudgingly now. "They've got two of the homeliest-looking kids you'd ever want to lay eyes on," he finished gleefully.

*Jessica fell back against the streetlight, holding her sides in laughter, tears running down her cheeks, at the picture of the elegant Marcy Evans being married to a clod like Willis Mercy.

"Ohhhh," she wailed, "that's priceless. Marcy Mercy! What a name for *her* to get stuck with!"

Jason's cool reserve finally broke as he found himself laughing as hard as she was, both of them in near hysteria.

Jason finally managed to regain some of his composure and was wiping his eyes on the arm of his blue shirt. His face wore a more tender expression as Jessica's laughter subsided. Soft violet eyes came slowly up to meet lazy green ones as he said in a gentle tone, "If you're asking me if I'm married, the answer is no. I'll be coming alone." He turned back in the direction of Jessica's truck and asked, "Do you think you can get that thing back home with no problems?"

"Oh, sure!" she cried exuberantly. "It isn't hurt at all!"

He shook his head and gave a mirthless laugh. "See you around seven then." He strode off in the direction of the bank.

"Sure, see you at seven," she whispered to herself as her eyes followed his strong, manly form down the street, "and at eight, and nine, and in all my dreams for as long as I can ever remember."

CHAPTER THREE

The old truck sped along home smoothly, as if in sincere repentance for its dastardly deeds of the afternoon.

Jessica made a hurried change into her cooler shorts and halter top, then flew around straightening the living room. It was a comfortable room with an Early American sofa and chair sitting before the large picture window, which flooded the plants Aunt Rainey had hung before it with sunlight. The maple end tables gleamed from the lemon furniture polish Jessica had just applied to them. A large bouquet of flowers, fresh from the yard, held the place of honor in the center of the large round glass coffee table in front of the sofa.

She moved on to the kitchen, feeding Tabby his dinner

and making a light evening meal for herself. The clock on the mantel was just chiming five thirty when Jessica finished her chores. The insurance matter had been taken care of, and fortunately her policy did cover her when driving another vehicle. She had decided to have a quick shower and shampoo her hair before Jason arrived.

"Isn't this silly," she told Tabby. "You'd think I actually had a date with him!" She hastened to remind Tabby that this was just a business meeting, nothing personal on her or Jason's part. She simply had the disagreeable chore of asking him to run this farm until she could receive her inheritance; then he would be gone from her life once again.

Tabby seemed rather bored by the whole conversation, but he dutifully heard her out, watching with his large yellow eyes, his tail switching slowly as he lay on his perch on the top of the sofa.

Jessica ran up the stairs and into the bathroom just off the hall from her bedroom. She had her halter top halfway off when it occurred to her that she was out of shampoo. Drat! She had known this morning that she was out, but in all the confusion of the day it had slipped her mind completely. Well, no problem. She still had plenty of time before Jason was due. She'd just jump in the truck and run on down to the drugstore and be back in fifteen minutes.

"Surely not one more thing could go wrong today," she assured herself as she grabbed her purse and ran back down the stairs, calling to Tabby on the way out, "Hold the fort, I'll be right back!"

The heat was terrible. The old seat in the truck was so hot on the backs of her legs it had her doing an obscene dance trying to get the key turned on. The motor sprang into life instantly, and Jessica praised it lavishly for its cooperation. She found a parking space directly in front of the drugstore. Things were finally going her way.

Jumping out onto the hot sticky pavement, she walked to the glass door of the drugstore and pushed it open. The smell of all the medicinal jars and bottles reached her as the cool air of the store washed over her.

Her eyes found the shampoo display immediately. As she paused to study the numerous assorted bottles before her a multitude of TV shampoo commercials flooded her mind. Biting her lip pensively, Jessica struggled with the age-old problem. Did she want her hair shiny, swinging, sexy, full, or just plain clean? The image of a tall good-looking cowboy skipped lightly through her mind as she glanced around sheepishly, then grabbed for the "sexy" brand. She hurriedly paid for her purchase and flew back out the front door.

She hopped back into the truck and turned the key once more. Nothing happened. The old gray relic just sat there mutely. "Oh, no! You can't do this to me," she threatened, jiggling the key insistently.

Apparently the truck did not respond to threats. It continued to ignore her. "You obstinant *jackass!*" Jessica moaned as she buried her hot, flushed face in her hands. Now what was she going to do?

Jerking the door handle back open, she got out of the truck, marched around to the hood, jerked it open angrily, and stood staring helplessly into the yawning chasm of wires, gadgets and doodads. Everything in the engine looked like it needed to be replaced. Well, she was no mechanic, of that she was absolutely sure. She jiggled a few wires, not having the least idea what their function was. She hopped back into the truck, praying for a miracle, and turned the ignition switch once more.

Rebellious silence from the old truck.

Jessica's temper was registering a 9.9 on the Richter scale as she stormed back out of the truck, her eyes catching a glimpse of a large wrench lying in the bed of the old truck. She grabbed it up and defiantly stomped to the motor again with a viscious glint in her dark-purple eyes as she began to bang on everything in sight. She leaned over into the motor, halfway burying herself in the engine, whacking unmercifully at the contents. The attendant at a nearby service station paused momentarily from wiping the windshield of a car to gape at the shapely set of legs and rounded derriere protruding from the hood of the old truck.

By now the sweat was literally pouring off of Jessica, who was growing madder by the moment. Giving one last vigorous whack to the battery, she straightened back up, her eyes disgustedly surveying the scene before her. Wiping her greasy hands on the bottom of her shorts, she climbed back in the truck, her eyes grimly warning the crass vehicle her patience had run out.

She turned the key once again, and the old engine purred sweetly to life. Jessica closed her eyes and slumped wearily over the steering wheel. This truck was going to be the death of her yet.

She got back out one final time to slam down the old hood, which took three tries, naturally, before she was able to get the lock to catch.

She jumped back into the truck and ground the gears into first, causing everyone on the sidewalk to grit their teeth at the grating, tearing sound coming from the old truck. She pulled out onto the main street, gunning the old truck for home, glancing nervously at her watch. She only had thirty minutes before Jason arrived, and she still had to take a shower. She felt as though she had worked on a chain gang this afternoon. Oh, well, she'd hurry.

The last stoplight caught her at the end of town. She sat tapping her nails on the steering wheel waiting for the green light. When the signal changed, she peeled out and was fairly flying along the road leading to the farmhouse. She eased up on the gas pedal, thinking the last thing she needed today was a speeding ticket. She was not too surprised to notice that the truck continued on at the same speed.

Here we go again, she thought.

She was stomping her foot on the pedal, trying to unstick it, as the driveway to Aunt Rainey's came into view. Jessica put her foot on the brake pedal hard, at the same time trying to negotiate the turn into the drive at break-neck speed. Aunt Rainey's few remaining chickens set up a terrible squawking, their feathers flying as they valiantly tried to fight their way out of the path of the careening truck.

Jessica shot into the farmyard at the speed of a bullet, her violet eyes widened in astonishment as she saw the long gray Lincoln Continental sitting in the drive. The thought barely had time to register in her mind before the truck came to a grinding halt, embedded in the Continental's rear end. The melodious tinkle of the lenses falling from the Lincoln's taillights was the only sound that could be heard as the old engine died a sputtering death.

The tall man standing on the old porch, about to knock on the door, spun around at the sound of all the confusion. A look of sheer incredulity crossed his face as he walked slowly down the steps, toward Jessica's side of the truck. He looked at the back of his beautiful car with a stunned expression and then turned back to face her.

Jessica looked up and in a very small, defensive voice complained, "You're early."

Still not taking his eyes from Jessica, he leaned casually back against the remains of his bumper, reaching in his shirt pocket for one of his small cheroots. He placed it in his mouth and, holding it in his strong, even teeth, lit it slowly.

Jessica was holding her breath, afraid to move.

He exhaled slowly and in a calm voice asked, "Jessica, would you mind letting me know when you're going to be out on the streets from now on?"

"Oh, Jason!" She let her breath out in a quick spurt. "It's that damn gas pedal again."

Jason shoved himself away from the truck and, showing the first signs of real anger that day, let out an expletive that would have made a sailor blush.

The tips of Jessica's ears turned fiery red. Suddenly it was just too much for her to contend with. Her violet eyes became pools of shimmering water. Her slight shoulders began to shake as she buried her face in her hands and bawled like a baby.

"Oh, hell," he muttered, opening the truck door. She became aware of a set of strong, muscular arms wrapping around her, lifting her out of the truck, drawing her against his hard, solid chest. *He smells so good,* she thought as the clean fragrance of soap and his aftershave drifted to her nostrils. She sobbed even harder.

"Oh, come on now, Angel," he consoled her, stroking the hot, sticky hair away from her forehead, "it can't be that bad."

"But it is, Jason. It is," she cried. "You can't begin to imagine what a nightmare this day has been!" Hot, salty tears were running in streams down her lovely face.

Jason laughed a mirthless laugh. "I think I can," he said sympathetically. "Mine hasn't been what you'd call a red letter day either." His eyes took in his wrecked car.

"Oh, I know, and I'm so sorry about your truck—and now your car. Then there was that ridiculous will." She sniffled loudly. "And then this—this—despicable piece of junk," she exclaimed as her foot shot out kicking the truck that was meekly sitting quiet now on its tires, "has done nothing but torment me all day!" She turned back to the haven of his arms, dissolving in a new round of fresh tears.

"Well, it could be worse," he said with not much conviction. "I don't think the car has quite as much damage as the truck."

"Really?" Her spirits lifted slightly.

Leaving the security of his arms for a moment, she looked up at him in earnest. "My insurance does cover me," she cried jubilantly, trying to improve his day.

A hint of amusement was in his eyes as he answered, "What do you say, let's go in now and wash that pretty face of yours. After that you can fix me a big glass of something cold to drink." With his arms still around her waist he tucked her closely to his side and began walking to the house.

Coming through the door of the living room, Jason pitched his Stetson in Uncle Fred's big reclining chair in front of the stone fireplace.

As Jessica entered the kitchen she asked, "Iced tea be all right?"

"Sounds good to me," he assured her as he sat down at the oak table. "Boy, does this kitchen bring back memories." He sighed, his eyes roaming around the room. "I'd like to have a nickel for every piece of Rainey's apple pie I've eaten in here." He laughed.

Jessica smiled, removing a tray of ice from the freezer compartment of the refrigerator. "You'd be a wealthy man," she kidded back, pouring his glass full of cold tea.

Jessica felt an unusual self-conciousness steal over her with him sitting so close here in the kitchen, his presence filling the room. One of her recurring daydreams crept into her mind. She would be standing here, fixing him something to drink, he, just coming in from the fields that day. Dinner would be simmering on the stove and his favorite apple pie bubbling hot in the oven. He'd come up behind her, putting his arms around her waist, and begin to nuzzle her neck, planting soft, searching kisses along her ears and throat as he reached down, turning off the burners on the stove. Then he would scoop her up in his strong arms, with all thought of food forgotten for the moment, and start carrying her toward their bedroom . . . Jessica's mind jerked back to his voice.

"I'm afraid I was neglectful in my visits to them in the last few years," he said softly to himself.

Jessica picked up his glass and carried it to the table. She felt so guilty about her previous thoughts that she could not meet his eyes as she asked, "Sugar?"

"No, this will be fine," he answered and took a long refreshing swallow. "That tastes good."

She walked back to the counter and picked up her glass, bringing it back to the table and seating herself opposite him, her back to the open window.

"Well, Jessie," he said idly, "how have you been these last few years? You're certainly as pretty as you ever were," he added in a light tone.

A pink blush crept into her cheeks as she replied softly, "Just fine, Jason."

"Rainey said you stayed on to teach in Austin when you finished school. What do you teach?"

"I teach home economics in high school there," she informed him.

"Is that right?" His gaze fastened unconsciously on the graceful curve of her slender neck, running down to the more than ample swell of her breasts in her skimpy halter top. Where had his little Jessie Cole gone? In her place sat a lovely, desirable woman. "I would have thought you'd be married again by now, with a couple of kids of your own to teach," he suggested coolly.

Jessie gave a short ironic laugh. "No, I'm afraid not." Her eyes dropped painfully away from his.

Picking up his glass of tea again, Jason asked curtly, "What did you want to see me about, Jessica?"

Jessica stood and walked over to the large window, gazing momentarily at the sweet-smelling flowers, trying to bolster her courage. Taking a deep breath, she turned back to face Jason.

"Uncle Fred and Aunt Rainey's will was read today."

"And?"

Jessica could feel his eyes resting lightly on her slim, tanned body, bringing old sweet, torturous memories flooding into her mind. Her eyes fell on his soft, sensuous mouth—that perfect mouth which had brought such unbearable pleasure to her that one night so long ago. She could almost feel the teasing yet demanding pressure as it had opened over hers in long drugging kisses. Jessica ran the tip of her tongue around her lips, lightly moistening them as the vague, familiar tightening inside her increased. For the second time that day her violet eyes met his soft, lazy green ones. The tension in the room increased as they both silently relived their brief but passionate wedding night. Jessica could feel herself drowning in the dark jade pools, alive with barely concealed desire as the quiet ticking of the old grandfather clock that sat in the hall filled the silent room.

Shoving his chair back from the table, Jason rose to his feet, striding over to the counter to pour another glass of tea for himself. Jessica jerked her mind determinedly back to the will. "It seems in order for me to inherit the estate, I have to return home and run this farm for six months," she blurted out.

Jason was still standing at the counter, his back to her. Jessica saw his muscles tense slightly before he took another drink from his glass.

"How do you propose to do that? You don't know anything about running a farm, do you?" He set his empty glass back down on the counter.

"Absolutely nothing. I've been gone so many years I wouldn't have the slightest idea what to do with all those cows standing out there."

Jason laughed quietly as he walked back over to the table and sat down. "You were raised here. You'd do better than you think."

"Jason, I don't want to come back here and run this farm! I want to start a catering business of my own, and it just burns me to think that Uncle Fred and Aunt Rainey, even in death, have managed to tear my life up once again . . ." She stopped in mid-sentence, a rosy flush coloring her face.

Jason looked at her pointedly, then shrugged his broad shoulders indifferently. "Then don't do it."

"But without the inheritance I wouldn't be able to start my own business." Jessica strolled back over to the table and dropped into her chair. "I can't for the life of me imagine why they wouldn't let me make my own decisions. My gosh, I'm twenty-five years old now—perfectly able to take care of myself," she finished heatedly.

"Perfectly," Jason responded sarcastically, his eyes on the Lincoln sitting in the drive behind Jessica's back.

Jessica's gaze followed his, and seeing his line of thought, she blurted out, "Jason, I said I was sorry! Believe me," she continued, "I've always had a perfect driving record!"

"Well, you sure blew it all to hell in one day, didn't you?" he said grimly, his eyes still on the vehicle sitting in the drive. Turning to face her again, his bold eyes appraised the graceful lines of her shapely body once again, and he asked with irony, "Aren't you sore from the beating you've taken today?"

"A little," she acknowledged sheepishly. "I probably won't be able to get out of bed in the morning."

"Well, I've always made it a point to help my neighbors," he teased, his eyes sparkling devilishly like the old Jason's, "so if you have any trouble, I'll . . ." He stopped, old memories surfacing in his eyes. "Send one of my men over to help you," he finished lamely.

Great, Jessica thought rebelliously, *just what I always dreamed of!*

Jason got to his feet once again as Jessica began to clear the table. "So what are you planning to do?" Jason asked her. Jessica's stomach fluttered, dreading the odious task before her.

"Jason," she started hesitantly, "you don't have any trouble running your big ranch, do you?"

Jason's features took on a guarded expression, his jade eyes narrowing. "No," he said cautiously. "Why?"

She'd play it safe and appeal to his business side right off, she decided. "It occurred to me you might want to take advantage of a rare business opportunity," she said brightly. "I thought maybe you'd like to run the farm for me!"

Jason's mouth dropped open. Jessica's heart thudded as she plunged on. "No, now wait, Jason. I know what you're thinking, because at first I thought the same thing. I know we didn't exactly part friends eight years ago, but," she rushed on, "we are two mature adults now, perfectly able to set aside our old differences . . ."

"Jessica, just hold it right there," Jason said tensely between clenched teeth.

"No, please, Jason, hear me out." She gulped breathlessly. Somehow she was going to *have* to *make* him run this farm for her! "I'll pay you ten thousand dollars. Just think, Jason! Ten thousand dollars! You could buy some new farm equipment, a new car." She looked guiltily out the window. "You could just consider it your mad money," she suggested helpfully.

Jason interrupted her again. "Look, Jessie, the last thing in the world I need is your mon—"

"Oh, Jason, *please!*" she pleaded, very close to tears now. "I don't know of anyone else to ask," she finished hopelessly.

Jason strode agitatedly back over to the window and began to pace back and forth. "Let me get this straight, Jessica. You want me to run this farm for the next six months . . ."

"For ten thousand dollars," Jessica inserted temptingly.

" . . . for ten thousand dollars," Jason conceded. "Now, I'm just supposed to hop over here every day, run your farm, and forget all about what happened eight years ago? Dammit, Jessica! Do you know what you're asking?"

"Well, you wouldn't have to see me much," Jessica promised resentfully. "I'd stay out of your way."

"That isn't the point, Jessica!" Jason stopped pacing, coming to a halt in front of her chair, pulling her swiftly to her feet, his eyes looking deep into her simmering, lavender ones. "There's not enough money in the world to tempt me to put myself back in that emotional blender you had me in years ago. I've spent eight long years trying to get you out of my blood, and I'll be *damned* if I'll let you do that to me again." A tense muscle worked along his smooth, clean-shaven jaw as Jessica stared back at the familiar loved face before her.

"You never did believe that I let you go because I had no other choice, did you?" she whispered softly.

"You had other choices," Jason said curtly, their faces still perilously close, making her bones turn to liquid jelly as his soft, clean breath fanned her face.

"Did I, Jason? What choices did I really have? I was under age, and Uncle Fred had a serious heart condition, not to mention the fact that I owed them a tremendous debt of gratitude for taking me into their home, loving me as their own child. I just couldn't break their hearts," she finished sadly, her eyes reflecting the deep hurt she was experiencing.

"So instead you broke mine," Jason said huskily.

"And mine, too," she said quietly.

"It doesn't matter, Jessie. You'll never have the opportunity to do it again," Jason stated firmly, stepping back from her.

Jessica felt the sun had gone behind a cloud as the warmth of his hard, granite body moved away from her. Her temper rapidly boiled to the surface, and her eyes turned to a dark purple as she whirled around to confront Jason. "Well, if you were so all-fired brokenhearted over me, why didn't you come after me—fight harder for me— *do something* other than just walk away? I never even *saw* you again until the other day at the cemetery, Jason Rawlings!"

"You made your choice that morning, right here in this room, *Ms. Cole!*" Jason made stabbing motions with his finger at the spot Jessica was standing in.

"If you had loved me, that wouldn't have stopped you!" Jessica blazed.

"If *you* had loved *me*, there would have been no choice!" Jason glared.

"I don't know how we got into this discussion in the first place," Jessica screamed. "Will you or will you not run this damn farm for me for the next six months?" Jessica's temper was boiling over now.

"I'll think about it," Jason shot back sarcastically, reaching for his hat.

"Well, by all means," Jessica responded snidely, "let me know when you reach a decision."

Giving her one last disgusted look, he slammed out of the farmhouse. When he reached his car, he shot another dirty look at the kitchen window, backed out of the drive, and with his back bumper dragging on the ground sped angrily toward his home.

Jessica had just stepped out of a hot bath an hour later when the phone rang. Wrapping the large fleecy white towel around her, she ran to answer it.

"Hello."

"I'll run your damn farm for you." Jason's tense, gruff voice said over the wire.

"Thank you," Jessica murmured politely.

"I'll be by in the morning to discuss the details. All right?"

"All right."

The loud click on the end of the line popped in Jessica's ear. Replacing the receiver gingerly, she did a happy little hop down the hall.

"I'll be here," she told Tabby exuberantly. Tabby opened one disinterested eye. It was apparent that he couldn't care less.

CHAPTER FOUR

The loud insistent knocking on the front door brought Jessica out of a sound sleep early the next morning. Fumbling for her robe, she groped her way downstairs, her head still fuzzy from sleep.

"I'm coming. I'm coming," she mumbled sleepily, jerking the door open angrily to confront a broadly grinning Jason. Leaning wearily against the doorsill, she glared purple daggers before reprehending him. "Jason, do you realize what time it is?"

"Gettin' late," he answered cockily, his eyes surveying her scanty attire appreciatively. "Almost six o'clock!"

Jessica sagged more heavily against the door. "I didn't even hear you drive up!"

Jason lifted one golden-brown brow ironically. "I haven't got anything to drive up in. I rode my horse over." Jessica moaned. "Surely," Jason continued brightly, "you haven't forgotten a farmer's day begins early, Jessica."

"I've tried my best to," Jessica confessed, smiling sheepishly.

"Well, Angel," he said matter-of-factly, "you'd better start remembering. We've got a lot of things to talk over." He turned her in the direction of the kitchen, and one large hand came down to give her a swat on her delectable fanny. Jessica whirled around in surprise as he continued pushing her toward the kitchen. "Isn't this going to be fun?" he heckled, giving her a sexy wink.

Boy, he sure was in a good mood this morning, Jessica thought as she filled the coffeepot with water. Setting it back down on the counter, she stood on tiptoe to reach the can of coffee on the top shelf. Straining hard, her fingers kept sliding the can back farther on the shelf, and her housecoat climbed up her shapely legs.

Jason was sitting at the kitchen table nonchalantly smoking one of his thin little cigars, the sweet aroma pleasantly filling the old kitchen. By now Jessica's short housecoat was nearly up to her bottom. Jason sat quietly, watching her growing frustration.

Whirling around angrily, she fumed at him, "Can't you at least help?"

Jason looked at her in total innocence. "You think I'm crazy? I'd much rather sit here and watch you make that coffee than I would drink it."

"Very funny, Jason. Now would you please hand me the can of coffee?"

Jason stood up reluctantly and handed her the can of coffee. Their hands touched briefly before he let go of the can. Jessica felt the familiar surge of desire course through her veins as she quickly jerked her hand away to spoon the grounds into the basket. As she plugged in the pot to perk she asked grudgingly, "Have you had breakfast?" If he was going to work for her, she was going to have to get along with him.

"Two hours ago."

"Oh." Jessica sat down opposite him at the table. "All right, then, what do we need to discuss?"

"First of all, I'm going to have to hire at least three more men to help run this farm."

Jessica yawned, laying her head down on the kitchen table. "That's all right with me," she said sleepily.

"Second—Jessica, look at me when I'm talking."

Jessica turned bleary eyes toward Jason, her head still lying on the table. "Is this permissible, sir?"

Shaking his head tolerantly, he continued, "Second of all, I won't have room for three more men to live on my farm, so they will have to stay here."

Jessica's head raised slightly as she cocked one perfectly arched brow. "Here?"

"That's right. In fact, if you have no objections, I'm going to move three of my own men in, too. My bunkhouse is too crowded as it is now."

"You want *me* to live here in this house with six strange men?" Jessica gasped, coming wide awake now.

Jason laughed at the look of consternation on her drowsy face. "No, you'll be coming over to live at my house. Next I'll have to know how much working capital you have on hand—there's some fence down in several areas—"

"*Wait a minute, Jason!*" Jessica was wide awake now. "Let's back up to the part where I come over to live at your house."

Jason looked at her blandly. "What about it?"

"You wouldn't care to humor me and elaborate on that just a hair more, would you?" She smiled with saccharine sweetness, her eyes darkening noticeably.

"Not at all. My housekeeper's sister has had to have major surgery and will need constant care for the next few months. Mrs. Perkins left last week and won't be back for several months at least." He stood to walk over to the coffeepot. "Now, if I have to run two farms, I certainly don't plan on taking the time to find a new housekeeper. So in essence, Jessica, if I'm going to do you a favor, you're going to do one for me."

"But, I'm *paying* you to run this farm," Jessica said hotly, not liking his logic one bit.

"All right. I'll pay you to run my house," Jason said simply.

Jessica sat staring mutinously at his broad back. What a mess! How could Uncle Fred and Aunt Rainey have done this to her, she asked herself again for the hundredth time. "I don't like it," Jessica told him, getting up to get herself a cup of the freshly brewed coffee.

"Take it or leave it," Jason said indifferently.

"Would you still run the farm if I refused?" she asked hopefully.

"No."

Jessica slumped dejectedly back down in her chair. "Then, I guess I'll take it," she said glumly.

"I thought you'd see it that way," Jason said, sitting back down at the table. "You get your things packed today, and I'll pick you up later this evening and take you over to the house."

"This soon? Why can't we wait for a few days?" Jessica gasped.

"I want to make the change as soon as possible," Jason told her sternly. "As soon as these living arrangements are settled, I can get on with my work."

"I thought you didn't want me around, or to be involved with me in any way, Jason," Jessica reminded him spitefully.

"I don't. But as you pointed out, we are two reasonable adults, and this is too good a proposition to pass up. Ten thousand dollars is a lot of 'mad money,' Angel!"

Jessica felt a stabbing pain of discomfort. Well, what had she expected? She had known all along he was doing it for the money. Then why did she feel such crushing disappointment?

Rising to his feet once again, Jason reached for her, pulling her up out of her chair. Slipping his arms around her waist, he tipped his head and studied her oval, pixie face in the early-morning sunshine streaming through the kitchen window. Jessica's blood began to pulse hotly through her veins as the faint smell of his aftershave filled her senses. Unbidden, her arms slipped cautiously up around his neck, her body unconsciously snuggling in closer to his. His hands began to trace light exploring patterns on the sheer, clinging material of her robe.

"You know, Jessica, I've spent more than my share of long, lonely nights waking up in a cold sweat wanting to see those lavender eyes of yours looking at me with hungry anticipation," he said quietly, his husky, deep voice barely a whisper, "and I swore that if I ever got you out of my mind, I'd never let you back in. No, you're just another woman now—a very desirable one, I'll admit—but I know lots of desirable women," he added, "so that shouldn't bother me." Jessica was beginning to feel light-headed, her body molded so tightly to his she could feel the first stirrings of his manly passion. "So," he continued, his eyes still locked with hers, "don't misunderstand the reason for your living in my home. You're my housekeeper—nothing else."

Jessica glared back at him boldly, still locked tightly in his arms. "I wouldn't have it any other way," she assured him.

"Fine. Just so we understand each other. As I said, you're a damn desirable woman, so if you ever feel the need for a 'one night stand,' I'd be more than happy to oblige you, but there will never be anything permanent between us again. Understood?"

Well, really! Jessica thought rebelliously. *Who does he think he is?* The big, conceited oaf thought that her main goal in life would be to get in his bed! Well, she'd play his stupid little game and happily come out the victor. Putting on the meekest of her faces, she lowered her eyes respectfully and said in a quiet, sedate voice, "I understand, Jason. I'll try to stay out of your way as much as humanly possible." Bringing her mouth close to his, she brushed her lips lightly over his, feeling his body tense instantly. "Thank you for being such a wonderful man. Running my farm, letting me come and live in your house."

Jessica released a long wistful sigh, then abruptly captured his mouth with hers, searing his lips with a bold, demanding kiss, her soft moist tongue scrimmaging playfully to meet his.

Jason, momentarily stunned, hesitated for a fraction of a second before his mouth took possession of hers. The room grew very silent as they stood locked in each other's arms, their mouths sweetly devouring each other. Jessica's knees began to tremble as Jason deepened the kiss, his lips moving hungrily against hers. His hands cupped her buttocks, moving her in closer against the lean tautness of his muscled thighs.

Jessica moaned softly as he broke the kiss, whispering huskily, "What in the hell do you think you're doing, lady?"

Jessica closed her eyes, savoring the feel of his beautiful, strong body next to hers. She ran her hands lightly over his heavily corded arms as he brought his mouth back down to merge helplessly with hers once again. What had started out to be a game had suddenly turned quite serious. Jessica had to put a stop to it immediately. She started to pull away determinedly, but Jason blocked her move effectively, his arms tightening like a steel vise around her slim waist. "Oh, no you don't, Angel," he breathed raggedly. "You started this, now I'll finish it!" His mouth caught hers one more time, leaving Jessica trembling at the intensity of his ravishing kiss. She leaned closer to his granite body, pressing herself tightly against him as he caressed the softness of her breasts. Jessica felt herself

72

drowning in his arms, powerless to keep her overwhelming feelings of love for him from rapidly surfacing again.

Jessica broke away violently, fighting to regain some semblance of composure. What had gone wrong? *She* was supposed to be in firm control of this situation. Jason's heavy breathing filled the quiet kitchen as his emerald-green eyes locked with her lavender ones obstinately. Drawing a shaky breath, Jessica pasted a condescending smile on her flustered face. "Well, now that we have that all settled, and I know what my place will be in your house, I'd better get busy," she said matter-of-factly, her heart still thudding out of control. "It will probably take me all day to pack. See you later, Jason!"

She bolted out of the room in a dead run, leaving Jason standing with a look of disbelief on his slightly flushed face and one terrific ache throbbing inside him.

Jessica was packed and ready when one of Jason's men dropped him by the farm late that afternoon. After a quick glance at her packed bags Jason advised her, "We'll have to take your truck." Jessica shrugged her shoulders unconcernedly, reaching down for her cosmetic bag.

As they started down the porch steps Jason held out his hand. Looking at it in bewilderment, Jessica asked, "What do you want?"

"The keys to the truck," he said firmly.

"Why? I can drive," Jessica told him sharply.

"Bet me!" Jason said sarcastically.

Disgustedly Jessica flung the keys to him. Brother! He would never let her live those car wrecks down!

They drove back to Jason's house in strained silence. Jessica's ride on the passenger side of the old truck was as nerve-racking as the rest of the cantankerous old relic. Her seat was loose at the bottom, swaying around and making a popping noise every time Jason stopped for a stop sign or started up after one, forcing her to grab for anything solid to keep from sliding out of the seat onto the floor.

She could never recall having to make so many stops while she was driving. Jason seemed to be determined to make as many as possible. She caught him once watching her from the corner of his eye, carefully concealing a devilish twinkle.

At last they turned into the winding drive leading to the farmhouse, which was lined on both sides with towering sycamore trees that made a shady canopy over the road. They traveled on for another mile or so before coming to the house itself—a lovely, homey, one-story brick house nestled in a stand of majestic old oak trees. The carpet of early-summer grass sparkled emerald green, and flowers bloomed riotously around the yard. A large red barn with a tractor and several pieces of farm machinery sat just to the right of the house, with several gleaming white out-buildings in the distance. The white fences surrounding the farm all looked newly painted and lovingly cared for.

Jason stopped the old truck, turned off the key, and said, "I thought you said you were having trouble with the gas pedal sticking on this?"

"It does!" She practically took his head off, but she had noticed, too, that the traitorous thing had purred along like a Cadillac with Jason at the wheel.

"Well," he said skeptically, "remind me to take a look at it before you drive it again. I'd hate to turn you loose on the townspeople again before it's fixed."

Jessica was getting out of her side of the truck, and with a slam of the door she retorted, "Ha, ha," in her most sarcastic voice. "How many times do I have to say, I'm sorry, Jason?" she continued. "What do you want— blood?"

Jason laughed and affectionately took a swat at her rounded derriere as they walked to the wide screened-in porch sitting off the back entrance to the house.

"What's the matter, hellcat, losing your sense of humor?" he taunted.

74

Jessica refused even to dignify his question with an answer.

A large golden retriever came bounding toward them, making a friendly lunge at Jessica and nearly knocking her off her feet in his exuberance.

"Get down, Alfie," scolded Jason. "You better start showing some manners around this ill-tempered lady. She's going to be the new hand that feeds your face," he teased the affectionate dog, who was licking Jessica's hands, his tail wagging so hard it was nearly throwing him off balance.

Jessica was returning pat for lick. "Don't believe a word this nasty man tells you, Alfie. I'll feed you manners or not," she assured the retriever. Looking at Jason, she added sweetly, "I'll have to feed your master, and he doesn't have any!" Satisfied he still had a meal ticket, Alfie wandered back toward the barn happily.

Jessica and Jason had started toward the house when they heard a shrill whistle down by the barn. Jessica saw a nice-looking man, around her own age, stride swiftly toward them from the barnyard.

"Hey, Jason, wait up!"

"What is it, Rick?" Jason paused beside Jessica, his eyes narrowing slightly.

Eyeing Jessica appreciatively, Rick approached the couple. "Who's the pretty lady, boss?"

"Jessica Cole, meet Rick Warner. Jessica is my . . . new housekeeper," Jason said lightly.

"Housekeeper! Damn, what agency did you get her from? I'm going to call and have them send me four right over for the bunkhouse." Rick grinned broadly.

Jessica smiled and shifted uncomfortably beside Jason.

"Cool it, Rick," Jason said sternly. "Don't let me catch you hanging around the house any more than necessary."

"Me?" Rick asked in mock innocence. "Do I look like the type that would hang around a gorgeous lady like this one when there's work to be done?" Rick's brown eyes twinkled merrily.

Jason's green eyes flashed him a silent warning. "Did you want something?" he asked briskly.

"Yow. The garage called and said it would be a couple of weeks on your car and truck. Man! How did you manage to tear both of them up all in the same day?" he asked in astonishment.

Jessica blushed as Jason's eyes caught hers briefly. "Just lucky, I guess," he answered flippantly, turning back toward the door.

"See you around, pretty lady," Rick promised optimistically.

"Glad to have met you," Jessica told him politely.

"Don't be taking up the men's time with a lot of idle chatter," Jason warned her as they entered the house.

"Oh, I won't, master! If you'll just throw me some stale bread and water in the door occasionally, I promise no one will ever know I'm around," she said brightly as she stepped into the kitchen.

It had been many years since she had been in this room, but everything was still as she remembered it. The rest of the house was much smaller, in general, than Uncle Fred and Aunt Rainey's, but Jessica had always loved this kitchen more than any other room in the whole house. It had a cozy, warm feeling with windows across one whole wall on the south letting in all the light and sunshine anyone could desire. The round glass kitchen table sat in front of the windows, with a large sliding glass door leading out to a covered patio. The windows had cheery yellow Cape Cod curtains, blending with the coppertone dishwasher, stove, and refrigerator. A long island bar ran almost the length of the kitchen, the butcher-block counter tops and sink providing enough space for any woman to "create" to her heart's content.

They walked on into the living room, and Jessica's heart fell as she saw the drab color scheme in here. She had always liked lots of color in her decorating, and although the furniture was of good quality, the tones were all drab browns and greens. Plain—that was the word she would use to describe it—just downright plain!

Jason noticed the expression on her face go from pleased to troubled after their entrance to the living room. "Mom always loved her kitchen best, so she never spent much time on the rest of the house," he said defensively. He had been born and raised in this house with his brothers, Eric and Randall, and had stayed on here when his parents had passed away several years ago. Eric had married and was living in Dallas with his wife and their small child, and Randall was working in the oil fields in Texas, never having married. That much Jason had told her on the way over, but little else. Trying to get anything personal out of him was like trying to pull hen's teeth. He didn't waste time on idle chitchat.

Jessica's eyes ran over the massive red brick fireplace that covered one whole wall on the north side, while wide, airy windows like those in the kitchen stretched across the south wall. The rays of the late-evening sun were pouring through them, falling on a monstrous plant that looked very out of place sitting in the room. Jessica felt it would feel more at home in a jungle. The poor, sick plant looked as though it had been through the ravages of war. The few leaves remaining on its limbs were limp and turning yellow. Just her eyes resting on it made it give up another leaf to the floor, and a most peculiarly unpleasant odor surrounded it.

Jessica approached it hesitantly. Peering into its large clay pot, she saw a huge glob of coffee grounds lying on the soil.

"What's this?" she asked Jason suspiciously.

He walked over to peer into the clay pot with her, deep concern written on his face. "My plant," he said. "It doesn't seem to be doing very well."

That *had* to be the understatement of the year!

"I don't understand what I'm doing wrong," he complained. "I've tried everything people have suggested, but I can't seem to get it back on its feet."

"What is that rotten, nauseous smell?" she asked in a puzzled tone.

"Oh, that," he said, very unconcerned. "It's fish emulsion."

"Fish emulsion? What is that?"

"It's plant food. The girl at Wal-Mart said it was a good one, but I'll tell you," he confessed, "the smell gets pretty rank in the heat of the day."

Jessica laughed. "Maybe you should take it out on the patio and let the sun absorb the smell on the days you feed it the plant food," she suggested helpfully. Judging by the look that came over his face, you would have thought she had suggested they take a gun and shoot Alfie.

"Move that plant?" he asked incredulously. "Why, there wouldn't be a leaf left on it!"

Jessica straightened slowly from where she had been bending over the diseased plant and looked up into troubled green eyes.

"You certainly have a point there," she conceded.

"Well"—he shrugged philosophically—"it's looking better than it did."

Turning his attention back to the tour of the house, he started down the wide green-carpeted hall, calling over his shoulder, "Come on, I'll show you our bedroom. You may want to freshen up a bit before we eat. I've got a couple of steaks we can grill—"

"*Our* bedroom?"

He stopped momentarily, a slightly cocky grin spreading across his tanned face. "I just got to thinking after I left you this morning, Jessie, as long as we're going to live in the same house for the next few months, and taking into consideration we *were* married at one time . . ." He paused, looking at her in amusement. "Granted, twelve hours isn't exactly a golden wedding anniversary, but since we both

78

agree we can keep ourselves emotionally detached, why shouldn't we enjoy each other's company during your stay. I'm sure you have needs, just as I do, so—we could just look at it as the 'fringe benefits' of this business arrangement."

Jessica stared at him aghast. "Are you serious?"

"Perfectly serious," he answered nonchalantly.

"And you think I'd go along with something so disgusting?" Jessica asked in disbelief.

"Why not? I'm a man, you're a woman. I'm willing to take full advantage of the situation if you are." He had a licentious smirk on his face.

Jessica stared at him, totally fed up. "That's really magnanimous of you! You have got the worst case of colossal gall I have ever encountered in all my life," she fumed heatedly.

His face fell. "What are you getting so hot under the collar for?" he argued back. "You think it's going to be easy living in the house with you like a damn eunuch for the next few months?"

"You're the one who thought up this stinking idea in the first place, Jason!" she pointed out bluntly.

"Well, of all . . ." Jason's temper was simmering now, his eyes shooting fire. "I suppose you won't even give it some thought?"

"When hell freezes over," she shouted, her temper matching his. Even though there was nothing Jessica would enjoy more than to partake of those "fringe benefits," as he so crudely put it, she still had her pride! She wasn't his love-sick little puppy anymore. She wasn't about to give herself to him under those revolting conditions.

"What's that supposed to mean, Jessica? Am I supposed to pray for a hard winter down there?" Jason stormed.

"Well, you sure had better if you expect me to sleep in that room with an arrogant oaf like you," she shrieked.

His mouth dropped in astonishment and he shouted, "Well, that tears it!" He threw open the door directly behind her and pointed into the room with swift jabbing motions. "You just plant your prudish little fanny right in there, and I'll stay in *my* room, and we'll just see who cries uncle first." With his sparkling green eyes flashing, he yelled, *"And it sure as hell won't be me!"*

Jessica drew herself up to her full five feet two inches, and with her lower lip jutted out she replied in a steely calm voice, "You don't have to shout."

Jason let out a snort of disbelief.

Picking up her cosmetic bag, she swept regally past him into her allotted cell. The last words she spat at Jason before slamming the door loudly in his face were: "Well, you can bet your sick plant it won't be me either!"

CHAPTER FIVE

The first few weeks of their "business arrangement" proved that the word *uncle* was not in either one's vocabulary.

The farmhouse had undergone an almost miraculous change. Bright throw pillows and paintings now enlivened the rooms with their vivid splashes of color. Lush green foliage adorned each room throughout the house. Even Jason's prized plant now showed signs of rapidly improving health.

Jessica had washed and ironed all the curtains that now hung freshly starched at the windows and had mopped and waxed the kitchen floor until you could see your face in the finish. She had shampooed the green, plush carpeting in the living room, bedrooms, and hall, bringing back the color to almost new.

The mouth-watering smells that reached Jason each night when he came home made him weak with hunger. He was overwhelmed the first time he came home to be greeted by a tall glass of iced tea waiting for him and his favorite apple pie bubbling hot in the oven.

His clothes now hung, cleaned and pressed, in his closet, buttons all replaced, and his socks were mended and lying neatly in his dresser drawers. That in itself was a source of amazement to him, the way she could mend those socks so neatly! He had asked Mrs. Perkins to mend several pairs for him one day, and for weeks he had felt like he was walking on rocks. Finally he had given up completely and in a fit of anger uncharacteristic of him thrown them all away and bought new ones. But when Jessica mended them, they were comfortable—really comfortable!

Jessica was living in her own corner of heaven these days. She had her dream house, with her flowers, and her Jason to cook for. Of course she didn't have her children, she thought wistfully, and this arrangement was only for such a short time; but she would always have these memories. No one could take that from her.

Although Jason totally ignored her as a woman—she could have had three eyes and four legs as far as he was concerned—they did get along nicely together in lots of other ways. No matter what mischievous thing she came up with, he would always play right along with her. Even so, they seemed to be engaged in a running battle of wills, neither one ever conceding a point on any issue.

Jessica was humming to herself this morning as she started a load of dirty clothes in the washing machine. She began to giggle, thinking of their first breakfast together, when she had gotten up early after hearing Jason in the shower, determined at least to make his home as pleasant as she could for the next six months even if she couldn't let herself join him in his bedroom. With Mrs. Perkins gone the house had turned into a shambles very quickly. Jessica recalled she had just set Jason's plate of bacon and eggs in front of him that morning when she noticed his plaid cotton work shirt clinging to his skin like Saran Wrap. She walked back to the oven, took out a pan of light, golden-brown biscuits, and placed them on the trivet sitting on the table. Walking to the large refrigerator, she removed the juice and butter. As she poured him a glass of juice her eyes returned to his shirt.

"What's the matter with your shirt?" she asked inquisitively.

He was spreading generous amounts of golden butter over his flaky, hot biscuit. He glanced down at his attire and shrugged his broad shoulders. "Damned if I know," he said unconcernedly, biting into the steaming biscuit.

"It looks like static electricity," she remarked, buttering her own biscuit and reaching for the honey sitting on the table. She smeared an ample amount on the biscuit, licking her fingers free of the sweet, sticky substance clinging to them. "Have you been doing your own laundry?" she ventured.

"Trying to," he grinned. "It's not one of my favorite things."

She stood up, reached for the coffeepot, and poured Jason's thick brown mug full of the hot liquid. "Do you use fabric softener when you wash?" she persisted.

He was busy eating his third biscuit when he said curtly, "I don't know what I use. It's sitting in there on the washing machine in a big box." He was getting a little tired of the conversation.

"Well, that's just the washing powder," she informed him. "Don't you use anything but that when you wash?"

He shot her a rather impatient look and said, "No, I just put a cup of that stuff from the blue box in the washing machine and turn it on. When it's through, I put it in the dryer, turn it on 'normal heat,' and press the start button," he muttered in a monotone voice, "just like Mrs. Perkins told me to."

Jessica shook her head and picked up her coffee cup. "Doesn't that bother you, clinging to your skin like that all day?" she continued.

"It's irritating," he agreed in a clipped tone.

"Well"—she sighed—"I'll do your laundry from now on." She picked up her juice glass and took a small sip from it.

Jason finished his meal, pushed away from the table, and stood up, reaching for his hat, which hung on the coatrack by the back door of the kitchen. "Well, I'd appreciate it if you could get it straightened out, Angel. My underwear has been taking a lot of indecent liberties with me lately," he said, giving her a broad wink as he walked out the door.

Exactly one month to the day after Jessica's arrival, her wonderful make-believe world came tumbling down around her. They had just finished supper, which Jason had eaten rapidly, leaving the room the minute he was done. She could hear the shower running as she cleared away the dinner dishes, wondering idly what his big hurry was tonight. Fifteen minutes later a red convertible pulled up in the drive and "beeped" loudly.

Jessica peeked out through the kitchen curtain, her heart sinking as she saw the pretty, brown-haired girl who smiled warmly at her. Jessica smiled back, then dropped the curtain. The clean, fresh smell of Jason filled the room as he walked through the kitchen toward the back door. Opening the screen, he told Jessica shortly, "I may be late. Just leave the back door unlocked."

Jessica watched as he walked out to the red car, leaned down and kissed the driver, then went around to the passenger's side and slid in. The car pulled swiftly out of the drive in the direction of town.

Jessica walked away from the window, sharp pangs of

jealously painfully coursing through her. Well, what had she expected? She had known there had to be other women in Jason's life. The last thing in the world he would be was a monk! But it still hurt, she thought, wiping at the unexpected tears that rose in her eyes. How different things could have been, she thought resentfully, if only she had had the gumption to stand up to Uncle Fred and Aunt Rainey concerning her marriage.

Wiping ineffectually at the streaming tears, she washed the last skillet, rinsed it, and laid it in the drainer. Turning out the light in the kitchen, she wandered back through the silent house, clicking on a small lamp in the living room, her eyes falling on one of Jason's shirts that he had carelessly draped there. She walked over, picked it up, and hugged it to her momentarily. The unique, special smell of Jason assaulted her nostrils, the faint aroma of his aftershave clinging to the soft fabric. Once again Jessica felt the wetness on her cheeks as tears slid rapidly down her face. Giving in to an overwhelming feeling of loneliness, she buried her face in the shirt, and her slender body shook with the force of her deep sobbing. She loved him more than life itself, but he would never be hers again. Only once in a lifetime could anyone feel the kind of love she felt for Jason. Jessica didn't know how she would ever bear the pain of losing him again.

It was very late when she finally heard the car pull into the drive. Jessica had been trying to concentrate on the book she had taken to bed, meeting with little success. With a deep sigh she reached up and switched off her bedside lamp. Snuggling down into her bed, she heard Jason let himself in the back door, not any too quietly. Banging his way down the hall, he paused before her door and peeked in, his tall form appearing very comforting to her.

"Hope I didn't wake you, Angel," he said insincerely.

"No, I was awake." Now that he was back, Jessica suddenly felt very hostile toward him.

He walked on into the room and sat down on the edge of the bed. The light from the hall formed a hazy glow in the dark room. Jessica sat up, modestly pulling the sheet up around her bodice. Jason's eyes followed her movements as though he enjoyed her discomfort.

"What did you do this evening?" he asked conversationally.

"Nothing as interesting as you, I'm sure," she replied in a petulant voice.

"Really? How do you know what I did?" Jason asked in surprise.

"I guessed." Jessica lay back down, pulling the sheet up around her neck. "Who was your date?"

"Monica Sawyers," he told her teasingly, obviously enjoying her barely concealed jealousy.

"She was very pretty," Jessica said grudgingly. "Have you been dating her long?" Drat! Why did she ask that? She didn't want to know anything about the woman.

"About a year." He confirmed her worst fear.

"Oh," Jessica mumbled weakly, "then it must be serious."

"It could be," Jason said evasively.

"If you don't mind, Jason, I'm very tired," Jessica said wearily. "Could we finish this conversation in the morning?" If she had to hear about all of Monica's attributes, she'd scream.

"You really ought to get to know Monica, Jessie. She's a nice person," Jason said earnestly, making no move to leave the room.

"I will, Jason," Jessica said with mock enthusiasm. "I'll bake her a cake one of these days and take it over to her."

"You wouldn't by any chance be jealous of her, would you?" Jason leaned down closer to her, his fresh, clean smell washing over her.

"Not at all. Good night, Jason," she tried once again.

"You're sure?"

Jessica bolted up in bed, her patience clearly at an end.

"Look, Jason, I don't want to hear about your overactive sex life, nor do I want to discuss your little playmates. Is that clear? Just please get out of here and leave me alone!"

"Overactive sex life?" Jason heckled. "What do you think I am, some sort of pervert?"

Jessica glared at him. "You said it, I didn't!"

"Oh, ex-Mrs. Rawlings, I believe you *are* jealous." Jason was definitely pushing his luck.

Shoving him away irritatedly, Jessica lay down again, trying to totally ignore him now. Jason followed her head to the pillow, his warm mouth teasing lightly down the side of her neck. "Let me try out the new 'perverting' techniques I've recently developed on you, Angel," he taunted unmercifully, his arms trapping her against the pillow.

"Jason Rawlings, let me go!" she threatened grimly.

"I can't do that," he said in mock sadness. "We perverts don't have any scruples at all." His hands reached up under her thin gown, firmly grasping both of her soft breasts in his hands. His bold touch caused Jessica to catch her breath sharply as she squirmed harder to escape his hold.

"Let me go, you scurrilous toad!" Jessica was barely able to conceal her mounting laughter.

"Toad? Now she calls me a perverted toad!" Jason's hands left her breasts to tickle her rib cage, sending her into a fit of uncontrolled giggles.

"Jason!" she pleaded, gasping. "*Stop!* I can't stand it!" Tears of laughter rolled down her cheeks and her sides were killing her. Jason was tumbling her around on the bed like a rag doll, both of them caught up in his playful antics. Suddenly his teasing hands came back in contact with the velvet smoothness of her breasts, this time lingering for an instant, the soft satiny mounds fitting perfectly in his large hands.

"Mmmmmm," he groaned, all signs of laughter fading from his deep voice. "I think the scurrilous toad has found the lily pad he wants to sleep on tonight." His mouth touched one of the pink pliant crests gently.

Jessica was instantly aroused by his searching mouth, her laughter dying a sudden death. "Jason, don't," she pleaded breathlessly. She couldn't stand this sort of teasing for very long. If he kept it up, she was afraid she would shock him speechless by ripping off his clothes and fulfilling *all* the fantasies she had dreamed up during the last eight years.

Jason moaned again, burying his face in the white fleshy mounds, breathing in the sweet, flowery fragrance of her soft skin. With deliberate slowness his mouth began to make its way toward her throat, his tongue tasting her, his breathing becoming heavier. His hand traced along the curve of her thigh, over the softly rounded hip, searching its way upward once again to claim the voluptuous mound of her breast. He could feel her heartbeat pounding against his fingertips.

Jessica's body had gone totally limp as waves of pleasure enveloped her, her hands reaching out to grip the sides of Jason's heavily muscled arms, her breathing matching his now as his lips moved up her neck, pressing slow, languid kisses along the way. When he reached her ear, the moist warmth of his mouth and tongue sent cold shivers coursing through her trembling body as he pleaded huskily, "Jessie, this is getting out of hand. Stop me—please!"

Jessica's arms came up around his neck as her body strained closer to his, her breath catching as she became aware of the hard warmth of his arousal against her bare leg. *Stop him? Who does he think I am—Wonder Woman?*

Closing her eyes in hopeless surrender, she reached to bring his mouth down to meet hers, murmuring, "I can't —I don't want to. I've waited eight long years for this night." She tightened her hold on him as she continued, "I *want* you to make love to me. Please don't make us stop."

Their eyes met for a fraction of a second as the fires of awakening desire burned brightly between them. Jessica sighed blissfully as his mouth lowered to capture hers in a tender, hesitant kiss, then opened more fully over hers, their tongues mingling in a sweet, rapturous reunion. She smoothed her hands over his head, entwining her fingers in the thickness of his hair, pulling his face closer, forcing the kiss to deepen, swirling them into a whirlpool of passion. Shuddering, Jason broke away shakily, then buried his face back in her neck, kissing her hungrily. "Do you know how long I've dreamed of doing this to you?" he rasped, his hands aggressively beginning to explore every inch of her body, sliding her gown up to give him better access to her perfectly shaped thighs.

Moaning softly, Jessica reached for the buttons on his shirt, aching to feel the touch of his bare skin against hers. She unbuttoned the buttons hastily, her fingers trembling in anxiety. She spread his shirt apart, her hands catching in the thick mat of golden-brown hair on his chest. Tears sprang to her eyes momentarily as she brushed her lips lovingly along his rough skin, feeling that she had at long last come home.

Jason brought her mouth back to his roughly in a series of hot fiery kisses, his hands assaulting her hips, her abdomen, her thighs in deliciously swirling motions. Cursing softly, he shrugged all the way out of his shirt, throwing it on the floor. He stood by the side of the bed to rid himself of his jeans and briefs, and Jessica watched with delight the lithe movements of his tall muscular form in the shadowy room, the faint rays of moonlight from the window touching his sun-bronzed body. *He looks like a Greek god,* she thought hazily—more desirable than she remembered. Her body ached, burned, for his return, her arms reaching out to touch his taut thighs with her fingertips, not wanting to lose a moment's contact with him.

As he crawled back into bed he impatiently jerked her

thin gown off and pulled her back into his arms, his mouth seeking and finding hers once again.

The night took on a magical glow as they lay in each other's arms in the small bed, their mouths hungrily devouring each other, their hands eagerly becoming reacquainted with the delightful secrets of each other's bodies. Jason, seeking the sweetness of her warmth, gradually created an overpowering tension within Jessica as she gently caressed his firm flesh with her fingertips. Jessica would not permit herself to think beyond this moment. She would face tomorrow when it came, but tonight was hers and Jason's and she would allow nothing to take that away from her.

Their bodies blended in perfect harmony as Jason moved to cover her slender body with his. He entered her swiftly, driving deeply as their desire for each other reached unbearable proportions. Soaring high on a swelling tide of rapture, Jessica dug her nails deeply into Jason's back, feeling his hard muscles as they tensed and flexed. Their bodies cried for release as they scaled the mountain of ecstasy together, their hot fires becoming consuming, searing, nearly intolerable, until they both found sweet ecstatic relief. Their quiet erotic moans of beautiful, torturous release blended together, and their mouths clung helplessly together. Jason held her securely and lovingly in his arms as they both tumbled gently back to earth.

The sounds of the summer night surrounded them from the open window as they lay locked in each other's arms, stunned by the intensity of what had just taken place.

Jessica sighed blissfully, snuggling in closer to his heavenly body, planting tiny kisses along his clean-shaven jaw.

"If you don't mind, this toad is going to sack out here for the rest of the night," Jason whispered tiredly.

"Not at all. My toad changed into Prince Charming, and who could refuse to sleep with Prince Charming?" Jessica teased lightly.

"Good night, Angel."

"Good night . . . toad."

Jessica was happily putting the biscuits in the oven when Jason came into the kitchen the next morning. Without saying a word he walked over to the coffeepot, pouring himself a large steaming cupful before returning to the table.

"Hi," Jessica said brightly.

"Hi," Jason grumbled.

"What's the matter? Didn't you sleep well last night?" Jessica's eyes sparkled mischievously. "Well, I did. The most relaxed sleep I've had in . . . a long time."

"No, I slept well . . . Damn it, Jessica! Last night should never have happened."

Jessica felt like he had thrown cold water in her face. "What . . ." she murmured, confusion racing through her mind.

Jason stood up straighter, slamming his coffeecup down. "I said, dammit, we shouldn't have slept together last night, Jessica!"

"But why? You asked me to sleep with you when I first moved in, Jason. What happened? Is it Monica?" She hesitated for a moment, searching his eyes for an answer. "It is, isn't it?" she persisted.

"Of course I'm concerned about Monica, but that isn't the main reason." Jason was visibly upset as he stalked across the room to stand in front of the patio door. He ran his hands through his thick golden-brown hair, the muscles in his back tensing.

"I thought I had made it perfectly clear when you moved in here, Jessica, that I do *not* plan on getting involved again . . . with you."

Jessica's eyes blazed. "We just slept together, Jason. I didn't hog-tie you and drag you to the altar!"

"No, but many more nights like last night and I'd probably be dragging *myself* down the aisle, and there's *no way,* lady, I'm going to give you a chance to walk out on me again!"

"Ohhhhh . . ." Jessica sputtered, grabbing the flaky brown biscuits out of the oven and slamming them down on the kitchen table. "Sit down and eat your breakfast, Jason. I certainly have no plans to molest you ever again. Besides, you're the one who started it."

"I sure didn't see you begging for mercy," Jason said tightly, reaching for a biscuit.

"Well, of all the . . . you're sure no gentleman!"

"Well, you're sure no lady!"

Jessica's temper was boiling as she slammed the plate of eggs and ham down violently in front of him. "Do you want more than one egg . . . *toad!*"

"One's fine," Jason said, calmly picking up his fork to eat, "and you can just simmer down. I simply wanted to get things straight with you . . . all right? No need to get all bent out of shape." He salted his eggs casually.

"I'll try to control myself," Jessica said sarcastically, reaching for a biscuit. "I can do anything when I put my mind to it."

"Fine, then how about hustling your fanny over to the refrigerator and getting me a glass of orange juice . . . housekeeper," he taunted.

"Sure . . . boss." Jessica shoved back from the table, causing his coffee to slosh all over his plate.

Grabbing to retrieve a biscuit, he shot her an infuriating grin as he got up from the table. "Changed my mind. I think I'll clear out while I can still walk!"

"You're a lot smarter than you look, Jason," Jessica heckled.

He breezed by her, giving her a pinch on the derriere before he bolted out the back door chuckling. A few minutes later he stuck his broadly grinning face back through the door, saying mischievously, "Remember, hands off, *Cole!*"

92

Jessica picked up a dish towel and flung it at the door as he banged it shut.

The month of June sped by with Jason keeping a safe distance from Jessica. Outwardly they laughed and talked, but inwardly they were both aware of a tension between them. Jason continued to date Monica, a source of deep irritation to Jessica. Rick Warner continuously hung around Jessica's doorstep, a source of deep irritation to Jason.

The Fourth of July dawned hot and muggy. Jessica sat in front of the kitchen fan, drinking a glass of tea, thumbing through her recipes. She was trying to decide what to take to the annual picnic and Fourth of July dance that had been a standing tradition in this small town for over fifty years. In fact it was the highlight of the year, second only to Christmas. Jessica was especially looking forward to it this year, having been away from home for so long. The meal was always served in the open air unless it rained, in which case it was moved to the covered pavilion. The tables groaned under every type of food imaginable, each woman bringing her own particular specialty. It had turned into an unspoken contest to see who had the most sought-after recipe at the end of the day. Cakes, pies, breads, jams, jellies, fried chicken, hams, big buckets of corn on the cob dripping with homemade butter, freezers of fresh-turned ice cream, watermelons—the list went on and on.

The men would all try to out-eat one another, and the women would throw their diets out the window for the day, only to pay a heavy penalty the rest of the week. Then, after every button on their pants had popped, the old fiddlers would start tuning up their instruments, along with the guitar and banjo players, getting ready for the dancing. Before long every foot would be tapping, hands would be clapping, and couples would start pairing off for the dance. From then on the old pavilion would fairly rock

93

on its foundation until around midnight, when the merchants of the town would put on a spectacular fireworks display, signaling the end of another happy, successful Fourth.

Then came the job of gathering sleepy, tired, slightly grimy children into parents' arms, rounding up all the empty dishes, and heading for home, tired but happy.

Well, she mused, she could always take her German chocolate cake. That always seemed to be a hit wherever she went. Just then she heard Jason's truck drive up and its door slam. A few minutes later he opened the back screen and poked his head in. "Can you come out here a minute, Jessie?"

Jessica looked up in surprise, since he rarely was around the house during the day. "Sure," she readily agreed, closing the recipe file. She got up from the table and trailed him out into the yard. She saw his tractor sitting by his truck, jumper cables lying beside it.

"The tractor's battery is as dead as a doornail. I want you to drive the truck. I'm going to try to pull-start it," he stated calmly.

Jessica felt the first stirring of panic rising in her throat. "I don't know, Jason," she began uneasily. "I'm not very good at things like this. Can't you get Sam to help you?"

"Sam's over mending fence in the south section today," he informed her curtly.

"What about Rick?"

"Everyone's busy right now, Jessie. Just do what I tell you, and you won't have any problems," he said, walking around to hook a thick, heavy cable to the front of the tractor. "Just jump in my truck and drive it. It'll only take a minute."

She walked slowly to the truck, still protesting, "I don't think this is such a good idea, Jas—"

"Just get in it and back it up to the tractor so I can hook this chain on."

She climbed onto the plush seat of the truck and turned

the key in the ignition. The motor started up with a smooth sound. She carefully backed the truck up to the tractor, her palms sweating. Jason hooked the heavy chain to the back of the truck and jumped up onto the tractor seat, giving her instructions. "Now just give it a little gas, ease off on the clutch pedal real slow until you feel the chain go taut, then let off on the gas when you hear the tractor start. Is that clear?"

Sweat was beginning to trickle down her back, and her hands were clammy. She was gripping the steering wheel so hard her knuckles had turned white.

"Pull me down toward the barn," he shouted. "Okay, go!"

"Jason"—she stuck her head out the truck window— "this really makes me nervous," she pleaded desperately one last time.

"Just do it, Jessie," he snapped and shifted the tractor into low gear. "I haven't got time to argue! Are you ready?"

"I guess," she said in a small voice.

"Okay," he ordered once again, "go!"

She started easing down on the gas pedal very slowly. She could hear the chain on the bumper making a popping noise like it was going to tear the whole bumper off the truck. She began crawling down the drive at a snail's pace, perspiration dripping off her face and arms.

"Faster," Jason yelled. "You got to get up more speed."

"Oh, God, I can't do this," she moaned, letting her foot slip from the gas pedal just a little. The heavy chain immediately went slack.

"Keep it taut!" Jason was shouting. "Keep the damn chain taut, Jessie!"

Her foot came back down hard on the pedal this time— too hard. She immediately let up on the gas again. That was a mistake! She now had the truck jerking Jason along on the tractor in giant hiccuping jolts.

"You've got to get the slack out, Jessie!" He was near

hysteria now, screaming at the top of his vibrating lungs. Her foot slammed down even harder on the pedal, and the truck surged forward at a rapid pace—the chain definitely becoming taut! Jessica heard a loud *snap* as the chain broke, catapulting the truck straight toward the barn at very nearly the speed of sound. *Oh, my God,* Jessica thought as she fought frantically to bring the truck under control. She put up a valiant fight, but the truck won. She felt the front end plow through the side of the barn as easily as a hot knife slicing through butter.

She glanced around sheepishly for a moment, then nonchalantly pulled the gear shift into reverse and backed slowly out of the yawning chasm. She hazarded a glance in the rearview mirror at Jason. He was standing up on his tractor, astonishment written clearly on his face. Coming out of his state of shock, he leaped off the tractor, running toward the truck, shouting, "Are you hurt?" with real concern in his voice.

By this time Jessica was shaking like a leaf and feeling like an utter fool again. "No," she said in a shaky voice, "I don't think so."

He let out a long breath and sagged against the truck. He took off his hat and wiped his forehead on the arm of his shirt sleeve. Knocking the dust from his hat on his jean-clad leg, he put it back on his head. "I know where we can make a fast buck, Angel," he said. "I can rent you out as a one-woman demolition squad."

Well, that did it! She was as mad as a wet hen now. Tears sprang to her eyes, and her temper flared. "*I told you I couldn't do it,*" she railed, "but, *no,* you had to make me try it—screaming at me, 'Faster, Jessie, keep the chain taut, Jessie.' By then you had me so nervous I could have died! Now you have the audacity to stand there and insinuate that it was my fault!" She jerked her door open and nearly fell out onto the ground. "Well," she said haughtily, her back stiffening in pride, "I don't have to stand here and take this." With the air of a queen going to hold court, she turned and flounced off toward the house, leaving him standing there in the rubble.

The sounds of hammering and sawing could be heard as the tantalizing aroma of the chocolate cake came drifting out through the open kitchen window. Jessica could see the wrecker pulling Jason's truck out of the farmyard and a ranch hand hammering away on the side of the barn. A feeling of foolishness swept over her again. Even if it wasn't her fault this time, Jason's men were probably thinking he had hired a refugee from a mental institution as his housekeeper. It was a standing joke among his men, the way she systematically went about destroying his vehicles.

She crossed over to the refrigerator and poured a large glass of lemonade, then stepped out through the back door. Jason came walking toward her, his face hot and flushed. "You got an extra glass of that tantalizing stuff?" he asked, eyeing the glass of cold lemonade.

"There's a whole pitcherful," Jessica replied coolly.

"Well, I was coming in to cool off, and by the sound of things I won't have any trouble." He grinned boyishly.

Jessica grinned back pertly. "Go on in the kitchen, Jason. It's nice and cool in there."

Jason stepped into the kitchen, and the heat from the oven nearly knocked him down. "Damn! It's like a furnace in here."

"Isn't it, though?" Jessica said serenely, forcing the laughter from her tone.

"How do you put up with this all day?" Jason asked in amazement, taking off his hat to wipe the sweat from his brow.

Jessica was pouring him a large glass of cold lemonade. "My 'boss' likes big, hot home-cooked meals, remember?"

Jason grinned sheepishly and took the glass of lemonade from her.

"Do you realize the 'boss' has gained ten pounds this month alone on those hot home-cooked meals?"

Jessica smiled proudly, noticing the tiny little tummy protruding slightly over the waist of his jeans. "I'd noticed."

"Why didn't you say something about it being so hot in here, Angel? I'm never in the house enough in the daytime to notice. I'll have one of the men put in an air conditioner first thing in the morning."

"I'd be eternally grateful," Jessica acknowledged.

"You ready for the picnic tonight?" Jason said conversationally, taking another long drink of his lemonade.

"Almost," Jessica replied, checking her cake in the oven.

"I'll try to wind things up soon today so we can get an early start."

Jessica looked surprised. "Am I riding with you?"

"How else did you plan on getting there?" Jason asked skeptically.

"I don't know—riding with Rick, I suppose. Aren't you taking Monica?"

Jason stared out the kitchen window, watching the hammering going on down at the barn. "She'll be there, but I'm not 'taking her,'" he said mildly.

Jessica removed her cake from the oven, the delicious rich chocolate smell permeating the hot kitchen. Jason looked at the cake and inhaled deeply. "Well, there goes another five pounds." He grinned.

"Have you ever thought about not eating any?" Jessica teased gently.

"Nope, that would be sacrilegious."

Jessica giggled. She had managed to find the way to his stomach. Now if she could just find the way to his heart.

"Well, back to the old grind." Jason picked up his hat and shoved it on his head, starting for the back door. He stopped at the door, his eyes catching hers briefly. There was something very unreadable in their soft green depths,

98

Jessica thought. She swallowed hard, longing to walk over and kiss him. If they were married, that's exactly what she would do every time he stuck that handsome mug of his in the door. But they weren't married, and Jessica didn't want to kid herself that they ever would be again.

"Did you want something else, Jason?" Jessica forced herself to ask lightly.

"No, I was just thinking . . ." His voice trailed off. "See you tonight, Angel."

"I'll be waiting," she whispered softly, her eyes shining with love.

The festivities were in full swing when they pulled up in Jason's Continental that evening. He got the picnic hamper out of the trunk, and they made their way through the crowd of friends and neighbors who were shouting their hellos with boisterous backslapping and bone-crushing handshakes.

"Jessica!" Rick Warner's voice caught Jessica's attention immediately. Jason stiffened involuntarily as Rick came bounding up to them, his face a wreath of smiles—all for Jessica.

"Hell-ooo, pretty lady." Jessica had to laugh at his comical elation over her appearance. "I sure hope you brought whatever was making that mouth-watering smell float around in the air this afternoon," he said earnestly. "I've been seriously thinking of offering to marry you all afternoon, just to be able to come home to your cooking every night—among other things." He grinned devilishly.

Taking Jessica's arm firmly, Jason began to steer her on through the picnic grounds. "Her cake will be on the table along with everyone else's, Rick," he mumbled rudely.

Trailing along beside them, Rick petitioned Jason boyishly, his eyes still openly flirting with Jessica, "Can she eat a piece of it with me?"

Jessica giggled again at Rick's obvious lack of fright at

Jason's grim expression. "That's entirely up to the 'pretty lady,' " Jason responded flatly.

"Well, Jessica?" Rick waited hopefully.

"I'll make it a point to look you up when I'm ready for dessert, Rick," Jessica told him smilingly.

Taking her hand in his, he looked at her adoringly. "I'll be waiting, Jessica."

Jason walked on through the crowd, grumbling irritably, "That punk kid gets on my nerves!!"

"For heaven's sake, he's not a kid, Jason. He's my age!" Jessica corrected.

"Then if you two 'kids' want to carry on a love affair, do it when I'm not around," he snapped testily.

Jessica started to retort hotly, then caught herself. Smiling sweetly, she answered, "I'm sorry, Jason. From now on we'll try to control ourselves in your presence. Maybe you and Monica would jot down a few pointers on how to act dignified and show respect to our employer while trying to control our animalistic desires for each other. That is, if you don't have anything more important to do."

"Oh, but you see, Angel, Monica and I *always* have more important things to do, so you and little Ricky will have to run on down to the library and do your own research," Jason responded sarcastically.

Jessica's eyes blazed purple as they walked on through the crowd. "I'll just bet you do, you . . . toad!"

Jason stopped walking and turned to confront Jessica's boiling temper. "Jessica," he said pointedly, "you remember what happened to you the last time you called me that?"

Jessica stared back at him boldly, her chin set mutinously. "You mean the night you made your 'big mistake'? No! I don't remember a thing about it!"

Jason met her bold stare, and then laughter began to rumble deep in his chest. "Unfortunately, Angel, I do."

Jessica's temper receded quickly in the wake of his

laughter, her pixie face breaking into an impish smile. "I lied. I do, too," she admitted calmly.

Jason shook his head tolerantly and reached for her hand. "Come on, wildcat, let's enjoy the picnic."

They walked on through the crowd, Jason still holding her hand. Several people stopped to chat cordially with them. While they were talking with the Ramseys, Jessica noticed Monica standing off to the side, admiring Jason with her big dark-brown eyes. She had the expression of a child staring into a pet-store window full of puppies. Jason looked up, and his eyes met hers. Giving her a cocky wink and a nod of greeting, he turned back to the conversation with Mr. Ramsey. Jessica felt a stab of jealousy tear through her. Would she ever get over the hurt at seeing him with Monica? She knew they were serious about each other, and Monica was really a nice person, so why did it hurt so? Down deep she knew why it hurt. To think of this lovely girl in Jason's arms—where she longed to be more than anything in this world—was like having a knife slice through her heart. She turned and slipped quietly away from Jason, wandering off through the crowd, trying to calm her mangled thoughts.

Everyone was gathering around the tables now, and there was an air of joviality that was catching. Soon everyone was caught up in the lighthearted holiday spirit. Jessica got in line to fill her plate, and Jason and Monica followed not far behind her. She walked over to a table and sat down.

Rick brought his plate over and sat down beside Jessica. "Mind if I join you, Jessica?"

"Not at all." Jessica smiled. Jason shot her a disgusted look as he and Monica joined them. Jessica turned her eyes back to her plate, trying to ignore their presence. For the next few minutes all thoughts of conversation vanished as they dedicated themselves to the feast sitting before them. Finally, after they all agreed they couldn't stuff one more deviled egg down, they sat around conversing in low tones, catching up on all the old gossip and some of the new, Monica and Jessica saying very little.

The women began clearing off the tables, and the musicians started tuning their instruments. Couples grabbed for each other's hands and headed for the pavilion. The really fun part of the night was just about to get underway. It would begin with a couple of hours of square dancing; then, when everyone was totally worn out, things would swing into a slower pace for the remainder of the evening.

The pavilion dance floor was usually jam-packed, and tonight was no exception. Bob Preston was going to do the calling, and he grabbed the microphone, shouting, "Now, listen up, folks. We're goin' to get this dancin' underway. Grab your partner."

Couples began forming squares all around the dance floor, and the band started playing "Cotton-Eyed Joe."

Jessica's eyes were shining and her foot was tapping as she watched the couples, young and old, two-stepping it up out onto the dance floor, the rollicking music filling the air.

"Want to dance the next square?" Jason stood by her side.

"Oh, could we?" she asked, as excited as a child on Christmas morning.

Jason's face broke into a wide smile. "I'm game if you are!"

For the next two hours, Jessica had more fun than she had had in years. It felt *great* to be back home again! She danced every square with a different partner, young and old alike, stopping only once long enough to gulp down a glass of cold punch which Jason had handed to her during one of the breaks in the music.

"Having fun, Jessie?" he asked with a look of tender amusement in his eyes.

"I haven't had so much fun in ages." She giggled, her mind reliving the dance she had just finished with Clevon

Johnson. He had about as much rhythm as a grade-school orchestra!

"Yoo-hoo! *Jas*—on!"

They both turned to see Marcy Mercy bounding through the couples on the dance floor, dragging Willis along behind her. Jessica had never seen a more mismatched couple in her life. Marcy had not lost any of her beauty. On the contrary, she was lovelier than ever, but Willis—Willis gave a whole new meaning to the word homely. There really wasn't an attractive feature about him. He was short and stocky, with a thatch of coarse red hair sitting on his head. He wore glasses so thick it almost made you dizzy just to stand and talk to him. Marcy and Willis looked like Beauty and the Beast together, but one thing was obvious. Willis adored his wife, and strangely enough she seemed to return his affection.

"There you are," Marcy was saying. "I told Willis I hadn't seen you all night. Where have you been hiding?"

"Hi, Marcy," Jason called to her. Under his breath he said to Jessica snappishly, "Stay close. She's like a bad case of poison ivy—hard to get rid of."

"Jessica, you remember Marcy and Willis Mercy, her husband?"

"Certainly," Jessica said. "Hi, Marcy. Willis."

"Oh, hi, Jessica. Why, you've hardly changed, after all these years. How lovely!" she said distastefully.

Jessica smiled tensely. "And neither have you, Marcy."

"How you doing, Willis?" Jason was saying.

"Fine, just fine, Jason. Fine night, isn't it? Everything's just going fine!"

Good heavens, Jessica thought, *he certainly has a limited vocabulary for a banker.*

The music was starting again, and Rick came over, grabbing Jessica's hand, claiming her for his partner. He swept her onto the dance floor and kept her moving at a breathless pace through the steps. She was happily allemande-lefting when out of the corner of her eye she caught a glimpse of the square directly next to theirs. Jason was dancing with Monica, his lean, lithe body keeping perfect time to the music. Monica's smiling face was turned up to his, her eyes shining with undisguised adoration. The night suddenly lost all its magic for Jessica, and her feet faltered in the dance steps.

"Whoa, I've got you, pretty lady," Rick assured her.

She smiled back gratefully, her heart not in the dance anymore. They finished the set, and the band swung into a change of pace with the fiddles playing the sweet, lilting refrain of "The Tennessee Waltz." Rick had automatically turned her around in his arms, and they were gliding back out onto the dance floor when she heard Jason's deep voice at her side.

"Mind if I cut in, Rick?" he asked respectfully for a change.

"Well, I mind, but since you're the boss . . ." he said, grinning, and turned her over to Jason's waiting arms.

She slid into his arms, and the magic glow of the evening came slowly back into the room. He pulled her up tight against his hard, lean body, her hands coming up around his neck. As she laid her head on his strong, solid chest she sighed. This had to be the closest thing to heaven here on earth for her. The fiddles were sweetly telling of someone losing their "little darling," but she had hers right here in her arms, if only for the moment. He guided her effortlessly across the floor, their bodies molded together in a perfect fit. She loved the smell of him—his soap, his tantalizing aftershave, the faint smell of smoke lightly lingering from the little cigars he smoked. The top of her head didn't quite reach to his chin, and he had to bend down just a little as he absently placed soft featherlike kisses along her hairline. His large hands cupped her softly rounded derriere and nestled her in closer to his taut thighs.

The picture of him with Monica surfaced momentarily in Jessica's mind, and she drew back slightly from his intimate embrace. He seemed suddenly surprised, as if he had been wool-gathering.

"What's the matter, Angel?" he asked with concern. "Am I hurting you?"

"No," she answered slowly. "Jason, why have you never married again?"

"Mmmmmmm . . ." he murmured drowsily, listening to the music. "What brought that on?" He pulled her closer into his embrace.

Jessica was feeling a little light-headed from the closeness of him. She could feel the contour of his manliness beginning to stir against her thin dress. "I was just wondering," she whispered weakly.

"Why haven't you?" he asked idly.

"I don't know. I guess I haven't found the right man yet," she said hesitantly, praying for the music to go on forever.

"I don't think I want to hear about the rejects," he said in a soft, husky voice, his hands starting to move seductively over her back in a slow, sensuous pattern.

"There were tons of them," Jessica lied boldly, shivering as his hands increased their rhythm, he being clearly aroused now.

"I'll bet there were," Jason agreed readily, his mouth beginning to search down her neck.

Jessica jerked away, her blood turning to liquid fire. "Aren't you afraid Monica will see you?" she blurted out.

He gave a short laugh and kissed her parted lips lightly. "Now, don't go getting yourself in a snit over Monica," he teased. She hasn't got a contract on me—yet."

"A snit?" she said in an injured tone, drawing back slightly from him again. She turned her soft violet eyes up to meet his jade-green ones, alive now with smoldering desire. "I'm certainly not in a snit, as you call it. I'm just a little surprised, that's all. I certainly wouldn't want you dancing with every woman in the room if you were mine," she finished lamely.

He threw his head back and laughed loudly this time. "Now, isn't it funny that you would see it that way? I used to be yours, and you casually tossed me away in favor of your aunt and uncle. What did you expect me to do, Jessica, wait until you decided there were things more important in life than going to school?" He felt her stiffen in rebellion against him and hastened to add quickly, "Besides, what difference does it make to you who I dance with?" he said in a boyish, teasing tone. "We have no ties anymore. You've had your share of fun with Rick this evening! Remember, honey, this is just a business arrangement. When the six months are over, I'll take my ten grand, and we'll part company. Now, isn't that what we agreed on?"

Jessica's heart sank. He had her there. She *had* said that. Why was her mind always in neutral and her mouth always in gear?

The band had switched to another waltz now, and Jason continued to hold her intimately, gliding around the dance floor, which was lit by hundreds of tiny multicolored lights strung around the pavilion.

"Jason," she said conversationally, "have you ever thought of what you're going to do with all your money?"

Jason tensed slightly and asked cautiously, "All what money?"

"All of the ten thousand dollars you're going to have," she said curiously. That had bothered her. What *was* he going to do with that much money? "Have you given it any serious thought?"

"Yes, I have," he said very solemnly.

"Well?" she prompted. "What are you going to do with it?"

"Well, the first thing I'm going to do is take part of it down to the bank and change it into hundred-dollar bills."

"Yes, and . . ." she urged.

"Then I'm going to carry those hundred-dollar bills around in my pockets, to light my cigars with."

She jerked back from his arms, looking directly into his serious, steady gaze. "You're what?" she exclaimed.

"I'm going to pull out those hundred-dollar bills and light my cigars with them," he said matter-of-factly. "I've always wanted to see the looks on people's faces under those circumstances."

She stopped dancing and looked up at him belligerently. "Have you gone mad?" she admonished. "Totally off your rocker?"

He looked at her in mock innocence again and reminded her, "You *said* to consider it my 'mad money'."

The excited shouts of the children filled the air as the merchants began their elaborate fireworks display as the evening began to draw to a close. Jason led Jessica to a soft grassy spot in the open field and spread out an old army blanket he had retrieved from the back of his car. He fell spread-eagled on his back on the blanket in mock exhaustion. She had to laugh at his exaggerated pose, lying there on the ground. He reached up and pulled her down on the blanket beside him.

"Let's call a cease-fire for the rest of the night, Angel. How about it?" he asked contritely, pulling her soft, feminine curves closer to him.

"Fine with me. Where's Monica?" she asked snidely.

"She left earlier," Jason informed her, adding lazily, "Now, isn't this better?"

"Much," she agreed and lay back to gaze up into the black, clear, beautiful sky. The stars were hanging so close to the ground Jessica felt she could reach out and touch one of them. The moon had just risen and was casting its soft beams over the dark shadows of this mystical night.

A favorite childhood song drifted softly through her mind as she gazed into the heavens trying to recall the words . . . about the stars being little candles and the angels lighting them at night.

She could hear the hushed *oohs* and *ahhhs* coming from the people around them as the magnificent exploding missiles showered overhead in a blinding array of brilliant colors, drifting back to earth lazily. If there were ever a time in her life when she had been more content or at peace with the world, she didn't remember it. If she could stop time right here, right now, she would happily do so. But she couldn't, she knew, so instead she breathed a silent word of thanks to the Lord for having been given this one precious night with Jason, to carry in her dreams for the rest of her life.

Jason stirred beside her, turned over, and put his hand on his chin, supporting himself by his elbow. "Penny for your thoughts, Angel."

"Oh, I was just thinking what a wonderful night this has been," she started, and for some reason unknown, even to her, tears slipped silently from her eyes. She didn't want this to end. She wanted to stay here forever in his strong arms. She wanted him to protect her, love her, cherish her, for the rest of her life. She wanted to have his children, grow old with him, play with their grandchildren together —she wanted a marriage like Judge Baker and Edna's, who after nearly fifty years still loved each other with the intensity of newlyweds, and maybe more deeply. They knew the value of true love, a love that would endure for over half a century. In a few months she would be alone again with only a dream once more.

Jason felt the tears dropping on his bare arm and gave a long sigh, lying back down and pulling her with him against the solidness of his chest. "Are you crying, Angel?" he whispered tenderly.

"No," she sniffed, trying to bring herself under control but only sobbing harder. She had her face buried in the front of his shirt, the soft curly hair on his chest tickling her nose.

"You know, that's the second time today I've made you cry," he reminded himself, "and I swear I didn't mean to either time, sweetheart. Here. Stop, honey, it's all right . . ."

108

She was sobbing in deep gulps now, the front of his shirt rapidly becoming wet and plastered to his broad chest.

"I know you didn't," she said, patting his chest lovingly, trying to console him now. "It's just that you seem to bring out the very worst in me at times. I'm so sorry about your barn today, and then I've torn your truck up again . . ."

"It's all right, Angel," he promised. "I shouldn't have made you drive the truck when you didn't want to . . ."

"But I could have done it for anyone else. It's only when I get around you that everything always goes wrong," she said, crying harder now. "You must think I'm a total idiot!"

Laughing softly, he began to nuzzle her neck, tracing a soft pattern of kisses down to her throat. "I've had a lot of thoughts about you lately," he said, his voice becoming husky and low, "but I've never thought you were an idiot."

She snuggled closer to him, and he reached a searching hand out and gently cupped her breast in it. She shuddered, and liquid fire raced through her veins as he stroked her nipple into a hardening peak. No other man had ever made her feel the way he could with just a soft touch or a fleeting glance.

"I think I had a pretty dull life before you came along," he murmured, touching the tip of his tongue, very gently, to her trembling mouth. She returned his soft teasing probes with her own tongue, running it lightly over his. She heard him moan softly before his mouth covered her vulnerable one in a kiss that was so devastating in its intensity they were both left trembling in its wake.

"Hey, Jason! You guys going to stay here and neck all night? The party's over," someone shouted good-naturedly. "Better take her home, where you can have some privacy," someone else offered helpfully.

They broke apart quickly, feeling a little guilty about

109

making such a public spectacle of themselves and got to their feet rapidly. Jason's face was a tense mask as he helped her into the car. "They're right, you know. Five more minutes and we would have made another 'mistake,'" he told her firmly.

"I know." She sighed wistfully, taking one last look at the pavilion and picnic grounds with its twinkling lights hanging in the soft night. "But I wish it didn't have to end," she said sadly.

"I think it's better that it does," he muttered softly.

He pulled her back to him for one last short, tender kiss, then gave her a playful swat on the bottom, saying teasingly, "We would have made a great team, sweetheart. Too bad things had to work out like they did."

CHAPTER SIX

The phone rang bright and early the following morning. It was Monica wanting to speak to Jason, who just happened to be walking in the back door, with his chores for the morning finished. Jessica handed the phone to him.

"For me?" he said, a puzzled look on his face.

Jessica nodded curtly, then went back to dressing for church. She could hear the rich timbre of Jason's baritone voice as he laughed at some stimulating comment Monica had apparently made. She looked in the mirror and mimicked his laughter in a sarcastic manner, jealousy shooting through every part of her body. She threw her hairbrush disgustedly back onto the dressing table. What was she going to do? It was becoming more apparent every day she lived here that Jason was bound and determined he was *not* going to ever give her a chance again. Her love for him was so complete now that she didn't know how she would ever be able to give him up again. Not that she had him, but at least she was in his home, able to see him every day, cook for him, take care of him. Monica was such a nice person—why couldn't Jessica simply reconcile herself to the fact that Jason would in all likelihood marry her, and she would probably make him very happy? Jessica groaned aloud as she thought of Monica wrapped in Jason's arms at night instead of her. Well, she had to try to do something about it. After all, he had been attracted to her years ago. Still was, if that one night they had spent together several weeks ago proved anything. No, she just couldn't sit idly by and let him slip through her fingers again without trying to win him back. She smiled smugly at herself in the mirror as a mischievous glint came into her eyes. No, Rawlings, you better head for the hills, because you are just about to be seduced in the most blatant manner!

The first thing she had to do, was get him to spend some time with her alone. She stood up and walked over to the window in the bedroom, pausing to look out on the farmyard. He was awfully skittish about being with her alone lately, so she would need something convincing to entice him.

She could still hear him talking in the other room as she plotted feverishly. Short of her death, she couldn't think of anything that would keep him home. She paused, her eyes lighting up. Well, she might not be dead, but she could be *near* death! Grinning triumphantly, she waltzed over to the bed, dropping spread-eagled onto the middle of it.

She heard Jason whistling as he came down the hall, stopping in front of her room with a wide grin on his face. "I'm going on a picnic, Angel. See you later."

"Have a nice time, Jason," she muttered weakly, her eyes drooping pathetically closed.

"Hey . . . you feeling all right?" Jason stepped into the room, concern showing in his face.

"Me? Oh, I'm fine—just fine. But before you go, could you bring me an aspirin?" she asked meekly.

"An aspirin? Sure. Are you sick?"

Jessica opened her eyes wearily and smiled pitifully. "I don't know what happened. I was feeling fine just a few minutes ago."

Jason walked over to sit down next to her on the bed, reaching up to feel her forehead. "You don't seem to have a fever. Where do you hurt?"

Jessica let out a long heartrending sigh. "Everywhere— my stomach—my head . . . but don't let me keep you from your date with Monica. If I need anything, I'll try to make it to the back door and call—Rick."

She closed her eyes again and let out a deep, shuddering breath.

"Well, hell, Angel! I'm not going to leave you here if you're sick! I'll just call Monica back and tell her I can't make it today."

Jessica cautiously opened one eye as he stood up and started for the phone. "Oh, Jason, no! I don't want to spoil your day," she protested valiantly.

He turned around, giving her a stern look. "I'm not leaving you, Jessie!"

"Whatever you say, Jason. I'm too sick to argue."

Jason left the room to make his phone call as Jessica quickly got out of her clothes and put on her nightgown. Then she snuggled down deeper in the bed. *This really is a dirty trick to pull on him,* she berated herself, but she was desperate.

Coming back into the room a few minutes later, he brought a cold cloth and placed it on her head. He brought out the aspirin, Alka-Seltzer, everything he could think of

113

to ease this strange malady that seemed to have overtaken her so quickly.

Jessica dozed most of the day, not quite sure where she was going with the plan from here. Granted, she had him there, but she wasn't quite sure what to do with him. He sat quietly by her bedside all afternoon reading a farm journal, granting her every request for a glass of water, juice, more aspirin. Jessica was running out of things to ask for toward evening when he suggested that he fix them some soup.

"Great, I'm starved!" Jessica said eagerly, then caught herself as Jason's face took on a surprised look. "I mean . . . I may be able to force something down."

"I'll be right back," he told her, eyeing her suspiciously for the first time.

By the time he brought the soup, Jessica was ravenous. She had had only a piece of toast for breakfast and no lunch, but she felt like she had had at least forty-five aspirins. She had to force herself not to ask for a third bowl of soup.

Jason sat watching her eat with gusto, a knowing smile on his face. "Do you want *my* bowl?"

Jessica looked up sheepishly. "I think I'm feeling better."

"Obviously," Jason said dryly.

Laying her spoon down carefully on the tray, she smiled at him beguilingly. "I'm through."

He cleared the tray away, then sat back down in his chair. "Do you want to watch some TV?" He inclined his head toward the small portable TV set sitting on the dresser.

"That would be nice," Jessica said sweetly. "Want to lie down on the bed with me?" She patted the space beside her enticingly. "You look uncomfortable sitting over there," she added hastily.

Jason studied her for a moment, then moved to lie down

114

next to her. "Sure, what have I got to fear? You're a sick woman, aren't you?" He glanced at her pointedly.

"Very!" she assured him.

They lay contentedly next to each other watching an old Disney outdoor film. Jessica wanted to snuggle closer to him, but he was keeping a discreet distance between them. By about nine Jessica was starving again. "Jason, doesn't popcorn sound good?"

Jason looked at her in astonishment. "You want greasy popcorn?" he asked increduously.

"Maybe just a small bowl," she said weakly.

"Whatever this sickness is, it sure hasn't affected your appetite!" he said, grumbling as he got off the bed to head for the kitchen.

While he was gone Jessica bounded off the bed to go to the bathroom and to do some quick calisthenics before getting back in bed. She was stiff from lying down all day. She was in the middle of her leg kicks when Jason walked back into the room unexpectedly, carrying a large bowl of popcorn and two Cokes.

"Well, hallelujah! I've witnessed a miracle," he said snidely, setting the bowl of popcorn down on the bed.

A crimson blush overtook Jessica's face as she climbed back into bed, her skimpy nightgown barely covering her bottom. "I told you I was feeling much better," she muttered defensively.

Jessica cursed herself for not listening more closely for his footsteps in the hall, but she had figured she had at least another ten minutes before he finished in the kitchen.

The late movie was just coming on when she felt Jason stir beside her later that night. She had dropped off to sleep during the ten o'clock news. She awoke to find her head lying on his chest, Jason dozing, too. She lay still for a moment, enjoying the feel of that solid wall of muscle. She slipped her hand up to play softly with the small tuft of hair showing where his shirt was unbuttoned. How she longed to run her fingers through that thick, wiry mass of hair on his chest!

"You having fun?" Jason's sleepy voice startled her as she jerked her hand back down to her side. He reached down, taking hold of her small hand, and brought it back up to the buttons on his shirt. "Be my guest."

Slowly she unbuttoned each small button, her pulse pounding as the front of the shirt gaped open to reveal the expanse of golden-brown hair on his chest.

Sighing softly, she buried her face in its depth, inhaling his unique and very masculine scent.

"You've got a thing about that chest hair, haven't you, lady?" He chuckled softly.

"Just yours," Jessica whispered quietly, running her fingers lightly over his chest.

"Well, don't feel bad. There's certain things about you that drive me out of my mind," he murmured suggestively.

"Such as?" Jessica placed his hands gently on her rounded breasts.

Jason groaned as his hands came in contact with the soft white flesh, burying his face deeply in her bosom. His mouth and tongue began to trace soft searching patterns, nibbling gently at the voluptuous mounds.

Jessica could feel Jason's hard arousal pressing hotly against her bare leg as his mouth came up to capture hers. They lay lazily exchanging tender kisses, their tongues playing lightly with each other. Jason's breathing became more and more ragged as his hands intimately explored the inner warmth of her femininity.

"Don't you think that's a little unfair?" Jessica whispered huskily.

"What?" Jason's tone was deep and drowsy.

"You still have your clothes on and I don't," Jessica reminded him.

"So?" He brought his mouth back to capture hers in a long, drugging kiss.

"So," Jessica murmured when he let her come up for air, "take them off."

"Why?" His hands moved gradually up her thigh to caress her stomach teasingly.

"Jason . . . you know why," she said timidly.

"No, I don't," he insisted infuriatingly. "Tell me."

She reached a hand teasingly to the front of his trousers. "Guess!"

He moaned as her hand lightly stroked his rigid body. "Too bad you're sick, Angel. I'm a starving man right now, but I wouldn't want to catch anything."

"Don't let that stop you," she whispered seductively. "I feel much better."

He chuckled intimately, pulling her closer for another passionate kiss. "Tell me the truth, sweetheart. You never have been sick, have you?"

Jessica squirmed uneasily in his arms. "Oh, Jason, I can't lie to you . . . no, I haven't been."

He continued to nibble along her neck, sending cold chills up her spine. "Then, you mean you just didn't want me to go out with Monica today . . . is that right?"

"Yes," Jessica admitted weakly, her hands running more firmly over his chest, along his sides, finally tracing the muscles of his firm back with her fingertips.

With one firm whack to her bottom Jason sat up, buttoning his shirt. "That's a pretty rotten thing for you to do, Jessica."

"But, Jason . . ." Jessica sat up in surprise.

"No buts, Jessica. That was rotten—pure and simple!"

"Jason Rawlings, you come back here!" Jessica screamed as he stomped to the door. "I just wanted to spend some time alone with you, you . . ." Jessica sputtered.

"Next time, ask me, Angel." Jason gave her a mock salute and slammed the bedroom door in her face.

"Of all the nerve." Jessica bounded out of bed, her

temper simmering, flinging her pillow against the closed door.

Well, she wasn't about to give up this easy! Tomorrow was another day, and she'd just see how long old Rawlings could hold out against the very intense pressure she planned to apply to him.

Time was running out, and she was a desperate woman!

The next day dragged by as she plotted her course of action for that evening. She gave herself a manicure, pedicure, facial—everything she could think of to make her mission less likely to fail.

Late in the morning the phone shrilled persistently. Jessica ran to answer it, fanning her hands in the air to dry the coat of fingernail polish she had just applied. Monica Sawyers's lilting voice drifted sweetly over the line again.

"Jessica?"

"Yes." Jessica took a deep breath, praying that Monica wasn't calling to involve Jason in any plans for this evening.

"How are you this morning? Jason said you had taken ill quite suddenly yesterday." Her voice held real concern.

Good grief, Jessica thought guiltily, why couldn't she be the bitchy kind of woman that Jessica could readily dislike? Instead she was a supernice person who, under any other circumstances, Jessica could easily have liked. Well, her rotten luck was just running true to form.

"Oh, I'm feeling much better this morning," Jessica said meekly into the receiver.

"I'm really happy to hear that, but are you sure there isn't anything I can do for you?"

Yes, Jessica thought, *take a slow boat to China!* Immediately she felt ashamed of her catty thoughts. "No, nothing," Jessica assured her politely. "I'm just fine—really."

"Well, don't hesitate to let me know if you need anything, Jessica." Monica paused. "I really mean that, you know."

"I know, and thank you for your concern, Monica."

A brief moment of silence followed on the line, and then Monica spoke once again. "Jessica, I wonder if you'd mind answering a nagging question for me. One that's been bothering me a lot lately."

Jessica swallowed hard as she heard the tone of seriousness in Monica's voice. "No—I wouldn't mind. What is it, Monica?"

Monica paused, then answered quite bluntly, "I really don't know any way to put this, Jessica, so I'll just ask you quite honestly. Do you and Jason still care for each other?"

Jessica sank down in the chair next to the phone, the frankness of Monica's question leaving her shaken. Monica was continuing on rapidly. "I know about your brief marriage, and I know how hard Jason took the annulment, but at times—" her voice dropped—"at times I really have to wonder if he's completely over you."

"I don't think you have any worries about that, Monica. He's over me," Jessica assured her sadly.

"Jessica, don't misunderstand me. I have no intention of prying into your private affairs, and I can readily see how hard it would be to get over a man like Jason. I *know*. I fell deeply in love with him myself, though I can honestly say I don't know if he returns that love."

Jessica twisted the phone cord in her slender fingers, mulling over Monica's words. How right she was! It *wasn't* easy getting over a man like Jason.

"I'm not blind," Monica continued. "I see the look that comes into his eyes when your name is mentioned, yet it seems he's constantly fighting within himself to stay away from you."

"Jason doesn't want to become involved with me again, Monica," Jessica told her honestly.

"And—what about you?" Monica asked softly.

"I—I still love him," Jessica admitted.

"But you really feel he *doesn't* want to get involved again?"

"That's what he's told me on a number of occasions," Jessica said gravely.

Monica's voice came calmly back across the line: "Jason's quite a man, you know. You never really know what he's thinking, but somehow I suspect he's not as over you as he believes he is."

Jessica's breath caught in sharp surprise at Monica's remark. "I thought you were in love with him."

"Oh, I am." Monica laughed shakily. "And as much as I like you, you can rest assured I will do everything in my power to keep him. But I can't fault you for loving him, too."

Jessica smiled, shaking her head unbelievingly. "Then you won't mind if *I* do everything in my power to get him back?"

"I'd mind," Monica said sadly, but then her lilting voice took on a cheerful tone. "Let's just say, may the best ma—woman win!"

Smiling brightly, her tone matching Monica's, Jessica replied, "Thanks, Monica. I'm sure going to try!"

As she replaced the receiver in the cradle she noticed the cord wrapped around her wet fingernail. "Drat!" she muttered audibly as she bounded for her room to reapply her polish.

Jason was late getting home, coming in hot, tired, and dirty. He headed immediately for the shower as Jessica nervously paced the floor, willing him to speed up. She threw a hasty cold-cut supper on the table and watched Jason's face drop at the unappetizing fare sitting before him.

"You been busy today?" he asked, wondering forlornly where his hot meal was tonight.

"No, not really," she said.

"What have you done all day?" he said conversationally, spreading his bread with mayonnaise before adding the strips of bologna she had placed before him.

"Nothing! Jason, could we hurry a little?" she said anxiously. "I'm really tired tonight and want to go to bed early."

He looked up at her in surprise. "What are you so tired from? You just said you didn't do anything today."

"Well, nothing big, I mean. Just the normal things." She had made her sandwich with one piece of bread folded over, reasoning that she could eat it faster that way. Jason was trying to spear the last bite of potato salad on his plate when she wisked it out from under his nose, threw it into the dishwasher, and slamming its door shut, turned to him, saying, "Want to go in the front room and rest for a while?" He looked at her like she was slightly deranged but followed her into the living room, sinking down into his recliner and picking up the latest edition of the *Farm Journal.* Jessica picked up an afghan she was knitting and worked quietly for a few minutes, her needles flying as she concentrated on the rapidly approaching drama.

She yawned, casting a glance at the grandfather clock in the hall. Good grief! It was only five fifty! He'd never buy her going to bed this early. For the next hour Jessica was in agony, looking at the clock every five minutes while Jason sat calmly in his chair, turning the pages of his magazine, watching her from the corner of his eye.

Finally, at seven, she threw her yarn into the knitting basket, gave two big convincing yawns, just for safety's sake, and announced in a bored tone, "I think I'll take my shower early tonight."

Jason looked up at the clock, then back at her and said dryly, "Kind of early, isn't it?"

"I said I was tired," she reminded him curtly.

Jason mumbled some incoherent remark and buried his face behind the magazine again as she sauntered casually out of the room. When she reached the hall, she sprang into action, racing down the hall, through her bedroom, and into her bath, leaving a jetstream of her discarded clothes along the way. Quickly she ran a tubful of hot water and sprinkled in the most seductive bubble bath she could find on her bathroom vanity. She jumped in, relaxing only long enough to wash and let the sensuous fragrance of the bubble bath penetrate her soft, delicate skin.

As the tub drained she dried herself with the large, thick towel she had laid out earlier and dusted herself generously with bath powder. She raced back into her bedroom, pulled open her lingerie drawer, dug back into its farthest recesses, and removed a filmy black negligee and matching robe. She drew the thin, sheer material over her head and turned to face the mirror.

She let out an audible gasp. This might be carrying things a little far! She and Sally Munson, a college friend, had gone shopping a couple of years ago and, being in a silly mood that day, had tried on the sexiest, most revealing negligees they could find. In fact they had gone to several different stores, each trying to outdo the other, until they happened on this particular one. They had stood in a fit of giggles for ten minutes with a most unamused salesclerk watching before each decided to buy the negligee set and took a solemn oath to wear it on her wedding night.

Jessica turned around slowly, looking at every angle in the mirror. Not much was left to the imagination, she thought. In fact she would class it as downright X-rated. How in the world was she going to go out there and let him see her like this? The robe did tone it down some, she mused, but it was still going to be tough walking out there like this. Taking one more hard look in the mirror, she shrugged her shoulders carelessly and thought, *I'll force myself!*

She ran a hairbrush through her loose, softly curled hair and added a touch of gloss to her lips, making them look wet and shiny. For the crowning touch she reached to her perfume tray and picked up the mate to her bath powder,

Hot Passion, and dabbed just a touch behind her ears, on her wrists, and between her breasts, hoping it wouldn't be wasted.

Well, Jessica, she said to herself, *up until last night you'd never tried to seduce a man, but there comes a time in a woman's life when things have to change. Let me be the first to wish you luck!*

One last check in the mirror sent her flying out of the bedroom and down the hall. Slowing to a stroll, she entered the living room, noticing by the clock she had been gone only twenty minutes.

Jason was still right where she had left him—probably still on the same page of his *Farm Journal.* He glanced up, his mouth dropping open before he quickly concealed his astonishment. His narrow green gaze focused on her black diaphanous negligee, sending his masculine instincts on a rampage. Gaining control of his emotions slowly, he let his eyes linger on her for a moment more before turning casually back to his magazine. A bead of perspiration appeared on his forehead.

"What took you so long?" he asked in a bored tone.

"Long!" she stammered, caught off guard by his question. She thought maybe she'd been a little too obvious.

"Yeah, I thought you were going to be in there all evening," he said nonchalantly, turning to another page of his journal.

Jessica looked at him warily. Had he caught on already?

He laid the magazine down on the end table and rose slowly to his feet, stretching. "Well, guess I'll catch up on some of my bookwork before turning in," he told her, heading for the study door. "Oh, by the way"—he stopped and turned to face her again—"I saw Willis Mercy today. I invited him and Marcy for dinner tomorrow evening. I hope you don't mind. Since I have to do a lot of business with him at the bank, I try to take them out for dinner every couple of months or so. I just thought it would be nice this time to show off my pretty housekeeper and what she's done with the house, not to mention her cooking," he added with a touch of pride in his voice.

A black cloud came up and hovered momentarily over Jessica's head. "I have to cook dinner for Marcy Evans?" she asked darkly.

"No, Angel, for Marcy Mercy, my banker's wife," he said patiently.

"Same difference," she muttered under her breath, then added quickly, "No, I don't mind. I could do that."

"Good, I thought you could." He made a move as if to leave the room.

"Jason," she said urgently, "just a minute." *Well, here goes,* she thought. *It's now or never!*

She slinked over to him seductively, contorting her body in as provocative a manner as she knew how and reached up to smooth the collar of his shirt. (She had seen that done on TV in an old movie.)

Jason backed away slightly, his eyes locked on the plunging neckline of her black negligee.

"Is there anything special you'd like?" she whispered a little breathlessly, rubbing her generous bosom against his broad chest. "I mean"—she paused, twitching her lips in a Marilyn Monroe fashion, breathing hot breath against his neck—"for dinner tomorrow night." She blinked her wide, soft violet eyes at his brilliant green blazing ones, giving him her most enticing look, her hands still moving lightly over his collar.

He shifted nervously, moving a little closer to her now, his arm coming around her waist lightly. "Oh, I don't know, Angel," he said, his voice taking on a husky tone. His hands tightened slowly, pulling her closer to his body. She squirmed against him, feeling his mounting desire for her spring to life as he began placing soft, sensuous kisses on the curve of her neck, running on down past her throat with his tongue, tracing moist patterns on her skin. She felt a great deal of her control evaporating as she tugged impatiently at his shirttail to free it from his jeans, in her haste popping the buttons off one by one. "Drat!" she muttered under her breath. *Maybe he didn't notice,* she prayed.

"I can think of a lot of things I would like to have right now—a new shirt, for example," he whispered softly, his tongue now reaching out to sensuously touch the curve of one white breast. The warm moistness of his mouth on her nipple made her catch her breath and wonder who was seducing whom—but she continued with her game plan, running her hands up under his shirt, lightly scraping her fingernails against his bronze skin.

Her legs were rapidly turning to jelly, and her breathing was beginning to become very labored as she felt the heat of his body through her thin gown, and his mouth on her sensitive lips. Her arms trembled beneath his shirt as his hands slipped her negligee from her shoulders, his mouth following its path again to close over her hardened nipple. She closed her eyes and breathed deeply, savoring the manly smell of his aftershave, touching her lips teasingly to his ear, and delighting in the sound of him sucking in his breath sharply at her touch. She felt smug, thrilled with the knowledge that she had him eating out of her hand.

He moaned softly. "What in the *hell* is that perfume you're wearing? That could drive a man crazy!" he whispered hoarsely.

Oh, goody! It worked! "I really don't remember," she said coyly, pressing closer to his warm body. Boy! This was going to be even easier than she had imagined.

"Wear it more often," he pleaded, lifting his head to bring his mouth down on hers, his tongue forcing her yielding lips open to wander aimlessly through the softest of the warm recesses of her mouth, her tongue joining his with abandoned fervor.

He broke away suddenly with a strangled groan, breathing heavily, and reached for her hand, bringing it down boldly to cover his obvious desire for her. "Do you want to know what I really want, sweetheart?" His voice was hoarse, his green eyes dripping with lust. Her hand was on fire from touching him.

"No, tell me, darling," she replied, barely able to breathe, her heart pounding like a jackhammer, torturous passion driving her crazy for release. She closed her eyes and tilted her face upward, parting her lips seductively, running her tongue along the edge of her teeth.

"Meatloaf," he whispered softly.

She bit her tongue as her violet eyes snapped open, wide with shock. "Meatloaf!" she gasped, jerking her hand from his hold.

"Yeah, meatloaf. It's one of my favorites. You do have a good recipe, don't you?" he asked with concern.

She stepped back aghast, irritably straightening her negligee to cover her bare shoulders and one obviously exposed breast, her eyes blazing at him as if he were a mad dog.

He turned and started toward the study again in a nonchalant manner, giving her instructions as he stuffed his shirttail back into his jeans. "Maybe a few potatoes, a nice big salad, some of those hot rolls you make—you know, just the usual stuff." He paused at the door and gave her a big, broad wink. "Fix us a meal they won't soon forget, Angel." He turned and cockily walked down the hall to his study whistling "The Old Gray Mare."

Jessica stood there completely stunned, her eyes following his retreating back. What had gone wrong? Meatloaf! Her eyes were turning a dark lavender now. "Oooooooo!" she screeched, and with a defiant stomp of her small foot she started marching militantly back to her bedroom. Tabby was just starting to cross the doorway, and a roaring voice made him jump for safety. "Get out of my way, cat!" she shouted as a puff of black smoke streaked by.

She muttered as she marched into her room, "Fix them a meal they won't forget. Well, you can bet your stinkin'

126

meatloaf on that, Jason Rawlings. Believe me, you can *definitely* count on that!"

Jessica was up bright and early the following morning, her blood still boiling from the night before. He had made her the world's biggest fool, and she was intent on revenge. She slammed the coffeepot under the kitchen faucet, spraying water all over herself and the cabinet in her haste. She had just plugged it in and reached for her coffee cup when she heard a noise at the kitchen door. It was Jason asking, "Jessica, where did you put my clean underwear?"

"Why, in your top drawer where I always do. Why?" she said as she turned to face him. It was *her* mouth that dropped open this time. Jason was standing in the doorway stark, raving naked! Her face felt like a four-alarm fire with him standing there naked as a jaybird.

They're not there," he replied calmly. "I just looked."

Jessica froze in her tracks. She could not take her eyes from his massive chest with the thick, soft curly hair running down to his waist and tapering off to—good heavens! He was magnificent! She *had* to get her traitorous eyes to move back up to his face.

Summoning every ounce of strength she possessed, she whirled back around, facing the kitchen window.

"What is the meaning of this disgusting display?" she said through clenched teeth.

"What are you talking about?" he asked bluntly.

"What do you think you are doing?" she screeched, totally out of control now.

"I think I'm looking for my clean underwear," he replied matter-of-factly. "Why?"

"You know very well why," she yelled. "You don't have one stitch of clothes on!"

"Oh." He glanced down at his nude condition with sorrow written mockingly all over his handsome face. "Well, I just thought after that gown you had on last night, you had decided we didn't have to be quite so formal around the house anymore," he said in a petulant tone of voice.

She slammed her coffee cup down on the cabinet and said in a tight voice, "Just because I had on an old gown and housecoat that I've had for years last night, you have to go and make some big deal out of it. And I certainly wouldn't call wearing your clothes being formal!"

"Well," he said, "I'll just run in there and check again. I could have overlooked them."

"You do that," she gritted out.

He turned and swaggered back down the hall to his bedroom.

Jessica had just poured her coffee, trying to steady her nerves, when his voice came floating down the hall sweetly: "Why, you were right, Angel, they're right here where you said they were!"

CHAPTER SEVEN

Jessica finished her work in the kitchen in record time. As she stepped out onto the back porch to shake a small area rug she noticed the air had a hot, stifling stillness to it this morning. She hoped they would get rain by tonight but added a silent prayer that there would be no storms.

Jessica had always had an abnormal fear of the storms that could sweep through this small Texas town. Although she had never actually been in a tornado, she had heard some hair-raising tales from Uncle Fred and Aunt Rainey concerning ones they had experienced. Jessica remembered listening, wide-eyed, to their tales, deciding that she would happily forgo that experience.

Just as she finished shaking the rug, she saw the mailman pull up to the mailbox and deposit the mail. She waved happily at him as he drove on down the dusty road. As Jessica gathered the handful of bills and advertisements from the big box she noticed one letter addressed to her. She smiled as she recognized the handwriting of old Mrs. Houseman, her landlady in Austin. Jessica had dropped her a short note last week informing her that she would be staying on here and giving her the new phone number where she could be reached in case of an emergency.

Jessica ripped open the letter, remembering fondly the kind elderly lady who had mothered her through the last few years. If Jessica was sick, Mrs. Houseman would always be the first to show up at her door with a jar of her homemade chicken soup and a big bottle of Dr. Caldwell's laxative. Mrs. Houseman had always contended that Dr. Caldwell's was the answer to anyone's ills, no matter what the diagnosis.

Her eyes scanned the pastel paper, trying to read Mrs. Houseman's scratchy writing. She was offering to pack Jessica's personal belongings and mail them to her. "Don't worry about the lease, dear," she had written. "There was a young girl by here this morning wanting to know if the apartment was available, and though I'll miss you something fierce, I know your place is at home right now," she concluded:

Jessica's eyes turned teary as she folded the letter back up lovingly. It suddenly occurred to her that she would, in all likelihood, have to return to her little home in Austin permanently—for, unless things changed, she would never be able to live here in this town when she and Jason parted at the end of the six months. She would never be able to live in the small town with him, seeing him married to Monica. No, she couldn't live through that!

She realized now that instead of coming out of this "arrangement" unscathed, she had succeeded only in falling in love more deeply with Jason. Jessica sighed. She would have to write Mrs. Houseman and tell her that she had better hold the apartment for her, just in case.

As she returned to the house with a heavy heart she knew she was going to have to make a decision soon, and not only about the apartment; she would have to let the school know whether she was returning for the next semester.

As she was passing through the kitchen on the way to the living room the phone shrilled. Muttering a small expletive under her breath as she turned back, she jerked the phone off its cradle. She wasn't in the mood for a phone conversation this morning. "Hello!"

"Wow, I'm sorry!" Maureen Winters's voice apologized. "The day this young and going so bad already?" she teased.

"*Bad* isn't the word," Jessica told her. "This whole week has been the pits!"

"Well, old Dr. Winters has just the right prescription. Let's go out to lunch and do some shopping."

"I can't," Jessica responded glumly. "Jason has invited Willis and Marcy over for dinner this evening. I have to do the marketing for that, on top of tear up the house," she finished absently.

"Tear up the house?" Maureen laughed. "Don't you mean *clean* up the house?"

"No, I meant *tear* it up . . . Listen, Maureen, I'm sorry, but I can't chat right now. I have to go to the market. Can I call you tomorrow?"

"Sure, no problem," Maureen said. "I'll talk to you then."

Jessica placed the receiver back on the hook, giving it a threatening look which forbade it to ring again, and hurried to the bathroom for a quick shower, after which she put on a pair of white slacks with a navy-blue top, applied a light coat of mascara to her lashes and a touch of gloss to her pink lips. She then twisted her thick hair into a knot, pinning it securely to the top of her head, letting a few wispy tendrils hang down the sides and back. Satisfied with her work, she picked up the keys to the Lincoln from the basket that was lying on the kitchen counter and let herself out the back door.

She cruised to the market slowly in the elegant luxury of Jason's air-conditioned car, listening dreamily to the elaborate stereo system playing her favorite tape, "Hooked on Classics." She parked the classy gray Continental in front of Mr. Sweeney's store and jumped out onto the hot pavement, grabbing a cart as she entered the store and started down the aisles, fighting the overwhelming temptation to squeeze the Charmin. She paused before the meat counter, selecting the hamburger that looked as if it had the most suet in it. She wanted her meatloaf to be just right . . . with enough grease to float a battleship. Continuing down the aisle, she handpicked the vegetables to go into the meatloaf. The green pepper was so limp and tough she was going to have to use the electric carving knife to chop it up. A cart of discarded lettuce sat next to the produce department—heads of brown wilted lettuce ready to be taken to the back to be dumped. She stopped her cart next to it and casually selected the sickest-looking head in the basket, smiling smugly as she plunked it into her cart.

When she came to the check-out stand, Mr. Sweeney greeted her warmly and started to remove the items from Jessica's cart. He reached for the head of lettuce and his face paled. "Jessica, my goodness," he exclaimed, "let me get you another head." He left his register and started for the produce counter.

"No, Mr. Sweeney, that one will do just fine."

Mr. Sweeney looked puzzled and tried to persuade her one more time. "But this was going to be thrown away. Let me just run and get you a nice fresh crisp head that we have just unpacked," he pleaded. "It won't take a minute."

"No." Jessica stood firm. "That's the one I want."

Mr. Sweeney looked helpless. "Well," he relented, "I'm certainly not going to charge you for it!" He proceeded to finish ringing up the items in her cart.

Leaving the store feeling satisfied, Jessica drove home humming under her breath. "This will *definitely* be a meal they won't forget, Jason!" she muttered tightly to herself.

Arriving home, she unloaded her groceries and brought them in, setting the brown paper bags on the kitchen counter. After she put the perishables in the refrigerator and the canned goods in the cabinet, she tore around the living room disarranging throw pillows, draping various items of their clothing over chairs, throwing newspapers haphazardly around on the floor. She sprinkled a sack of popcorn on the floor and threw a couple of pairs of Jason's boots, covered with cow dung, next to his chair. She set several glasses full of ice around on the end tables, hoping the ice would be melted by the time the guests arrived. Standing back and looking at the mess she'd created, she decided it would do and went into the kitchen. She spent the rest of the afternoon working on the meal itself, not bothering to wash up any of the dishes she was using, leaving them sitting around on the cabinet to grow dry and crusty. The floor looked like it had snowed, from all the flour she had scattered around baking her cake. She was having a great time, humming under her breath, working as hard as a beaver.

When Jason opened the door that evening, he wasn't sure if the predicted approaching storm hadn't already hit. His eyes widened in astonishment before he pulled a calm mask over his face. He stepped lightly into the room, calling over his shoulder, "Come on in, Eric. Jessie must be in the kitchen."

Jason's younger brother, Eric, followed him through the door, talking as he walked. "I can't wait to see her after all these years. I bet she'll be surprised. She doesn't know I'm here, does she?" he asked, his eyes mirroring surprise as he surveyed the living room.

"Yes, I bet she *will* be surprised," Jason agreed. "I tried to call her this morning when I found out you were flying in, but I couldn't reach her."

"Well, I sure wish Rena could have made the trip, but Scottie had a summer cold, so she thought she had better stay home with him this time," he explained, trailing Jason on into the room.

Eric had the same good looks as the other Rawlings boys. He was not as tall as Jason, but he had the same golden-brown hair and luscious green eyes, his not quite as vivid as Jason's but nonetheless very attractive.

"Maybe the next trip," Jason offered, pitching the cat's bowl out of his chair. He motioned to Eric to take a seat.

"Want a cold beer, Eric?" he offered.

"No, I'll hold off till supper," he answered distractedly, his eyes roaming around the room with a puzzled look.

"Jessie has changed things quite a bit," Jason was saying as he stretched out in his chair, relaxing for a minute. "You wouldn't recognize this old house," he added tiredly.

Eric looked around warily again. "No, I sure wouldn't," he agreed.

The door opened from the kitchen, and Jessica stuck her head out. "Are our guests here yet, Jason?"

"Part of them, Angel," Jason called sweetly. "Why don't you come on out here. I've got a surprise for you."

"In a minute, Jason," she responded just as sweetly. "Let me check my meat one more time first. I want everything to be perfect!"

"Well, hurry, Angel. We're waiting!" Jason snickered under his breath.

A moment later the door swung open, and Jessica stopped dead in her tracks. "Eric?"

"None other, sweetheart." Jason beamed.

Eric jumped up from his chair, crossed the room, swooped her off her feet in a tremendous bear hug, and swung her around the room.

"My Lord, you're prettier than ever." He was grinning from ear to ear.

Eric had always been the biggest tease of all the boys and usually said the first thing that popped into his head, regardless of decorum.

"Why in the world would you want to get hooked up with this bum again?" He was pointing at Jason and grinning broadly.

Jessica looked at Jason and replied gaily, "Oh, we still hate each other. I'm only working for him now. It's strictly a 'business agreement'!"

Jason gave her a big grin and a mock salute with his hand. "Touché!" he acknowledged.

"Well, if I had known you weren't too particular who you worked for, I would have been down here trying for you myself," he stated boldly.

"What would Rena think about that?" Jason responded dryly.

"Rena who?" Eric asked innocently.

"Rena who?" Jessica echoed, puzzled.

"My sexy little wife"—Eric grinned—"and she's a mean woman when she gets her hackles up!"

Jessica gave him one big hug before letting go of his neck. "I am so happy to see you," she exclaimed. "I had no idea you would be here tonight." She shot Jason a dirty look.

Jason held up both hands in mock surrender. "I tried to call you this morning, but you weren't home," he chided.

"Didn't know I was coming myself until the last minute," Eric soothed as he seated himself on the sofa once again. "I had some papers that needed Jason's signature, so I just hopped a plane and flew down this afternoon."

"Well, Eric, how have you been?" Jessica asked, nonchalantly trying to stuff a pair of Jason's dirty socks under the cushion of the chair she was sitting in.

135

"Can't complain," he replied, leaning forward, his puzzled eyes roaming the cluttered room once again.

Jason pushed himself back up out of his chair. "Come on, Eric. You can wash up before dinner if you'd like. Just put your bags in the guest room." He turned to Jessica. "Eric's going to spend the night here and take the early flight out tomorrow morning."

"That's fine," Jessica replied, her heart sinking as she thought of poor Eric's reaction to the house and the coming dinner.

Eric stood, picked up his suitcase, and followed Jason down the hall. "Your cat not trained?" he asked innocently as his eyes took in all the newspapers lying on the floor.

"No, it's trained," she heard Jason's deep voice say as they reached the guest room. "Just put your things in there, and we'll let you know when dinner's ready.

The peal of the doorbell brought Jessica back to her feet, scurrying for the kitchen at a run.

"I'll get it, Angel," Jason called sweetly.

"Thank you, Jason," she responded in the same sweet tone as she slammed through the kitchen door.

"Ms. Vogue" and her "brown shoe" were smiling brightly as Jason opened the door and let them into the cluttered room. Marcy's eyebrow rose immediately in distaste, but she tactfully recovered her composure. Willis was obviously just along for the ride. Judging by the expression on his face, all was as it should be.

"Jason, darling," Marcy was saying, clutching his arm, "how nice of you to have us in your home!"

"I'm glad you could come this evening, Marcy, Willis," he was saying. "Come in and sit down. I think dinner's almost ready."

Marcy started to seat herself in a chair beside Jason, but discovering the seat full of cookie crumbs, she immediately moved to the sofa.

Willis sat down in the pile of cookie crumbs.

"Well, Willis," Jason said pleasantly, "could I get you something to drink?"

"No, Jason, thank you, I'm fine, really. Yes," he assured him again, "I'm fine—really, just fine. I don't drink too much. It gives me a sour stomach." Jason looked at him and nodded, a small look of annoyance on his face.

"Nothing for me, darling," Marcy piped up. "I still have to watch my figure, you know. I was just telling Willis on the drive over here, just because I have children now doesn't mean I can let myself go. No, most people are *shocked* when they find out I have children. Isn't that what I was telling you, sweetie?" She turned to Willis.

"Yes, dear. She *was* telling me that, Jason, she really was. But I told her she looks just fine to me, don't you think? I mean really fine?"

"Yes, she looks just fine." Jason could have kicked himself. They sounded like a room full of parrots.

As the men stood Jessica came through the kitchen door. Jason took her arm, pulling her over next to him. "Everything going all right, Angel?" he asked. "Do you need any help in the kitchen?"

"No, I can handle things just *fine,* thank you. Good evening, Marcy. Willis."

"Good evening, Jessica," Willis was saying. "Jason certainly has a lovely home." He reached out to shake her hand. Jessica felt like she was squeezing a nerf ball. "It's just so homey-looking," he said sincerely.

Their eyes took in the disarray in the living room.

"Yes, that's what I told Jessie," Jason piped up. "Now, this is a room a man can really be at home in!"

Jessica couldn't believe her ears. He was actually enjoying this!

Willis had always had the annoying habit of sucking on his front teeth. It drove Jessica crazy, that sucking, squeaky noise. Many was the time when she could have cheerfully strangled him. He was beginning to do just that as they stood talking while waiting for Eric to join them.

137

Jessica was never so relieved as to hear Eric's voice booming out.

"I don't know about anyone else, but I'm starving. I've had to put up with Jason's bragging all afternoon about what a hell of a cook his—uh, housekeeper is. Now I'm ready to be convinced!" he finished loudly. "When do we eat?"

Jessica smiled weakly. "Everything's ready now. We can eat anytime."

"Then, madam, if I may?" Eric held out his arm gallantly to Jessica and led her into the dining room.

Jason escorted a chattering Marcy, with Willis trailing along behind, sucking on his teeth.

The table was lovely in its simplicity. A fresh bouquet of late-summer flowers nestled elegantly in a peanut-butter jar in the center of the table, gaily flower-patterned Melmac was placed lovingly in front of each chair, with sparkling clean jelly glasses catching the light from the glittering chandelier, waiting to be filled with the cherry Kool-Aid Jessica had made to complement the meal. Two candle stubs were in the brass holders sitting next to the flower centerpiece.

Jason seated Marcy and dramatically lit the candle stubs before Jessica brought in the food. "The table looks lovely, Jessie."

How do I get myself in these messes? she thought while slamming pots and pans around in the kitchen with such force she was sure the people in the other room thought there was a war going on in there. *Eric thinks I'm an absolute basket case,* she wailed to herself. Why did everything have to backfire on her like this? She was so mad at herself!

She began dishing up the vegetables and potatoes in all the mismatched bowls she could drag out of the cabinet. Defiantly she marched back to the dining room, slamming bowls down on the table, going back for more in a militant mood.

138

The guests sat quietly, the expressions on their faces ranging from mild surprise to deep puzzlement to outright astonishment. Jason's eyes, however, held only mild amusement, carefully concealed by his lowered lashes.

Jessica shoved the large bowl of potatoes under Eric's nose and asked in a curt tone if he would mind passing them, then, turning to Jason, said, "I'm bringing in the meatloaf now, Jason. Would you mind serving?"

"Of course not, Angel. I can hardly wait to taste it." Turning to his guests, he said, "Wait until you taste her meatloaf. You're in for the treat of your life."

Jessica fired him a disgusted look and returned to the kitchen, emerging a few minutes later with a meat platter, bearing the nearly charred remains of the meatloaf.

She looked at the blank expressions on the four faces as they surveyed their meat course, and said defensively, "Jason hates his meat rare."

"She's right," Jason said, backing her up, "I don't like any pink left in my meat!" He picked up a large carving knife and began slicing generous servings for each plate. "Ahhhhh . . . just the way I like it, Angel." He looked up and smiled adoringly at her.

Eric picked up the bowl of potatoes and spooned some onto his plate, leaning down to peer closer at them. "Are these mashed or fried, Jessie?" he said, puzzled.

"Mashed," she clarified curtly.

He passed the bowl on to Marcy, who, in turn, immediately passed it on to Willis.

"You know, Jessica taught home ec in high school while she was in Austin," Jason was saying conversationally.

"You must be kidding!" Jessica heard Marcy mutter under her breath.

As Jason picked up Marcy's plate to serve her meat she practically shouted, "Just a very *small* serving for me," then qualified her request with, "I try not to eat too heavily in the evening."

"Oh, but you must let down just for tonight," Jessica urged.

The table was ladened with a dazzling array of starches, all for Marcy's benefit. There was a large bowl of corn, one each of hominy and pork and beans, and a bowl of creamed peas so thick you could easily have hung wallpaper with them. The tossed salad looked like someone's garbage, and the jello salad had large chunks of pineapple floating around in it, the gelatin not quite congealed yet.

Eric was surveying the table with awe now as he said, "Damn, Jessica, you got enough starch here to start a Chinese laundry!"

Jessica flushed a bright red.

"You haven't given Eric his meat, Jason," she said, turning to him.

"Oh, sorry, Angel. Pass your plate, Eric, and take it like a man." He grinned.

"Could I have some catsup, please," he pleaded. "I always eat my meatloaf with catsup," he finished meekly.

"I'll get you some, Eric." Jessica could hardly keep a straight face, Eric was being so pathetically obliging about eating his meal.

"Jessica," Willis was saying as she brought the catsup back to the table and set it before a grateful Eric, who was trying to work his way through the gooey peas, "this is really a nice meal. Marcy is a fine cook, but she rarely fixes so many fine things at one time." Willis looked up and gave her an angelic smile. She grabbed her napkin and covered her mouth before she let out a stifled giggle. Willis had little black pieces of the meatloaf stuck between all his teeth.

"Why, that's sweet of you, Willis, but I don't want to mislead you, I don't cook quite this heavy a meal for Jason *every* night—just on special occasions, like tonight," she purred sweetly.

Eric, looking up from his plate, was starting to say something, but thought better of it. Instead he just gave

Jessica a devilish little grin and turned regretfully back to his food.

The ghastly meal finally came to an end, with everyone eating very lightly except for Willis, who took seconds of everything.

Jason suggested they have their coffee and dessert in the living room. They all left the table with the zeal of refugees leaving a war zone.

Jessica brought the tray with coffee and cups in, placing it on the low coffee table in front of the sofa. She left briefly, returning with the chocolate cake that had fallen in the middle when she had iced it hot from the oven. Four sets of eyes immediately focused on everything in the room but the cake. Jessica had used so many toothpicks to hold the cake together it looked as if it had been shot with a pellet gun.

Jessica handed Marcy her coffee first. "Oh, hot tea," Marcy remarked, looking at the almost clear liquid in the bottom of her cup. "How nice for a change."

"No," Jessica answered coolly, "it's coffee. Jason can't sleep nights if I make it too strong."

Eric sat up straighter, peering into his cup. "Well, hell, Jason, you ought to sleep like the dead tonight!" he stated firmly.

Willis was starting to squeak and suck on his teeth again. Jessica felt her nerves were at the breaking point. Would this night ever end?

Jason shot Willis a dirty look and reached over to the cake, withdrew a toothpick, and offered it to him silently.

Why doesn't he just leave him alone? Jessica thought irritably. *It would be a vast improvement if he managed to get the black out!*

They made small talk for another hour or so before Willis and Marcy said their good-byes, and Eric retired to his room early.

Jason saw the Mercys to the front door, closing and locking it behind them. He switched off the large yard light and turned back to Jessica, still sitting in the devastated living room.

He crossed the room to her, reached down, and drew her into his arms for one tender moment before tipping her face up to his and placing an affectionate kiss on her trembling lips.

"Angel," he said softly, "your meal was outstanding tonight. Everything was just as I knew it would be."

Giving her bottom a loving swat, he started toward his bedroom. She could hear him whistling "Auld Lang Syne" as he walked down the hall. Jessica sank back down on the sofa, her eyes falling on the hideous chocolate cake on the table before her. Tears welled up in her eyes like soft violet pools. Laying her head on her arm, letting the tears come freely now, she sobbed her heart out.

Finally her tears subsided, and she made her way wearily to her bedroom. This plan had gone down the drain along with the others.

The violent clap of thunder caused Jessica to jerk violently up out of a sound sleep. She could hear the wind rising and see the limbs of the old tree by her bedroom window making grotesque patterns on the wall in her room, against the security light left burning all night in the farmyard.

A jagged streak of lightning forked through the sky, followed by a deafening boom which shook the entire house.

Jessica lay very still, her heart pounding. The rain had not started yet. It seemed to be one of the violent electrical storms that came up occasionally.

Another lightning bolt shot across the sky. When she was small, she would always run into Uncle Fred and Aunt Rainey's room, crawling between them, burying her head under the covers. Aunt Rainey would pull her close, patting her back, telling her not to be afraid. "It's just the angels' potato wagons falling over," she'd say comfortingly. Then another deafening clap would come, and Jessica would make the observation that they sure must have big potatoes. As she grew older she would lie in a petrified state until the storm passed.

The wind was whipping the branches of the old oaks violently now. She got up cautiously to peer out the window. The streaks of lightning were following almost on top of one another, with the thunder sounding like sonic booms.

Cringing, Jessica let the curtain drop back down across the window, ineffectually blocking out the raging storm. She was a big girl now with nowhere to run.

She climbed back into her bed and pulled the pillow up over her ears. A few minutes later she was startled when she felt the bed give under a heavy weight. She pulled the pillow off her head, her eyes barely making out Jason's form in the stormy bedroom. "What are you doing in here?" she asked incredulously as she watched him very casually remove his pants, leaving on his underwear, then slide between the cool sheets beside her.

"I woke up and happened to remember a little violet-eyed pixie who has an unnatural fear of storms." He reached over to enfold her in his arms comfortingly. "And I just thought she might welcome some company along about now."

The deafening boom of another loud clap of thunder shook the house again as she eagerly accepted his arms, burying her face tightly in his neck.

"How did you know I was afraid of storms?" she asked wonderingly, pressing tight against his wonderfully warm body.

"I was there one day when you came running in the back door of Aunt Rainey's, your face as white as a sheet, during a spring thunderstorm." He chuckled tenderly.

"Oh, I know it's silly, Jason." She sighed. "And it's something I've tried to overcome, but I'm still deathly afraid of storms," she finished shakily, her words fanning softly on his smooth cheek.

"It's all right, Angel," he whispered back tenderly as the storm raged on in its full fury. "How many times do I get the opportunity to sleep in a beautiful woman's arms?" he teased, brushing her mouth ever so lightly with his.

A woman's arms! He finally thought of her as a woman —not "little Jessie Cole."

Her eyes filled with tears at his kindness, her arms wrapping more tightly around his neck. "Jason, thank you for coming—for caring." She raised halfway over him, gazing intently into his eyes. "Would you care if I kissed you? I just want to have you here with me tonight . . . just for tonight." Her face was precariously close to his in the dark room with only occasional bright flashes of lightning illuminating the surroundings.

There was a moment of silence, then he whispered softly, "I don't mind, Angel."

Jessica lowered her mouth hesitantly at first, then let it settle gently over his. The rain pelted hard against the windows as their mouths merged together tenderly, the kiss one of the sweetest they had ever shared.

Jessica ended the kiss reluctantly and laid her head on his broad chest. "Thank you, Jason."

Jason patted her arm lovingly as he murmured tiredly, "I don't know what in the hell I'm going to do with you, Angel, but I'm too tired to figure it out tonight. Go to sleep."

And she did—peacefully, calmly, and most contentedly in his arms.

CHAPTER EIGHT

The rain was still falling softly as she heard Jason leave the room long before daybreak the next morning. She snuggled down deeper into her bed to enjoy another few hours of sleep before she faced the new day. As she was drifting back to sleep she heard him and two of his farmhands slam the doors of their trucks, start their motors, and drive out of the farmyard.

The next sound she heard was that of Eric shaving in the hall bathroom. She lay there in lazy limbo for a few minutes, thinking of the night before, and poor Eric's face through the whole nightmarish part of the evening. She giggled softly as she thought of what must be going through his mind this morning: the pigsty of a house, the horrendous meal.

She jumped out of bed, pulled on a pair of old jeans she took from her closet, and grabbed a soft yellow cotton T-shirt on the way to the bathroom to wash her face and brush her teeth. Picking up her hairbrush, she brushed rapidly through the tangled black silk until it crackled in the early morning air. Satisfied she was presentable, she turned from the mirror and hurried to the kitchen.

The smell of coffee perking and ham frying in the large iron skillet on the stove assailed Eric's nostrils as he entered the kitchen a little later.

"Good morning, pretty lady," he said cheerfully. "What's got you out of bed so early on a dreary morning like this?"

"Good morning to you," she called back, her voice showing the affection she had for Jason's younger brother. "How about some breakfast?"

Eric's face paled slightly before he pleaded, "Just coffee, please. My stomach is a little queasy this morning."

"Nonsense." Jessica smiled. "I owe you a decent breakfast after what I put you through last night. Sit down, Eric, I promise you your meal will be different this morning."

He let out a long breath as he pulled out the chair at the kitchen table and settled his long frame in it. "I got to tell you, Jessie, that meal hung heavy on my stomach all night. I'm afraid I've cleaned you out of Alka-Seltzer," he added shamefacedly.

Jessica giggled as she placed a thick mug of hot coffee before him. He sat up straighter and peered intently into his cup. Assuring himself it wasn't of the same quality as the previous night's, he picked up the cream pitcher and added a liberal portion to the strong black liquid. Jessica turned back to the counter, preparing to mix batter for hot cakes. She set the large cast-iron griddle on the burner to heat, walked over to the refrigerator, and removed the eggs and milk she needed. She broke the eggs into the batter and added some cooking oil before asking, "How long have you and Rena been married?"

"Three years last month. You would really like her, Jessie. She's the best looking blonde you've ever laid eyes on, believe me," he said adamantly.

Jessica smiled as she picked up a wooden spoon and began beating the thick batter in a rapid motion, her rounded derriere rotating in rhythm with the wooden spoon. "You wouldn't be just a little partial, now, would you, Eric?"

Eric's eyes were on Jessica's motions. Picking up his coffee cup, he took another sip of his coffee before commenting, "You know, it's a shame old Jason's not here this morning. I think he'd rather watch you mix up those hot cakes than he would eat them!"

Jessica whirled around, looking at him in surprise. "Why, Eric Rawlings, you dirty old man!" she teased.

Eric grinned broadly. "Yeah, ain't it the truth—and Rena loves every minute of it."

Jessica shook her head tolerantly as she spooned out the batter onto the sizzling hot grill. They puffed up slightly before becoming bubbly on top. She flipped over the golden-brown cakes, which gave off a mouth-watering aroma. Removing the first two cakes, she generously spread them with the golden butter sitting beside the stove and handed the plate to Eric before spooning two more cakes onto the hot griddle.

"How old is your little boy, Eric?" Jessica asked.

Eric had a bottle of maple syrup in his hand and was completely drowning his cakes in the gooey, sweet substance. "He's a year and a half." He grinned exuberantly. He laid his fork down, reached into his back pocket, and produced a wallet that had at least fifteen pictures of a smiling, chubby, blond-haired boy.

Jessica's eyes turned misty as she looked at the beautiful child, who bore a strong resemblance to his father and uncle. Is this what Jason's baby would look like? she wondered as she turned the pages of the wallet, seeing the chubby baby go from an infant to a very endearing toddler. Would she ever have the honor of carrying his children, seeing the proud look on his face that was now radiating from Eric's? The last picture was of a very lovely blond-haired woman holding a baby, her eyes shining with the proud love of a mother. She had the look of a very contented woman, one who had found her place in life with her child and her husband.

"This must be Rena," Jessica said softly, feeling a pang of envy shoot through her as she gazed at the picture of this woman who seemed to have everything important in life.

"Yeah," Eric said reverently, "that's her." His love for Rena was waving like a red banner.

"She's very beautiful," Jessica assured him, "and Scottie's a real angel."

"Kids are great. We want at least six," he said, sitting back down to his hot cakes. "What about you and old Jase—you thinking of gettin' married again? Jason isn't getting any younger, you know."

Jessica was removing the last hot cake from the grill as she felt the tears welling up in her eyes. They started running down her cheeks faster than she could wipe them away.

Eric looked up with surprise, his expression turning to a worried frown as he saw the river rolling down her face. "Well, for goodness sakes, Jessie, did I say something wrong, honey?" he asked with tender concern. Grabbing a napkin from the table, he began awkwardly mopping at her tears. "Sit down, Jessie," he said, pulling her over to the table and placing her in the chair across from his, still wiping ineffectually at her tears. She was a total basket case now, the flood gates of the dam completely opened.

"Jessica!" Eric was getting panicky now. "Will you please tell me what in the world's going on. I feel like I've

148

stayed overnight at the zoo—in the monkey cage!" His voice was getting a little edgy.

"Oh, Eric, I'm so miserable," she sobbed, "and I'm making Jason miserable. Everything is in a miserable mess." Her slim shoulders shook violently as she sat at the table, beginning to pour her heart out to the one man she hoped could tell her what to do.

"What are you talking about?" he asked tenderly. "Are you and Jason having a little quarrel? Good heavens, that's nothing to get so upset over. Hell, Rena and I average one a day, but that doesn't mean I don't love her," he told her reassuringly.

"Oh, Eric, you just don't understand," she sobbed. "Jason doesn't love me, period! The only reason we're together at all is this stupid business arrangement. I paid him ten thousand dollars to stay here and run my farm for me until November, when I can collect my inheritance," she sobbed, stopping momentarily to blow her nose. Her face was red and puffy now from all the crying. "You see, Uncle Fred and Aunt Rainey stipulated in their will that I had to come home and run the farm for six months or all my inheritance would go to the church. I wanted to come back here anyway to start a small business instead of staying in Austin to teach this year. So I offered Jason the opportunity to make extra money if he would help me out." She blew her nose again loudly, then continued. "He agreed to the arrangement, I guess, partly because he felt sorry for me, partly because he needed the money."

"Needed the money!" Eric interrupted. "Jessica, this is getting crazier by the minute."

Jessica sniffed hard, then looked up at Eric. "What do you mean by that?"

"Hasn't Jason told you anything about his finances?" he asked increduously.

"No, but I haven't asked him either. We just haven't ever talked about that sort of thing."

Eric reached up and ran his fingers through his thick

brown hair, clearly disturbed by this mind-boggling conversation. "Jessica, it's not my place to tell you Jason's business, but you two should stop fighting and sit down and have a long talk. I can't believe he's never told you anything about his life after you left."

"Why should he?" she hiccuped. "I'm nothing to him but a business arrangement."

"Damn it, Jessica. You mean to sit there and tell me that my brother, Jason, who is the most level-headed one in this whole family, is just doing this for you as a favor? Sorry—for ten thousand dollars." Eric shook his head pathetically. "Then he's going to up and walk out on you in November, going his own separate way? Now, honestly —do you think you can make me believe that? That's a hell of a lot of hard work for Jason."

"Well, it's the truth, whether you believe it or not," she challenged.

"Then you've missed your calling," he said firmly. "You should be selling ocean-front property in Kansas."

Jessica laid her head on the table now, saying desperately, "Oh, Eric, what am I going to do? I love him more than anything in the world."

Eric shook his head in disbelief as he got up to pour himself and Jessica more coffee. "Wish I could tell you, honey, but I can't make heads nor tails out of any of this." Suddenly his eyes softened, "You really love the guy, don't you, Jessie? In fact I've always known you loved him, since you were a child. It was always there, plain as the nose on your face."

"Oh, I love him more than life itself, Eric, but I've lost him forever. He can't forgive me for letting the annulment take place," Jessica sobbed.

"Well, I think you're borrowing trouble. Jason doesn't take his personal affairs lightly. Who knows, he could still be in love with you. There's something that must be inspiring him to stay around."

"Oh, Eric, I wish I could undo the past, but I can't!

Now he's involved with a woman named Monica, and I don't know—he may be in love with her. She certainly is with him—but that's perfectly understandable," she said miserably, "with his devastating good looks."

"Jessica," Eric said kindly, "did you ever stop to think that not everyone sees him through your eyes? Jason's just an average guy, no better, no worse than the next guy. You're looking at him through the eyes of love, honey."

"But, he *is* good-looking," she said hotly, her violet eyes sizzling.

"Of course, he's good-looking. I mean, I guess he is— he's really not my type. But what I'm trying to say to you, Jessie, is you've got to take him down off that pedestal you've had him on all these years. You're just as lovely a woman as he is a man. If you want him, go after him."

"Oh, Eric, do you really think I would ever stand a chance with him again?" she asked, hope lighting up her eyes.

"I really don't know, Jessie, but I can tell you this. I think I know my brother well, and I have never—I repeat, never—known him to do *anything* unless he knew exactly what he was doing. I have a strong hunch that things are not nearly as dark as you picture them."

Jessica poured her fourth cup of coffee that day after Eric left to catch his plane. Her mind kept running through the conversation they'd had that morning. Would she really ever have a chance to become Jason's wife again? Was she looking at him only through the eyes of love? She didn't know—all she knew was she did love him and it hurt!

CHAPTER NINE

The weeks crawled by, the intense heat of the summer blending slowly into fall. The six-month "business arrangement" crept steadily toward an end as October opened its arms to the world. Jason seemed more grimly determined to keep his distance from Jessica than ever. After one or two more subtle attempts at seducing him, she scratched that plan when she caught his mocking eyes openly laughing at her. No, Jason was a tough bird—one that couldn't be led down the garden path very easily.

Jessica was in the kitchen lovingly patting a very pregnant Tabby who had been renamed Tabacina, as Jason came through the kitchen on his way to pick up Monica for their date that evening.

Jessica looked up as he came in, the tired lines on his face showing clearly. Her heart turned over with love for him as she realized that he had had very little time for his personal life the last few weeks. He had worked from before sunup until long past sundown to keep the two farms running efficiently. No matter how he had teased about the way he was going to spend his ten thousand dollars, he must really be in great need of it to put himself through all this misery, Jessica thought tenderly. Maybe she could manage to slip an extra thousand in his pay envelope when this job was over. It would undoubtedly come in handy for whatever he had in mind.

As Jason knelt down beside her his clean smell washed over her, causing a tight knot to form in her throat as she closed her eyes momentarily, fighting the urge to throw herself into his arms.

"How's the expectant mama coming along?" Jason asked lightly, running his large hand smoothly over Tabby's soft shiny fur.

Jessica envied the cat as she watched Jason's strong hand tenderly stroking her. She wet her lips with the tip of her tongue, her mind unwillingly remembering his hands on her body, stroking and exploring, gently showing her the difference between heaven and earth.

"Just fine," she answered, striving to keep her voice steady. "I've warned her that's what happens to 'loose' women."

Jason chuckled softly, giving Tabby one final pat before rising to his feet again. "Now, what would you know about 'loose' women?"

"Not too much." Jessica grinned honestly. "Tabby could probably curl my hair with some of her varied experiences."

Jason leaned back against the counter, crossing his husky arms, apparently in no big hurry. "When's the big event due?"

"Very soon—I think. I'm not too sure when her night

153

of passion was spent." Jessica giggled, her eyes coming up to meet his shyly.

His emerald gaze held hers for a moment. Jessica's heart thudded. Finally he spoke in a quiet, serious tone. "You know, Jessie, I used to lie awake nights for the first few months after the annulment wondering if anything had ever come out of that 'night of passion' we spent together."

Jessica looked surprised, asking softly, "Come out of it? What do you mean, Jason?"

Jason continued to hold her eyes with his. "I wondered if maybe you were carrying my baby," he said bluntly.

Jessica was flabbergasted now, her temper slowly rising. What did he take her for, some nitwit who would deny her child his father! No, if that had happened—and she was heartbroken it hadn't—she would have told the world to go to Hades and been back in Jason's arms so fast it would have made everyone's head swim! It hurt her feelings something fierce for him to think she wouldn't have informed him about such an event.

Looking up at him, her eyes flashing, she said in a tight voice, "Jason, I really don't know how to tell you this." She paused effectively before continuing, her pixie face deadly earnest. "I have good news, and bad news."

Jason straightened, his arms falling to his sides, his face assuming an expectant air. "What's the good news?"

"Well," she said, dragging out the announcement with agonising suspense, "I *was* pregnant with your child—in fact I had quadruplets!"

Jason's face was a mask of horror now. "Quadruplets!" he choked out.

Jessica nodded her head proudly.

Jason managed to get himself under control and asked skeptically, "What's the bad news?"

Jessica hung her head in shame. "I gave all four of them away as Christmas presents."

Jason let out a snort of exasperation. "Dammit, Jessica, that's not funny! You had me going there for a minute."

Jessica was laughing delightedly at the look of consternation on Jason's handsome face, her bubbly giggles catching. Jason began to grin sheepishly, taking a playful swat at her. Jessica dodged his hand as he grabbed for her, capturing her arm. He pulled her up roughly to him, their faces only a breath apart. "I'll make you pay for that," he whispered huskily.

Jessica's laughter caught in her throat as she saw the deep pools of jade darken as desire sprang alive in them.

"I'm not afraid," Jessica whispered bravely, her hands creeping up around his neck. "Do your worst, Rawlings."

Jason's shimmering green eyes looked into her luminous violet ones as he brought his mouth down to capture the sweetness of hers. The kiss started out slow and sensuous, his mouth moving lazily but firmly on hers. Suddenly the tranquility of it ignited into a raging inferno as Jason forcefully jerked her slender body up tightly against him, violently molding her soft breasts to the granite surface of his broad chest, his fingers burying deep in her thick hair, pulling her roughly toward him. A small whimper escaped her lips as he crushed his mouth on hers, hungrily devouring the sweet moistness.

He broke away just as abruptly as he had brought her to him, his face registering painful mixed emotions as he gazed into the lavender pools of her eyes. He let his breath out slowly, pressing his lips against her hair, his warm breath sending shuddering rivulets of delight through her veins.

"Jessica Cole," he rasped hoarsely, "do you know what you're doing to me?"

She slowly tilted her face upward to tenderly kiss each eye in an attempt to ease the clouded confusion she saw, whispering softly as her lips brushed his eyelids, "I know what I'd like to do with you."

He paused a moment, searching the depths of her eyes,

overwhelmed by the innocent honesty he saw there. "Damn, Jessie! You *know* I can't go on much longer like this."

She tightened her hold on him, overcoming his hesitancy, their mouths again joining, this time in a softer, more tender embrace. Jessica moved against him, moaning sweetly as his tongue united hotly with hers, the familiar ache of passion sweeping riotously through her. How she loved this man! She would move heaven and earth if only he were hers to love once again.

"Angel," Jason grunted breathlessly, his lips breaking away momentarily to kiss her eyes and nose, then reclaiming her mouth once again passionately. The kiss was so intense that Jessica sagged weakly against his taut frame, her hands burying deep in his thick hair, their breathing becoming ragged and uneven as the loud knocking on the back door echoed through the room.

Letting out a soft curse, Jason pulled away from her and agitatedly walked over to yank open the back screen. A smiling Rick stood there, a bouquet of autumn flowers grasped foolishly in his hand. "Hi, boss. Where's the pretty lady?"

Jason jerked his head impatiently toward Jessica, still standing breathless in front of Tabby's box. "In there," he mumbled shortly as he brushed rudely past Rick and stormed out the back door.

Jessica's heart sank as she watched him go, her senses still achingly alive for him.

"Have I come at a bad time?" Rick asked hesitantly.

"No, of course not, Rick. What can I do for you?" Jessica brought herself regretfully back to earth.

"These are for you, pretty lady." Rick extended the bouquet of flowers proudly.

"They're beautiful, Rick. Thank you!" It was hard for her to stay angry with Rick. He was always all sunshine and light when he was around Jessica.

"Well, there's a catch to them." Rick grinned broadly.

156

"And what might that be?" Jessica returned playfully.

"You have to agree to be my date for the hayride Saturday night."

"What hayride?" Jessica looked puzzled.

"The one Jason always has every Fall. Hasn't he said anything about it to you?"

"It seems he did mention it awhile back. Is it this Saturday night?"

"Sure is. Every couple in love, engaged, or just 'hoping' will be there. What do ya say? Will you go with me?" Rick's face wore a hopeful expression.

Jason would undoubtedly be taking Monica, she thought silently, so why not. "I'd love to," she assured him, putting the flowers in a vase of water.

"Fantastic," Rick shouted, scooping her up in his arms and whirling her around the room until both of them were laughing and breathless. He stayed around for another fifteen minutes, having a glass of tea with her before returning to his chores.

Jessica waved good-bye, then closed the back door slowly, leaning against its hard surface wearily. Her mind drifted lazily over Jason's heated kiss before Rick interrupted them. The torture of being around him, yet so far away from him, was becoming unbearable. She couldn't go on much longer like she was. She was going to have to throw in the towel soon, but her stubborn loving heart just wouldn't let her do it—yet.

The week flew by with the farm crew preparing for the hayride Saturday night. The big hay wagon had been brought up to the farmyard, and bales of hay quickly covered it. One of the large farm tractors had been attached to it and stood ready and waiting for the happy couples. Rick told her they would go about five miles down the road, where they would have a barbecue dinner awaiting them. Jason hired several people to come in and cook for the boisterous group. Apparently Monica had helped him plan the whole affair, since he had barely mentioned it to Jessica.

He had asked her if she was going with Rick, and when she confirmed she was, he had turned and left the room in a dark mood. Jessica had sighed deeply, wishing he had asked her to go with him. Somehow she would have found a way to comply with his wishes. But of course he hadn't. Jessica was sure who she would see beside him Saturday night, and it wouldn't be her.

Jessica finished her chores as quickly as possible Saturday afternoon, hoping to be the first one in the shower this evening. The old relic of a hot-water heater had been causing some trouble lately, providing only enough hot water for one person, leaving the other to shower rapidly in a stream of ice-cold water. With a triumphant smile on her face she barely managed to scurry past Jason that evening as he headed for the bathroom. Smiling pertly, she moved to close the door. "Sorry . . . I was here first!"

Jason stepped back slightly, eyeing her suspiciously. "Couldn't you have showered earlier?"

"Nope! I've been busy, too," she said, trying unsuccessfully to close the door in his face.

Jason stuck out his hand, effectively blocking her move, a mischievous twinkle invading his eyes. "You use all that hot water, and you're a dead woman."

Jessica smiled back innocently. "Would I do a thing like that to you?"

"You have three times this week already," Jason told her dryly.

"Tough luck, Rawlings," she retorted, throwing her slight weight against the door.

Jason held his ground solidly, his muscled arms easily blocking her attempt. "You fool with me, and I'll come in there and supervise your shower personally. Then I'll *know* I won't have to freeze my buns off again tonight, Cole." It was Jason's turn to smile triumphantly.

A small pucker of indecision crossed Jessica's face as

she mulled over his threat. *That wouldn't be half bad,* she thought wickedly. But, not wanting to see that knowing look in his eyes if she dared him to, she settled for heckling him a little. Sighing dramatically, she batted her black spiky eyelashes at him seductively and said breathlessly, "I've just decided to take a nice *cold* shower anyway. I feel it will help me control my lustful tendencies around Rick tonight. You know how romantic hayrides can be," she finished theatrically.

Jason looked disgusted. Jessica seized the advantage and slammed the bathroom door loudly in his face. Giggling impishly, she quickly stripped her clothes off, leaving them in a heap on the floor as she turned the shower knobs on full blast and hopped into the shower, letting the hot water soothe her tired body. Humming softly, she closed her eyes dreamily, the steam from the hot water softly filling the room. A piercing scream tore from her lips as a glass of ice-cold water, thrown over the top of the shower stall, hit her full blast.

"*Jason, you dog!*" she screamed at the top of her lungs.

He arrogantly jerked the shower door open, grinning at her belligerent face. "Just thought I'd help you and Rick out, Angel!" he said brightly. His eyes fastened appreciatively on her nude form as she stood there sputtering, grabbing for the wet washcloth, which she angrily threw at him, barely missing her mark as he slammed the shower door shut and, laughing fiendishly, left the room at a dead run.

She finished her shower in a fit of anger and blazed out of the bathroom, still boiling. Jason was nowhere to be seen. She whirled around, stomped into her room, and slammed the door, jarring the windows in the whole house.

She had just finished her makeup and slipped into a pair of western designer jeans and a soft yellow top when she heard the water running in the shower again. Throwing down her hairbrush, she rushed into the utility room, took a large pail down from the top shelf, and filled it with cold water. Proceeding on to the kitchen, she dumped three trays of ice into the pail and tiptoed back down the hall to the bathroom, her face a mask of concentration as she sloshed the heavy pail along beside her, plotting feverishly.

She stopped in front of the bathroom door and turned the doorknob slowly, hardly believing her luck. The dummy had left the door unlocked! Creeping stealthily into the bathroom, Jessica stopped just outside the shower door and listened to Jason singing a boisterous version of "Blow the Man Down," unaware of his impending doom.

With a screeching karate cry, Jessica swung the door open and heaved the pail of ice water on an astounded Jason, causing the last note of his song to sound like the mating call of a banshee. With a loud bellow of rage he bounded rapidly out of the shower, reaching the door before Jessica could, locking it firmly, and turning to stalk a wide-eyed Jessica.

"Now, Jason"—she grinned shakily—"don't do anything rash! Turn about's fair play," she reminded him in a panicky voice. He continued, undaunted by her sense of fair play, his magnificent body still lathered in white soap. "Jason," she warned, trying her best to sound stern, but at the sight of his mean scowl her laughter threatened to bubble over. He made one powerful lunge at her and dragged her, clothes and all, into the shower with him, turning the hot water off completely and letting the cold water slice down on them unmercifully. "I'm already dressed, you toad!" she shrieked.

"You want to play rough, do you, wildcat?" He pushed her head firmly under the hard spray, her clothes becoming drenched in the onslaught. Struggling wildly to break his steel grip, she dissolved in a fit of uncontrollable giggles as his grip only increased.

Jessica's ear-piercing screams could probably be heard for miles as they romped and scuffled in the cold shower,

Jason showing his captured prey no mercy. Flinging her hands out for support, she encountered Jason's wet body, the effects of their horseplay evident in his blatant arousal.

"Let me out of here," Jessica petitioned halfheartedly as she pushed ineffectually at his hard body.

"Not until you've paid for your sins," Jason told her determinedly, shoving her head back under the water. His hands came in contact with her wet breasts, the clinging fabric of her blouse revealing all of her "assets" clearly.

Just as Jessica let out another ear-piercing scream a loud pounding on the bathroom door shattered their mini-war instantly. They both stopped struggling, Jason holding her tight up against him as he heatedly shouted, "Who is it?"

"Jason, what in the world is going on in there?" Monica's agitated voice reached them above the pounding water of the shower.

"Aw . . . *damn!*" Jason muttered. "What's she doing here this early?"

"I don't know." Jessica giggled, her mouth pressed tightly against his neck. "Want me to yell out there and find out?" she whispered sweetly.

"Hell, no, I don't want you to yell out there!" he hissed. "I don't want her to know we're in here together."

Jessica laughed even harder, her body shaking seductively against his. "I think you're out of luck! I believe she may have already figured it out on her own."

"Jason!" Monica yelled again.

"Be right out, Monica. Nothing to worry about." Jason reached up to shut off the shower, whispering in a low voice, "Just stay in here after I leave. I'll handle it."

Jessica tiptoed meekly out of the shower stall and sat quietly on the seat of the commode, grinning broadly as she watched a muddled Jason towel off briskly before slipping on his briefs and his tight jeans.

Noticing her roving eyes, he grinned recklessly. "Wipe

161

that smile off your face, Cole. You're not seeing anything you haven't seen before."

Grinning back at him smugly, she shot him a mock salute. "Aye, aye, sir. Can't blame a girl for enjoying the view!"

He gave her an affectionate peck on the nose as he slipped out the door, issuing a firm, "Stay here!"

Closing the door firmly behind him, he confronted a bewildered Monica.

"What in heaven's name is going on in there, Jason? Is Jessica hurt?"

Looking her directly in the eye, his face as innocent as an angel's, he asked calmly, "What are you talking about, Monica?"

Monica's mouth sagged slightly. "What am I talking about? I'm talking about all that loud screaming going on. What was that all about?"

"Oh, that," Jason said unconcernedly. "That was Jessica."

"Jason"—Monica sent him a penetrating stare—"I *know* it was Jessica. I *don't* know what her problem is. Is she hurt?"

Shrugging his broad shoulders nonchalantly, he brushed passed Monica, her eyes openly admiring his massive body and thick hair, which was still wet and glistening from his exuberant shower. "Monica, you're making a big deal over a few little screams," he said blandly.

"A few *little* screams?" Monica plainly thought he was nuts.

"Jessica just spilled a pail of water in the bathroom, and she was mad because I asked her to clean it up." Jason closed the door to his bedroom, leaving a perfectly dissatisfied Monica staring daggers at his closed door.

The hayride had gotten off to a roaring start with everyone in high spirits. Close to thirty couples showed up, Willis and Marcy among them. Jessica had to smother a laugh when she first saw Willis. His new jeans bagged unmercifully, his western shirt was outrageously loud, and his new Stetson hat made him look like Quick Draw McGraw on the Saturday morning cartoon. *He was about as exciting as a cello player at a rock concert,* Jessica thought amusedly.

The night flew by rapidly with all the laughter and high spirits, but as Jessica let herself into the dark house long after midnight a sense of deep depression settled over her. Her thoughts turned back to the hayride. Rick had been at his most charming all evening, making her laugh with his lighthearted foolishness. Just as the ride was about to start, he had held her down and stuffed hay into every available pocket of her jeans and shirt. She had squealed with delight, but her laughter had died quickly as her eyes caught the deep scowl on Jason's face. He had been talking to the driver of the hay wagon, going over the route with him. At the sound of her pealing laughter he had jerked his head around, shooting her a *very* irritated glance before continuing the conversation. But Jessica hadn't let that spoil her fun. They had all indulged in the huge barbecue, then later had a horseshoe tournament, a sack race, and a rolling-pin contest, in which the woman throwing the rolling pin the farthest (indicating bad news for the boyfriend or spouse) won the prize. A red-faced Marcy Mercy took the trophy home while a grinning Willis, his hands jammed in his jean pockets, quietly beamed on the sidelines.

It was very late when they all piled back on the wagon for the return trip home. The wagon became quieter as the moon crept higher in the sky, the couples busy, wrapped in each other's arms. A man with a beautiful voice sang the sweet strains of "Moonlight Bay." Rick had pulled Jessica into his arms but was still keeping a respectful distance from her. She didn't want to encourage anything romantic with him, no matter how hard she teased Jason about him. He was a friendly, happy person to be with, but like all his predecessors, he left Jessica feeling empty. There was only one person she loved. She shifted around on the hay, turning over to lie on her side more comfortably. Her breath froze momentarily as her eyes locked with Jason's. He was beside them on the hay, sitting close to Monica, who was snuggled contentedly against his shoulder. Jessica unconsciously looked to see where his hands were, blushing when his eyes followed her searching gaze. Satisfied they were decently draped lightly around Monica's waist, Jessica dropped her eyes sheepishly. Monica's eyes were closed dreamily as Jessica hazarded another glance at Jason, his steady gaze still on her.

Electrical currents surged through her body as she began to slowly drown in the liquid fire of his beautiful jade eyes. Becoming slightly breathless, she fought an overwhelming urge to reach out and simply touch him. With sudden clarity it occurred to her that she had reached her breaking point. No amount of money on earth could make her stay on here, dying a little more each day. Without Jason life held no meaning for her. She knew at this moment what she had to do. Tears began to drip, like a soft summer rain, from her eyes, which were violet pools of living torment. She would give up the inheritance, go back to Austin, and try once more to fit the torn shambles of her life back together. This one last night she would allow herself to drown here in his eyes. The agony of not being able to lie in his arms, breathe his unique fragrance, touch his soft, full mouth, which had brought such unbearable pleasure to her, caused the tears to fall swifter.

Jason was aware of her tears, his eyes tenderly caressing hers, visually beginning to make love to her without ever touching her. The vocalist began to sing a beautiful, tender love song as the tractor crept silently toward home. Jason and Jessica lay under the stars together, yet alone, trapped in their own corners of hell. The words wrapped painfully around Jessica's heart as the prophetic lyrics filled the quiet moonlit night, the singer's deep, melodious voice proclaiming that this might be the loving couple's last night together, that someday they would have only memories of each other. . . .

Jessica remembered the hay wagon pulling quietly into the farmyard long after midnight, depositing its sleepy occupants. She felt emotionally exhausted as she climbed out of the wagon and longed only to reach the privacy of her room, where she could cry her heart out alone, but Rick had insisted on walking her to the door, sensing the change in her mood. He pulled her into the comfort of his arms and gave her a reassuring hug, placing a light kiss on her temple. "I don't know what the problem is, pretty lady," he said in a comforting voice, "but things will look different in the morning."

"I doubt it." Jessica gave a shaky laugh, the hot tears pricking her eyes once again.

"Would you like to talk about it?"

"No, thank you, Rick. It's something that I have to work out alone . . . but thanks."

"Anytime you need someone, Jessica, I'll be here." Jessica remembered how serious Rick's face had been as he shifted uneasily in the soft moonlight. *Oh, Rick,* Jessica had thought tenderly, *how I wish that I could fall in love with you. How I wish I could take a surgical knife and literally cut all the painful memories and the love I have for Jason out of my heart.* But instead she had given Rick an affectionate pat and told him good night at the door.

Jessica sat wearily in her bedroom, fighting to make her mind a total blank, trying to erase the memories of tonight. She took a quick shower before slipping into her nightgown and brushing the loose hay out of her hair. Her mind seemed determined to keep her imprisoned as her thoughts once again drifted back to Jason's eyes as they had held hers tonight. As she replaced the brush slowly on her dressing table the dam of self-control finally broke. She switched off the light and fell across the bed, burying her face in the pillow, the hateful tears overcoming her once more.

A loud bang as the door to her bedroom was thrown violently open brought her abruptly to her feet, the hot tears still streaming down her face. Jason stood in the doorway, dressed only in his jeans, his large frame blocking out the light from the hall. He stood perfectly still, his eyes moving painfully over her soft rounded breasts, which heaved with every sob, then traveling languidly on down her slender length.

Jessica's lavender eyes found his emerald ones as he walked calmly to her, still not saying a word. With a frightening determination written on his face he literally jerked her up into his arms. Jessica had been barely holding her breath, afraid to move. As she became aware of his naked chest and his lean, muscular body, pressed to hers, she let out a deep shuddering sob, burying her face in his neck, clutching tightly to his shoulder.

He carried her silently down the hall to his bedroom, kicked the door closed behind him, and stood her before him, his eyes locked rapturously with hers. He stripped off his jeans, his eyes never leaving hers, and with trembling hands reached for her. "Dammit, Jessica, I may hate myself in the morning, but I can't fight this any longer!"

He brought his mouth down on hers roughly, devouring her lips, almost bruising them with his intensity. She heard the sheer fabric of her gown give way as he ripped it from her trembling body.

Jessica's heart froze. She had never in all her years seen Jason so disturbed. "Jason," she murmured helplessly, "why are you doing this?"

"Why! Because you're driving me out of my mind!"

He grabbed at her forcefully as she cringed in terror. "Jason, please don't do this. You're hurting me . . . scaring me," she whimpered.

Jason stared at her frightened face, shocked back to normalcy. His shoulders sagged apologetically as he gently pulled her to his chest, whispering raggedly, "I'm so sorry, Angel. I don't know what got into me. I'm half crazy wanting you. I've never wanted anything like I want you tonight."

Their bodies moved as one toward the large bed as they murmured each other's names, their mouths seeking and hungrily finding each other. As they lay side by side, seeking out the secrets and pleasures of their bodies, Jessica came to him with an eagerness that pleased and astounded him, her supple, warm body complying with his every demand. His tongue chased hers in sweet, provocative play as their mouths clung together, their soft sighs mingling in the quiet room. Helplessly she arched her hips toward him, pressing her body closer, and with her hand caressed the firm curve of his back as it dipped to form the sensuous slope of his buttocks. He eagerly surrendered to her touch, his tongue moving inside her warm mouth as though he was afraid that if he stopped she would disappear from his arms.

His mouth grazed her tender breasts, causing her nipples to strain toward his tongue as wave after wave of desire coursed through her body. Her small hands clutched fervently at his thickly corded arms, his muscles tensing with a need for her too strong to be denied. "I want you—I need you," Jason whispered huskily as his hand moved between her shapely thighs.

A hard knot rose in her throat as her hot salty tears mingled with their kisses. "I know, my darling Jason . . . I know."

He slid his fingertips against the sensitive flesh of her inner thigh, causing Jessica to writhe in sweet torment at the exquisiteness of his touch. As the intensity of her shuddering increased he pulled her beneath him, his merging with her fiery and deep. Their need for each other was so great that neither one could move as the tide of blinding passion devoured them. It was over almost as soon as it started. Jason carried them to a frantic plateau, their need building higher and higher, their satisfaction reaching far beyond the physical. The fires deep within them burst together, each one feeling a sense of acute disappointment that it could not last forever. Jessica clung to Jason, her face buried in his broad chest as they spiraled helplessly back toward sanity.

As their ragged breathing slowed and the sounds of the quiet night resumed Jason spoke. "Do you know what you put me through out there tonight on that hay wagon?"

Jessica kept her eyes closed, a sweet languid feeling pervading her. "You're the one who started it," she said in weak defense.

Jason began running his hands slowly over her, stopping at her breasts to flick her nipples lightly with his fingers, then moving to the roundness of her hip, reacquainting himself leisurely with all her feminine curves and secrets. Jessica shuddered at the boldness of his hands as his fingertips sought the warmth of her femininity, and she reached out to examine the pleasurable planes of his body.

"I wanted to take you in my arms so damn bad . . ." He moaned, his hands tightening possessively around her derriere. "But I had to sit there and watch you in some other man's arms."

She sighed deeply, brushing her mouth over his, kissing him tenderly as she felt him press deeper against her silken thigh. "I *imagined* I was in your arms."

"But I didn't have you in my arms, and I plan on correcting that. From now on I want you in this bed every night with me, Jessica. You belong here." Jessica's heart soared, then plunged to the ground with his next words. "There is no reason to deny what we both feel for the next few weeks," he whispered hoarsely, his mouth searing hers again with a coaxing kiss.

"You mean until our 'business' is over with," Jessica said sadly.

Jason's tongue played lightly with hers, the embers igniting rapidly again for them both. "Let's not talk about business tonight, sweetheart," he whispered softly.

Talk about business! Jessica's mind scoffed at his choice of words. He certainly didn't plan on committing himself! Why should he, she reasoned, when he had her *and* Monica? Jessica loved him, but she would not settle for second best. She wanted marriage and a home with his children, or nothing. Her thoughts froze as his mouth began to trail over the hollow of her neck and down to the softness of her breasts, his tongue licking wet circles around their pink crests, causing a delightful tautness to invade her entire body. She held her breath as his tongue continued its searing path, hesitating for one brief second as he placed soft, lingering kisses around her navel before retracing his way back to her mouth and whispering against her lips, "Now, can't you think of something you'd rather do besides talk?"

She smiled in the darkness as her hands reached to guide him over her slender body once again. "Shut up, Rawlings. Hasn't anyone ever told you you talk too much?"

Their mouths met in fiery kisses, blotting out all other coherent thoughts.

This time their merging was a slow tender union, the unrestrained joy of being in each other's arms overriding their differences for the moment. They floated together through hazy, sensuous hillsides, moaning blissfully, before the fires of passion captured them a second time, leaving them clinging weakly, wrapped in each other's arms, a thin sheen of perspiration covering their bodies.

Jason rolled over on his back, bringing her with him. "I'm not going to ask you where you've learned some of those things you've just so expertly put to use . . . but you damn well better never use them with anyone but me, ever again." His breath was coming in short ragged spurts.

Jessica brought her mouth down to trail featherlike kisses across the side of his neck. "Why, don't you remem-

169

ber? I owe all my expertise in lovemaking to you. You taught me all I know," she whispered intimately in his ear.

"I'd love to take the credit for that, but I only spent one night with you," he said skeptically.

"As you once said, I'm a fast learner," Jessica reminded him, playfully tugging at his lips with her teeth.

His mouth caught hers in another long drugging kiss before he shifted her over next to his side. "You should have caught me when I was younger, Angel. I'm getting too old for these all night love-a-thons," he said sleepily. "Let's continue our—uh—conversation in the morning."

Jessica lay very still. He had not said he loved her. He wanted her, but he didn't love her. Things had not changed one iota. She simply had one more night to put in her memory box.

"Jason," she whispered quietly.

"Ummm . . ."

"I'm going home—back to Austin—in the morning."

Jason opened one eye. "Why?"

Jessica closed her eyes, willing herself to deceive him. "I need to check on my apartment—do a few things I've been putting off," she lied boldly.

Jason closed his eyes again, weariness etched deeply in his tanned face. "That shouldn't take very long, should it?"

"No, maybe a couple of days."

"Well"—he turned over, taking her in his arms again—"don't stay any longer than necessary. The nights could start getting long without your tempting little body next to me."

"Will you take good care of Tabby and her kittens?" Jessica asked sorrowfully.

"Sure," Jason agreed readily, then cocked one eye open again. "What do you mean by that? I thought she wasn't due for a while."

"Oh, I just meant, in case she had them while I was gone," Jessica said, catching her error.

"Don't worry about anything, honey. I'll take care of it." Jason's breathing became slow as Jessica lay in the warm comfort of his heavily muscled arms, savoring her last few hours with him. She wouldn't return from Austin; she'd go to the bank and try to obtain a loan to pay Jason for running the farm for her and mail him a check. It no longer mattered to her whether she got the inheritance. Life would go on whether she wanted it to or not, and right now she didn't care.

CHAPTER TEN

The large jet sat its cumbersome body down, light as a feather, as it landed gracefully on the runway of the Robert Mueller Municipal Airport in Austin that early evening in October, bringing Jessica back to what had been her home for the last eight years.

The plane rolled gracefully to a stop as she began gathering her things in preparation to leave the plane. After stepping into the terminal she fought her way over to claim her baggage. She never ceased to be amazed by the way people's manners deserted them in a hurried situation like this, but she had learned to be as aggressive as the next person, reasoning that if you had to live in the jungle, you needed to be able to hold your own with the animals.

She stepped back out into the still, warm evening and hailed a cab. Giving the driver the address, she climbed in and leaned back sadly in the seat as the driver pulled swiftly away from the terminal.

The capital of Texas was a lovely old city, boasting schools for the deaf and blind, the University of Texas, which Jessica had attended for four years, as well as the LBJ ranch, sitting just fifty miles to the west. They were now passing the campus where she had spent long hours sitting in the large LBJ Library, cramming for tests with Sally Munson, her closest friend throughout her college years.

She smiled now as she thought of all the good times they had had together . . . those late night jam sessions they'd had in Jessica's room—Sally either in the clouds from her latest love or in the depths of dark despair from the lack of one. They would consume large quantities of Coke and potato chips, sitting in the middle of Jessica's bed, agonizing over Sally's unquestionable fate of forever being a bridesmaid but never a bride. Sally would get so desperate about the prospect of becoming an old maid she would wave the potato chip sack wildly over the bed before Jessica's distressed eyes. By the time Sally would leave forlornly for her own room, Jessica would have to drag out the little Dustbuster she kept in her closet and vacuum out her bed before going to sleep that night.

Jessica laughed openly as she thought of her good friend now, very happily married, expecting a child any day. She wondered fleetingly whether she had remembered her vow to wear the black negligee they had bought together that day two years ago, and if so, whether she had had any better luck with it than Jessica had.

The taxi was pulling into the drive of Mrs. Houseman's house, her homey little bungalow with its flowers and shrubbery looking very peaceful in the gathering twilight. Jessica paid her cab fare, adding a generous tip as the cab driver removed her luggage from the trunk of the cab and set the suitcases on the drive. Jessica picked them up and walked around to the back of her landlady's house and rang the bell. Mrs. Houseman threw open the door, enveloping Jessica in a maternal hug and expressing her delight to see her again.

"Things have just not been the same around here," she was complaining to Jessica. "I'd look up at your little apartment every night, and there would be no lights on, and I'd have such a lonely feeling," she said wistfully. "You had me spoiled, young lady, spending so many of your free evenings together with me," she scolded Jessica lovingly. "Now I'm going to have to find someone else to tell all my problems to."

Jessica hugged her affectionately. "There's a lot of people that would be more than happy to take my place. Mr. Hawks, to name one," she teased.

"Oh, my, Mr. Hawks, my foot!" Mrs. Houseman became quite flustered. "Now, why in the world would I want him around underfoot every evening?"

Jessica grinned mischievously. "Why, I don't think he'd mind keeping you company in the evenings. Doesn't he just 'happen by' almost every night, anyway?" she asked innocently.

"Oh, flitter, I can't seem to step out my back door that he doesn't show up, looking for a piece of that lemon cake he's always been so fond of," she complained good-naturedly.

"Well," Jessica replied tactfully, "it's a good thing you find time to bake a fresh one a couple of times a week, or he'd be up that proverbial creek without a paddle, wouldn't he?"

Mrs. Houseman flushed prettily, her wrinkled face glowing. "Let's just forget about Mr. Hawks for now." She hastened to change the subject. "Come on, I'll fix us a glass of fresh lemonade. I know you must be tired from your flight."

They stepped into the house, going into the large kitchen that still held the smells of the fried chicken Mrs. Houseman had fixed for her dinner that evening. There was a covered plate sitting on the table, still containing pieces of the golden-brown, crispy meat.

"If you're hungry, I'll fix you a plate, Jessica," she was saying. "I know how you've always loved my chicken." She smiled proudly. "Just sit down and help yourself."

Jessica couldn't resist the temptation, so she reached for a fat drumstick, bit into the tender meat, and rolled her eyes up toward the ceiling. "This is fantastic! I don't know how you do it. I've tried fixing it just as you told me, and it doesn't taste nearly this good," she said reverently.

"Oh, it's just always a treat to eat someone else's cooking, dear, that's the only difference." She beamed, setting a plate with a blue willow design down in front of Jessica as she pushed a bowl of fresh green beans, from her summer garden, toward her. She opened the refrigerator and took out a plate of thick slices of juicy red tomatoes, removing the Saran Wrap that was covering the plate. "The tomatoes didn't do so well this year," she fretted. She reached over and put a thick slice on Jessica's plate. "The garden just dried up from lack of rain. I tried to water it, but it just made my water bill run too high." She sighed.

"I know," Jessica sympathized, munching on her chicken. "It was dry everywhere this year."

Jessica ate the remainder of her dinner engaging in pleasant small talk, with Mrs. Houseman hovering over her, offering her more than she could possibly eat.

Jessica pushed back from the table, taking her plate over to the sink and running water over it. She noticed all her plants lovingly arranged on a table in front of one of the kitchen windows. Mrs. Houseman had been caring for them while Jessica was gone, and they all had such a green healthy appearance—her tiny baby's tears was thick and full in its pot and the bridal veil bloomed in gay profusion. The large yellow "pocketbook" plant, as Jessica had always called it, was blooming in glorious bright colors, its fat little "pocketbooks," speckled with red, hanging lightly on the stems. The love Mrs. Houseman had given the plants was very apparent.

"Mrs. Houseman," Jessica said suddenly, "would you mind keeping these plants forever. I'm afraid if I move them now, they'll not do as well. I can always get new starts."

Mrs. Houseman's face lit up in a bright smile. "Why, I would love to keep them, Jessica. If you're sure," she added. "I've become quite fond of them. They're almost like my children now." She grinned sheepishly. "That one philodendron and I have a long conversation over breakfast every morning," she confessed.

Jessica smiled tenderly. "I couldn't think of a nicer home for them to 'grow up' in. Please take them with my blessings."

Mrs. Houseman crossed over to the plants sitting happily on the table. "Well, now, see what I told you, children. Everything always has a way of working out for the best!" she said elatedly.

Jessica let herself into her dark apartment, reaching for the light switch as she set her bag inside the door. The three-room apartment came to life as the light from the lamp flooded the small area. Jessica walked over to open the window, letting the fresh air in the stuffy room, and continued on into her bedroom, turning on the bedside lamp and sinking down on the bed. As she lay on her back looking up at the white ceiling and thinking of Jason, a sense of loneliness crept over her. He was nearly seven hundred miles away from her now! She closed her eyes, remembering the feel of his arms and his kisses the night before. She bit her lip to keep the tears from falling, which was something strange for Jessica. Until she had returned home for Aunt Rainey's funeral, she had never been one to burst into tears at the drop of a hat, but for the last few months that was *all* she had done. How could you love someone so much and be so miserable?

The apartment was beginning to lose its musty smell as she sat back up on the corner of the bed. What she needed now, she surmised, was a hot shower and a good night's rest. She hadn't gotten over having just three hours of sleep the night before. *I'll bet Jason's tired tonight,* she thought as she unpacked the things she had brought with her. She would have to send for the rest of her belongings later.

Jessica released a long sigh as she stepped into the small blue-tiled bathroom for her shower. She would have to try to get through one day at a time, but for right now she was too tired to think. Maybe tomorrow would be brighter.

Up bright and early the next morning but dreading to face the long day ahead, she dumped out a bowlful of the cornflakes Mrs. Houseman had sent over, poured the donated milk over them, and made herself a cup of instant coffee from the supplies she still had in her cabinet. After eating the simple meal she washed the bowl and cup and set them in the dish drainer to dry. It was going to be a long, long day.

She picked up the phone to call Mr. Samuels, the principal where she had taught school. Jessica proceeded to tell him that she was back and available for her old job when she was needed.

Mr. Samuels sounded flustered as he said kindly, "I'm afraid it will have to be after the Christmas break, Jessica. Quite frankly we didn't expect you back."

"I know that, Mr. Samuels," Jessica assured him, "but I decided to come home after all."

"What about your farm?"

"It's being taken care of," Jessica told him.

"Well, enjoy yourself, Jessica. Take advantage of this little rest. You'll be thankful for it when you come back," he cautioned with a chuckle.

"Thank you, Mr. Samuels, I will," Jessica murmured, replacing the phone in its cradle, overwhelming sadness washing over her. How she longed to be back home with Jason right now.

She dressed in a pair of jeans and pulled on a blue T-shirt, tied her hair back in a ponytail, and let herself out of the apartment to go down to the garage directly below. She swung open the heavy door and saw her little red Datsun sitting patiently waiting for its mistress to return.

"Boy, have I missed you," she assured it lovingly. "I've got a truck I want you to meet someday. You're not going to believe it," she told her car seriously.

She sat down on the familiar seat, started the engine with no difficulty, backed it slowly out of the drive, and headed toward the local supermarket. She returned an hour later with the little car overflowing with supplies for the kitchen.

Well, she thought optimistically that evening as she sat alone in her newly scrubbed apartment, *I've used up one day of the rest of my life without Jason.* She looked around the lonely room, a tight knot forming in her throat. One day! And it seemed like a week. How could she ever make it? Grabbing a light sweater, she ran out of her apartment, intent on a long walk which would make her so tired she wouldn't be able to even think afterward.

Two hours later a weary Jessica let herself into the apartment, took a hot bath, then stared misty-eyed at the dark ceiling for the rest of the night . . .

The next few days blurred together for Jessica. She was barely able to control her emotions, bursting into tears at odd moments of the day. She had gone down to the local drugstore one evening looking for a new paperback to read—anything to take up the empty hours of the endless lonely days. She had selected the book and was idly looking over the large display of colognes when out of the

178

corner of her eye she glimpsed the aftershave display. With faltering steps she walked over slowly and picked up the dark amber bottle, holding it with reverence in her hands. She removed the top of the bottle and inhaled deeply, breathing in the rich masculine scent . . . the one Jason always wore. A river of tears cascaded down her face as she stood cradling the aftershave, her hands trembling violently. Dragging a Kleenex out of her purse, she wiped her eyes and replaced the lid on the bottle. She started to put it back on the shelf but paused, then carried it to the check-out counter along with her book. It was a small comfort . . . but at least it was something.

She drove home with tears still in her eyes and let herself into the small apartment just as the phone rang.

Jessica's heart leaped into her throat as she snatched it up swiftly, praying silently to hear a deep manly voice begging her to return home. Instead she found herself explaining irritably to a persistent salesman that she didn't *need* aluminum siding for her house—she didn't *have* a house.

Jessica had been gone eight days. Had it been eight thousand she couldn't have been lonelier as she stood at her window looking out at the approaching twilight. The dark night was beginning to take on a stormy appearance, the promise of much-needed rain hanging heavy in the sultry air. Jessica could hear the distant roll of thunder and smell the faint scent of coming rain in the muggy breeze blowing in her window. A sharp streak of lightning briefly lit up the living room as the storm drew closer to the city. Jessica cringed as a loud clap of thunder shook the small apartment. She looked down into Mrs. Houseman's yard. Some of her webbed lawn chairs had been turned over from the wind, which was beginning to gust strongly. She could see the little patch of garden with its beans hanging limply on their vines from lack of water.

Jessica stood there absently massaging hand cream into

her hands, her mind wandering back to Jason for the thousandth time that day. "I wonder what he's doing right now," she muttered longingly. Had he missed her even a tiny bit? She laughed a short, ironic laugh. "Probably not." He was no doubt enjoying a return to sanity from the life he had led the last few months.

She heaved a deep sigh. Today had not been one of her best days, what with the annoying little problem she had had with the Datsun on the way to the market this afternoon. She wished now she had walked the short distance. Then she wouldn't have had to be without her car for the next couple of days.

She pulled the window down a little before going to her bedroom, glancing once more at the approaching storm. Maybe it would just be a good rain this time instead of a storm, she wished hopefully.

Sliding between her sheets, she picked up the paperback from the nightstand by the bed and for over an hour tried unsuccessfully to concentrate on the hero and heroine. Finally she threw the book back down on the table in disgust. How could she expect to read about a man's hot, passionate lips taking control of a woman's trembling, vulnerable lips, their eyes meeting in bold, smoldering desire, and keep her mind off Jason?

Switching off the bedside lamp, she settled down tensely, listening to the mounting fury of the coming storm. There was no doubt left in her mind now—it was clearly going to be a full-blown storm. Being more fatigued than she realized, she drifted off quickly into an uneasy sleep, one ear tuned to the wind, lest it take her roof off.

Jessica had been asleep for only a few minutes when her subconscious mind registered a loud pounding noise. She turned irritably at the disturbing sound, snuggling deeper into her soft pillow. The persistent banging became louder and louder. Someone was obviously trying to beat a wooden door down with his bare hands.

"Jessica!"

Jessica's mind slowly came to the surface. That was *her* door they were trying to beat down!

"Jessica, damn it, you'd better be in there!" a deep voice threatened, almost hysterically, the banging increasing in intensity.

She sat up, her heart pounding as she put her feet on the floor, fighting to overcome her grogginess. She staggered into the front room, groping for the light switch. If this was Avon calling, they had gone berserk.

"I'm coming, I'm coming," Jessica mumbled. "Just hold on a minute!"

She reached the protesting door, which was now groaning under the battering assault. As she reached up to slip the chain off the safety lock, she demanded, "Who is it?"

"Dammit, Jessica, you'd better open this door—*NOW!*"

"Jason?" she asked in astonishment.

She quickly pulled the chain off and flung the door wide open, the warm rain blowing in on her.

"Jason," she repeated blankly.

Jason was standing there in the doorway, his clothes plastered to his body, rain running in rivulets off the brim of his hat, his large frame sagging weakly against the doorframe. His face was lined with fatigue, and heavy dark circles smudged his eyes. He heaved a deep sigh. "Damn, Jessica, I was beginning to think you weren't in there," he said in a weary voice.

Jessica was still too stunned to make any kind of reasonable response to him. "Jason, what's the matter? Is something wrong at home?" She studied his troubled face for a moment, then exclaimed, "It's Tabby, isn't it? She's had her kittens!" It was the only reason Jessica could think of at the moment for Jason to be standing here in Austin at her front door.

Jason looked at her in dumbfounded astonishment. "Had her kittens?" he asked, flabbergasted.

"How many did she have, Jason?" Jessica was excitedly awaiting the news.

"You think I flew seven hundred miles to tell you the damn cat had her kittens?" Jason bellowed, his eyes turning wild.

Jessica stepped back uncertainly. "She hasn't had her kittens?" she asked meekly.

Jason shot her a look of pure disgust. In a low, tightly controlled voice he said, "No, she hasn't had her kittens!" He brushed past her, walking into the small living room. Jessica followed behind him, still trying to figure out what had brought him here in the middle of the night, nearly hysterical.

"Jason," she tried again, "is there something wrong?"

He looked up in a daze, as if he were just now seeing her for the first time since she opened the door, his jade eyes flashing angrily.

"Wrong?" he sneered sarcastically. "Wrong, Jessica? Why, hell, no, nothing's *wrong*, unless you'd consider my being in a plane half the night last night trying to get here, then traipsing around this damn town in total confusion all day trying to find out where you lived, then spending the last two hours wandering around in this—this—damn monsoon looking for your address as *wrong!*" He began pacing the floor like a caged animal, his boots, which were filled with rainwater, making a squishing noise.

"But—but why are you here?" Jessica stammered meekly, her pulse beginning to pound, her heart taking on new hope.

"Why am *I* here?" he shouted loudly. "That's what I came to ask you! Why in the hell are *you* still here?"

Jessica dropped her eyes sheepishly, unable to meet his penetrating gaze. "Does it matter?" she whispered softly.

"Matter? Of course it matters! You told me you'd be back in a couple of days. What in the hell's holding you up?"

Jessica stiffened, bringing her eyes up to meet his. "I'm

not coming back, Jason," she said, holding her breath for a moment before releasing it slowly.

"You wouldn't like to lay odds on that, would you, *Cole?*" Jason said tightly, his eyes never leaving hers.

"Oh, *Jason!*" Jessica wailed. "Why didn't you just let things alone. You don't love me—don't want me around, except to fill your bed at nights. Why couldn't you let us part with the memory of our last night together, instead of coming here to tear my life up again?" She began to pace the floor, following in Jason's footsteps.

"What do you mean, don't love you?" he sneered as he passed her going the opposite direction. "Where did you get a stupid idea like that?"

Jessica stopped in her tracks and jammed her small fists on her hips, her mouth dropping open. "A *stupid* idea like that?" she taunted. "When have you *ever* told me you loved me? It's always been *me* dogging *your* steps ever since the first day I met you, you—you—you *toad!*"

Jason stopped in front of her, his hands coming up sharply on his own hips. "I told you on our wedding night, you—you *toadess!*"

Jessica's purple eyes blazed back at him. "You did *not!* You said you *wanted* me! You said you loved my eyes, my nose, my face . . ."

Jason flailed his hands through the air. "Wanted? Loved? What's the *difference?* Aren't your eyes, your nose, your face—you? You know perfectly well I've never gotten you out of my system." His voice was full of irritation as he resumed pacing in a huff, bellowing above his squishing shoes, "Lord knows I tried—and I almost made it. Then you came back and set out to systematically destroy every means of transportation I own!" He whirled sharply, his face just inches from hers. "I'm damned surprised you didn't run over my horse!"

She clenched her teeth, her eyes shooting purple daggers into the green blazing depths of his. Frustration washed over her as she doubled up her tiny fists and shook them wildly in his face. "I'm sick of hearing about those wrecks! When I get some money, I'll buy you a car agency of your very own!"

He turned from her, snorting as he continued pacing, ignoring her last remark. "Then you used our 'business arrangement' to try to seduce me—which was really, pardon the expression, hitting below the belt—pretty rotten, if you ask me, when you *knew* what your body does to me—*knew* I hadn't gotten over you!"

"You *said* you had!" Jessica held firm to her argument, the tension thick in the small apartment. "You plainly told me the day I *hired* you that you didn't care for me any longer. Then, the first night we made love after I moved into your house, you said it was a mistake!"

They both began their pacing again, passing each other in heated silence.

"And what about Monica!" she yelled triumphantly. "Just explain why you've continued to see her all these months if you love me, Jason Rawlings!"

"What about Rick? You threw him in my face enough in the last few weeks, Jessica Cole!"

"You know perfectly well I didn't care for Rick romantically!"

Jason snorted disgustedly as he passed her. "It didn't look that way to me! And I'm *sure* I told you that I loved you the night after the hayride," he said tensely, getting back to the original subject.

"You did not!" Jessica screamed again. "You only said you *wanted* me—wanted me in your bed every night," she added lamely, her temper starting to cool somewhat, her pacing slowing.

Jason stopped again, pulling her around into his arms. "Do you honestly believe for one moment that I don't love you, Angel?" His voice had dropped to a low, husky whisper.

"Oh, Jason, I want so desperately to believe that you do." Jessica froze, barely able to breathe, as they stood in

184

the middle of the small room staring at each other, the rain pattering against the windowpanes.

"Well, you can believe it, or not—I'm tired of fighting. I want you to come home with me. I love you and I want you. If I can't have it all, then I'll take what I can."

"Why would you think that you couldn't have it all? I've always been yours."

"Then why were you able to give me up so easily eight years ago?"

"Easily? Is that what you think? Jason, you'll never know how many times I walked to the telephone those few days before I left for college wanting desperately to call you and beg you to come for me. I realize now I was young and I felt like I owed Uncle Fred and Aunt Rainey their dream that I go to college—but if I could put back the hands of the clock—and, Jason, I'd give my life to—then there would be no power on earth that could separate me from you. Don't you know I've loved you from the first day I set eyes on you?" She moved closer in his arms, her hands sliding around his neck, her eyes looking pleadingly into his. "I know I've hurt you, but believe me, Jason, my hurt is as great as yours. I love you beyond belief—and you can believe that, or not!"

His emerald eyes were drinking in her loveliness, his hands trembling slightly as he pressed her closer to him.

Those disgusting tears swam into Jessica's eyes once more as he enfolded her lovingly in his arms, his cheeks becoming wet, too.

"I thought I'd never hear you say those words, Angel. I'm sorry for what I've put you through," he whispered raggedly as his mouth descended to take hers.

"Shhh-shhh," Jessica comforted, holding him close.

"No, let me say this—I love you, I *love* you," he rasped emphatically.

They stood locked in each other's arms, their kisses and tears washing away eight years of pain and loneliness.

They were laughing and crying at the same time, both trying to convey their love for the other.

"Oh, hell, Angel," Jason said, hurriedly jerking her up into his arms. "I can show you better than tell you! Where's the bed?"

"Jason!" Jessica teased. "Surely you can control yourself a little longer. We have a lot of things to discuss . . ."

His lips cut her off as he kissed her soundly. "Talk, talk, talk. You're always wanting to talk! Give me a break—I haven't seen you in eight days. We can talk later." Flashing her one of those knee-weakening grins of his, he said seductively, "You're talking to an overheated toad, lady!"

"Well, for heaven's sake," Jessica said with a dramatic sigh, "why are you standing here wasting time—talking! Just start walking, Rawlings, and I'll point the way!"

The soft patter of rain falling on the roof made a melodious backdrop for the two lovers, who eagerly sought each other. Gone was the shy, timid bride of eight years ago as she confidently brought her hands effortlessly and swiftly up to remove his wet shirt, tossing it carelessly across the room.

Jason smiled down at her through passion-laden eyes, his arms hanging limply at his side while she methodically and diligently unbuckled his belt and pulled it through the loops with a snap with one hand while with the other she snapped, unzipped, and stripped off his jeans.

"You've been practicing," he noted dryly, clasping his hands behind his head and parting his legs slightly, grinning deviously. Jessica felt her cheeks warm as it dawned on her that she *was* acting a bit impatient. *Drat!* she said to herself. *I wanted to be so sophisticated!* She hesitated for a second, marveling at his composure.

"Well?" he asked.

"Well what?"

"Haven't you forgotten something?" He motioned to his briefs with his eyes.

"Oh," she said, her mouth forming a wry grin as her thumbs hooked under the elastic waistband. She gave him a seductive wink and murmured, "Don't be afraid, Jason. I'll take it nice and slow. I'll show you the beauty of becoming a man."

He grinned broadly, enjoying every minute of her silly reenactment of their wedding night.

She gave his briefs a gentle tug and slid them to the floor, trailing little nibbling kisses up his legs as she rose with maddening slowness, lingering to kiss the taut, flat expanse of his stomach, making little circles with her tongue.

Jason drew his breath in sharply, his grin turning to an agonized mask as his desire for her became firm and rigid. *Now where's your composure, Rawlings?* she thought wickedly, stepping back to arm's length and resting her hands on his hips. Her eyes widened with delight. "Holy cow! You're not bad for a toad!"

A deep rumbling laugh burst from his throat as he grabbed her and fell onto the bed, pulling her on top of him. She kissed him lightly on his nose and whispered cunningly, "Jason, darling, my clothes are going to have to come off before we can have our . . ."

"Okay. All right! You're driving me crazy," he said, reaching to pull her gown off. She held his hands in check. "I'll do it," she told him. "You might take too long." With that her gown became a cloud of silk floating through the air to land in a far corner of the room.

Her warm, sensuous curves blended with his sinewy form as she melted into his embrace. "Since I've taken care of all the preliminaries," she whispered, "you take it from here."

"Mmmmmm, and just when I was enjoying myself," he said, a smug grin pasted across his face.

Jessica bit her bottom lip pensively, then ran her tongue around her mouth, moistening her lips before breathing sexily against his. "Well, on page fifty of the . . . uh

. . . research manual I was reading the other night, I came across a new technique I might try out."

"Research manual?" His voice rose in astonishment. "What in the devil were you researching?"

She slithered down his body with torturous precision. "I can show you so much better than I can take the time to explain it."

Jason writhed in agonizing pleasure as her lips nipped the flat of his stomach around his navel. "Damn!" he said huskily. "Can I read that manual when you're through with it?"

Her mouth worked its way down the heated path, muttering between bites, "If you liked page fifty, you're going to lo-ove page fifty-one . . ."—and he did!

Gasping uncontrollably, his hands wildly pulling her on top of him, he positioned her hips to accept his eager desire and their bodies blended rapturously in a mounting haze of fiery bliss. They moved in tandem as they reached simultaneous delight. Jason breathed a quivering moan as he clung desperately to her shuddering body, glowing with a sheen of perspiration. Clinging together through a maze of kisses and whispered love words, they glided gently back to earth from their dizzying heights.

Jessica fell limply to his side, snuggling down deep in his arms, wrapping her arms around his middle, loving the feel of his bare skin next to hers.

Wriggling seductively, she squirmed closer to him, biting playfully at his ear as his large hands cupped her rounded derriere.

"I can tell I'd better start learning to sleep while I'm on my tractor, once we're married again," he said dryly. "It's plain I won't be getting any sleep at night."

"Why, Mr. Rawlings, are you asking me to be your wife again?" She nipped at his lips, moving her mouth slowly over them.

"One more time!" Jason told her, slapping her bottom.

"This time there'll be no getting out of it. You're stuck for life."

"Fine with me," Jessica said, bringing her hand down to intimately caress his relaxed body.

"I wouldn't get too carried away, lady," he groaned painfully, his mouth covering hers again. "There's still a lot of life left in this tired old body."

"Oh, Jason, I know you're tired," she said sympathetically, her fingers fluttering lightly over his taut stomach, causing him to draw his breath in sharply and emit a low, shuddering moan as he rolled over on top of her.

"Not that tired," he rasped huskily.

"My darling Jason," Jessica whispered, nearly breathless with overwhelming happiness. "I love you so much!"

Jason slowly and gently maneuvered their bodies into one, their very souls blending passionately as they once more sailed the sea of ecstacy.

As they lay in the mellow afterglow Jason tenderly cradled Jessica in his arms, his hand running down her velvet arm until it reached her delicate fingers. Holding her hand close to his lips, he kissed the tip of each finger, whispering between each nibble, "Mrs.—Jason—Rawlings—Jessica—Rawlings. Has a nice ring to it, doesn't it?"

"Ummmm . . ." Jessica moaned sleepily.

"I love you, Angel."

Jessica raised her drowsy lids. "Now, that *really* has a nice ring to it."

"I love you, I love you, I love you," Jason whispered over and over in her ear, lulling her into semisleep.

Just before she drifted off, she gave him one last kiss on the cheek. "And, darling," she offered, "when we're married, you can have *all* my money to do with as you wish!"

A low rumble of laughter came from Jason's throat as he smoothed her dark hair back from her face lovingly. "I don't need your money, sweetheart."

"But you're welcome to it," Jessica insisted. "You've

nearly killed yourself the last few months working both farms."

Pulling her head closer, he whispered in her ear lightly, "I guess that was my way of telling you I loved you—every day for the last five months, Angel. I needed that ten thousand dollars like I needed another day's work."

Jessica looked puzzled, sitting up in bed, suddenly wide awake.

"Jessica, listen to me, Angel," he explained, sitting up to face her. "Just before my dad died, they found oil on the five hundred acres he owned in Dallas. It made us all millionaires. Eric stays up there and runs the business for us because I wanted to work the farm." He took hold of her shoulders, looking her straight in the eyes. "Jessica, I've got enough money to burn a wet mule! So every day I ran that farm for you was a labor of love. I was doing it because I loved you and couldn't let you walk back out of my life again. Do you understand? Do you believe that, honey?"

Jessica brought her hands up, running her fingers along his smoothly shaven jaw, her eyes shining with love. "Yes, my darling Jason. I believe you and—thank you." She wrapped her arms around his neck and hugged him tightly.

"You're more than welcome, Angel."

They kissed tenderly, savoring the sweetness of the moment.

"Just one more thing, Jason," Jessica said. There was one more question clouding Jessica's otherwise tranquil mind. "About Monica . . ."

Jason heaved a sigh and lay back on his pillow, pulling her face toward his hair-covered chest. "What is it?"

"Did you—well—did you love her?"

He paused for a brief moment. "I'll be very honest with you. I tried to—I wanted to—and maybe there was a time when I thought I did, but I think she knew all along how I felt about you. She is really a nice person, Jessica, but it's you I love, and I told her just before I flew down here, and she understood."

Jessica had to fight the urge to jump out of bed and shout *"Finally Jason Rawlings loves Jessica Cole!"* She showered his face with a multitude of feather kisses, lulling him into a peaceful glow.

"Right now, Angel, I think we need some sleep. We have a long trip ahead of us in the morning."

A tiny frown crossed Jessica's glowing face. "Uh—Jason . . ."

"Ummmm . . ."

"Well, you know I have my car here . . ."

"I know, sweetheart," he said, on the verge of sleep. "I'll drive it for you—we'll go home together." He patted her stomach lovingly.

"Well . . ." she said hesitantly. "There's just one *small* thing . . ."

"What's that, honey?"

She rose up on her knees in the middle of the bed, her bright violet eyes sparkling in extreme agitation. "Jason, you're not going to believe this, but on the way to the market this afternoon, some *idiot* pulled out in front of me . . ."

One large hand reached out and pulled her back down on the bed. Jason's mouth covered her sputtering one one final time before they both dropped contentedly off into a peaceful sleep, wrapped in each other's arms forever.

A TEMPTING STRANGER

CHAPTER ONE

The sharp bite of the early evening wind nipped angrily at the attractive, slender blonde stepping out of the waiting cab and hurriedly paying the driver with shivering fingers. As she breezed by the courteous doorman smiling pleasantly at her, the sultry scent of her very enticing perfume filtered softly through the crisp night air.

Chandra Loring paused to catch her breath as she walked into the elegant lobby of one of the oldest but most exclusive apartment buildings in all of Oklahoma. She gazed around the massive room, its beauty and festive decor holding her spellbound. Although it was barely a few days into December, the room resembled an enchanted Christmas fairyland. Enormous wreaths of pine greenery tied with bright red satin bows adorned the stately old walls, and tiny miniature Christmas trees twinkled brightly throughout the lobby. Long strings of garland were draped about the room, their fresh, clean, woodsy smell filling the air along with the sweet sounds of Christmas carols coming from the intricate stereo system.

Chandra closed her eyes for a moment, drinking in the sounds and smells of the season, and for just that small moment elation replaced her feeling of apprehension. Christmas had always brought out the small child in her. She would rush madly around the crowded shopping malls, enjoying the happy, carefree attitude that seemed to descend over the people, turning Scrooges into baby lambs and even the most cynical into believers—if only for a season. Her apartment would come alive with the smells

9

of holiday baking, and her fingers would fairly fly as she wrapped each present in bright-colored paper, eagerly awaiting the time when she could hand them lovingly to the ones she had purchased them for.

Casting one last admiring glance around her, she walked over to the old elevator and pushed the button. The sounds of the old lift squeaking into motion caused her to tilt her head upward, watching in fascination as it slowly started to descend from the very top of the building.

Chandra stepped back to await its arrival, her stomach twitching nervously at the thought of why she was here. If she had one ounce of sense she would turn around and run for the hills! How she had ever let her brother Darrell talk her into this perfectly ridiculous scheme still astounded her. She bit her bottom lip apprehensively as she glanced up again to watch the progression of the small cage. It was parked on the fourth floor, and the sounds of boisterous male voices echoed faintly through the old lobby. *Seems as if someone is celebrating a little early,* she thought as she heard the door clang and the cables start up again.

She nervously tapped her foot. She just hoped she'd get through this night. All she had wanted was to come home a couple of weeks early and have a long mother-daughter talk about her upcoming wedding that was to take place on the thirty-first of this month. She realized now she should have called and let her mother know she was coming, but at the time she had decided to come, she'd just thrown her things in a bag and caught the first plane. She had arrived home to an empty house and found that her mother had gone with her dad on a business trip. Chandra began to pace the small waiting area, thinking back to last night when her brother had come over to keep her company. With the cunning of a wolf he had manipulated her into the wildest farce she had ever heard of—within thirty minutes of his arrival she had agreed to pose as his best friend Cecil's wife!

Her two-inch heels clicked heatedly on the floor as her impatience mounted, her hazel eyes searching for the gold cage that

10

now sat quietly on the second floor. She still had time to back out, she reasoned. She certainly didn't have to go through with this! After all, she was engaged to Phillip and, although he was a fun-loving type of man, she was sure he wouldn't be too happy about any of this should he ever find out. It was totally out of character for her to even consider such a plan, much less become part of it—but in a moment of great weakness she had succumbed to her brother's urgent pleas. Cecil, it seemed, was trying for a top position in an aeronautical company and had heard through the grapevine that the owner would be more favorably impressed by a married man. Out of desperation Darrell and Cecil had cooked up a half-baked plan for her to pose as his wife this evening at a party that was being thrown for the prospective candidates. If it wasn't for the fact, as her brother had so pathetically put it, that "poor shy Cecil" couldn't find a "substitute wife" of his own for the evening, she would never have agreed to the plot in the first place.

Darrell had explained that after Cecil secured the position the owner and his wife were leaving town again. Cecil could eventually announce that his marriage had not worked out. He would have his job, Chandra would have done her brother's friend a great humanitarian service, and everything would be dipsy doodle again!

What upset her most about the whole deal was that she had never even laid eyes on Cecil, and all she had to go on was a very limited description of him.

Chandra ceased pacing, a frown of irritation marring her lovely features. No, she had promised Darrell she would do this, so she would. But if he were standing before her right now, she would cheerfully strangle him and never blink an eye. If this Cecil was half the loser her brother had painted him to be—bad luck with women, jobs, life in general—she didn't see how this one night would change anything for him. But at least she would have done her share to set his feet back on the road to happiness.

The elevator gradually reached the first floor, coming to a jerky halt as an elderly operator made a couple of stabs at bringing the cage in line with the lobby floor. With a loud clang of metal he threw open the door and three slightly inebriated gentlemen staggered out.

"Well-l-l-l, Merry Christmas, little lady!" cheerily greeted one heavy-set man carrying a champagne glass in one hand and clutching a bottle under one of his chubby arms. "Would you mind holding my drink for me, sweetie? We're just going around the corner to get some more of the bubbly." He leered at her drunkenly.

Before Chandra could stop him one fat hand had thrust an overflowing glass of the sparkling liquid into her hand. She glanced down at the glass with surprise, then back to the retreating figure of her benefactor, weaving on out into the lobby with his two friends. *Now what in the world am I going to do with this,* she thought irritably. Two couples entered the lobby and came forward hurriedly to board the waiting elevator. The two women stepped around her in disdain as they viewed the glass of champagne in her hand. Chandra gripped the glass more tightly and quickly stepped into the small cage, fearing she would miss the ride if she waited any longer. The operator stood up and started to close the metal doors, his movements slow and laborious.

The lobby door opened once again and a tall, well-dressed man emerged with a gust of cold night air. He strode swiftly across the lobby, motioning for the elevator to wait. He stepped into the lift and Chandra caught a whiff of a very masculine aftershave and the clean smell of soap as he stood close to her in the crowded cage. The heavy door closed as the operator seated himself on a small stool and set the car in motion. Trying to be as discreet as possible she examined the handsome newcomer out of the corner of her eye. He was wearing an expensively tailored gray suit with a shirt that almost perfectly matched the color of his eyes—a beautiful, clear blue. He had on a coordinating gray and blue striped tie with a gold tie tack in the shape of a tiny airplane secured neatly in the middle. The large hand that casually straightened the leather overcoat on his arm had strong manly features, the nails immaculately clean and clipped short.

His thick brown hair was just a tiny bit unruly from the fierce evening wind, a hint of natural curliness against the deep tan of his neck. Her eyes cautiously worked their way down his lean, masculine, athletic form, ending on his perfectly styled, gray suede dress shoes.

"What floor, people?" the old man asked tiredly as the car ground upward.

"Third," grunted one of the men from the party behind her, shuffling around uncomfortably in the close quarters. His arm bumped Chandra's slightly, causing a bit of the champagne to slosh out of the glass onto the elevator floor. The man standing beside her turned aloof blue eyes on her as he stepped back hurriedly to avoid the splashing liquid.

Chandra dropped her embarrassed gaze from his, shifting the glass into her other hand. "Fourth, please," she replied tensely. She could feel her face flushing a bright pink as the man coolly turned his attention away from her to stare straight ahead. She could well imagine what he was thinking! His haughty attitude told her that he thought he was standing next to a lush who couldn't wait until she got to a party to begin drinking!

The elevator rose agonizingly slowly, passing the second floor without stopping. Chandra stood uneasily next to the tall, handsome man, her mind going back over the sketchy set of instructions Darrell had given her in a short phone conversation early that morning. He had called before leaving on an unexpected charter flight to tell her Cecil would be standing next to the punch bowl that evening at exactly seven o'clock. She was to look for a tall, dark-haired man around six feet tall. After giving her the address he had hung up abruptly, leaving her no time to ask questions. *Why didn't I just let Cecil pick me up at the house,* she berated herself angrily. Darrell had offered to arrange it, but Chandra had quickly declined his offer. At the time she hadn't wanted to involve herself any more in this farce than was totally necessary, but now she could see the folly of being so independent!

The elevator jerked suddenly to a halt as they reached the

13

third floor, throwing all the occupants forward awkwardly. Chandra quickly cupped the glass of champagne with her other hand to keep it from splashing out onto the floor again. The tall man beside her made another slight move away from her, watching warily from the corner of his eye. The door squeaked open and Chandra felt herself being jostled as the four passengers in back tried to get around her. She fought to keep the glass from spilling but was shoved up against the man next to her and a tiny bit of the liquid spilled out onto his perfectly tailored gray slacks.

His blue glare dropped to the darkening wet stain in distress as the other four occupants exited roughly and the door swung shut again.

"Sorry," Chandra muttered uncomfortably under her breath as the cage continued its climb.

"That's perfectly all right," the man clipped out curtly, his blue eyes fairly sizzling now as he stared stonily ahead of him. "I'd suggest you drink that damn thing," he added in a tense afterthought.

"Oh . . ." Chandra glanced back down at the glass in her hand. She didn't even like champagne! Giving him a small, guilty smile, she took a long drink out of the glass, nearly gagging at its sour, vinegary taste. She took a deep breath as tears sprang momentarily to her eyes, then exhaled loudly. "That's good," she said defiantly to the man beside her. With a cold gaze of dismissal he turned back to stare at the closed doors.

Conceited snob! she thought heatedly, balancing the glass with both hands. She wished she didn't have to be standing here next to him. It didn't really matter, though, she consoled herself, she would be getting off on the next floor. The first thing she was going to do was pitch this glass as far as she could!

"Fourth floor," the old man announced blandly, jerking the cage to a halt once again. He stood up and tiredly swung the doors open, muttering softly under his breath as he saw the fourth floor was some three inches above the floor of the elevator. "Wait a minute," he said resignedly, his hand reaching for the lever that operated the car. They shot up past the floor, missing

14

their target by a good three inches in the other direction. Chandra grabbed for the railing with one free hand, the drink sloshing around dangerously in the other.

"Nope, hold on," he ordered gruffly, grimly determined to hit his mark. He eyed his goal critically, then shot the elevator like a speeding bullet to within an inch and a half of his intended spot.

This time Chandra had been totally unprepared for their rapid descent and came sailing across the car, nearly knocking down the man standing irritably beside her. The remaining contents of the glass dumped out sickeningly all over his suede shoes.

"Oh, hell!" he shouted disgustedly, watching the dark stain spread rapidly across the suede.

"Ohhhh. . . . I am sorry!" Chandra choked out in embarrassment. He had looked so perfectly groomed when he'd stepped on the elevator five minutes ago. Now he had a wet stain on his slacks and one shoe looked like he'd tried to stomp a mud hole dry.

"You should register that glass as a lethal weapon, lady!" he said hotly as he stepped up out of the elevator, trying to shake the excess liquid off his shoe.

Chandra swallowed hard and followed in his steps, the elderly man reaching out to push her upward. "Thank you," she murmured politely, watching the long strides of the handsome man disappearing down the hall. She immediately sat the empty glass down on a table in the hall and tried to wipe the sticky liquid off her hands. She really felt bad about spilling it all over that poor guy, but he was so . . . so uppity! It served him right. *Thank goodness Phillip isn't like that,* she thought gratefully as she started down the carpeted hall. Maybe he and Chandra didn't share as much in common as she hoped they would, but at least he was a perfect gentleman at all times. He would never have made a lady feel as . . . small as that man had just done. No, Phillip was going to make a perfect husband and a perfect father to her children. If they had boys he would be more than perfect. His obsession with sports—all sports—nearly drove her to distraction at times, but she was sure any boy would be thrilled to have such an athletic father. She was thrilled and proud to have him as her fiancé . . . wasn't she? She shook her head stubbornly. *Now, don't start thinking in that vein again, Chandra,* she scolded. *You just have a bad case of marital jitters, that's all.* Her eyes were carefully scanning the numbers written on the doors, searching for Apartment 4. Pausing for a moment in the dim hallway, she rummaged around in her small handbag and extracted a white scrap of paper. Apartment 4, 14789 Yearling Street. Yes, this was it. Chandra suddenly developed a case of weak knees and began to tremble inwardly. She would gladly give someone all she owned to get out of this mess right now!

She nervously straightened the simple, black crocheted dress she was wearing and touched her hair lightly to make sure no strands had come loose in her harried elevator ride. Satisfied that she looked fairly presentable she licked her lips nervously, took a deep breath, and pushed the doorbell. It was answered immediately by a butler who looked as if he were suffering from a terminal case of hemorrhoids.

"Good evening, Madam," he said stiffly.

"Good evening," Chandra returned pleasantly.

"Your coat, Madam."

Chandra handed him her short white fur jacket. He took it ceremoniously and motioned for her to follow him.

The tinkle of glasses and low murmurs of laughter reached her ears as she was ushered into a large room lit almost entirely by tiny, flickering candles. The room was done tastefully in shades of blues and white and the entire apartment reeked of money. Chandra's feet sank into the thick, white carpeting as she made her way lightly across the crowded room, following the butler.

"Your host and hostess should be with you shortly," he said, politely handing her another glass of champagne. "Please make yourself comfortable."

"Thank you. I'm supposed to be meeting someone here," she replied, her eyes searching for the punch bowl.

16

"Very good, Madam." He bowed slightly and turned to glide back across the room.

At the moment there was no one standing anywhere near the punch bowl, so she walked over to a small settee and sat down where she would have a clear view of the meeting area. She glanced at her thin gold watch and saw that it was still a few minutes before seven. Her gaze caught the glass of champagne in her hand, and her face reddened again as the picture of the tall, blue-eyed man in the elevator skipped lightly through her mind. Although it didn't matter—she would never see him again —it still made her uncomfortable to realize what an absolute fool he thought she was! She sat quietly watching the guests mill around the room, her mind going over the million little things she needed to do before the wedding. The last thing she needed to be doing was sitting at this party waiting for some stranger! There were invitations to mail out, she needed to talk to the caterer again, she still had the bridesmaids' gifts to buy . . . not to mention all the work that awaited her after her marriage. Chandra had just moved into a new apartment last week, leaving her roommate of the last three years by herself. She and Phillip had decided to live in an apartment until they bought a home, and now there were boxes to unpack and a hundred last-minute details to attend to. Since she worked in Phillip's law office as one of the legal secretaries she never seemed to have enough time for anything anymore, coming home too tired at night to do anything but fix a light meal and collapse when she didn't have a date with Phillip. The nights they were together were sometimes a little disappointing to her. It seemed they always ended up at some basketball game or hockey event.

The sound of sultry feminine laughter caught her ear, and Chandra's gaze was drawn to a stunning woman dressed in a tight, shimmering, red satin dress. Her figure was flawless and the low cut of her gown hid nothing from a man's roving eye. Chandra's eyes widened suddenly, her pulse pounding rapidly in her throat as she noticed the tall, brown-haired man standing next to her at the appointed punch bowl. Good heavens! It was

17

the same man who rode up with her on the elevator! He was smiling down on the sexy woman, his even, white teeth flashing brightly in his tanned, rugged face, thoroughly engrossed in something "Red Satin" was saying to him. The deep tone of his amused voice reached Chandra as she glanced down suspiciously at her watch. It was exactly seven o'clock. Surely Cecil hadn't arrived yet and it was just a strange coincidence that the snob on the elevator was standing there talking to that woman at the appointed time. Chandra slid back on the small settee, trying to fade into the dark blue upholstery. Another five minutes passed before "Red Satin" reached up and touched "Blue Eyes" on the face seductively, murmuring something low and suggestive. Chuckling softly he brought her hand to his mouth and kissed it lightly while winking at her sexily. With a promising look she left his side to make her way across the floor, leaving him standing alone by the punch bowl. Chandra noted the time again, biting her lip in exasperation as she saw that it was now seven minutes after seven.

The brown-haired man at the punch bowl looked down at his watch, a small frown on his forehead. He seemed to be waiting for someone now as he turned around and filled a small cup with the fruit punch from the sterling silver bowl.

Chandra closed her eyes in hopelessness. It was no use—THAT was Cecil! It didn't matter to her what he would think when he found out who she was, but she did hate to embarrass Darrell. She had no doubts Cecil would make a point of telling her brother that he had met her on the elevator "boozing it up" before she even made it to the party.

With a sigh of defeat she rose and started walking toward the punch bowl, her heart thudding painfully against her ribs. As she sauntered toward him she studied her intended target intensely. Darrell had said Cecil was painfully shy around all women, finding it hard even to ask one out for a date. *That just goes to show you how dense a man can be at times,* she thought snidely as the picture of "Red Satin" staring up at him invitingly a few minutes ago invaded her mind. Maybe "poor Cecil" had gotten lucky, but she seriously doubted it. The man standing before her gazing at the dancing couples looked about as shy as a dog in mating season. No, Chandra knew his type all too well. He was used to calling the shots with women, and with his looks they wouldn't mind at all. Well, he might fool Darrell but he certainly couldn't pull the wool over her eyes—or anything else! *Sorry, Cecil ole man,* she mused delightedly, *party's over for you and your little satin playmate tonight. Your "wife" has just arrived!*

CHAPTER TWO

Chandra reached the punch bowl at the same time Cecil's satin lady was making her way back from the other side of the room. Taking a deep breath Chandra walked up to him and took hold of his arm possessively. "Hello, darling. I'm sorry I'm late." She smiled sweetly up into his guarded face.

When he had seen her approaching him, his body had tensed, and his eyes had grown instantly defensive. When Chandra had reached out and taken his arm, he had stepped back momentarily, surprised at her actions. "Late?" he now asked blankly, wondering what this dippy broad was up to now.

"Red Satin" finally reached them, her eyes hostilely surveying Chandra's arm looped casually through his. "I wasn't aware you knew anyone at this party," she told him coldly.

"Oh, do you know my *husband* ?" Chandra smiled brightly, her hold tightening on the man next to her. "You didn't tell me you had met anyone, darling. Shame on you!" She grinned smugly up at her "husband." It felt good to let some of her apprehension drain out of her. If her brother and this man wanted a good show, she'd be more than glad to give them one. It was worth her time and trouble to see Cecil's hope for a little "action" on the side go down the drain for the evening!

"Wife! Is this some joke? You certainly never mentioned having a wife!" "Red Satin" was becoming angry, her voluminous breasts heaving in agitation.

"Well . . . I . . ." The man's blue eyes widened as Chandra moved in closer, taking one large hand in her small one.

20

"He must have blanked out temporarily," she said icily. "He does that once in a while." *You would think the woman would take a hint,* she thought nervously, wishing that this fiasco were over and done with.

"Well, really!" "Red Satin" turned on her heel and flounced angrily away. The man's blue eyes regretfully watched her walk across the floor.

Turning to face him Chandra said in a low voice, "Look, I'm sorry I didn't know who you were on the elevator. I hope you don't find it necessary to mention that silly champagne incident to Darrell—but if you do, I want you to know that it wasn't my wine. I was holding it for someone."

"Of course," he agreed dryly. "Now, would you mind telling me what the hell's going on?"

"Well, I really don't know," Chandra admitted, glancing around the room thoughtfully. "I suppose the best thing for us to do is to get this over with as quickly as possible. Why don't you introduce me as your wife, then we'll sort of play it by ear from then on."

"Introduce you as my wife!" He looked at her blankly again. "To whom?"

Chandra glared back up into his handsome face. "To whom! Why, to the man you're trying to get the job from, I suppose! Do you have a different plan?"

"No, I really can't say that I have a *different* plan, but whatever we do I want to warn you I only have one suit with me. I'd appreciate it if you would put that glass of champagne down and leave it there for the rest of the night," he said sarcastically, eyeing the drink she was still clutching in her hand.

"Oh . . . yes, I forgot about that." Chandra sheepishly set the glass down on the serving table.

"Now let me get this straight. You want me to take you over and introduce you to John Rhodes as my . . . wife? Right?" he asked grimly.

"If that's the man's name you're trying to get the job from. Why are you asking *me*, for heaven's sake! Isn't that what you

21

and Darrell said to do? I thought the plan was to make him think you were married so you would have a better chance at the job."

"Hey, now look, Rhodes couldn't put that sort of requirement on this job. In case you haven't heard of it that would be called 'job discrimination,' lady," he answered tightly, removing her arm from his roughly.

"Look! I'd be more than happy to leave right now, mister, so you don't have to be so . . . so . . . cocky about this! All I know is Darrell said the man would be more favorably impressed if you were married. Now do you want to go through with this or not? Personally, I think the whole idea stinks!" Chandra was getting fed up with his superior attitude.

The tall, dark-haired man looked thoughtful for a moment, then let out a long, low whistle. "Darrell said that, did he?"

Chandra looked up at him in exasperation. "I thought you guys had worked this all out?"

He looked at her, flashing her a questioning grin that made her knees turn to water, his white teeth sparkling brightly in his tanned face. "Well, lady, you better be a good actress because the curtain's going up. Turn around and put your prettiest smile on because you're just about to meet the big man himself!" His mood had changed from defensive to agreeable in a matter of seconds.

Chandra caught a glimpse of a large, expensively dressed man threading his way through the crowd, a lovely, silver-haired lady on his arm. Chandra felt light-headed as her companion pulled her close with one arm resting possessively around her waist.

"Mr. Rhodes, how are you tonight?" The young man extended his right hand and firmly shook hands with the older gentleman.

"Fine, Morganson, and how are you this evening?"

"Couldn't be better, sir, and Mrs. Rhodes, you look lovely as usual."

Mrs. Rhodes smiled and took his hand. "So happy to see you again." Her eyes looked questioningly at Chandra.

"Mr. and Mrs. Rhodes, I'd like you to meet my beautiful wife

. . . uh . . ." He looked at Chandra helplessly. "Uh . . . Mrs. Morganson," he finished lamely.

"So happy to meet you, dear." Mrs. Rhodes took Chandra's hand in hers. "We were very impressed with your husband this afternoon at the meeting." She turned to her husband. "You didn't say anything about Mr. Morganson being married, John."

"To be honest, Sara, I was under the impression that he was a single man. There must have been an error on your application blank, Morganson." John Rhodes took Chandra's hand and pumped it vigorously. "You don't know how happy this little piece of information makes me, son."

"A single man?! Well, I'm afraid you're very much mistaken," Chandra said merrily, snuggling in closer to the large man at her side. She felt him pull away slightly as if she were a pesky fly that had landed on his arm. Determined to make a go of this mission she glared at him sweetly and moved even closer. "Isn't that right, darling?"

His clear blue eyes had turned as cold as sheets of ice, but his voice was calm and cool as he replied hesitantly, "That's right, Mr. Rhodes. We are a happily married couple." He subtly took her arm from his and shoved it back down to her side.

Chandra looked at him in surprise, but kept her arm to herself. If the dodo wanted to blow his chances at this job, that was his problem.

"Well, well, well, this *is* encouraging. I was just telling my wife that it was hard to make a decision from the field I have to choose from, but this may make my choice a little easier. I have always liked my men to be married and settled down, not that that would necessarily be the deciding factor, but"—Mr. Rhodes smiled assuringly—"it sure isn't going to hurt anything. No sir, it sure isn't going to hurt *your* case at all, Morganson."

"I wasn't really aware you were looking for a married man, sir. I figured a man's qualifications would speak for themselves."

Chandra glanced up dumbfoundedly at the man beside her. Why was he saying he didn't know they were looking for a married man when that was the only reason she was here at this moment!

"Oh, don't read me wrong, Garrett. My decision *will* rest upon the man's qualifications alone, but it would just be an added bonus for me if the man is married."

Garrett? Chandra looked at Mr. Rhodes sympathetically. Didn't the poor man even know which one of his prospects he was talking to?

"I have always said that a good woman is the key to a successful man." Mr. Rhodes patted his wife lovingly. "Without my Sara, I would not have come through life so easily. Oh, we've had our rough times, but we made it together, always able to overcome the obstacles together. Yes sir, a good woman stablizes a man!"

"That may be true for some men, sir, but not necessarily for all men." The blue-eyed man standing rigid beside Chandra spoke tensely. As far as Chandra was concerned he was making a terrible impression, practically telling his potential boss that he didn't much care for marriage. Mercy! She wished the floor would open up and swallow her, she was so embarrassed!

Giving him a swift jab in his side she tried to change the topic of conversation. "Darling, I'm really getting thirsty. Could I have something to drink?"

"That's a good idea. Let's find a table and sit down for a chat." Mr. Rhodes steered the small group through the crowd to a quiet table in the corner of the room. "What's everyone drinking, Morganson?"

"A beer would be fine, sir."

"Coke for me," Chandra replied as her "husband" seated her next to Mrs. Rhodes.

"One beer and two Cokes, John," Mrs. Rhodes told her husband.

"Coming right up." John Rhodes disappeared happily into the noisy crowd and was back in a few minutes carrying a tray with four drinks on it. Setting it down on the table he took the chair

24

opposite Chandra and continued the conversation in a friendly tone. "Where are you two staying?"

"Holiday Inn."

"My parents' house."

They both looked at each other in alarm and began again.

"Her parents' house!"

"Holiday Inn!"

The Rhodeses looked at each other in puzzlement. "Well, which one is it, son?" John asked, beginning to smile.

The young man cleared his throat nervously and took a sip of his beer. Looking sharply at Chandra he said sweetly, "All right, sweetheart, you win. We'll go ahead and stay at your parents' house. I just didn't want to put them out in any way, so I suggested that we stay at the Holiday Inn."

"Put them out," Mrs. Rhodes repeated, laughing. "Why, I'm sure they would feel as we do if our children came to visit us. We would be insulted if they didn't stay with us!"

Chandra's "husband" grinned sheepishly. "Mrs. Morganson and I haven't been married very long, so this is all new to me."

Sara Rhodes smiled in understanding. "How long *have* you been married?"

They glanced at each other and answered in unison.

"Six days."

"Four weeks."

Chandra piped up again. "Oh, stop it, darling—you're such a tease!" Good grief! These people were going to think that she and her "husband" had both fallen out of their trees.

"I'm sorry, darling. Of course you're right. It only *seems* like we've been married only six days." He grinned beguilingly at her. Chandra shot him a snide look and took another drink of her Coke.

Couples were beginning to move into the center of the room to dance as strains of music floated into the room. Grabbing for her hand the tall man helped Chandra from her chair. "If you'll excuse us, I'd like to dance with my wife."

25

"Why certainly. We'll just sit here and enjoy the music," John Rhodes said hurriedly. "You two lovebirds enjoy yourselves."

He dragged Chandra out to the middle of the room and swung her into his arms. Chandra instantly became aware of his broad chest as he pulled her up tight in an almost crushing embrace. She could smell the tantalizing fragrance of his aftershave and the very faint odor of cigar smoke clinging to his shirt.

He danced her quickly to the far side of the room, away from the watchful eyes of Mr. and Mrs. Rhodes. "What in the hell is your name?" he gritted out between clenched teeth as they reached safety.

Chandra looked up at him in wonder. "Chandra."

"Chandra. Chandra what?"

"Chandra Loring, of course! What's wrong with you?" This man definitely had problems.

"Well, Chandra Loring, we had better start getting our stories straight or this whole thing's going to go up in smoke."

Well, honestly—you'd think he'd be more grateful to her than this! He was being downright rude!

He danced her right on through the crowd out into the dimly lit foyer and pressed her intimately up into a dark corner. His face was barely inches away from hers as he looked deeply into her hazel eyes.

"I'll say one thing. I've inherited a damn good-looking wife!" he said huskily, his eyes roving intimately over her face.

"Thank you," she murmured politely, growing weaker by the minute.

He brought one long, tanned finger out to delicately touch her soft skin and trace a light pattern around and down her chin. His sweet, clean breath fanned against her cheeks. "You've got the most beautiful skin I have ever seen on any woman," he whispered wonderingly, his finger absently tracing the outline of her lips. "And your mouth"—his finger moved quickly and lightly across her mouth—"you have the kind of mouth that makes a man want—" He broke off the sentence, his hand dropping down to her shoulder.

26

Chandra's pulse was racing at a frantic pace. His tall, lean body was close to hers, pressing her breasts tightly into his broad chest. She was sure he could hear the pounding of her heart, as near as he was to her. This night was turning out to be crazy! Here she was, standing in a dimly lit hall in another man's arms, afraid—no, half hoping—that he would kiss her. Where was her sense of right and wrong? Why wasn't she shoving him back and thinking of Phillip?

"Look, Chandra," he said as he stepped back away from her, running his fingers through his thick, slightly curly brown hair, "just let me do the talking, okay? Whatever I say, you just go along with it."

Chandra drew a deep breath and reached up shakily to straighten her hair. "Yes, that's fine with me."

He turned around and faced her again. "All right. Now this has turned into one hell of a mess, but we can carry it off." He took a deep breath and drew her back into his arms. "Shall we continue this dance?"

Chandra nodded mutely and went back into his arms. He seemed to hold her even closer as they danced back out onto the floor. What was happening to her? She was experiencing feelings she had never had before. She was going to have to get herself under control, starting right now!

Pushing back from him slightly, she said primly, "Please don't hold me so close."

He looked amused and pulled her even closer. "Why not?" he asked dryly. "Don't you think we should strive to look like the happily married couple? After all, you're the one who started this fiasco. I think I should have a few fringe benefits, don't you?"

Chandra squirmed to get free from his strong embrace, his arrogance making her madder by the minute. "I don't know what you're talking about! May I remind you that this was yours and Darrell's idea, not mine!"

"Who in the hell is Darrell?" he said without interest.

"Darrell—Darrell Loring—my brother—your friend."

"Afraid not, sweetheart. I've never heard of the man."

Chandra suddenly felt as if she were going to lose her dinner. Her feet stopped dancing and her heart started hammering wildly as she sagged against him. "You don't know Darrell . . . ?"

"I said I didn't. Can't you understand plain English?" he said rudely as he set her feet in motion once more. "Stand up and dance!" he ordered roughly, nearly dragging her around the floor. "Everyone's looking at us."

Chandra willed her feet to follow his as her mind whirled in rapid confusion. She finally managed to stammer out a weak, "You're not Cecil."

The tall, brown-haired man turned mocking blue eyes on her. "BINGO!"

Chandra definitely did feel ill now. Who in the world was she dancing with—whose wife was she pretending to be? Garrett Morganson? From the sneer on his face he wasn't any happier about this situation than she was.

"But—who?"

"Garrett Morganson, but does it matter who I am? Hell, you got us in one fine pickle, lady, and it's up to you to carry this thing off for the rest of the evening. I'm warning you . . . Chandra . . . I don't know what your game is, but this job is the chance of a lifetime for me, so don't do *anything* that's going to blow my chances at it. Do you understand?" His hands gripped her wrists like a steel vise.

"Let me go," she hissed under her breath. "You're hurting me!"

"Not until you promise me you'll carry on with this ridiculous charade." He tightened his hold even more on her fragile wrists.

"All right! I'm not going to do or say anything that will hurt your chances for this stupid job!"

His grip loosened as he pulled her back into his arms, the strains of a slow waltz filling the room. They danced quietly for a few moments, lost in their own thoughts.

"I'm sorry," Chandra said softly, striving to explain, "I thought you were a friend of my brother's who wanted the job."

"Your brother must be one hell of a friend to loan out his sister to be another man's wife," he answered tensely as they glided around the dance floor.

"I didn't *want* to do it!" she defended hotly.

"What did your brother do? Hold a gun to your head?"

"Certainly not! He just felt his friend, Cecil, needed a break, that's all! I was simply trying to give him one."

"Is that a fact? Well, Cecil isn't the only one in life who needs a break. Keep that in mind, lady. I want that job too," he said tightly.

"All right, you don't have to use that tone of voice with me. I said I would help you."

"You bet your sweet tush you will," he mumbled, but seemed to relax as he loosened his grip. She was floating lightly in his arms under the hundreds of tiny candles flickering brightly in the elegant room. It was almost like dancing in fairyland, except "Prince Charming" was not so charming. Chandra relaxed against him, his soft breath fanning her cheek. She gradually became aware of his hand moving gently along the base of her spine.

"You've gotten awfully quiet. What are you thinking up now?" His voice was heavy with sarcasm.

"I'm not thinking—I'm dancing," she muttered. She was really just enjoying the feel of his muscular arms around her, but was too ashamed of herself to admit it. She *should* be thinking of Phillip. And she most assuredly *would*, in just a few more minutes.

"Look, I'm sorry I came down on you so hard, but this little act of yours is a bit disconcerting." His voice sounded less harsh now.

"It's all right," she managed to reply shakily. It wasn't all right! This had to be the single most disastrous blunder she had ever made in her otherwise sane, orderly life. Darrell Loring was a dead man as soon as she got her hands on him! "I'm sorry I upset you," she added lamely.

"Don't misunderstand me, Chandra. This job is important to me, but I don't like the idea of some broad coming up and introducing herself as my wife. I've managed to successfully avoid marriage for thirty-six years, and I sure don't plan on picking up a wife at some lousy cocktail party!"

"I said I was sorry," she snarled through clenched teeth, her fists doubling up in anger. She definitely did not like to be referred to as a broad. "Don't worry, you're *still* as pure as the driven snow," she added snidely. "I haven't exercised my marital rights!"

He pulled back slightly, his blue eyes meeting her wide hazel ones. "Let's not get carried away now. Pure I'm not!"

"I don't doubt that one bit," she readily agreed. "I should have known you were not a shy 'Cecil' type the minute I first saw you."

Garrett pulled back from her, his face a mask of mock sincerity. "Now what makes you say that? For all you know, I may be an A-one, clean-cut guy."

Chandra smiled up at him coolly. "I didn't ride into town on a load of hay, mister. I know what type you are. 'Shy' would be the last word that I'd use to describe you."

His bold blue eyes locked with hers. "If we were not standing in a room full of people right now, Ms. Loring, I'd show you just how right you are." He winked seductively at her.

"You really are quite sure of yourself when it comes to women, aren't you?" Chandra sneered. "Have you ever stopped to think that not *all* women find you appealing?"

He made a pretense of mulling the question over in his mind for a moment. "I hadn't really stopped to think about it. I really don't care one way or the other what women think about me." He smiled down at her smugly. "I manage to struggle along with the women I know."

"I'm sure you do." Chandra wished this dance would end. She was beginning to tire of her dancing partner.

"What do you do with your time, other than running around to parties and posing as some strange man's wife?"

"I was *not* posing as some stranger's wife! Cecil is a very close friend of my brother's." This guy was really getting on her nerves. He might be one of the best-looking men she had ever met, but his personality was zero in her book.

"Sorry. I forget how touchy women are. . . ."

"I am not touchy!" she fired back rapidly. "And, not that it's any of your business, but I work for a law firm in Kansas City. I'm a legal secretary. What do *you* do whenever you're not out trying to scrape up a job?" she returned snidely.

"I'm not trying to 'scrape' up a job." His eyes had turned a cold, haughty blue. She had finally managed to get his goat. "I happen to be a damn good test pilot."

Chandra's pulse quickened. A test pilot! That sounded extremely dangerous. She caught herself quickly. What did she care what he did? He could risk his fool neck if he wanted to. It wouldn't make any earth-shaking difference to her one way or the other.

"Really," she taunted. "Then why are you trying so hard for this job?"

She felt his shoulders lift in a show of indifference. "It's a good opportunity. I suppose it's time I was settling down somewhere. At my age, I should be putting down roots."

"Does that include looking for a wife?" Chandra asked softly.

"Me?" He threw his head back and laughed loudly. Chandra stared at him stonily. She didn't find the question all that funny.

"I take it that means you're not in the market for a wife."

"Not me, lady! You'll never find me caught in the marriage trap."

"Marriage trap? Do you really view marriage as a trap?" Chandra asked in amazement. *It's probably just as well,* she thought. *No woman would ever be able to live with your arrogance for very long.*

"Let's just say I'm more than content with the way my life is —freedom with no complications from a woman. I don't have

31

to put up with tears, tantrums, or someone telling me what to do. No commitments. If I don't like a woman, I simply tell her to 'hit the road.' "

"Hit the road!" Chandra shook her head in disbelief. "Gee, you're every woman's fantasy in a man. I'd be surprised if you could find a woman who would even have you. You and I are exact opposites. *I* want a marriage with all the ties," she told him heatedly.

"Good luck," he returned flippantly. "You're welcome to my share of marital bliss."

He seemed so smug. Chandra would have loved to have been the woman to bring him to his knees in surrender. She might just have tried, too, if she weren't in love with another man. It would be sheer delight to watch some woman come along and make him eat his words! She suddenly had had enough of this foolish conversation . . . and his company.

"I'm going back to the table," she mumbled hotly and whirled out of his arms. She was suddenly jerked to a dead halt. "Let go of me!" she hissed under her breath. The conceited oaf was going to make a scene out here on the dance floor!

"I'm not touching you," he spat out nastily. "Hold still, dammit!"

"Will you *please* stop that disgusting cussing!" She glared emphatically at him over her shoulder.

"Don't be telling *me* what to do, lady!" He was working frantically with the clasp of his belt buckle, holding her tight against him on the dance floor. "I'll cuss if I feel like it. Your damn dress is stuck on my belt buckle."

She glanced back nervously at the entangled dress, her face flushing a dark pink. "Oh my gosh—what are we going to do now?"

"Just keep moving," he said tightly. "I'll see if I can get it loose."

For the next few minutes Chandra was sure everyone in the place thought he was molesting her on the dance floor. She had never been so embarrassed.

Disgusted, he finally backed her into the foyer, smiling pleasantly at the other dancers. Reaching the safety of the dark hall, Chandra let out a long, angry sigh. "That's the most embarrassing thing I've ever had to endure," she spat out, her back still turned to him.

"You think I'm enjoying this, lady?! Just calm down—no one saw us."

"No one *saw* us! There was an old man in a blue suit whose eyes were hanging out of his head!"

"That's just your imagination. Look, why don't you try to undo it? Your fingers are a lot smaller than mine," he said from behind her.

Chandra tried to look back at him, sputtering, "You're joking!"

"No, I'm not joking. I can't get it undone, so you'll either have to try or we can stand here all night. . . ." He stopped in mid-sentence. "Or . . . I can just slip these pants off right here."

"You wouldn't dare!" Chandra glared at the wall she was facing.

"As you said, honey, I'm not shy."

"This is simply disgusting," Chandra murmured helplessly as her hand slipped around her back and between them. She worked uselessly for a few minutes trying to twist the stubborn dress out of the belt buckle. A crimson flush crept up her neck as she felt the first stirrings of his desire against her fumbling fingers as she kept brushing the front of his trousers. She glanced back into his innocent, sky-blue eyes, a look of consternation on her pretty face.

He shrugged his broad shoulders, grinning boyishly. "Sorry, this happens every time some good-looking woman fumbles with my belt in the dark."

By now there was definitely a prominent show of his aroused passion.

"Oooooooh . . ." Chandra jerked angrily away from him, ripping a large hole in her dress.

33

"Hey, watch it!" he advised shakily, his hands grabbing hers. "*Now* look what you've done!"

Chandra could not make her eyes look at the front of his trousers. "What did I do?"

He stared down, repulsed at the numerous pieces of her dress sticking out of his belt buckle. He looked back up at her in annoyance. "You think *this* isn't going to attract attention?"

Her eyes unwillingly fastened on the pieces of black yarn standing out like a sore thumb against the pale gray of his slacks. "Ohhhh, I'm sorry!" she apologized sincerely.

"What a hell of a mess. I'm not going to stand here and let you dig out that yarn." He took hold of her shoulders and turned her around. "Come on, let's get out of here before one more thing happens. You walk in front of me. We'll make our apologies to the Rhodeses for leaving early, then grab a cab. You didn't drive over by yourself, did you?"

"No, I don't have a car. I came in a cab. But what about the hole in my dress?

"At least you've got one of those black things on under it and the hole's not so noticeable. Just keep your hands to your side and stay close to me. Okay, now start walking nice and easy, just as if nothing was wrong. I'll do all the explaining."

Chandra groaned helplessly as they stepped back out of the small foyer onto the crowded dance floor, smiling innocently at the questioning stares. He kept Chandra against the front of him, his arms draped around her waist casually. If she could get her hands on Darrell right now, she would throttle him alive!

Threading their way over to the Rhodeses' table, they stopped in front of the smiling older couple, Chandra indecently close to her "husband."

"John, I hope you'll excuse us, but my wife has developed a terrible headache and wants to go home."

John observed Morganson's intimate embrace of Chandra and gave him a knowing smile. "That's perfectly all right, son. I'm not too old to remember what it was like to be a newlywed." He winked friskily at Chandra. "We were just about to leave ourselves. We'll give you a ride home."

Chandra's blood froze. Oh brother, now he thought they couldn't wait to get home and alone with each other. The last thing she needed was for this "hotshot" to go home with her.

"Oh, that's all right, sir. We'll just grab a ca—" Morganson started.

"Nonsense, my boy. Where is your parents' house, Mrs. Morganson?"

"On Thirty-ninth Street, but really, Mr. Rhodes, we can easily call a cab." Chandra was beginning to panic.

"We're not staying three blocks from there ourselves." He turned to his wife. "Isn't that right, Sara?"

"Of course, we'd be delighted to drop you off. I'll just get my wrap." She stood up and took her husband's arm.

Still walking with Chandra in front of him, Garrett eased their way across the crowded room. "You're going to have to let me go so I can get my coat," Chandra gritted between clenched teeth.

"All right, but you'll have to get mine while you're at it." He looked around uneasily. "I don't want to take the chance anyone will see this damn yarn."

"What about the hole in *my* dress?" Chandra protested. "Couldn't you be enough of a gentleman to get *both* coats?"

"Come on, Chandra, give me a break!" He looked disconcerted for the first time that evening.

"This is a nightmare," she grumbled, just before asking the maid for their coats. "What are we going to do about them taking us home?"

"We'll just have to let them," he said distractedly as he draped the coat over his arm, discreetly covering the front of his trousers. "I'll grab a cab from your house and go on to my hotel."

"I don't know . . ." Chandra suddenly looked blank.

"Well, well, well, are we all ready to depart?" Mr. Rhodes walked up behind them with a fatherly smile.

"Ready sir," the young man grinned.

35

"You better put your coat on, dear," Sara cautioned Chandra as they walked through the gaily decorated lobby. "It's terribly cold out there tonight."

"Oh, I'll just drape it around my shoulders." She smiled brightly. "I love this nippy weather!" She would gladly freeze to death before she let them see that gaping hole in the back of her dress. She shifted the coat a little more to the back.

They walked out the front door and a huge gust of wind tore through Chandra's dress. By the time they reached the car her teeth were chattering like a typewriter and she was clinging to her mystery man for some small shred of warmth. She fell into the back seat of the cold car, as her "husband" gave her a mocking grin. He pulled her over to him and wrapped her coat snugly around her as they sat in the dark. She gratefully snuggled close to him, suddenly wanting to be in his arms again. He brushed her ear with his lips lightly. "Are you warm now?"

"Yes, thank you," she whispered against his smooth-shaven cheek.

"Just a small, husbandly duty," he dismissed lightly.

After giving Mr. Rhodes the street number Chandra settled back in Garrett's strong arms and enjoyed the ride home. The night was about to end, and she suddenly felt very tired.

Ten minutes later the Cadillac pulled up in front of her parents' dark house. "Here you are, folks. Safe and sound." Mr. Rhodes left the motor running as the two climbed out the back door.

"Thanks again, sir," the young man told Mr. Rhodes as he took Chandra's hand and helped her out.

"Glad to do it, Garrett. I'll pick you up in the morning around nine. There're several things I'd like to go over with you before I make my final decision."

"In the morning, sir?"

"Right. Nine o'clock sharp. Good night, Mrs. Morganson."

"Good night, Mr. and Mrs. Rhodes." Chandra smiled bravely.

The big black car sped away into the cold night as the two

young people stood in the middle of the street looking at each other.

"He wants to pick you up here at nine o'clock in the morning," Chandra told him, stunned.

"I heard!" he snapped tersely.

The wind was whistling around her skirt tail, making her absolutely miserable. "Well, I'm freezing. Let's go in and call your cab."

They hurried up the walk as Chandra dug in her purse for the key to the front door and handed it to him. He inserted it into the lock and they let themselves into the heavenly warmth of the house.

She switched on the lamp beside the sofa, flooding the room with soft light. The dying embers in the fireplace surged rapidly back to life as Chandra threw a couple of sticks of wood onto the fire. She removed her coat and laid it on the arm of the chair.

She suddenly felt very shy and ill at ease watching him warm his hands in front of the fireplace, his tall, solid frame casting a shadow over the rug on the floor. He seemed to be mesmerized by the dancing, flickering flames as he stood staring down into the fire.

Chandra perched on the arm of the chair, not quite knowing what to say. Finally taking a deep breath, she offered lightly, "Did you want me to call you a cab?"

Coming out of his trance he turned to face her. "Chandra, you know how much this job means to me, don't you?"

Chandra took a deep breath before answering. "I think so."

"Then you won't be too surprised to learn that you're going to have a house guest tonight. As late as it is I'd no more get back to my hotel than it would be time to turn around and come back here to meet Rhodes. Like it or not I'm staying here tonight," he told her bluntly.

Chandra was on her feet in a flash, clearly disturbed by his statement, her patience finally coming to an end.

"No, I won't be surprised, because I'm not going to let you stay here! I *admit* I have made a total fool out of myself tonight, stupidly introducing myself as your wife, but *I* have played out the charade for the evening, which is *all* I promised to do, Mr. Morganson, so you can just call your cab and be on your merry way. You are not welcome to stay in my house for the night!"

Garrett watched her raving with the bored calm most husbands possess when they have angered their wives.

He walked over to the chintz-covered couch and sat down, making himself at home. "Are you through with your mad fit?"

"Are you leaving?"

"Hell, no!"

"Then I'm not through!" She walked over and shook her fist in his face for emphasis. "I'll scream to high heaven until you leave!"

"Go ahead. You won't bother me." He grabbed her flailing fist with one large hand. "But I'll tell you what *will* bother me— losing a shot at the Vice Presidency at Rhodes Aircraft. Now as I've tried patiently to tell you all evening, you got me into this mess and you're going to get me out of it!"

"Patiently! Well, you've got your nerve. You have been nothing but downright rude to me all evening!"

"I'm going to get ruder," he warned, his blue eyes snapping, "if you don't calm down. All I'm asking is to stay the night in your guest room. I'm not asking for bed 'privileges' with you."

"If you were I'd turn you down flat!" Her hazel eyes stormed at him.

He jerked her up more tightly to him, his eyes catching and holding hers. In a calm voice, he stated, "Honey, there are a lot of women who would fight you for that invitation—*not*," he emphasized, "that it was ever extended to you. You have to be patient, Chandra. Wait until a man invites you into his bed."

Chandra flushed a bright red, trying to jerk angrily away from him. "You arrogant—"

His hold on her tightened as he began to chuckle menacingly. "Don't start calling me names or you may never get the pleasure of sleeping in my bed. And make no mistake about it, Chandra Loring," his voice had dropped to a husky timbre, "I do make it a pleasure for my women!" He suddenly thrust her roughly away from him and walked back over to the fireplace. "Now that you understand that I'm not after your body, why don't you show me where you want me to sleep tonight." He turned back to face her and said in a more reasonable tone of voice, "After tonight, this will be over. I'll figure a way out of all this tomorrow, but right now I need some time to think."

Rubbing her wrists angrily Chandra stared at him, trying to decide what to do. He was right—she had gotten him into this mess, and if one night could rid her of him then she supposed she would have to relent and let him spend that night here. Anything to get this farce over with, and this Garrett Morganson out of her life! She could never be attracted to such an egotistical snob. Phillip suddenly seemed a warm refuge for her after being with Garrett all evening.

"All right, Garrett, but I want to warn you, in case you try anything funny, my parents are asleep in their room upstairs," she stressed as she swept swiftly by him. She wasn't about to let him know she was in the house alone.

"I *am* sorry, honey, but you're just not my type." He smiled at her sympathetically.

"And you *certainly* are not mine," she shot back angrily.

"Now let me guess what type you like—one that sends you flowers and writes you poetry. Right?" Garrett fell into step behind her.

"You wouldn't have the vaguest idea of what kind of a man a woman would like. I'd love to see what attracts you! Oh, pardon me, I forgot. I did see one of them. 'Red Satin' at the party was looking at you awfully hungrily tonight."

"Yes, and if it hadn't been for you, I would be . . . enjoying her company right about now," he responded crudely.

"I just bet you would," she spat out as she started to climb the stairs rapidly.

"You didn't say what kind of a man you went for," he reminded Chandra as he climbed the stairs behind her, trying to keep up with her angrily flying feet.

39

"I like a man who knows how to treat a woman like a woman. One who sends me flowers, treats me kindly, whispers sweet nothings in my ear, sends me love notes—all those silly things you have probably never even thought of doing for a woman. And, yes, I *love* poetry!"

Garrett paused on the top stair, a small grin on his face. "Now how would you know how I treat my women?"

Chandra stopped and looked him square in the eyes. "Women mean one thing for men like you," she flashed. "You would never appeal to me, Mr. Morganson. Sorry."

Garrett's face was uncomfortably close to hers as he leaned negligently against the top rail of the stairs. His eyes roved intimately over the straining bodice of her dress, and her pulse began to pound. The soft curve of her breasts caught his appraisal, his eyes lingering for a brief moment on them before traveling on down her body. Chandra felt as though he had virtually undressed her while they were standing there on the stairs. She would never admit it but at that moment she was sure he would be every woman's fantasy in bed.

He finally spoke in a quiet tone, his words clipped and concise. "If I had time, lady, I'd show you what it meant to be my woman. You would have all those things you want"—his eyes surveyed her suggestively—"and more. I promise you that."

Chandra's knees felt rubbery as she tore her gaze away from him and proceeded down the hall. She pointed to a closed door. "You can sleep in there tonight."

She heard his soft chuckle as he opened the door to the guest room. "No good-night kiss, wife?"

"You are to be out of here by nine o'clock tomorrow morning," Chandra returned sternly, her back turned to him as she continued down the hall.

Garrett stood watching her walk, her slender hips swaying provocatively in the black clinging dress. He quickly smothered an unwelcome feeling of desire as he watched the petite, good-looking blonde enter her own bedroom and slam the door loudly. *Careful old man,* he cautioned himself under his breath as he entered his own room and sank down onto the bed. *Dames like that are nothing but trouble. They want the marriage, home, and baby-carriage routine, and will settle for nothing less.* Garrett Morganson wanted no part of marriage. When he walked out of that dippy blonde's life in the morning, that would be the end of that!

Garrett shrugged tiredly out of his clothes and was asleep five minutes after his head hit the pillow.

CHAPTER THREE

Chandra spooned fragrant coffee grounds into the paper filter in the basket of the percolator and plugged it in. Within seconds the stimulating aroma of coffee filled the small kitchen. She pushed back the freshly starched curtain hanging at the window of the small breakfast nook and looked out on the gray, frosty morning. The stark, bare branches of the large old oak that stood beside the kitchen window swayed lightly in the gusty, early morning wind. She poured a cup of coffee and sat down at the table, her mind mulling over the events of the previous night.

It had taken her a long time to fall asleep; the image of a tall, handsome man with clear blue eyes appeared every time she closed her eyes. She would be relieved when she saw the last of Garrett Morganson. She sighed and took another sip of her hot coffee. She wasn't going to spend her day worrying over Garrett. Today she would sit down and tackle the wedding invitations. She would address them all this week and mail them the next.

"Good morning."

Chandra jumped at the sound of the deep male voice greeting her. She glanced up quickly to see Garrett standing in the doorway, his hair still damp from the shower.

"Good morning," she murmured coolly.

"I hope you don't mind, but I used the shower in the hall bathroom a few minutes ago and shaved with a pink razor I found in there."

Chandra couldn't help smiling as she watched him rub his large hand over his face. "That's mine. I'm sorry I neglected to

42

show you where the bathroom was last night." Chandra stood up and walked over to the kitchen cabinet. "How do you like your coffee?" she asked as she opened the cabinet door, pausing as her eyes rested on the coffee cups sitting on the second shelf. Her mother was a good three inches taller than Chandra so the cups were no obstacle in her kitchen, but they were way beyond Chandra's reach.

"Black is fine," he said, watching her drag a small step stool over to the cabinet and climb up on it.

Chandra was preoccupied in her search for a cup, unaware that he'd come up to stand behind her. His eyes lazily inspected the bare expanse of the slender leg that was propped up on the cabinet for support.

"Can I help you with something?" He reached out and held Chandra around her small waist with his hands. Chandra was startled at his touch, and her hand knocked over the cup she had been reaching for. The heavy mug came tumbling down, hitting him squarely on the forehead.

"Son of a—" he yelled, grabbing at the inch-long cut on his head. Bright-red blood covered his fingers instantly.

"Oh, my gosh!" Chandra hopped down off the stool and reached for a paper towel. She wet it with cold water, then steered Garrett over to the table to set him down gently. "I'm so sorry. I had no idea you were behind me!" she exclaimed, dabbing frantically at the open wound.

"Ouch! Take it easy!" He twisted around in his seat like a two-year-old with a skinned knee. "How bad is it?" he asked, his face turning pale.

Chandra examined the wound carefully, then assured him, "You'll live."

"Come on, Chandra, it's not funny. It hurts like hell." He reached up to feel a bump the size of a goose egg swelling up instantly beside the cut.

Chandra swallowed her giggles and made an attempt to look serious. "Just hold still while I get the first-aid kit." Chandra disappeared through the door, returning momentarily with a small Red Cross medical kit. "Does it still hurt?"

His blue eyes looked at her painfully. "Yes."

Chandra patted his arm mockingly and leaned over to gleefully wipe away the slight trace of blood with a cotton ball dipped in alcohol.

He sucked in his breath and let go with a shocking expletive as the cold, stinging antiseptic penetrated the cut. *What a coward,* Chandra thought as she steadied his head with her hands and smoothed first-aid cream over the cut. She slapped a small Band-Aid across his forehead. "There! Good as new."

She started to move away when Garrett pulled her roughly up against him and brought her face next to his. "You enjoyed that, didn't you?"

"Who, me?" Chandra asked innocently, her hazel eyes sparkling.

"Yeah, you," he teased, his mouth dangerously close to hers. "Sadistic little witch, aren't you?"

Chandra was finding it increasingly hard to breathe standing so close to him, her thin robe barely considered decent. She wet her lips with the tip of her tongue, mesmerized by the deep sound of his voice as he continued to chide her gently.

"I think the least you could do is kiss it for me and make it better. That's what my mother used to do."

"I'm not your mother, Garrett," she reminded him nicely.

"I'd noticed that," he grinned cockily, pulling her closer.

Chandra's eyes met his. He was looking at her, desire clearly written in his face. Chandra would never know why she reached over and started to hesitantly kiss the small wound on his forehead. All of a sudden her face was grasped between two large hands that steered her mouth downward. Her heart fluttered wildly as Garrett's mouth closed over hers. His kiss started gently, playfully, as his lips and teeth tugged lightly at hers. She was so stunned by his action she slumped against his broad chest, her hands coming out to encircle his neck.

He growled low in his throat and pulled her down on his lap.

44

Chandra could feel the lean hardness of him as he drew her tighter into his arms. His mouth reached out to capture hers more roughly this time, his tongue gently pushing its way inside. Chandra began to tremble as he brought his hand up, running it lightly over the smoothness of her neck and face, stroking the lobe of her ear gently between his fingertips. His mouth moved sensuously with hers and his breathing deepened. Chandra could feel the hard ridge of his muscled thighs straining against her thin gown. Her insides churned with butterflies as her arms tightened her grip on his neck. In the year she had been engaged to Phillip, not once had he ever kissed her like this. Her blood was rushing and pounding in her head, and a strange gnawing ache was developing deep within her, a need that had to be fulfilled, not by just any man, but by this particular one.

Garrett broke the kiss off, breathing raggedly as he met her eyes. "I was wrong. Now I have pain in two places," he said, moving suggestively against her bottom, making her aware of his unquestionable desire for her.

Chandra caught her breath and buried her face into his neck, breathing in the fresh, clean smell of him. "Garrett, please . . ."

He ceased his teasing movements and stroked her blond hair tenderly. "I'm sorry, sweetheart." He pulled her face around and kissed her eyes, nose, cheeks, working his way around to her neck, murmuring huskily, "You know you're a damn appealing woman." His mouth searched eagerly for hers again. Chandra met him halfway this time as their tongues mingled hotly together. He reached up to run his fingers through her thick, honey blond tresses, pulling her mouth firmly against his. Groaning deeply in his throat, he hungrily devoured the sweetness of her mouth. Chandra moaned deliciously as wave after wave of desire washed over her, her hands gripping his hair tightly.

"Chandra—sweetheart . . ." he breathed passionately, his hands stroking her body urgently.

"Garrett . . . I . . ." Chandra had lost all sense of reality; all

45

she could think of or feel was his mouth drugging her with long, warm kisses. "We have to stop," she pleaded.

"Who says we have to?" His hands became bolder, slipping under her thin gown to run lightly down the length of her leg.

Chandra struggled to regain her sanity, pulling away from him. "*I* say we have to stop!" Chandra was trying to catch her breath as she reached out to grab his persistent hands.

Pulling her back for one more long, drugging kiss, he pleaded softly, "We're two adults—what's the problem?"

Chandra pushed away from him and stood up breathlessly, unable to break out of his hold. This was sheer madness. What had gotten into her! "Garrett," she threatened weakly, realizing that at this moment she was as helpless in his arms as a newborn babe, "I don't fall into bed with every man I meet. . . ." Her voice trailed off helplessly.

Garrett pulled away reluctantly, his breathing heavy and irregular. "You wouldn't want to make an exception this one time . . . would you?" His slumberous eyes were misted with desire.

"No," she murmured firmly. "I don't make exceptions."

Garrett shuddered, releasing her instantly. "Sorry," he muttered tensely. "Forget I ever asked."

"Forgotten," Chandra muttered, her voice unsteady. She felt unreasonably disappointed—he had given up so easily!

The loud shrill of the telephone startled them both. Garrett walked over and shakily poured himself a cup of coffee, then sat down at the table as Chandra confusedly picked up the receiver next to the kitchen stove. "Hello?"

Dead silence met her ear for a moment, then she heard a very meek voice asking, "Ms. Chandra Loring, please."

Chandra was puzzled. Who could be calling her here? Very few people knew where she was right now.

"This is she."

"Oh my goodness, Chandra. This is Cecil Burgess."

"Who?"

"Cecil Burgess. Darrell's friend. I'm so sorry I haven't called

46

before now, but I was only released from the hospital a few minutes ago."

"The hospital?" Chandra's mind couldn't grasp the situation yet. Garrett was quietly drinking his cup of coffee, leafing nonchalantly through the morning paper.

"Yes, on the way to the party last night some drunk hit my car and I spent the night in the hospital. I hope you weren't inconvenienced too much by my not being there." Cecil's voice held a note of despair.

"No, I . . . made it just fine. I hope you weren't hurt."

"Just a few bruises, but I'll be without a car for a while. The other driver wasn't insured."

Naturally, Chandra thought fleetingly. *With Cecil's luck, what else could he expect!?*

"I certainly appreciate what you tried to do for me, Chandra. Maybe I can thank you in person someday," Cecil said kindly.

"That would be nice, *Cecil,*" she emphasized. Garrett's eyebrows shot up. "I'll look forward to that. Thank you for calling." Chandra replaced the receiver on the hook and glared at the dark-haired man sitting at the table.

"Boy," he observed as he casually turned the paper to the sports section, "there're more Cecils around here than a cat has fleas!"

"Don't be so smug. I told you there really was a Cecil," she said heatedly.

Garrett leafed absently through the paper. "I didn't doubt that there was a Cecil."

Suddenly the strong emotions of the last twenty-four hours caught up with Chandra as she felt silent tears begin to slip down her face. It was bad enough to make such a stupendous mistake, but why did it have to be with a man as appealing and virile as Garrett?

Garrett glanced from behind the paper and saw tears sliding down Chandra's pretty face. With a deep sigh of exasperation he got to his feet and came over to kneel by her chair.

"Now what did I do?"

"Nothing," she sniffed.

"Nothing, hell! Why are you crying?" he asked.

"Why didn't you stop me last night from making such a fool of myself?" She turned tear-filled hazel eyes on his serious face.

Shaking his head wearily he answered, "I didn't know what you were up to, Chandra. Hell, for all I knew you were just some pushy broad looking for a good time!"

"Don't call me a broad. I hate that." She blew her nose into a wadded-up paper towel she had in her hand. "And stop cussing," she reminded him again curtly.

"Damn! Anyway, when you walked up and introduced yourself as my wife . . . well, dam—darn, Chandra, what was I supposed to think?"

"What did you think?" Chandra couldn't resist asking.

"Do you really want to know?"

"Yes," she answered bravely.

"I thought you were crazy as hel—heck. But when you said Rhodes was looking for a married man, well . . . I would have answered to Rover last night if it would have gotten me the job. That's what makes me so mad, Chandra. I *had* that job in the bag with my qualifications. There was no way Rhodes could pass me up. Then you came breezing in and announced to the world that you were my wife . . . well, it made me mad—damn mad!"

"I said I was sorry. I can't undo it Garrett, or I assure you I most certainly would," she sobbed.

"Why in the world didn't you get your facts straight . . . or have Cecil pick you up here?" he raved, beginning to pace the room restlessly.

"Darrell called before he left on a flight to give me Cecil's description—he was just too sketchy and *you* were tall, had brown hair, and were standing next to the punch bowl at seven o'clock. That's where he said Cecil would be. You even looked like you were expecting someone after that hussy left. You even glanced at your watch once," she defended angrily.

"Well, hell!" he sputtered in exasperation. "I wanted to know what time it was. I had had a long day." He stopped his pacing and reached into his back pocket to pull out a large, clean white handkerchief. "Will you please knock off that crying? It drives me up a wall. That's one of the reasons I'd never marry. Women and their up-and-down moods. Always blubbering all over the place—it gets on my nerves."

"I'm sorry, Garrett," she sniffed. Chandra was sitting quietly as he kneeled down and mopped at her face, none too gently. "I don't cry very often."

"Just control yourself when I'm around," he mumbled sternly as he stood back up.

His sudden kindness made Chandra dissolve in a new round of tears. "I don't know what Phillip's going to say about all this."

Garrett jammed his fist on his lean hips and looked at her in frustration. "Now, who in the hell is *Phillip*?"

"My fiancé."

"Your what?!" Garrett's mouth dropped, his face growing tense.

"He's my fiancé," Chandra said. "We're supposed to be married at the end of this month. What's he going to say when he finds out I've posed as your wife and you stayed all night with me?"

"Don't get so shook, dammit. We didn't stay all night—together." Garrett looked disgusted. Chandra sniffed and reached for a paper towel to blow her nose, fingers trembling. "You really going to marry this guy?" Garrett's blue eyes had lost their twinkle.

"Yes," she whispered softly. She couldn't look at him.

"Well, I still say there's nothing to get so upset about. Phillip" —Garrett hesitated when he spoke the other man's name— "doesn't ever have to know about last night."

"What will you do about the job?" Chandra asked him tearfully.

"With a little luck I should wrap it up this morning." He looked at her slim figure sitting so forlornly in the chair. Her blond hair was tousled and her face was flushed from tears. He put a large hand out to touch the softness of her cheek, wiping away a stray tear with his thumb. "Come on, Chandra," he said huskily. "It tears me up to see you cry, honey."

"I'm sorry . . . Garrett." The sound of her soft voice saying his name tugged at his heart. What would it sound like whispering softly in his ear while he was making love to her?

Chandra's eyes drank in the handsomeness of Garrett's features, her stomach fluttering. The way he had said her name just now—Chandra—she had never heard it said in such a deep, melodious, rich tone. She fought the urge to reach out and stroke his strong, firm jaw.

The sound of a car horn in the drive brought them both back to the present.

"That's Mr. Rhodes," Chandra said peering out the curtain at the new Cadillac sitting in the drive. She let the curtain drop back in place and walked over to Garrett. "Let me at least get you one of Dad's clean shirts," she offered, stalling for a little more time. "It's going to look strange if you show up this morning wearing the same clothes you had on last night."

"Thank you," he smiled, "I'd appreciate that."

Chandra flew out of the room and was back momentarily with a clean white shirt and gray striped tie. "I think you and Dad are close to the same size," she said, quickly handing him the fresh apparel.

Garrett shrugged out of his own shirt and began to put on the borrowed clothes. Chandra's pulse jumped erratically as he bared his broad chest thickly covered with light brown hair, his powerful muscles flexing as he first buttoned the shirt, then unbuttoned his trousers and stuffed the tail of the borrowed shirt into them.

"I see you got the black yarn out of your belt," she offered lightly.

"Yeah, but it was a lot more fun when you tried," he teased.

"I'll bet you say that to all your women," she parried softly.

"No, not all of them. Only the pretty, hazel-eyed blondes." He grinned tenderly as he tied the striped tie in a perfect knot.

Chandra blushed. "Let me get your coat," she finished lamely. He was making her feel so . . . different, almost light-headed.

The sound of the horn reached their ears once again.

"I've got to go," Garrett said with resignation, his eyes never leaving hers. "Thanks . . . for everything."

"It's all right. I'm sorry I made such a fool of myself." Chandra didn't want him to leave. She wanted to hold on to this brief moment forever.

"Well, thanks again. Maybe we'll see each other sometime. Are you going to live here after your marriage?"

"No, I'll be going back to Missouri."

"Oh." Garrett drank in her loveliness one last time. "Well, thanks again . . . Mrs. Morganson," he whispered quietly. "I'll have the shirt laundered and delivered back here."

"That's fine. I hope your head heals okay," Chandra told him helplessly.

Garrett reached up to feel the small bump on his forehead. "It's nothing," he assured her. "I think your kiss made it well. . . ." Their eyes locked once again.

The third, insistent beep of the horn warned Garrett that Mr. Rhodes was losing his patience.

"I have to go, Chandra."

"Good-bye, Garrett."

Just before he turned to leave, he winked suggestively. "When your dad comes home, tell him thanks for the loan of the shirt."

Chandra's cheeks reddened at the realization that he knew all along they had been alone.

When he was gone Chandra sat down at the table and stared out the window on the cold, bleak morning. It was as if all the warmth had left the room. Why did she suddenly feel such a sense of loneliness? How could one man leave such emptiness behind him? Chandra shook her head to clear her thoughts. Was she losing her mind? Why was she thinking of Garrett Morganson when she had a hundred wedding invitations to address? She was going to marry a man by the name of Phillip Watson, and she'd better start remembering that! Last night and this morning had been an interesting interlude in her life, one she would never forget, but it was over. She had seen the last of Garrett Morganson, test pilot, the most gorgeous blue-eyed man in the world.

The remainder of the day dragged by as Chandra dutifully addressed all the wedding invitations. Her mind constantly wandered back to Garrett, and she wondered if he'd managed to secure the job that was so important to him. Late in the afternoon she went up to her bedroom and lay down across the bed, her mind desperately fighting the loneliness. She thought about calling Phillip at his office but quickly discarded the idea when she remembered he had tickets to a hockey game that afternoon. She closed her eyes wearily and had just dozed off to sleep when the phone by her bed rang.

"Hello, honey? This is Garrett!" His sunny voice sang over the line.

"Garrett?" Chandra sat up abruptly. She was sure she was dreaming!

"Were you asleep, sweetheart?"

"Yes . . . I was taking a nap." What was the matter with him? He sounded strained.

"Mrs. Rhodes wanted me to call and tell you that one of the engineers' wives is hosting a formal get-together tonight in *our* honor. As the newest member of their firm they naturally want to get to know my *wife* better!"

"Garrett," Chandra's voice was stern. "You know that's impossible!"

"Yes, it is—it *is* formal. Now you'll have a chance to wear that dinner dress I like so much."

"Garrett, is someone with you?"

"That's right, sweetheart." Garrett's voice was tense.

"Garrett, we have to tell them the truth. I can't keep posing as your wife. This has got to stop somewhere." Chandra bit her lip in frustration.

"Excuse me for a minute, sweetheart, I want to change phones."

Chandra could hear the rumble of voices in the background as Garrett changed phones. In a few minutes he was back on the line speaking in a low tense tone. "Chandra, are you still there?"

"Yes, what's going on?"

"Trouble. This party is in my honor tonight. Rhodes hired me this afternoon."

"Congratulations!"

"Thanks, but it will all go down the drain if I show up without a wife." Garrett's voice held desperation.

Chandra simmered inside. She didn't want him to lose the job, but she couldn't keep this charade up forever. "So you want me to go with you."

"Just this one last time, Chandra. I promise I'll figure a way out of this mess, but I have to have time to think."

"Garrett, I really want to help you, but you surely can see my side of it. Phillip would have a *fit* if he found out."

"I know, but he's not going to find out."

"I can't take the chance that he will," Chandra snapped.

"Look, one more night, that's all I'm asking. Come on, Chandra, you came this far with me. Don't desert me now."

Chandra closed her eyes in miserable surrender. "All right, Garrett, I'll go, but I'm warning you right now, this is absolutely *the last time*. Is that clear?"

"Right! I'll be home in thirty minutes."

"Wait a minute. You're surely not planning on staying over here again tonight!"

"Just one more night. What's it going to hurt? Besides, Rhodes insists on picking us up again. I've already checked out of my hotel room."

This was getting more involved every moment. "I thought you said Mr. Rhodes would leave town as soon as you were hired."

There was a brief silence on the other end of the line. "I didn't say that. Darrell must have said that. I have no idea what Rhodes's schedule is. Look, I've got to go. I'll be home in a little while and we'll thrash this all out."

"I don't know, Garrett. . . ."

"Chandra!" Garrett's voice was stern and left no room for argument. "I haven't got time to fight with you. My job's at stake right now, and you're going to go to this party with me!"

There was a sharp click as the line went dead. Chandra lay on the bed with the phone still in her hand. What had she gotten herself into? *Well, I know one thing for certain,* she told herself as she replaced the receiver in its cradle. *Garrett Morganson better get it through his thick skull that tonight will absolutely and unequivocally be the last time I pose as his wife!*

CHAPTER FOUR

"You look simply lovely this evening, Mrs. Morganson," John Rhodes complimented Chandra as she and Garrett stepped into the back seat of the black Cadillac.

"Yes, she does, doesn't she," Garrett agreed promptly, a devilish twinkle in his eye as he surveyed the emerald-green gown she was wearing. Chandra had barely spoken two words to him since he had arrived by cab earlier, suitcase in hand. She could only hope that all her parents' neighbors had been struck with temporary blindness. She cringed when she thought of what her father would say about this whole ridiculous arrangement.

"You do, you know," he tauntingly whispered close to her ear. "You've got the disposition of a witch and the tongue of a shrew. *But*"—he hastened to add—"the body of an angel. That dress is designed to do strange things to a man." His arm went around her shoulders to draw her closer.

Pulling away from him discreetly Chandra edged over to the corner of the seat. *Disposition of a witch!* she fumed inwardly. *Why couldn't he have just said I looked nice and left it at that.* Glaring at Garrett pointedly, Chandra let him know she didn't appreciate the compliment.

"Thank you, *darling*, but I thought *red* was your favorite color," she returned snidely, thinking of the voluptuous woman in shimmering satin.

"Well"—he paused for emphasis—"only on some women." He made the motion with his hands of a very busty woman, his

55

cocky grin taking in her small rounded breasts. "On you, green looks better."

Her hazel eyes let him know the intensity of her anger, and with a smirk of repentance on his face, he pulled her over in his arms, his mouth moving close to her ear. "All right, I really meant what I said a minute ago about you being a witch and a shrew, but"—he hastened to add—"your body isn't lacking in any area that I can tell. That dress lets a man know you're all woman beneath it."

Pulling away from him again, Chandra edged back to her corner of the seat. The man was incorrigible! She'd like to shove his backhanded compliments back into his gorgeous, well-shaped mouth.

"Well, I trust you're as excited about your husband's new position as we are," Mr. Rhodes said as he drove down the quiet, residential street.

"Yes, I'm very happy—for him," Chandra replied, still rather put out.

"We believe that Garrett has a great future with Rhodes Aircraft," Sara Rhodes pointed out nicely. "It has to be exciting to be newly married with your whole lives stretching out before you."

"It certainly is," Garrett said, trying to get Chandra's attention without alerting Mr. and Mrs. Rhodes. "Living with Chandra is always . . . exciting. She's already added more unexpected thrills to my life than a man could ask for." He gave her a look of agony.

"Oh, darling, you give me too much credit! Why, without you, my life was empty." She childishly made a gagging noise in her throat. She was becoming increasingly uneasy around him. He was a totally different breed of man from Phillip. She couldn't let his good looks and virile charm distract her. His type of man spelled nothing but trouble for a woman who wanted anything permanent.

They glared stonily at one another in the dim light, each determined to outstare the other.

Unaware of the tension in the back seat, Mrs. Rhodes asked innocently, "I'll bet you two newlyweds would rather be alone than at a noisy party tonight, wouldn't you?" she laughed. "But John and I have so little time to get to know our employees that we didn't want to pass up this opportunity to know the two of you better. You remind us so much of our son and his wife," she added warmly.

"Yes," Mr. Rhodes agreed with a chuckle, "it's hard for a new groom to keep his hands off his new bride, isn't it Garrett?"

"Very," Garrett muttered dryly, still glaring at Chandra. He raised his hands as if to strangle her.

"Now that you have the job, Garrett, have you and Chandra given any thought to where you'll want to live?" Mrs. Rhodes asked conversationally as the car sped along the highway.

"I suppose we'll find a small apartment," Garrett answered vaguely, finally breaking his defiant gaze away from Chandra's.

"You know, Sara, the thought hit me this afternoon after Garrett left the meeting, that he and Chandra would probably be interested in the house that the Millers vacated several months ago."

"Why, John! I hadn't even thought of that. Ed and Felicia's house would just be perfect for Garrett and Chandra." Turning to face Chandra, Mrs. Rhodes beamed brightly. "Oh, my dear, you are going to love that house. It's less than two miles from the plant. Why, Garrett could practically walk to work. It needs a little repair, but nothing major . . . and the price . . . well, didn't the company buy that house back from them, John?"

"Uh . . . Mrs. Rhodes," Chandra began tentatively, casting a panic-stricken glance over to Garrett. "Really . . . I think just a small apartment—"

"Nonsense, Chandra," John Rhodes broke in. "Why would you want to take a small apartment when you could have a lovely, spacious home for the same price? We'll work the payments out to suit your budget, don't worry about that! You and Garrett will need a large house to do all the entertaining that will ɔe required of you in his new position. No—I think that Ed Miller's old house would be just perfect for the two of you."

Chandra's fingers dug into Garrett's leg frantically, silently pleading for him to put a stop to this conversation.

Dislodging her fingers from his thigh, Garrett winced and said huskily, "That's awfully nice of you, Mr. Rhodes, but—"

"Then it's all settled. After you and Chandra see the house, you'll fall in love with it. I can guarantee it!"

"Oh, it will be so much fun to see that house come alive again." Sara Rhodes was brimming over with excitement. "Of course, you'll probably need new furniture—you don't have your furniture yet, do you?"

"No—" Chandra started.

"Well, no problem. I'll help you shop for some. The house already has almost-new drapes. Ed's wife had just had new ones made when he was transferred out to the coast with a satellite company of ours."

Chandra squirmed uncomfortably in the back seat. If Garrett wasn't going to put a stop to this, she would! "Mrs. Rhodes, I think you should know—" she began just as a strong band of steel clamped down on her leg—Garrett's large hand signaling for her to "cool it."

"What Chandra means, Mrs. Rhodes, is that we want you to know we appreciate the generous offer, and we'll be more than happy to take a look at the house."

A small gasp escaped Chandra's lips as Garrett's steel-blue eyes shot her a look of annoyance. What was he doing? They were not going to buy a house!

"Oh, my goodness, we'd love to help you get settled. I'll get the key to the house, and we'll all take a look at it in the morning." Sara Rhodes turned around in the seat to face Chandra again. "Isn't this exciting! I can hardly wait to get started on it."

Chandra gave a shaky laugh. "I don't want to trouble you, really . . . don't you and Mr. Rhodes have other plans? I mean . . . I thought I heard someone mention you traveled a lot."

"Yes, we do," she sighed, "but I've talked John into staying here at least a week before we go on to England. That will enable me to help you some."

"You were the one who made plans to spend Christmas with your sister, Sara, not me," John Rhodes gently reminded his wife.

"I know, but after this trip, John, I'd like to settle down somewhere for a while. I'm tired of all this traveling."

The long, black car was pulling up in front of a low, sprawling brick home, the neatly trimmed shrubbery in the front yar aglow with strings of Christmas lights.

Mr. Rhodes parked the car in one of the last remaining parking places, and they walked to the entrance of the house, huddled against the brisk north wind that was whipping savagely around them.

The door was opened by a white-coated servant, and they all stepped inside the elegant foyer of the house.

"John and Sara!" A woman's high voice reached them as they took off their coats and handed them to the servant.

"Darlings, how nice to see you." She reached out to take Sara Rhodes's and Chandra's hands in her slender, jeweled ones. Chandra noticed she had rings on every one of her fingers. "You must be Chandra Morganson," she said happily.

Sara Rhodes beamed. "Yes, Gwendolyn, this is the wife of our new Vice President of Research and Development—Chandra Morganson. Chandra, this is the wife of one of our top engineers —Gwendolyn Parsons."

Chandra shook her hand politely. "Happy to meet you," she murmured.

"And this"—she grabbed for Garrett's hand and pulled him forward excitedly—"this is her 'hunk' of a husband—the man behind the big title—Garrett." Mrs. Rhodes blushed furiously, aware of the term she had just used to introduce John's newest employee.

Garrett smiled pleasantly as he took Gwendolyn Parsons's hand. "A pleasure to meet you, Gwendolyn. I met your husband this afternoon, and I'm looking forward to working with him." He pulled Chandra beside him, his arm nonchalantly around her waist.

"Michael has spoken quite highly of you, Garrett. We're so happy to have you as one of us now. Come on in and meet the rest of your coworkers. After all, this party's for you and your lovely wife."

They moved on into the crowded living room, and for the next hour Chandra smiled and shook hands with at least fifty people. Garrett kept her close to his side, the two of them presenting the picture of a happily married couple.

By the middle of the evening Chandra had grown quite accustomed to Garrett's arm draped casually about her waist or his hand holding hers lightly as they stood and talked with other couples.

Chandra had nursed a single drink along almost all evening, carrying it with her as they moved through the crowd chatting casually. Garrett had been too preoccupied with meeting his fellow employees to notice how many drinks he was putting away, but Chandra had. Every time a waiter had walked by and offered Garrett a drink he had taken one. By the middle of the evening, Garrett was clearly "feeling no pain."

"Don't you think you're drinking a little too much?" Chandra murmured with a smile as they walked away from an older couple they had been visiting with.

"Me?" Garrett asked innocently, giving her a silly grin. "I haven't had over two or three drinks."

She looked at him in disbelief. "Three drinks?! Really, Garrett. You'd had three by the time you took your coat off. You better take it easy, you didn't eat any dinner, you know," she reminded him cautiously.

Garrett playfully pulled her around the corner into the empty kitchen, trapping her against the wall with both arms and leaned down, his face only inches from hers. "Now you're sounding like a wife again. Are you trying to tell me that not only can I not cuss—I can't hold my liquor either?"

60

"I'm not trying to tell you anything," she replied indifferently, a little disconcerted at his closeness. "I just pointed out you were getting awfully happy." Chandra pushed at his chest, trying to escape.

"And why shouldn't I be?" he asked brightly, pressing in even closer. "I just landed a hell of a good job—I've got a knockout of a broad—'scuse me . . . *lady*," he amended, bowing courtly to her, "for a wife. That's enough to make any man happy!"

"Garrett, you're getting cross-eyed drunk," Chandra told him sternly, trying in vain to push him away.

"Aw, come on, sweetheart, loosen up. If you're going to be a good wife to ole what's his name . . . Philpott . . ."

"Phillip!" Chandra corrected curtly.

"Ah, yes, Phillip! Well, as I was saying—if you're going to be a good wife to ole Phillip, you're going to have to loosen up a little." He dropped his arms down around her waist, pulling her in closer to blend into the lean, hard contours of his body. "What you need, lady, is for some man to teach you how," he said, bending his head down to nuzzle her neck gently.

"Garrett, stop that," she whispered sharply, his lips trailing light kisses around her ear, sending cold shivers rippling up her spine.

"Ummmmm . . . you smell good," he sighed, his mouth searching down her neck sensuously. "Why don't you get off your bandwagon, sweetheart, and take a break." His mouth was slowly making its way to her lips.

"Garrett . . . ummmmmm . . ." Chandra's remark was cut off by his lips as they found hers. She could faintly taste the liquor as his mouth opened over hers, his tongue reaching out to brush gently with hers. For some reason Chandra gave no thought to resisting his kiss this time. On the contrary, her arms came up to circle his neck as she leaned into his strong body, her tongue joining his with a sigh of ecstasy.

"See how much nicer this is," he murmured in a low, husky growl as his mouth left hers to wander over her eyes, her nose, then back to capture her lips again. His hands were running lightly across her back, his fingers gently caressing each place that they touched.

"Garrett, I've got to get you home," she groaned softly. He cut off her next words with another long, seductive kiss. Chandra knew she should pull away from him, but all her powers of reasoning had simply vanished. Even though she knew he was slightly drunk and it was the liquor that provoked his amorous mood, she couldn't will herself to break the close embrace.

"Thasssss a good idea, sweetheart—let's go home. I want to make love to you," he agreed in a slurred tone of voice, his hands becoming more aggressive. This time as his mouth found hers it did so with a hungry urgency, his kiss growing from a gentle, exploring inquiry to a hot, demanding explosion of desire. Chandra swayed against him, her knees turning watery as he pressed her up close to his taut thighs. She could feel his mounting desire for her pressing into her leg. Her hands gripped the solid wall of his chest as she forced herself to push away from the kiss.

"Stop it!" she rasped out curtly, her breath coming in short gasps. "I've got to get you out of here before anyone notices just how drunk you are."

Garrett laughed stupidly, his voice becoming more slurred with each word. "I think you may be right, cupcake! I think I may have had one too many." He leaned against her heavily, pinning her against the wall again with his solid, heavy frame. His slightly muddled blue eyes met hers intently. "Will you do something for me, honey?"

"It depends," she told him skeptically. "What do you want?"

Garrett giggled and buried his face in her shoulder. "Get me another drink on the way out!"

Chandra pushed him away disgustedly. "You're not having anything more to drink tonight but black coffee." She led him over to an empty chair in the corner of the kitchen and sternly sat him down. "Now you sit right there until I get back. I'll go in and tell the Rhodeses we've decided to leave early, then I'll call a cab." She paused and looked at him unrelentingly. "I mean it, Garrett, don't you move from that chair," she cautioned sharply.

Garrett looked up at her from his chair, his brown hair tousled, his blue eyes slightly glassy, giving her an angelic smile. "I won't move," he promised sincerely.

"You'd better not if you don't want to embarrass yourself," she warned again grimly as she walked over to the kitchen door. "I'll be right back."

Hurriedly she made her way through the boisterous crowd, looking for Mr. and Mrs. Rhodes. She finally found them in deep conversation with the Parsonses. After a somewhat vague explanation had been given for her and Garrett's early departure, she excused herself and found the nearest phone. She gave a sigh of relief when she was assured a cab would be there momentarily. Gathering up both their coats, she hurried back to the kitchen.

Garrett was still sitting placidly in the chair she had put him in. When she walked through the door a smile lit his face again. "Are we still going home so I can make love to you?" he asked brightly.

"We're going home, but not for that reason," she told him sharply, trying to get his coat on him before the cab came.

"I thought that's why I had to sit there in that chair while you were gone," he grumbled disappointedly, doing little to assist her in getting his coat on. "So we could go home and—"

"Just hush up and get this coat on, Garrett!" Her patience had run out. If the Rhodeses should happen to wander in here and find their new Vice President in this drunken condition, Garrett could kiss his new job good-bye. *Which, come to think of it, might not be a bad idea,* Chandra thought spitefully. *At least this whole charade would be over with and my life could return to normal.*

With both coats finally on Chandra led him out the back door, the blast of cold, winter wind hitting them full force. The cab had just pulled up at the back entrance as the couple emerged. She managed to push Garrett into the back seat before curtly giving the cab driver her address, then climbed into the back seat beside him. Garrett immediately had her in his arms again. "Come here and keep me warm, sweetheart," he invited in a low, sexy voice, his hands going into the warm confines of her coat, reaching for her intimately.

Slapping his hands away irritably Chandra took hold of them and held them prisoner in her lap. "If you weren't so drunk you'd have your face slapped for all this pawing."

He jerked his hands loose and grinned at her angelically in the dark interior of the cab. "But I'm drunk, so you'll have to overlook my bad manners." He brought his hands back around her waist, burying his face in her neck and kissing his way down the front of her dress. His breath was warm and sweet on her bare skin, sending tiny shivers of longing through her body. Chandra felt his hand brush against her breast exploringly.

"Have you forgotten that I'm engaged to another man?" she snapped, jerking his hands away once more. She was becoming increasingly uneasy at the wild, wanton feelings he was bringing alive in her.

"No—but I could, dammit, if you would quit reminding me of it!" he mumbled testily, his mouth moving along her neck once again. "Why in the hell do you want to go and get married? Wouldn't you rather have your freedom than be tied down to one man for the rest of your life?"

Chandra closed her eyes, savoring the feel of his warm mouth moving seductively along the sensitive part of her ear. She caught her breath as his tongue began to trace wet circles around the lobe. "I happen to want just one man in my life. I want to keep house for him, have his children. . . ." she whispered weakly as his tongue worked its way down into the valley of her breast. He trailed feather kisses intimately around the gentle swell of her bosom, his breathing heavier now. *Phillip! I have to think of Phillip,* she chanted silently, her eyes squeezing tightly closed as wave after erotic wave of longing washed over her. How could she sit here like this and enjoy what he was doing!? What was it about him that could turn her knees to jelly and make her forget that she was soon to be married? Right now he was making her feel as if she were the most desirable woman in the world. Funny, although Phillip was every ounce a man, he had never aroused her in the wild, crazy way that Garrett so easily accomplished.

"You can have my children," he suggested huskily, his breathing matching hers.

Chandra's heart leaped wildly at his softly spoken words. "Careful, Garrett, you'll sober up and find yourself with a real wife," she murmured, her mouth playing moistly with his.

"No wife!" he groaned firmly. "Just come and live with me—be my lover," he whispered, his voice ragged. "I'll give you everything a wife should have, sweetheart, I'll take care of you. It could be good between us. . . ." He paused. "Hell, it could be more than good between us, it could be dynamite!" His mouth closed hungrily over hers.

"No . . ." she whispered helplessly, squirming away from his advances and his soft words. "No, I want more than that out of life. We would never make it together, Garrett, we are too different. Oh, why am I even trying to talk to you when you're in this condition," she snapped irritably as he slumped tiredly against her shoulder.

The cab pulled up in front of the deserted house, and Chandra maneuvered Garrett out the door. She hurriedly paid the fare, and the cab sped off into the dark night.

"How would you like to hear my version of 'Man of La Mancha,' " Garrett offered generously, stepping ahead of her to position himself in front on the steps. He let out the first, deep, loud note of a song before Chandra had firmly clapped her hand over his mouth.

"Garrett! The neighbors," she warned bleakly.

"I'll sing loud enough for them to hear it too," he assured her belligerently, his voice sounding miffed because she wouldn't let him finish the song.

"Just turn around and walk quietly into the house," she encouraged, pushing him ahead of her firmly.

Chandra unlocked the door and flipped on the lamp in the

living room. She shrugged out of her coat and laid it across the back of the sofa, then helped Garrett remove his.

"Thank you," he said courteously. "Let me help you with yours," he offered blindly.

"Mine's already off, you imbecile," she scoffed.

"Well, then," he slurred, swaying slightly toward her, "let me give you a little kiss for helping me with mine."

"No more kisses tonight. It's time we were in bed," she said firmly, turning him in the direction of the stairs.

"I agree—let's go to bed," he grinned, draping his arm around her neck. "Your room or mine?"

"Both—you're sleeping in yours, I'm sleeping in mine," she said, as they started up the stairs.

"Well, maybe you're right. I need to be more in control of my facultite . . . flacxitiv . . . more sober when I make love to you," he relented, stripping off his jacket and throwing it over the banister. He reached up to loosen his tie, then jerked it off, throwing it on the floor as he walked. By the time they reached his bedroom door and Chandra turned to face him, she saw with despair that he was standing behind her clad only in his brief underwear, a challenging grin on his face. "I knew you would want me to be ready for bed the minute we got here," he told her reasonably.

"Good grief!" she exploded, her face flushing a bright pink. "Couldn't you have waited until you reached your own room?"

"Don't be mad at me," he grinned sweetly, reaching out to pull her up against his broad, heavily haired chest. "You *know* how drunk I am," he reminded her again petulantly.

This was more than she could take! He buried her face in his chest with his large hands. Her stomach fluttered in despair as the fresh, clean, male scent of Garrett reached her. Her hands were trembling as she once again pushed him back regretfully. He had one of the most attractive bodies she had ever seen. Tall, broad shouldered, lean waist and hips, powerful thighs. . . . Her eyes stopped momentarily in another area, the skimpy briefs leaving nothing to her imagination. He certainly had nothing to apologize for there. Dragging her eyes on down, she noticed his entire body was coated heavily with light brown hair. All she could think of to say at the moment was an inadequate, "You're so hairy."

Garrett's mouth was on the move again as he turned her face up to meet his. "Yeah, hope you like your men hairy," he whispered, kissing her nose gently.

"No. I don't. Phillip . . . isn't hairy," she murmured, trying to avoid his searching lips. "I—I like men just like Phillip," she lied.

"Damn! Why do you always bring up that man's name?" Garrett dropped his arms, and it was he who pushed her away this time.

"I'm going to *marry* Phillip. Can't you understand that?" she told him.

"You're a fool," he stated calmly, walking on into his bedroom. "I'll bid you good night now." He bowed again to her, and Chandra smothered a smile at the picture he presented. A very courtly knight bowing to his lady in his briefs! "Foolish lady," he continued, "may your dreams be filled with nothing but hairless Phillips." Chandra stepped back as the door slammed loudly in her face.

With a weary shrug of her shoulders she made her way on down the hall to her own bedroom. After a quick shower she fell into bed, exhausted by the events of the evening. She assumed Garrett was asleep since she hadn't heard anything more out of him. She smiled to herself, thinking of the hangover he would have in the morning. *It would serve him right,* she thought smugly, *if he couldn't get out of bed for days.* He had better be properly thankful that she had gotten him away from the party before he made a complete fool of himself.

Unwanted thoughts of his kisses sprang up in her mind as her body began to relax slowly. No matter how she tried to deny it she knew that his kisses and caresses had been something new and totally thrilling to her. Maybe it was because he was so experienced, for she had no doubt that a man like Garrett would be a pro in the area of making love. Phillip had excited her . . . to a small degree, but comparing the two, well . . . she was afraid Garrett won, hands down. *What a total waste of such a beautiful man,* she thought wearily, her eyes closing. No woman would ever be able to claim him as hers alone. For some unknown reason, Chandra's eyes grew misty with unshed tears. That thought seemed to tug at her heart—an annoying ache tightened in her throat. She had to put him out of her mind and out of her life. She would be married in a little over three weeks. That's what she had to concentrate on now. She turned over on her side and punched her pillow roughly. *Darn you, Garrett Morganson!* she fumed.

A loud, shrill whistle suddenly filled the air, its abrupt sound startling Chandra. She sat straight up in bed and listened intently. Again the shrill whistle echoed through the quiet house, this time followed by a deep voice, "Chandra! Hey . . . Chandra Loring!"

Garrett! She had thought he was asleep an hour ago. She lay back down, hoping if she didn't answer he would leave her alone.

"Come on, Chandra, answer me, honey. I know you're awake. I heard you turning over," he told her bluntly.

"What do you want, Garrett?" she sighed tiredly, knowing that if she didn't answer him now he would only persist until she did.

"I've been lying here thinking. You like men who recite you poems, so I've decided I'll recite you one. Are you listening, sweetheart?"

"That's all right, Garrett," Chandra called back. "You don't have to right now—maybe in the morning." He was still obviously drunk as a skunk.

"No, if you want poetry—you'll get poetry! I'll even buy you some flowers if you want them," he offered good-heartedly.

"Go to sleep, please," she tossed back uselessly. By the tone of his voice she knew she was going to hear his poem, regardless!

There was a brief moment of silence from the other room, raising Chandra's hopes that he had given up and gone back to sleep. That illusion was shattered instantly as his tipsy voice floated back to her once again. "There once was an old farmer's daughter. Who knew a lot more than she oughter." He pronounced his words very concisely and clearly, intent on wooing the lady.

Chandra sat up in her bed, the phrase "old farmer's daughter" catching her ear. He surely wouldn't be telling her one of those horrible risqué poems the boys used to recite in school, would he?

Garrett's deep voice droned on with his recitation. "The boys made a pass"—Chandra's mouth dropped open wider with indignation the longer he spoke—"as she wiggled her—"

"Garrett Morganson!" Chandra's voice shot through his room like a speeding bullet.

"Yes, ma'am!" he shouted back instantly, his voice filled with obedience.

"Don't you say another word of that poem—do you hear me?!"

There was dead silence from his end of the house, then a small male voice floated through the air. "You didn't like it," he said disappointed.

"It was disgusting," she told him bluntly. "Go to sleep!"

Silence reigned over the house once again as she lay back down in her bed. The nerve of that guy, reciting a poem like that. He was nothing but a rowdy, crude . . . test pilot. For the life of her, she couldn't think of what was so bad about being a test pilot, but there must undoubtedly be something, since he was one!

Again, a loud whistle filled the air.

"What now!"

"I'm cold. There aren't enough blankets on this bed," he complained loudly.

"There's one in the closet next to your bed." He was worse than a child. They were never going to get to sleep at this rate.

"I can't find it," he yelled irritably, a few minutes later. "You'll have to come in here and find it for me."

Muttering some very explicit ideas on what Garrett could do

69

with his blanket after she found it, Chandra threw back her covers and slid out of the bed. She literally stomped down the hall to the guest room and yanked the door open loudly. "It's in plain sight, Garrett. . . ." Her voice trailed off as she was forcefully tackled around her knees and pulled over onto the bed by a pair of strong hairy arms.

"I know it—I was lying to you," Garrett confessed, his hands trying to still a squirming Chandra. "I was lonesome for you, little wife. I don't want to sleep alone."

"You . . ." Chandra sputtered, "you let me go!"

"Not until you tell me you're not mad at me," Garrett told her, holding her down tighter on the bed. She shoved at him roughly, knocking him off balance for a moment. But her strength was no match for his, and he easily flipped her over on her back and pinned her flatly to the mattress, holding both her wrists in one large hand.

"Now, I'm waiting," he breathed patiently, his eyes locking into hers.

"What am I supposed to say I'm not mad at you for?" she asked tightly, the fight draining out of her. He had her practically nailed to the bed. She couldn't move a muscle if she tried.

"For reciting that awful poem to you. You're right—that was a nasty thing to do, and I most humbly ask your forgiveness." His voice had dropped to a low whisper now, his hand gradually releasing its hard grip on her wrists.

"I'm not mad," Chandra said softly. "I just don't like for you to treat me like one of your . . . well, the kind of women you're used to," she finished lamely.

He chuckled softly, his face moving ever closer to hers. "Is that what I've been doing? If it is, I'm sorry—although the majority of the women I'm used to are just like you." He paused, then added gently, "Well, not *just* like you. Somehow, I've never met anyone just like you, Chandra Loring." His voice was deep, almost musical, as he tenderly stroked the blond wisps of hair away from her face. "You will forgive me for my deplorable actions tonight, won't you? To tell you the truth, sweetheart, I *am* more than a little drunk at this moment," he confessed wryly.

"You're forgiven," Chandra dismissed lightly, wanting to break the close contact with him again. "Can I go back to my bed now?"

"No," he coaxed quietly, "stay here with me for a while." His fingertips began to trace the outline of her face, touching it gently and wonderingly.

"I really shouldn't . . ." Chandra began, then lost even the will to argue anymore. She was tired of kidding herself. She didn't want to leave him. Reaching up to touch his face hesitantly, she let her fingers wander along the plains and hollows of his features, marveling at the feel of his skin against her hands. "You know you won't remember any of this in the morning, don't you?" she whispered shakily, her fingers trembling lightly. That was the only reason she was allowing this nonsense to go on—the only reason she was allowing herself the luxury of gently stroking his face in the dark. Her hands dropped down to bury themselves in the thick hair on his chest.

A low groan escaped him as she gently began to massage his chest, her small hands kneading his firm flesh in soft, exploring caresses.

"That's a strong penalty for a man to pay for drinking too much," he rasped weakly, her motions arousing him to fever pitch. His hands slid up underneath her gown, drawing her warm body nearer to his naked flesh.

"You haven't got any clothes on!" she accused guiltily, as his body met the feminine curves of hers with nothing in between.

"You haven't either," he defended, just before he slipped her gown over her head and let it drop onto the floor.

Every defense Chandra ever had against him seemed to dissolve. As Garrett's body blended with hers, a hot fire surged through her veins. This went against everything Chandra had ever been taught or believed in her life, but she was his to do with as he wanted. Somehow the name Phillip never entered her mind. All she could feel was the strength of Garrett's passion and

71

the uncompromising demand that his hunger for her be assuaged. His hands reverently worshiped her trembling body, his eyes gazing into hers with a blaze of unconcealed desire.

"I want to make love to you, you know that?" he pleaded huskily.

"Yes, I know that," Chandra yielded softly.

The blue of his eyes suddenly turned dark as his passion flared brighter. Then a strange look of pleading indecision came into them as he whispered tormentedly, "No ties . . . no strings attached . . . I can't promise you . . ."

She placed her hand over his mouth, stopping his flow of words. "No ties, no strings, Garrett," Chandra said lovingly. Not for him at least, but for Chandra, he would be the first man who had ever made her feel this way, so she couldn't honestly tell him that this was not an important time in her life. No, she would always remember him. How could one forget paradise?

Their lips met hesitantly as Chandra felt tears well up in her eyes. Even though he didn't love her, she would make this a night for him to remember, this hour a sweet, sweet memory.

He moaned quietly as he buried his face in her neck, squeezing her tightly. "Damn," he muttered miserably. "Remind me never to drink again."

Chandra smiled and hugged him tighter. What was happening to her? Was she actually falling in love with this man? That would surely lead to heartbreak.

She waited for his kiss, eager for his caresses to begin again. She waited, and she waited, and she waited.

"Garrett?" she nudged softly.

The sounds of soft snoring reached her ears as she sat up slightly in the dark and stared at the limp form draped over half her body. "Garrett?" she murmured more loudly this time.

The snoring grew louder as Garrett rolled over onto his stomach and covered his head with his pillow.

Chandra stared at the wilted form in bed beside her. He was asleep! Passed out! Here she was, ready to give herself to him in the throes of passion, and he had passed out cold. She didn't

72

know whether to laugh or cry. Then she started to do both. Gales of laughter erupted from her as tears of frustration slid down her face. She should be down on her knees thanking her guardian angel that she hadn't made a fool of herself, but here she was sitting in bed with the best-looking, most virile man she had ever met in her life, and he was peacefully sleeping away. She picked up her pillow and smacked him hard across his rump. "Darn you anyway, Garrett Morganson. You have been nothing but a thorn in my side from the minute I laid eyes on you. How could you do this to me, you . . . you . . . test pilot!"

She hopped out of bed and disgustedly threw the covers back over Garrett's sleeping form. Slamming out of his room loudly (who cared, he couldn't have heard World War III), she marched furiously back to her room and threw herself across her bed in misery. How could she have lost control? Did her commitment to Phillip mean so little to her? The thought scared her. Maybe, just maybe, she wasn't really in love with Phillip at all. She closed her eyes, her temper dissolving rapidly. She had to get hold of herself. Nothing had happened between her and Garrett. She could still marry Phillip without the slightest twinge of conscience . . . well, almost. Tonight was going to be put behind her and never thought about again. Chances were Garrett would never remember this evening, and she sure wasn't about to enlighten him on the events that had taken place. No, she had learned a valuable lesson tonight—one that would stick with her for the rest of her life.

Chandra crawled under her covers, suddenly very tired. She lay back wearily, her thoughts finally churning to a halt. Yes sir, she had learned something very valuable tonight, and she wouldn't forget it. For the next two hours she stared at the ceiling of her dark bedroom trying her best to figure out what it was she had learned.

CHAPTER FIVE

Even after her perfectly wretched night, Chandra was up bright and early the next morning making a fast trip out to the mailbox in her robe, dropping the wedding invitations in and hurrying back into the warm house. Considering the night she had had Chandra felt surprisingly well this morning, zipping around her mom's kitchen, exhibiting some of the old enthusiasm that had been so sadly missing in her life of late.

I don't know why I should feel so different this morning, she mused to herself as she wiped away the heavy steam on the kitchen window to peer out into the early frosty morning. After last night, she should really be feeling down in the dumps, but for some strange reason she wasn't. Deciding to enjoy the feeling, whatever the reason, she walked over and put on the coffee pot. *I wonder how* he'll *feel this morning,* she wondered as she slipped a piece of bread into the toaster. She shuddered slightly as she remembered how close she had come to disaster with Garrett last night. Chandra had always viewed sex as something very personal, not to be given lightly. She had always felt that no matter what the morals of the day were, she was a bit old-fashioned in feeling that the man had to be someone special. For her, going from bed to bed would be a shallow, empty life. It wasn't what she wanted.

The toaster shot her piece of toast up in the air, and Chandra retrieved it before it hit the floor. *That old thing needs to be replaced,* she pondered idly as she spread the bread with butter and jam. She brought the toast up to her mouth and was just getting ready to take a bite when Garrett appeared at the doorway.

"Hi!" she greeted exuberantly. "Are you hungry?"

Garrett's face was ashen gray, his eyes looked like road maps, his hair was tossed wildly about his head, a dark stubble outlined his sagging jaw, and his stance pleaded for mercy. In essence he looked like death warmed over. "Do you have any aspirin?" he managed sickly.

"Sure!" she grinned cheerfully. "Have you got a headache?"

Garrett sagged against the door frame holding on tight for support. "You might say that," he agreed sourly. "It's either that or a brain concussion." He walked slowly over to the kitchen table and wilted into a chair.

"Oh," she moaned in mock sympathy, "are you not feeling up to snuff this morning? Maybe you're coming down with a bug," she heckled, biting her lip to keep from laughing in his face. He looked awful.

"Just get me the damn aspirin, clown. Can't you see I'm dying?" he pleaded, holding his head in his hands.

"Okay—you hold my toast." She handed him the sticky piece of bread covered in butter and orange marmalade. "Don't eat it," she warned as she went in search of the aspirin bottle.

Garrett's face turned varying shades of green as he stared at the rich glob in his hands. With a muttered expletive he threw it down on the table, his stomach churning violently.

Chandra was back in a few minutes shaking out a couple of aspirins into his trembling hand. She poured a glass of orange juice, handing it to him silently. He downed the pills, then took a small sip of the juice.

"How about some coffee?" she offered. "It might help."

"I'll try anything," he said defeatedly.

Chandra poured him a cup of hot coffee and set it before him. She really did feel sorry for him this morning. Apparently he wasn't used to drinking in the quantities he had consumed last night.

As if he had been reading her thoughts, he asked guiltily,

"What happened last night? The only thing I remember is getting to the party. From then on, my mind's a blank."

Chandra felt a small stab of disappointment that he didn't remember anything of the night before, but then reasoned that she really hadn't expected him to. It was better this way.

"I hope I didn't make a fool out of myself," he was continuing morosely. "I should never drink that many martinis on an empty stomach." He paused and took a sip of the black coffee, then looked at Chandra pleadingly. "Well, did I?"

"Did you what?" she asked innocently.

"Make a fool out of myself, dammit!"

"Watch your language," she reminded sweetly. "No, I don't think so . . . unless you want to count the incident when you had Mrs. Rhodes down on the floor trying to Indian wrestle her—"

"Oh, Lord!" A groan of agony erupted from Garrett. The look of sheer panic on his ashen face was too much for Chandra to bear. She broke out laughing, reaching over to give him an assuring pat. "I was only teasing you—no, we left the party before anyone realized how much you had had to drink."

Garrett's blue eyes filled with gratitude as he caught one of her hands in his. "I suppose I have you to thank for that," he said gratefully.

The feel of his hand on hers was warm and reassuring, and Chandra treasured the loving feeling that swept over her. "I knew you had drunk more than you realized," she answered gently.

"You're quite a lady, do you know that?" His eyes still held hers tenderly.

"Thank you—you're quite a man," she returned truthfully.

"What fool's firing a shotgun this early in the morning?" he asked, changing the subject abruptly, his eyes still locked with hers.

Chandra smiled up at him sweetly, her eyes never leaving his. "No one, that's the coffee pot perking again."

He dropped his head back down into his hands miserably.

"My head is splitting." The shrill ring of the phone caused him to bury his head even deeper—his face a mask of discomfort.

Chandra picked up the receiver hurriedly to ease his pain. The sound of Phillip's voice stunned her for a moment. "Hi, honey. Were you sitting right by the phone?"

"No . . . yes . . ." she stuttered uneasily. "Phillip . . . I wasn't expecting you to call until this evening."

At the mention of Phillip's name, Garrett raised his head to look at her.

"There's no law that says a man can't call his girl anytime he wants, is there?" Phillip said happily. "Miss me, honey?"

"Yes, I miss you, Phillip," she fibbed slightly. "Everything going smoothly at the office?"

"It goes smoother when you're here, but the business is still intact," he replied. "How are the wedding plans coming along? Have you got the invitations all mailed out?"

"I mailed them this morning. There's nothing left now but the last-minute preparations." Chandra felt strangely uneasy, talking with Phillip while Garrett was in the room. He was listening to every word she said.

"Just a few more weeks, honey, then we'll be man and wife. Does that make you as happy as it does me?"

Oh, Phillip, she despaired quietly. *I don't know what to say to you. My thoughts are as jumbled as my life right now.* Trying to answer him honestly she replied, "Any woman would be proud to be your wife, Phillip."

Garrett's blue eyes locked momentarily with hers before he calmly walked over and poured himself a fresh cup of coffee. He leaned back on the kitchen counter and surveyed her casually as she continued her conversation with her fiancé.

"I'm a lucky man." Phillip's voice had dropped to that of a lover. "Do you love me?"

Chandra bit her lower lip. She did love him . . . but not the way she should. Oh, dear Lord! Was she really willing to admit that to herself? "Oh, Phillip, you know I do," she answered lightly.

"Well, then say it!" he encouraged. "You're always saying I don't tell you enough—now I want to hear you say you love me."

Chandra cleared her throat nervously. Phillip *never* was vocal in expressing his love. Why did he have to pick this time to ask her to declare hers? "I love you . . ." her voice trailed off weakly as she saw the blue of Garrett's eyes darken to a stormy coolness.

"That's better. Well, I got to run, honey. I'm due in court at nine. I'll call you later next week—I'll be out of town the rest of this one and part of next."

"Oh, yes, the Marcell case," she responded absently, remembering the hours she had spent typing the depositions on the case.

"Yes, I hope to wrap it up before the honeymoon. I don't want anything to spoil that time for us. I have tickets to most of the sporting events in Ontario that week."

"Oh, really. . . . How nice." She was trying her best to fake some sort of enthusiasm. "Well, call me when you get back."

After a few more personal remarks to her Phillip's end of the line went dead. She replaced the receiver in the cradle slowly, relieved that the conversation was over.

"I take it that was Philbert," Garrett issued tightly as he walked back over to seat himself at the table.

"Phillip," she curtly reminded him. "Yes, that was him."

"I suppose he's champing at the bit to get his little bride off on the honeymoon."

"That's right," she agreed pleasantly.

"I suppose he's everything a girl could want in a man," he continued almost to himself, "steady, wants a vine-covered cottage, kids, the whole shootin' match. A veritable paragon of virtue," he spat out.

"That's right," she agreed again. Phillip was all those things and those were all the things that Chandra wanted—so why didn't they sound more ideal coming from Garrett's mouth?

The phone loudly signaled another caller as Garrett winced slightly in pain from the unexpected noise.

With a sigh Chandra picked up the phone once more. This time it was Sara Rhodes calling to say they would be by in an hour to show them the Miller house. Chandra had nearly forgotten their promise to take a look at it.

"What are we going to do about that?" she asked grimly as she hung up the phone. "They want us to look at the house this morning."

Garrett shrugged unconcernedly. "I suppose we'll take a look at it."

"What are you going to say when they practically throw the house in your lap? They want us . . . to have it," her voice trailed off in despair. She *would not* let herself think about what it could be like if she and Garrett were really married and looking for a home of their own. That thought was becoming too painful for her.

"I'll probably have to buy it," he said flatly. "I'll need somewhere to live. One place is as good as another."

"You'd want a big house . . . all by yourself?" she asked wonderingly, her eyes meeting his again.

"Who knows—maybe you're right. I might decide to find someone permanent one of these days and bring her home to live with me." He straightened to leave.

"Just bring her home to live with you . . . no marriage." Chandra's tone of voice was flat. He was a hopeless case.

Garrett paused beside her, looking at her coldly. "Why worry about my affairs? I should think you would have your hands full planning your own wedding."

Chandra stared back at him, her pulse fluttering weakly. Even in this morning's disreputable condition, he was so handsome he took her breath away. She longed to put her arms around his strong neck and kiss away the pain of last night. If she could just feel his arms around her again . . . Her thoughts dwindled. She was chasing rainbows. Instead of looking at his fine points she was going to have to find something about him she didn't like.

"Garrett," she said firmly.

"What?" He was still looking at her as they stood in the doorway.

"Do you like sports?"

Garrett's face turned a total blank for a moment. "What?"

"Do you like sports," she repeated. "It's a simple question. Sports—you know—football, baseball, bask—"

"I know what the damn question was! What I don't know is how it came flying out of left field like that," he said disgustedly. "I thought we were discussing the house."

"Just answer the question," she returned curtly.

"No, I don't particularly like sports. I can take them or leave them. Sometimes I'm interested in who won or lost—but I can get that out of the paper. Does that answer your question?"

Chandra's face fell to the floor. There went that theory. "Yes, that answered my question," she said in a depressed tone.

"I'm going up to clean up before the Rhodeses come. Give me a couple more of those aspirins, will you?" Garrett asked her as he turned to leave the room.

Chandra shook the pills out into his hand once again, her fingers trembling slightly. It might take her a while to find something about him that she really didn't like, but she was determined she was going to.

The next few hours were the most exciting, yet depressing, Chandra had ever spent. The Rhodeses had taken them to the Millers' house, and Chandra had fallen in love with it immediately. Its spacious, Spanish-style construction won her heart before the door was unlocked. She had excitedly explored every room of the house, forgetting for the moment that she would not be living here. She had grabbed Garrett's hand and shown him the different parts of the house she was so thrilled with, exclaiming over all the beautifully draped windows. She had paused with him in front of the large master bedroom pointing out all its splendid features, blushing a soft pink when he had looked at her with a grin on his face. "I take it you like the house."

"Oh—well . . ." Chandra caught herself, trying to stifle some of her exuberance. "Of course, it doesn't matter if *I* like the house. . . ." Then her excitement broke loose again. "Oh, Garrett, I *love* the house. You will too," she promised eagerly. "It's the perfect house for you. Any girl you bring home . . ." She paused, fighting the jealousy that surged through her, then continued more sedately. "Any girl you bring home would love this house."

Garrett smiled at her teasingly. "Now, be honest, Chandra. Do you like the house or not?" He was amused at the excitement she had radiated from the minute they had stepped inside the door.

"Oh, Garrett," she hung her head in embarrassment. "I know I'm acting like an idiot. Please, don't tease me. I love this house."

He tipped her face up by the chin with one of his long fingers. "Then I love it, too. I'll buy it on one condition."

"What's that?" she asked, drowning in his look.

"That you'll help me furnish it, before you cut out on me."

"Garrett . . ."

"No buts. What're a few more days going to hurt," he reasoned softly. "Satisfy Mrs. Rhodes's maternal instinct and let her help you shop for furniture. They'll be gone in a week, then you can get back to"—his clear eyes grew cloudy—"to your life," he finished gently.

"All right," she agreed reluctantly. She couldn't find the words to refuse him. She knew it was wrong, she knew that she would be the one to come out of this with the battle scars, but it suddenly didn't matter. If she could spend a few more days with him, she would. She'd pay the piper later.

"That's my lady," he told her huskily. His mouth descended to meet hers slowly. She moaned softly in her throat as their tongues met in sweet reunion, her arms going up around his neck. He pulled her tightly into him as he hungrily devoured the softness of her mouth. His kiss was different this time. It seemed to take on an urgency between them. He held her close, his large body nearly absorbing her slender frame. His hands moved restlessly across her back. It was as if he didn't want to let her go, as if there wouldn't be a next time for them.

The sound of the Rhodeses moving down the hall caught Chandra's ear, and she tried to pull away from his kiss. He caught her back to him roughly, murmuring her name once.

"Chandra . . . come back here. . . ." His mouth took hers roughly this time, his passion nearly out of check. She could taste the saltiness of the blood from her lip as his mouth ground almost violently into hers. She wondered if he was giving the kiss in desire or in punishment.

"Ooooops, excuse me," John Rhodes called merrily as he sauntered down the hall. "Hate to break this up, but I wanted to see the master bedroom again."

Chandra smiled shakily as Garrett hesitantly broke the kiss. His eyes were a cold, icy blue as he looked at her. Chandra wondered if she had done something to anger him. "That's all right, Mr. Rhodes, I was just showing it to Garrett myself."

Garrett seemed to be having a hard time bringing himself under control. He had walked on into the bedroom, keeping his back to them as he stared moodily out the large window.

"What do you think, Garrett, do you like the house?" John Rhodes asked hopefully.

Garrett didn't answer for a moment, then in a tense voice he acknowledged Mr. Rhodes's question. "Chandra loves the house."

"Well, good, good, I knew you would. You can have possession today if you want it. If the price is right with you, we can wrap this up quickly."

"Chandra?" Garrett turned, his eyes meeting hers for approval.

"That's fine with me," she said softly, her eyes lovingly caressing his.

"Then, I guess it's settled. The Morgansons have just bought their first home," John Rhodes beamed. "Wait 'till I tell Sara." He left the room at a dead run.

"You will keep your promise and stay, won't you?" Garrett asked quietly, never moving from the window.

"Yes, I'll stay a few more days, Garrett." Her heart felt very heavy at the moment. Her love for him was bursting at the seams, and she prayed he wouldn't be able to read it in her eyes.

"But only until the Rhodeses leave," she added gently. "I only have a few more weeks before—"

"The wedding," Garrett finished tiredly. "I know. This will all be over in time for your wedding, Chandra. I'll see to that personally."

"Thank you," she answered calmly. Her mind was screaming for him to ask her to forget the wedding, but he showed no signs of doing that.

He stood looking at her for a few more minutes before he crossed the room and pushed coldly by her. "We might as well get this wrapped up," he said curtly, walking out into the hall.

Yes, we might as well, Chandra thought forlornly as she followed his broad back down the hall of their new home. A few more days was all she had, but she would have her memories forever.

Events moved so rapidly from that moment on that Chandra could scarcely believe that within twenty-four hours she and Garrett were starting to move into their new house. She couldn't help it, that was how she had started to view the house. She knew it was wrong, she berated herself religiously for daydreaming, but she didn't have the strength to stop herself. When he walked into a room her day brightened, her world suddenly felt right. It was all going to end, but for now it was her home, and he was her husband.

"What is this, Chandra?" Garrett's deep voice reached her from the front door as she was putting away a few dishes they had bought earlier at a department store. Garrett was holding up a tightly rolled blanket in his hand as she walked into the living room.

"My bed," she grinned pertly.

"This thing?" Garrett was looking at the sleeping bag warily. "You don't think I'm going to let you sleep on this, do you?"

"Sure! I figure I can make my bed right here in front of the fireplace. I love fires on a cold winter night," she told him sincerely.

"Aren't they supposed to deliver the bedroom furniture to-day?" he asked, ignoring her declaration of independence.

"Yes, but you sleep—"

"You can take the master bedroom for right now," he broke in curtly.

"No!" She stood up to face him defiantly. "No, I will not sleep in that bedroom. I want to sleep in here, Garrett . . . please." Her eyes pleaded silently with his to grant her request. She would die before she slept in that big, lonely bed without him.

"Dammit, Chandra . . . have it your own way," he relented heatedly. "I was only trying to . . ." His voice fell off in despair. "If you want to sleep in here, then do it."

What's his problem, she thought irritably. It was *his* house, *his* bed. He had been testy all day. Actually, he had been in a bad mood ever since they had looked at the house yesterday. Chandra supposed it was because he was saddled with a house now, on top of a fake wife, but that wasn't her fault. He was the one who kept insisting that they play this charade out. If he wanted her to leave, all he had to do was say so!

"It's your house, Garrett. I'm not going to take your bedroom," she snapped testily.

"All right, all right!" He threw up his hands in surrender. "Sleep on the damn floor. I'll be a real gentleman and take the only bed in the house," he sneered.

"Fine," she agreed, turning back to finish her unpacking. "What's all the fuss about anyway?"

"You're as stubborn as a jackass, that's what the fuss is about," he answered in a surly tone of voice, throwing the bed-roll down in front of the fireplace.

"So? That's not your problem. You aren't going to have to live with me," she chided flippantly, walking back to the kitchen.

"Thank God," he muttered sarcastically, following right behind.

"Praise the Lord," she mocked back arrogantly, placing the dishes and coffee cups neatly in the cabinet.

They worked quietly and alone for the rest of the afternoon, putting away the household items they had bought in a frenzied shopping trip the night before. By the time the evening meal had been eaten, and Chandra had had her bath, she was totally exhausted. She was almost glad that Phillip had agreed to live in her apartment for a while after their marriage. She didn't think she would have the stamina to go through this again anywhere in the near future.

She lay down in her sleeping bag, wiggling her toes in delight. It felt so good just to stretch out and relax. Garrett had given her a dirty look as she'd passed him on the way out of the bathroom, his look clearly telling her he was still put out with her.

She yawned and stretched again, mentally going over a checklist in her mind. She had called Darrell's office this morning and left a message for him when he returned. She had simply told him she had decided to stay with a friend until Mom got home. With his work schedule he wouldn't have time to question her message. With any luck at all she would be back home before he started to wonder where his sister had disappeared to. Phillip was gone on a business trip and wouldn't call until next week— the same with her mom and dad. She could afford to stay here with Garrett another four or five days at the most. After that the game would be over.

The fire hissed and popped merrily in the fireplace, casting its rosy shadows across the room. The wind had come up again outside, blowing blustery and cold. Chandra snuggled down deeper into her bedroll, relaxing in her warm "bed." She could hear Garrett moving quietly around in his room. The department store had delivered the bedroom furniture they had picked out together the night before. It was dark, heavy oak, suitable for any man's taste, yet furniture that any woman would fall in love with. He had insisted that she make the final choice, and she had happily picked what now sat beautifully in his room. Chandra sighed and turned over on her back to stare at the flames flickering on the ceiling. This was going to be a lot harder than she realized, picking out the furniture for his home. It was proving to be a bittersweet experience. It hurt terribly to think that she was decorating this house for some nameless woman who would soon be its new mistress. The woman who would someday have Garrett's children, sleep in that big lovely bed with him—she broke her thoughts off quickly. She could not afford to think in this vein. Phillip! That's who she had to think of. As the fire burned lower she finally floated off to a sound sleep, with visions drifting through her mind of hockey players skating around rudely, trying to knock each other's brains out, sitting in their little penalty boxes.

With a start, Chandra sat straight up. What was that noise? She listened intently to the rising wind, then she heard it again. It sounded as if someone were trying to get in the front door.

Breaking out in a cold sweat she crawled carefully out of her bedroll, her eyes never leaving the creaking door. On hands and knees she crawled silently across the living room, reaching the safety of the hall. Still on her knees she crept silently down to Garrett's bedroom, her heart racing madly. She could still barely hear the strange scraping and thumping above the sound of the whistling wind. Pushing open the bedroom door she crept silently up to the side of his bed. She could hear his quiet heavy breathing as he lay in bed, totally unaware of the danger that confronted them both.

"Garrett!" she whispered loudly.

Garrett mumbled something under his breath and rolled over in the bed to the other side.

In exasperation she crawled quickly around to the other side of his bed, determined to get him awake without alerting the impending intruder. She didn't dare stand up and turn on a light; she was too afraid. Maybe she shouldn't even be whispering, she thought belatedly, as she stopped by the side of the bed once more. Deciding to reach up and shake him awake, she extended her hand up over the bed and grabbed the bare arm that was hanging limply over the side.

As her cold hand closed around his bare flesh, Garrett sat straight up in bed as if a bolt of lightning had hit him.

"What the hell—" He was on his feet in an instant, groping wildly in the dark for the unknown assailant.

"Garrett!" Chandra hissed angrily. "Shhhhhhhhh, there's someone trying to get in the front door." She was still on her hands and knees peeking over the side of the bed.

"Chandra . . ." Garrett was fighting for a clear head after being awakened from a sound sleep. "What in the *hell* are you doing on the floor in the middle of the night, grabbing my arm in the dark? You realize what I could have done to you?" he challenged angrily.

"I'm sorry," she whispered back snappishly, "but there's someone trying to break in the front door."

"Are you sure?" he asked irritably.

"Do you think I'm going to come crawling in here in the middle of the night and make up a story like that? Of course, I'm sure," she blazed.

"All right! Just calm down. I'll go check the noise out." He reached for his trousers lying on the bedroom chair.

"Garrett . . . be careful, I'm scared." Chandra's voice sounded very small in the dark room.

"I'm sure it's just the wind," he grumbled, angrily zipping up the fly of his pants. "Just one more reason *I* avoid marriage. Women's wild imaginations," he growled, looking at her pointedly.

"There's a ball bat one of the Miller children left in the hall closet. You'd better take that with you," she urged, ignoring his antimarriage theory.

"Stay right here," he snapped curtly as he slipped quietly out of the bedroom door.

Chandra hopped up into his bed to get warm, her feet feeling like chunks of ice after crawling around on the cold floor. She couldn't hear any sounds coming from the dark hall and living room. What if the burglar had actually gotten into the house while she was trying to wake Garrett? He could be lying in wait for Garrett to come walking into the dark room.

Chandra wrung her hands in anxiety. She really shouldn't be

such a coward—she should be in there helping him! Slipping out of the warm bed, she stepped onto the cold floor. She had to help him. If anything happened to him she'd never forgive herself. She crept silently back down the hall, holding her breath, listening for any sign of struggle. She peeked carefully around the door and, seeing no sign of Garrett, bolted on over to her sleeping roll and climbed into it quickly, covering up her head. The fire had died down to embers, casting a very dim light into the room. She lay as still as a statue as she waited for Garrett to make his rounds through the house. Peeking out of her hideout a few minutes later she could barely make out his tall form sneaking quietly out of the kitchen, a child's ball bat clutched tightly in his hand.

He approached her bedroll and instead of alerting him to her presence she simply reached out and latched onto his bare ankle, calling his name softly. "Garrett, I decided to come in here—" The words were nearly crammed back down her throat as he literally pounced on her, pinning her to the floor tightly. His heavy weight nearly knocked the breath out of her.

"Garrett, stop it!" she yelled, fighting to get his dead weight off her aching body. "Get off me, you big oaf!"

"Dammit, is that you again, Chandra?!" His voice was shooting fire.

"Yes, it's me—get off!" she bellowed. "You're breaking my arm!"

"I'm going to break every damn bone in your body if you don't quit sneaking around in the dark, grabbing out at me. Is that clear?!" He shoved off her in extreme agitation.

"Did you scare the burglar away?" she asked hurriedly as she sat up in her bedroll to face him.

"There wasn't any burglar. It was the wind flapping a loose shutter around," he hissed shortly. "Come on—you're coming with me." He took her by the arm and jerked her to her feet.

"Where are we going?" she asked resentfully. He didn't have to treat her so nastily. She was sure there was a burglar!

88

"You're sleeping in my bed for the rest of the night," he replied tensely, pulling her along behind him.

"What . . . ? I certainly am not," she protested indignantly. "What would I tell Phill—"

"I don't give a damn what you tell Phillip," he exploded, yanking her on down the hall. "You've scared ten years off my life tonight, lady, and I don't plan on lying back down in that bed until I make damn good and sure where you are."

"You're cussing again," she reminded curtly as he stalked on into the bedroom, shoving her none too gently onto the bed.

"Tell it to the wall, lady. I'll cuss if I want to."

"You're nothing but a bully—a mean, cussin' bully," she tossed back defiantly as she landed in the middle of the bed.

"That's right. I'm a mean, low-down, cussing bully! Now go to sleep before I call your fiancé and have him come take you off my hands," he threatened, jerking his trousers back off irritably.

"Don't you dare get in this bed," she warned hysterically.

Garrett stonily climbed into the bed, completely ignoring her shouting tirade. Chandra sat up on her side of the bed, her arms crossed, staring daggers at his broad, bare back. He was such a . . . brute! How could she have ever thought she was in love with him? Phillip was an angel compared to this gorilla. Well, he could only push her so far. She was going to have the last word in this little border skirmish.

Reaching over, she maliciously jerked the pillow from beneath his head and slammed it down between them. She did the same with her own pillow, creating a foam barrier. Garrett didn't move a muscle as she made her protective fence. He was completely ignoring her temper tantrum.

"Don't you dare cross over that line," she warned, raising up to see if he was listening to her. "Understand?"

"That not only was childish," he commented dryly, "it was a waste of time. I have no intention of trying to seduce you. I'm leaving it all for good old virtuous Phineas."

Chandra's temper boiled. She leaned over and pecked him

roughly on his shoulder with her fingernail. He turned over and his sleepy eyes met hers. "Now what?"

"'Garrett, look at my lips. Now watch me carefully." She enunciated carefully. "My fiancé's name is Phillip. Phillip Benjamin Watson the third."

With a short snort of disgust Garrett rolled back over. "You would have thought his parents could have come up with something better than that," he jeered.

"You're impossible!"

"And you're a dippy broad. Now, pipe down and let me get some sleep."

"I'll pipe down," she said wiggling down on her side of the bed, "but I'm going home in the morning, so just don't try to talk me out of it."

"I won't," he assured her sleepily.

Drat him anyway, she thought tearfully. *Things were going so smoothly until today. Oh well, it's for the best.* Things couldn't go on forever like this. Tomorrow she would go back home and think of nothing but her upcoming wedding to Phelan . . . Phillip!

Chandra could hear the cold wind whipping violently around the bare branches of the trees as she pushed away the barrier blocking her heat and snuggled closer to the warm object lying next to her. She buried her face into the soft warmth, breathing in the clean, tantalizing smell that reached her nostrils. She wrapped her arms around the source of such radiating heat, delighting in the soft, sensuous feeling of lying next to something so wonderful, so comforting. She could feel light touches on her neck, then down her shoulder, feather-soft kisses following the same path. She sighed blissfully, arching her neck for easier access.

The kisses strayed gently across her breasts, pausing, then becoming soft nibbles on her nipples, making their tips grow taut and hard. Chandra groaned, her mouth searching for fulfillment. An eager, moist mouth met hers and she responded anxiously. Her tongue mingled playfully then passionately with the other.

90

The hands that were intimately exploring her body held her captive in a world of sensous pleasure, sending shivers of longing rippling through her body. Her hands began to move slowly, her fingers acquainting themselves with the ridges of sinewy hard, rippling back muscles. She heard a low, agonizing groan as her hand traveled downward, touching everything within its path—molding, caressing—until it was grabbed firmly and stopped. Feeling slighted, Chandra groaned disappointedly, bringing her hand back down to gently caress once again.

"Chandra—dammit . . ." A male voice came to her. "Do you know what you're doing to me?" The same warm mouth closed back over hers, capturing it with a rough urgency.

"Mmmmm . . . Garrett . . ." she whispered between heated kisses, her hands working slowly through his hair-roughened chest. "You feel so good," she told him drowsily as his mouth began to wander back down her neck, exploring every inch with fevered kisses. Once again his mouth found her breasts, his tongue flicking lightly over them. Groaning, he buried his face in them, breathing in the sweet, flowery fragrance of her.

"Honey, are you awake?" he whispered in a strangled husky-sounding voice, his hands stroking down the curve of her satiny hip. "I don't want to take advantage of you, sweetheart, but I'm not drunk this time," he murmured helplessly. "I can't take much more of this, Chandra." He began working his way back up her body, leaving a trail of urgent kisses in his wake.

"I want you, Garrett," Chandra murmured, only vaguely aware of his strange statement. She stroked his buttocks gently, feeling his passion for her mounting steadily. She was still groggy but awake enough to know who the comforting warmth had become.

"Oh, baby, I want you, too," he groaned painfully, his mouth searching hungrily again for hers. They kissed long, slow, drugging kisses, the fire inside them building into a raging inferno. They touched each other's bodies eagerly, their hands stoking the fire higher. Garrett's hand touched and lightly stroked Chandra's secret hidden places, urging her to match his own overpowering needs. *I shouldn't be letting him do this,* she thought languidly. *I'm going to be married soon—but I love him. . . . Oh, dear Lord, I've fallen in love with him!*

Garrett slid on top of her urgently, his kisses hot, fiery, and completely out of control.

Chandra could feel his body trembling as he posed over her, supporting his weight from her body with his arms.

"I want this to be something special," he whispered, his eyes glowing with desire for her. "I've wanted you from the first night I saw you."

She reached up and drew his mouth back down to hers, eager for his touch once again. "I want you too, Garrett. I want to always remember the time we have together," she whispered, her fingers stroking the thick mass of his brown hair.

"You'll remember it," he growled low. "I promise you that. You'll always remember me."

He began to move gently with her. Together they began to climb to heights only dreamt of before. Wave after wave of sensation enveloped Chandra as Garrett more than amply proved his words. She would remember this as long as she lived, she thought languidly as she clung to him, her body blending in rapture with his. He took them both to a point where she knew she would explode with desire for him. She arched against him, begging for fulfillment. When she thought she could bear no more, he took her beyond all her expectations, their bodies both bursting with agonizing pleasure at the same time.

Garrett held on to her tightly as they both descended from their mist of passion, still exchanging heated kisses. Chandra was breathing raggedly as she buried her face in his shoulder, murmuring his name over and over again when she finally caught her breath. He stroked her hair tenderly, pushing back the moist, wet tendrils from her face. His fingers felt the wetness of her tears as he pulled her tighter into the shelter of his arms.

"Regrets already?" he asked gently, his hands moving over her bare back consolingly.

"Never," she murmured, raising her face up to meet his, kissing him again. "I'll always remember tonight, Garrett."

"You're one hell of a woman, do you know that?" he said admiringly, his eyes moving gently over her flushed face.

"I hope I made you happy." She reached out to trace the outline of his lips with her finger. She would give anything to hear him say he loved her, show any indication that he cared for her.

"You made me happy, sweetheart, and you're not leaving in the morning," he said firmly, pulling them both down into the bed, covering them with a light blanket.

Her heart soared. "You don't want me to?" she asked hopefully.

"I think we ought to forget about that fight we had and"—his voice faltered—"see this thing through."

Chandra fought back the tears as his words washed over her. He wasn't going to tell her he loved her. All that mattered to him was his job and to carry on this ridiculous fake marriage. Well, she was a fool of the biggest kind, and she deserved everything she got. He made no bones about his feelings on marriage. Garrett Morganson would belong to no woman—least of all her. The tears slipped silently down on her pillow as sleep overtook them both, still wrapped in each other's arms.

CHAPTER SIX

"It is truly hard to believe what you have done to that house in such a short time." Sara Rhodes complimented Chandra, taking a sip of her hot tea as they sat in the cheerfully bright restaurant. "At the rate you're going, you'll have the house decorated in no time at all."

Chandra smiled, picking up her own teacup and taking a drink. *I'd better have it decorated in record time,* she thought, *because I can't spend more than another few days in Garrett's house.* Something close to pain tugged gently at her heart as she realized her parents could be back sometime late this week from Europe and she'd have to return home. She no longer felt it necessary to have that talk with her mom about her coming marriage. She was beginning to realize that she and she alone had to be the one to decide if she loved Phillip enough to go on with the wedding.

Her eyes fixed on the single red rose sitting in the crystal vase on the small table where she and Mrs. Rhodes sat as the older woman chattered on about the simply breathtaking dining room furniture they had just seen. Chandra's thoughts wandered back to this morning when she had awakened to find Garrett's side of the bed empty. She had rolled over, gathering his pillow to her and breathing in the faint, musky smell of his aftershave. She buried her face in the deep, downy softness, recalling his love-making of the night before. It was true that she had no regrets. She knew she should have. Very soon she was supposed to become the bride of another man. Where was her conscience?

Phillip certainly deserved more than she was giving him. One thing she knew for certain, she would not marry him now without first telling him *all* that had taken place. He would be too much of a gentleman to ever question her about the details, but she would know. That was the problem. Would she ever be able to be the wife Phillip deserved? She was beginning to think not. In her mind she knew that after last night she would always dream of a tall, blue-eyed man holding her tightly, whispering words of passion, no matter whose arms she was in.

". . . do you mind?" Sara Rhodes's voice broke back in on her thoughts.

"I—I'm sorry, Mrs. Rhodes, what did you say?" Chandra smiled at the other woman apologetically.

"I asked to see your ring, dear, do you mind? It is really quite lovely."

Chandra's eyes dropped down to her hand, where Phillip's large, two-carat diamond ring sparkled impressively. She sat staring at it for a moment as if she were looking at a stranger's hand. "It is lovely, isn't it," she agreed distantly, holding her hand out for Mrs. Rhodes to have a closer look. The last few days had seemed like a dream to her. The Chandra who was engaged to Phillip was a different person from the one sitting so quietly having tea.

"Where is your wedding band?" the older woman asked casually, her eyes admiring the sparkling gem.

"Wedding band? Uh . . . it was a little too large for me, so I'm having it sized," she fabricated quickly, letting her hand drop back down to the table.

"You're such a lucky girl, being married to that man of yours," she grinned impishly. "Not only is he the best-looking thing I've ever laid eyes on, John says he's one of the best pilots in the business. Do you know he plans on doing his own testing on all the mock-up models he designs? Of course, John is having a fit! He says Garrett's much too valuable to the company to lose . . . well, I mean . . . there are other men available to do that job," she finished lamely.

"Garrett's job is dangerous?" Chandra asked softly, her stomach fluttering lightly at the thought of him being in any type of danger.

"Oh, no, dear, it certainly doesn't have to be. His job is to just design our new planes, but men like Garrett," she smiled weakly, shrugging her shoulders, "you know how they can be sometimes."

"Yes," Chandra sighed, "I know how they can be."

"Now, it's certainly nothing for you to worry about," Mrs. Rhodes said, patting her hand consolingly. "I probably should never have mentioned it to you."

"I won't worry," she promised, knowing that in a few more days it wouldn't make any difference anyway.

Deciding that they had accomplished all they could for that day, Chandra and Mrs. Rhodes agreed to meet again tomorrow to shop for the rest of the living room furniture. Mrs. Rhodes dropped Chandra off at her house twenty minutes later, promising to pick her up early the next morning.

Chandra had just dropped her coat and purse on the kitchen counter when she heard the doorbell. Wondering who it could be, she hurried through the living room to open the door. She wasn't expecting Garrett until later this afternoon. Although he didn't assume his duties until after the first of the year, he had left a note this morning telling her he was going over to familiarize himself with the plant, then sit in on several meetings in the afternoon. She opened the door, her mouth dropping open in surprise when she saw a delivery man from the florist holding a gigantic bouquet of yellow roses.

"Chandra Loring?"

"Yes, I'm Chandra Loring," she stammered out. It was the biggest bouquet of roses she had ever seen!

"Sign here, please." The delivery man held out a clipboard with a receipt attached to it.

"How many roses are there?" she asked disbelievingly as she scribbled her name across the piece of paper.

"Four dozen, ma'am. Someone must really like you." He smiled, tipping his hat.

Chandra closed the door with her backside, her arms full of yellow roses. She couldn't begin to imagine who'd sent them. Phillip had no idea she was here, and even if he did she doubted that he would be sending her flowers. Not four dozen worth.

Her hands shook as she reached into the middle of the large bouquet and pulled out a card. Opening it quickly, she read the bold handwriting scrawled on it. "Since you didn't like the poem I still have love notes and flowers to fall back on. Last night was beautiful. Garrett."

Chandra buried her face in the fragrant petals, fighting the overwhelming urge to bawl like a baby. He did remember that night when he was drunk! She didn't know whether to brain him or kiss him to death. She only knew this was the sweetest thing any man had ever done for her. Pulling herself together she walked into the kitchen looking for something to put the beautiful flowers in. The only thing she had was a small plastic utility pail which she filled with water. She placed the flowers lovingly in the pail and positioned them on the fireplace hearth, next to her bedroll. With a sigh of exhaustion, she laid down on her "bed" and stared happily at the flowers. Their lovely fragile petals were just beginning to open, pouring their heady fragrance out into the room. So beautiful, yet so fragile. Exactly like her love for the man who had sent them. In that moment Chandra came to a new decision in her life. For the little time remaining with Garrett she was going to live it to the fullest. She had no idea what tomorrow held for her, but for today she would spend it with the man she loved. She was too tired to insist that she really loved Phillip. She didn't. That had been a heavy burden on her ever since she had accepted his engagement ring several months ago. It wasn't that he wouldn't make her a fine husband, because he would. They just didn't seem to have anything in common, nothing that they could share together other than their mutual attraction. Phillip loved all types of sports, and Chandra was miserable always sitting on the bench. She didn't want to spend the rest of her life being a football "widow." She wanted a man, she sighed softly, a man like Garrett in her life. One she could laugh with, talk with, argue with, and make love with for hours on end. But she knew that she would never have a future with him. Oh, maybe if she wanted to hang around and live with him he wouldn't have any objections to that. It was obvious that he had enjoyed her company in bed last night, but she would never be willing to settle for that type of relationship with him. It would break her heart to know that he would replace her in that same bed someday. No, when she left here she would do so with the knowledge that it had been beautiful, but recognize it for what it was—only a brief affair. Her eyes closed heavily, the lack of sleep from the night before catching up with her, dreaming of a world without Garrett—cold, miserable, and bleak.

It seemed she had only closed her eyes for a moment when she became aware of a pair of strong arms around her, the faint smell of musky aftershave, and a warm mouth moving caressingly over hers. She opened her eyes to meet azure-blue ones looking at her desirously.

"What are you doing back in this bedroll?" he asked tenderly. He was lying beside her, his arm propped up on his elbow, just staring at her.

"Hi," she smiled sleepily, "I guess I fell asleep."

Garrett reached out to lightly trace the outline of her nose with his finger. "You have a big night last night?" he murmured, his finger moving on down to touch her bottom lip.

"The biggest," she whispered, her tongue reaching out to touch his finger lightly.

"I see you got the roses." His eyes were searching hers intently now, looking for any signs of regret from the night before. "Do you like them?" he asked, his voice deep and smooth as velvet.

"They're beautiful, Garrett. Thank you." Her insides trembled as his finger continued to caress her lips sensuously.

"Thank you?" he murmured, cocking one eyebrow. "Is that the best you can do? I was hoping you would show a little more gratitude than that."

98

"I should consider breaking your neck for fibbing to me about not remembering the night you were drunk, but I'll restrain myself." She rolled over on her side, her arms encircling his neck, then pulled his mouth down to kiss him provocatively.

He gave a low, throaty chuckle as he pulled her up close to his long, sinewy body, burying his face in the contour of her neck. "I don't remember all of it—just parts of it—the nice parts," he added, returning her kiss sexily.

He began to kiss her slowly, running his mouth up her neck with agonizing slowness until he found the point behind her ear that made her shudder and arch in closer to him. "Don't you think you might be able to come up with something to show how much you liked my poetry and flowers?" he said, beginning to tug at her earlobe with his teeth. "You said you liked your men to do those kinds of things—poems, flowers, love notes. . . ."

Her hands came up to slowly unbutton the front of his shirt, trembling as they reached in to bury themselves in the thick, wiry hair on his broad chest.

"I do," she agreed silkily. "Any ideas on where I should start?"

Chandra heard Garrett's quick intake of breath as her hands smoothed across the hard ridges of his muscles, stroking them lightly. She thrilled at the power she seemed to hold over him at this moment.

"Careful, lady," he breathed raggedly, clasping her more tightly, "this could be over before it even gets started."

"But I thought I was supposed to show you my undying gratitude for the lovely roses and your inspiring poetry," she teased, running the tip of her long nail lightly along the edge of his belt line.

"I didn't say stop. I just said slow down," he groaned, his breathing heavy and labored as he lay nearly limp beside her. Her hands moved over his body in smooth, exploring movements. "Damn!" he swore throatily as her hand became even more intimate with him.

"How many times do I have to tell you—stop cussing," she chided as she pulled his mouth over to meet hers again. The world seemed to explode as his mouth captured hers in a searing kiss, his hands reaching out to unbutton the front of her blouse. His long fingers closed around one of her breasts as he slipped his hand into the inside of her lacy bra. He kneaded the soft flesh almost roughly as the hungry urgency of his kiss sent waves of pleasure coursing through her body. A sharp rap on the front door broke the fiery kiss, and Garrett let out a cuss word that turned the air blue.

"Garrett!" Chandra scolded as they still lay locked in a tight embrace.

"Who in the he—devil, could that be," he asked tensely. "Whoever it is, has sure got poor timing."

Chandra grinned, pulling his mouth down for one last quick kiss. "No, they have good timing—have you forgotten we're going Christmas shopping tonight?"

Another loud rap on the door brought Garrett rapidly to his feet. "You'll have to answer it," he said disgustedly, trying to cool his ardor.

"Can't you?" she objected. "I need to start supper."

"In this condition?" he asked, turning around to face her.

Chandra blushed openly as her eyes surveyed the front of his trousers. It would definitely be up to her to open the door. With an impish grin she swept by, patting him intimately as she headed for the door. "I really did love my flowers. Thanks again!"

He caught her arm, his blue eyes sparkling. "I'm not through with you, lady. We'll continue the 'thank you's' later on." He kissed her hard on the mouth, then pushed her gently toward the front door.

Chandra swung the door open and nearly burst out laughing. An adorable little girl stood there with a Girl Scout hat perched on her small head, her big, husky father standing protectively right next to her.

"Ya wanna buy some cookies, lady?" the big, burly man asked

Chandra harshly. "You can help send a Girl Scout to camp this summer."

"Girl Scout cookies—gee!" Chandra turned around to Garrett and grinned wickedly. "Are you in the mood for Girl Scout cookies, Garrett?"

Garrett shot her a look that left no doubt as to what he thought she should do with the cookies.

As Garrett took a quick shower Chandra made them each a bowl of soup and a grilled cheese sandwich. She still had several gifts left to buy for Christmas and Garrett had agreed to accompany her shopping that evening.

"I have to make a fast trip back to Texas," he told her as they ate their simple dinner. "My car and most of my clothes are still down in Arlington."

"Texas? Is that where you're from?" Chandra asked, realizing that until this very minute she hadn't known where he'd lived before.

"I'm actually *from* California," he told her, taking a bite of his sandwich, "but I've worked in Arlington for the last two years for a company that designs helicopters."

"That's interesting. Do you test those too?"

"I test anything that flies, and I've tested a few that didn't— unfortunately."

Chandra continued eating, her heart fluttering only slightly at Garrett's implication. "Is there someone special . . ." she paused, choosing her words carefully. "Someone you're leaving behind in Arlington?"

He looked up from his plate, his eyes catching hers silently. "Not particularly. Why?" he answered smoothly.

"No reason," she lied. "Just making conversation."

"Have you talked to Phillip lately?" She noticed he had managed to get his name right this time.

"No, he's on a business trip. I'll talk to him next week." She avoided looking at him now, spooning her soup into her mouth.

"Your big day's not far off now, is it?" Garrett's voice had dropped to a low timbre.

Oh, Garrett, ask me to tell Phillip to go fly a kite, her eyes begged mutely. *Tell me that you love me—that you'll fight any man who tries to dispute that fact. Ask me to marry you, rob banks with you—do anything but sit there and casually ask about my wedding day to another man.* "No, it's not far off now." She put her spoon down, her appetite vanishing swiftly.

Garrett pushed his half-eaten meal out of the way, too, and stood up from the table. "I suppose we should get started."

"I'll get my coat," she murmured, rising to her feet as well.

"Chandra," he said, catching the sleeve of her blouse.

"Yes?" She paused, looking up at him sadly.

He seemed to be waging a war within himself, a look of pain in his clear blue eyes. They stood looking at each other in their new little kitchen, so many words unsaid between them. Chandra wanted to reach out and touch him, but she kept her hands clenched tightly to her side. If Garrett did love her, and oh God, how she prayed he did, then he had to tell her so.

His hand dropped back down to his side, his eyes dropping away from hers. "Nothing . . . just, Chandra," he said tiredly as he walked away. "I'll call a cab."

"Thank you," she answered, managing to get past the hard lump in her throat. "I'll be ready when it gets here." He wasn't going to say the words she longed to hear.

The sights and sounds downtown didn't hold their usual thrill for Chandra that night as they shopped virtually in silence. After an hour of them both brooding quietly, Chandra decided to try to change their mood. Apparently they were at an impasse, so she was going to try and make the best of it. Pulling him over to the large toy department in one of the gaily decorated stores, she put a silly, orange, glitter-covered band on her head with two big antlers flopping around on top. Resembling something from outer space (or a slightly loony twenty-five-year-old) she sneaked up behind his back and pecked him on his shoulder as he stood looking at a toy train display.

"Pardon me, mister, can you tell me when the next bus comes

by here?" She imitated Groucho Marx as she wiggled her eyebrows and flicked an imaginary cigar.

Garrett turned around to look at her blandly. "The last one left for the funny farm ten minutes ago."

"Oh my," she groaned. "I guess I'm an orphan now. Will you take me home, mister?" She dramatically threw herself into his arms.

Garrett looked around uncomfortably. "Damn, Chandra, everyone in the place is watching us."

"I know." Her hand came out from behind her back, and she extended another silly antler headgear, a ridiculous glowing-pink, and stuck it on his head. "Let's give them something to really talk about!"

They left the store a few minutes later five dollars poorer. Garrett mumbled under his breath about the cruel twist of fate that had brought Chandra into his sane, orderly life—but she noticed he was smiling.

They spent the next two hours carefree and laughing, munching on ice-cream cones and red-striped candy canes, still wearing the ridiculous antlers.

"I sure hope there's no one from Rhodes Aircraft out here shopping tonight," Garrett told her worriedly as they walked along the crowded sidewalk sharing a caramel apple. His big pink antlers didn't exactly personify the average vice president in a large aircraft corporation.

Chandra laughed and reached up to wipe some caramel off his nose from the last big bite. "I think you look dignified," she told him sincerely, then burst out in peals of laughter.

"Chandra!" A tall, very good-looking man moved rapidly through the crowd to where Chandra and Garrett stood looking at a mechanical Christmas scene in one of the department store windows.

"Gary!" Chandra said in surprise. "What are you doing here?"

Gary picked her up in his arms and swung her around a couple of times before he sat her back down on her feet and kissed her soundly. The antlers came off Garrett's head in record time, his face turning to a cold, stony mask as he watched Chandra being kissed by this strange man. When she showed no signs of protest, he stepped forward and literally jerked her out of the other man's embrace.

"Look, fella, the lady's with me," he said coldly, pulling Chandra up next to his side.

"Hey, sorry, old man, but Chandra and I go back a long way. I ran around with her brother all during high school, and she's been like a baby sister to me." Gary grinned, not the least bit intimidated by the glowering stranger before him. "You must be Phillip." He reached out and grasped Garrett's hand soundly.

"Gary," Chandra said, laughing nervously, "this isn't Phillip. This is a good . . . friend. Garrett Morganson. Garrett, this is Gary Norris," she smiled, "another—good friend."

Garrett reluctantly shook Gary's hand, then stood back as he and Chandra chatted about old times.

Chandra tried to hurry the conversation along as Gary repeatedly reached out and hugged her or gave her brief little kisses. To Chandra this wasn't unusual, he had always been overly affectionate, but judging by the look on Garrett's face she had better get rid of him—and fast.

A few minutes later they walked away in the other direction after Gary gave Chandra one final kiss. Garrett pulled her close to him roughly. "That guy's got one hell of a nerve, mauling you like that in public. He's lucky he's still able to walk out of here," Garrett ground out tensely as they walked along the lighted sidewalk.

Chandra was thrilled at this blatant show of jealousy from Garrett. Even though she knew it was wrong she couldn't help goading him just a little. "Well for goodness sake, Garrett, we're just friends. He's almost like a brother," she said innocently. "Why should you care how Gary treats me?"

"Brother my— You're engaged to be married, Chandra! That guy knows that, but he still had his hands all over you. His kind burns me to a crisp." He was practically dragging her down the street now, his temper boiling over. Chandra had to smother a cry of outrage. He was worrying about her fidelity to Phillip. After what she had done with him—that was a big laugh.

"Well, excuuuuuuse me! I'll certainly make it a point to tell Phillip how well you protected my virtue," she hissed nastily.

Garrett stopped and jerked her around to face him. "Make a joke out of it if you want to, lady, but when you're in *my* company, other men damn well better keep their hands off of you." He pulled her to him, his mouth coming down hard on hers in a kiss of undeniable possessiveness. He ground his lips into hers roughly, grasping her hair with both hands. Chandra fought to break his hold, but as quickly as the violent kiss started it rapidly turned into a hungry, passionate exploration. Chandra moaned softly as his hands released their punishing grip on her and gently began to stroke her hair lovingly, his hands trembling violently. He broke away murmuring her name incoherently as he kissed her eyes, her nose, her cheeks. "You're driving me crazy—I don't know what's happening to me, Chandra. Ever since you walked into my life I can't think straight." He brought his mouth back down to hers pleadingly. "What kind of curse are you, lady?"

"Oh, Garrett, don't you know? Maybe, just maybe, I'm more than a passing fancy in your life." She cried as they exchanged brief, desperate kisses.

"No, Chandra, no! Dammit! I don't want marriage. . . . Yes, I'll admit I want *you*, but I've seen marriage tear up more than one good relationship. Isn't what we've got together enough?" he said looking down at her, his eyes pleading for understanding.

The cold night wind caught them in its breeze as tears rolled down Chandra's face. "No, that isn't enough, Garrett. That could never be enough."

"Don't do this to us, Chandra." His lips kissed away the salty tears, his arms enfolding her gently. "Let me love you."

"That isn't love, Garrett. When you love someone you feel secure. You want to be with them forever," she sobbed painfully.

"Is that what Phillip's offering you?" he said, still holding her close. "Security for eternity—that's a tall order, you know."

Chandra leaned against him weakly, wanting so much to give in to her love for him, wanting so much to tell him that she would live with him, follow him to the ends of the earth if that's what he wanted, but she couldn't love that kind of life. She would be torn apart living in limbo like that. Yes, that was what Phillip was offering and maybe, just maybe, she should accept it.

"Yes, that's what he's offering," she whispered tenderly, her heart breaking. "The same thing offered in every *good* marriage that you see."

"Then I guess we don't have anything more to say to each other, do we?" Garrett said, releasing her slowly.

Chandra reached in her purse for a tissue, wiping her nose shakily. "I think it would be better if I went back home in the morning." She paused, watching for his reaction. "I think it would be best that way."

Garrett turned his back to her and she saw his broad shoulders tense slightly. "Yes, I think that probably would be the best."

Chandra held back a sob at his words. Well, there it was. He wanted her to go. It was finally over and she felt a strange sense of relief that it was. All she had to do now was go back to her old life and forget there ever was a Garrett Morganson. *Oh Lord,* she cried silently as she followed the tall, handsome man striding impatiently to the waiting cab, *this time you gave me a mountain.*

A cold, fine mist of rain had started to fall as they rode home in heavy silence. Chandra had tried unsuccessfully to engage Garrett in polite, impersonal conversation, but he had stared moodily out his side of the cab, barely responding to her words. After the first few tense minutes she had stopped even trying.

She could never recall feeling as miserable as she did at this very moment. It suddenly occurred to her that she didn't want their relationship to end on such an antagonistic note. Not only did she love Garrett, she liked him as well. She liked him very much. The time they had spent together held special meaning for her. When they were not at each other's throats they had developed an easy, warm relationship with each other, laughing at the same things, disagreeing respectfully over small things. He had never tried to force his likes on her, nor had she resented him when he hadn't seen eye to eye with her on different occasions. They both accepted each other as they were. As far as Chandra could see they only had one "small," insurmountable problem. Garrett didn't view their relationship in the same light. He was willing to let it go.

The rain had turned to a freezing, light sleet as the cab deposited them in front of their house. Chandra left Garrett to pay the fare and hurried ahead of him to unlock the door.

Determined that they wouldn't part in the morning with bad feelings, she tried one last time to clear the air between them.

"Would you like some hot chocolate?" she asked brightly "Nothing tastes better than hot chocolate on a cold night like this."

"No, thanks. I'm going to bed. I have to be at the plant early in the morning," he answered curtly and walked straight into his room, not even glancing in her direction. Chandra sank tiredly down on the fireplace hearth and reached out to lovingly touch one of the yellow petals of the roses. He didn't even want to talk it out with her. She knew that he would be gone in the morning before she woke up, so if she didn't talk to him tonight she wouldn't have the opportunity again. A streak of resentment began to build in her as the sleet intensified, pinging its ice crystals at the windows loudly. How dare he be so rude that he couldn't at least give her a decent good-bye? Even though they had their differences, *she had* helped him out of a bad spot. True, she'd put him in that spot, but she'd certainly not had to get him out of it.

She stood up abruptly, a look of rebellion in her stubborn hazel eyes. *Well, test pilot, you're not going to get away with it. The least you owe me is the courtesy to say good-bye decently!*

With the zeal of an invading army she marched briskly down the hall to the master bedroom. The sound of running water told her exactly what she wanted to know. The enemy was taking a shower, so he could hardly walk out on her if she confronted him in there. Stripping off her clothes rapidly before she lost her nerve, she threw them in a heap by his bed and walked bravely into the small bathroom. She forced her hand to reach for the shower door handle, then taking a deep breath she jerked the door open and stepped in.

Garrett stepped back in momentary astonishment, his hair and face lathered heavily in white soap. The steamy water beat down on Chandra as she wiped the strings of wet hair out of her eyes and began casually as if they were sitting in the parlor drinking tea. "Garrett, I want to talk to you."

He cracked one eye open, his large hands pausing in their vigorous rubbing. "I'm using this shower right now, Chandra. I'll be out in a minute," he said dryly.

"I know you're using it," she shot back. Surely he didn't think she was that dense. "I said, I *wanted* to talk to you."

With a disbelieving shake of his head he went back to his lusty scrubbing. "I'm busy right now." He reached for the bar of soap.

"I won't take but a minute of your time," she said stubbornly, and politely jerked the soap out of his hand and pitched it over the shower door. It landed in a wet plop on the other side. "Now, first of all," she continued purposefully, "I want to tell you that I'm perfectly aware I have been nothing but a thorn in your side from the first night we met."

Garrett leaned back arrogantly in the shower, his hair and body still thoroughly soaped, and crossed his arms. "You hit the nail on the head there," he agreed shortly.

"And I know that you don't want any permanent ties in your life," she continued, trying to ignore the broad, naked expanse of his body in the tiny shower stall, willing her eyes to stay on his face and not wander elsewhere, "and I want you to know I don't blame you for that. I just feel that since I won't be seeing you before you leave in the morning"—her voice broke, her bravery slipping fast—"I just wanted to tell you good-bye." She looked at his familiar face, love filling her eyes along with stray rebel tears. "No matter what you think of me, I'll never forget you. You'll always be a special . . . friend to me. I didn't want to leave with you mad at me," she finished hurriedly, relieved that she had had her say.

The heavy spray of water was washing the remainder of soap from Garrett as he still stood with his arms insolently crossed, listening to her gush the words out, his face giving no indication of what he was thinking.

"Friends? You want me to consider you as a friend," he finally answered above the sound of the water.

"Yes, I would value that very much," she told him truthfully, aching for him to discard his aloofness toward her.

Garrett reached around her and shut off the stream of water, then with both arms on either side of her, he backed her against the wet, tiled wall. His face was very close to hers in the confines of the small, quiet stall. Blue eyes searched her face for a moment before he spoke in a low voice. "Well, that's too damn bad, Chandra, because for some reason I just can't feel that way about you!"

Chandra stifled a sob at his harsh words, her heart sinking low. He wouldn't even consider her friendship, let alone anything else between them.

"Why do you dislike me so," she whispered miserably. "I made an honest mistake the night we met. I've tried very hard to make it up to you, Garrett."

"You think I *dislike* you?" he asked seriously, his face moving still closer to hers.

"Well, don't you? You're always yelling at me," she reminded him.

He let out a short snort of disgust, shaking his head slightly. "Women," he muttered under his breath. He brought his face back up to look at her intently. "Yes, I like you—too much for my own damn good."

"You do?" Hope flared up in her eyes. "You don't know how much better that makes me feel, Garrett," she glowed. "Now I can go on with my life knowing that at least you don't hate me. If I marry Ph—"

A large hand reached out and clamped over her mouth harshly. "I don't want to hear that name mentioned in my presence again. I am sick to death of hearing about your fiancé," he snarled between clenched teeth.

Chandra was surprised at the venom in his voice at the mention of Phillip. "I'm sorry, Garrett," she apologized hurriedly. "I didn't know you resented Phillip."

"Resent him." Garrett leaned in closer, pulling her wet, slick body up against his. Chandra gasped softly—having forgotten their state of undress—as her soft curves met the hard lines of his manly body. She became aware of his stirring manliness pressing into her side. "Resent him," he repeated again almost hatefully. "It tears my guts out, lady, every time I hear his name! When I think of Phillip being the one in your bed, Phillip taking what I want—" His voice broke off angrily as he slammed his fist into the wall next to her head in heated defiance of his words.

Chandra reached up and lovingly stroked the line of his clenched jaw. "Garrett, I had no idea. . . ." She searched for something to say, confused by the intensity of his words. "You never told me. . . ."

He jerked her up tightly to him, his fingers biting into the tender flesh of her arms. "Told you what? That you've got me just where you want me? That I go crazy inside every time you turn those innocent eyes toward mine? That I wake up nights thinking of you—wanting you? Is that what I haven't told you?" he ground out, his eyes burning angrily into hers.

"Don't be angry with me," she pleaded, drawing his lips down to meet hers, trying to make up for whatever had angered him so. "I don't want you angry."

"Damn you, damn you," he groaned helplessly as his mouth captured hers in agonizing, searing kisses. Chandra arched hopelessly against him as he hungrily devoured her mouth. His tongue reached out for hers, and as they met she felt an uncontrolled shudder assault his trembling body. She didn't know what unknown devils Garrett Morganson was fighting, she only knew that she loved him and she would be there if he ever needed her.

His hands searched her body with frenzied urgency, his mouth and lips telling her of his overpowering need for her at that moment. He lifted her tenderly in his arms, his mouth finding her breasts as he held her close to his heart. Gently he kissed the rising peaks to a taut hardness, his tongue flicking over them, claiming each one as his own. Chandra drowned in a world of love and longing as her hands played across the broad, wet expanse of his back, her fingers trying to ease the taut, straining muscles that rippled tightly as he held her slight frame off the floor.

"I love you, Garrett," she gasped deliriously against his compelling mouth. The words of love came pouring out of her mouth, tumbling over each other. If only he could admit his love for her, she thought miserably as his hand moved caressingly between her legs to passionately touch her warmth. She knew men could be casual about sex, but she also knew that what Garrett was experiencing at this moment was much more than casual sex. No, fight it as he may, he was in love with her whether he knew it or not.

His desire had become overwhelming. She heard him moan her name, suddenly sliding his body into hers. All semblance of control evaporated for Garrett as he became lost in a wild, fiery burst of scorching intensity, unable to wait for her to join him. Chandra buried her face in his broad neck, holding him tightly as his body convulsed in deep shudders.

"I'm sorry . . . I'm sorry," he whispered apologetically, burying his face in her hair. "I didn't expect that to happen. . . ."

"It's all right," she soothed, stroking his wet hair lovingly, her desire for him still flaming brightly. "I understand."

His mouth found hers again eagerly as he let her slide back down to the shower floor. "You don't have to understand, sweetheart," he murmured huskily. "I'm taking you to bed now where I plan on spending the night making it up to you." He lifted her in his arms, his mouth hotly proclaiming that he'd lost none of his desire for her as he pushed open the shower door and stepped out anxiously, eager to carry her to his large bed.

All of a sudden Chandra was flying through the air, the sound of Garrett's angry swearing filling the small bathroom. She landed in a tumbled heap in the middle of the floor and sat up stunned, wondering what had happened. A loud groan from Garrett snapped her out of her state of shock. He was lying sprawled on the bathroom floor holding his back painfully. "Oh, my gosh!" she exclaimed, crawling rapidly over to him on her hands and knees. "Garrett, darling, are you hurt?"

"I think my back's broken," he grimaced in agony, trying to sit up.

"Ohhhh . . . let me help you," she offered quickly, tugging at his arm.

"Wait!" he gasped, knocking her hands away hurriedly. "Just give me a minute to catch my breath."

"Sure, darling. Here, let me get you a cold rag to wipe your face with. What happened—did you trip?" she asked, crawling over to the bottom of the shower stall to retrieve Garrett's washcloth.

"No," he gritted out between clenched teeth. "I slipped on that damn bar of soap you threw out!"

Chandra stopped dead in her crawling tracks. Darn it! Every time she thought she was getting somewhere with him, something like this always cropped up to show her stupidity. Why had she thrown that soap? Wringing out the washcloth, she crawled back over to tenderly wipe his perspiring brow. "There, does that feel better now?"

"My head doesn't hurt," he told her crossly, "it's my back that's killing me. You know, Chandra, I used to fly bombing missions when I was stationed in Vietnam. I've had to ditch three planes in my career as a test pilot. I've been in numerous helicopters that malfunctioned. I've lived through two plagues and one severe drought while I was in Texas." He paused and took a painful deep breath. "I was even in the middle of an outbreak of malaria over in the Congo one time, and through it all, *not once* did I have so much as a Band-Aid on my finger."

Chandra tensed, her eyes growing stormy. She knew what was coming next.

"Now, it just occurred to me," Garrett continued calmly, "I've known you somewhere in the vicinity of one week, and so far I've had a one-inch gash on my forehead, a hangover that would have knocked the average horse off its feet, my nerves have been shot to hell from chasing your phantom prowler the other night, and now . . . now"—he paused again—"it looks like I'll probably be in a wheelchair the rest of my life, if the pain in my back is any indication of the extent of my injury. So if you don't mind, let me just lie here and die in peace."

"That's not fair, Garrett," she said crossly. "I'll admit I'm responsible for some of those things, but not all of them." She jumped up and wrapped a thick towel around her in sarong fashion. "Do you want me to help you up or not?" she asked again petulantly.

Garrett sat up slowly, sucking his breath in between his teeth at the stab of pain that shot through his lower back. "Take it easy, Chandra," he said, reaching for her outstretched hand.

She pulled him to his feet carefully, hurting almost as much as he did when she heard his groans of pain. Supporting most of his heavy weight on her slight frame, she moved cautiously toward the bed, staggering under his weight.

"You weigh a ton," she grumbled, stopping to catch her breath.

"Stop your griping," he grunted. "I should be lighter after eating your cooking the last few days."

"My cooking! What's wrong with my cooking?" she fumed. "You never said anything before about my cooking." Boy, he could sure burn her to the core at times.

"I didn't say anything because I didn't want to hurt your feelings," he grouched, moving at a snail's pace across the room.

"You didn't like it?"

"I've tasted better out of a vending machine." He sank down weakly on the side of the bed. "Help me lie down."

Chandra reached over and very deliberately shoved him back against the pillow, his howls of pain filling the room. "Sorry," she smiled angelically. "I figured it would just hurt worse if you tried to do it slowly. Is there anything I can get you—aspirins, back rub, gun to blow your conceited brains out?" She hovered over him protectively, then plopped down heavily on the bed, jarring it violently. "Maybe you'd like for me to fix you one of my famed ten-course meals before you doze off."

"Just get out of here and let me suffer in dignity," he groaned, trying to find a position that wasn't so painful. The anger instantly drained out of Chandra as she saw the look of pure agony on his face.

"I'm sorry, Garrett," she relented, kneeling down beside the bed. "Really, is there anything I can do to help you?"

"I don't know, sweetheart, all I know is it hurts like the devil." He reached over and pulled her head over on his chest, stroking her hair tenderly. "I'm sorry I made that nasty crack about your cooking."

"That's all right. I know I'm a lousy cook," she admitted. "I made my dad and brother deathly ill sometimes when I lived at home and helped Mom cook." Her arms went around him to hug him tightly, but she instantly eased her hold at his flinch of pain. "I make good Christmas candy and cakes though," she added encouragingly.

"Well, if a person didn't mind living on peanut butter fudge and fruitcake, that wouldn't be too bad," he said thoughtfully. "But I want you to know, I'm sorry about that other matter too," he whispered sexily against her ear.

"Not as sorry as I am," she grinned, raising her face to meet his. She kissed him sweetly, then abruptly left his arms. "I'll see if I can find something for your pain."

"We don't have anything in the house, you know that," he said, wincing.

"I know. I'm going to walk down to the corner drugstore," she replied absently, thinking of the cold, wet sleet hitting the windows.

"I'm not letting you go out alone at this time of night," Garrett said angrily, "let alone walk in this kind of weather."

She looked back at him with determination on her face. She wasn't going to sit by and watch him suffer all night. "I'll be back before you even realize I'm gone," she tossed over her shoulder as she scooted out the bedroom door.

"Chandra, come back here!" Garrett yelled irritably, trying in vain to raise up out of bed. He sank back down in a sea of pain as he heard the bedroom door close.

Sighing painfully he threw an arm up over his eyes. "Crazy, dippy broad," he mumbled to himself heatedly. "Crazy, wonderful, lovable, sexy broad . . ."

CHAPTER SEVEN

The light, freezing sleet had turned to a heavy, freezing rain by the time Chandra returned from the drugstore. Her hands were half frozen as she handed Garrett a heating pad and a bottle of aspirin, her teeth chattering.

"If I had the strength, I'd get up and turn you over my knee," he grumbled sharply as he accepted her offered relief. "That was a stupid trip!"

"But you don't have the strength," she said as she searched for an outlet to plug in the pad. "Roll over," she told him in a no-nonsense voice.

Garrett rolled onto his stomach painfully. "What are you going to do?"

"Just rub some of this pain reliever on your back." She took the cap off the small red and white tube and squeezed some white cream out into the palm of her hand. Carefully she placed her hand on the center of his lower back, moving gently as if it were something she did every day.

"Son of a—moose!" He came up halfway out of the bed, his hands gripping his pillow violently. "Your hands are like two blocks of ice!"

"Just hush and hold still," she scolded, her eyes fascinated with the play of muscles rippling across his broad back. By the time she had massaged the ointment into his back Garrett had measurably relaxed, his voice growing drowsy with sleep. Tucking the blankets around him snugly she reached over and switched on the small bedside lamp and stood up to leave.

116

"Where do you think you're going?" he mumbled sleepily.

"To bed," she whispered back, not wanting to disturb his relaxed state.

"Aren't you going to sleep in here with me?" he asked groggily, groping for her hand.

"No, I don't think I should, Garrett. We decided I should go home in the morning, remember?" she reminded softly, squeezing his hand gently.

His slow breathing reached her ears as she leaned over and kissed him tenderly on the side of his neck. He was sound asleep now, his tall, lean body relaxed in slumber. Chandra smoothed away the unruly brown wisps of hair on his forehead. He looked like a little, innocent boy in his sleep, but Chandra knew better. He wasn't a boy any longer, he was a fully grown, very desirable man. She stared down at him, wondering about his parents, where they were, if he was close to them. There was so much she didn't know about him, and her time had run out ever to find out. Something in Garrett's life had soured him on marriage. *What a shame,* she thought, rising to her feet slowly. *He would make the perfect father, the perfect lover, and whether or not he wanted to believe it, the perfect husband—perfect, but unwilling.*

The air seemed alive and popping as Chandra opened her eyes early the next morning. The room had a funny, bright light to it as she sat up in her sleeping bag and looked around. The rain had stopped sometime in the night, the temperature dropping rapidly. She jumped up and went over to turn the heat up, shivering as she walked over to look out the front window. The world that met her eyes was one of solid ice. The branches of the trees in front of the house were sagging under their heavy icy coating, causing the more fragile ones to snap off loudly. A thin, weak sun was glistening brightly off the shrubbery, and the ice-covered walks turned the small, residential street into a veritable glittering fairyland.

Chandra stood framed in the front window, squinting her eyes in awe at the magnificence of the gigantic icicles hanging in long

117

rows across the front of the houses, some of them as tall as she was. The icy prison seemed to have the whole world locked in its powerful grip as she noticed there was no sign of traffic moving on the quiet street. The only signs of life were the gray puffs of smoke coming from the chimneys of the houses along the street.

There was certainly no question of her leaving for home today. With a resigned sigh she let the heavy drape drop back into place and walked over to pick up her robe. Tying the belt tightly around her waist she stepped into the kitchen and picked up the wall phone to call Mrs. Rhodes. There wouldn't be any shopping trip this morning either. As she chatted with the other woman Chandra filled the coffee pot and put it on to perk, dragging the long phone cord around the kitchen as she worked. She explained that Garrett had hurt his back—leaving out the details, of course—and was told to keep him in bed until he was feeling better. *Ha!* she thought as she hung up the receiver, *wouldn't I just love to!*

She ate her breakfast quickly, then arranged an attractive tray with scrambled eggs and bacon (she didn't burn it for once), toast, jam, and coffee for Garrett. After she added a small glass of orange juice, she whisked it off the cabinet and headed for his room.

He was reading a magazine as she knocked lightly on his door. Hearing a curt "I'm awake" she pushed the door open and walked in.

"It's time to torture the patient," she grinned enchantingly, holding the tray up. "I know you can hardly wait to dig in to one of my home-cooked meals."

"Do I get a pain pill first?" he asked, grinning wickedly. "It might ease the shock of your burnt bacon."

"You're the one going to be shocked," she said, arranging his tray on his lap. "It isn't burnt this morning."

"No kidding!" His interest seemed to pick up as he peered hopefully at his tray. She unfolded his napkin and handed it to him. "You going to join me?" he invited.

"Nope—I've already eaten, but I'll keep you company while you eat," she offered, reaching over for a piece of his bacon. "How's your back this morning?" she asked, crunching the crisp bacon.

"It's a little better. I think I just twisted a muscle." He dove into his scrambled eggs hungrily.

"Good! I called Mrs. Rhodes and told her. She said for you to stay in bed until it's better. Can I have a small sip of your juice?" she asked politely, reaching over for the small glass.

"That's exactly what I plan on doing," he said, watching her down the juice, then absently reach for a piece of toast.

"I don't know if I'll be able to leave today or not," Chandra told him, reaching for the other slice and spreading it thick with strawberry jam. Garrett watched blandly as she reached over and took a sip of his coffee. "I don't think there're any cabs running," she explained.

"Why? What's the problem?" he questioned, scraping the small jelly dish for enough jam to spread on his toast.

"You should look outside," she said excitedly. "We had a big ice storm during the night." She finished off the last of his orange juice. "There is virtually nothing moving outside."

"I thought it felt colder in here this morning," Garrett answered, fighting her for the last bite of his eggs.

"I turned the heat up—it should be warmer in a few minutes." She dusted the crumbs off her hands, eyeing the cup of coffee Garrett had raised to his lips.

"You want the last swallow?" He raised his eyebrows and held out the cup.

"No, really, I'm not hungry. It's your breakfast—enjoy it," she smiled sincerely.

"I'd *like* to . . ." He finished the cup off smoothly, then replaced it on the tray.

"Are you through already?" she asked in surprise, noting the empty tray without a single crumb remaining on it. "Your injury hasn't hurt your appetite!" she exclaimed, removing the tray from his lap.

Garrett looked at her ironically. "Yes, it *is* hard to believe I ate the whole thing by myself."

"Well, let me know if you need anything. I'm going to start gathering my things up. I'm going home today, you know . . . if I can." She was watching his face intently, hoping he would suggest that she stay longer.

He picked up his magazine again and settled back down on his pillow comfortably. "Don't leave before lunch," he cautioned sarcastically, "and let's eat earlier than usual. I have a feeling I'm going to get hungry quick."

Sheesh! she thought irritably as she carried the tray back to the kitchen. *Men and their monstrous appetites! He had just eaten enough breakfast to feed* two *people—now he was already thinking ahead to lunch.* Well, she probably wouldn't be able to leave until late afternoon anyway. She poured herself another cup of coffee and started the breakfast dishes.

She worked quietly around the house the rest of the morning, stopping only fourteen or fifteen times to get him something to drink, aspirins, help him to the bathroom, rub his back, make a couple of phone calls for him, fix him a mid-morning snack. An hour later, he wanted lunch, *insisting* that she stop work and eat when he did. That set the pattern for the rest of that miserable day. By the time Chandra sank wearily down on her makeshift bed that night she was seriously considering the thought of giving up all men and becoming a nun.

The next morning dawned cold and bleak, with no sign of the weather easing so she could call a cab and go home. It would have to let up soon, she had to be home by Friday at the latest.

Garrett was as worrisome this morning as he had been the previous, but Chandra managed to keep calm, seeing to his wants with a cool, controlled efficiency, then letting out a scream of frustration when she left his room.

Her patience was worn thin when thirty minutes after lunch she again heard his voice bellowing for her.

"What is it now?" she called, her voice dripping with impatience. She poked her head back into the bedroom, her hands and nose covered with flour. She had decided to prove her amazing culinary skills with Christmas cookies while she waited for any sign of a thaw in the weather.

"I'm getting bored. Do you know how to play poker?"

"No—I don't know how to play poker!" She turned around and started for the kitchen again.

"Hey!" A shrill whistle followed his exclamation. "Come back here for a minute."

Counting to ten under her breath she turned around and stuck her head back in the doorway. "You whistled?"

"No kidding, don't you know how to play *any* kind of cards?" he asked hopefully, his bored face full of expectation.

"I'm sorry—I really don't. But I'm making you a surprise for your dinner," she said encouragingly.

His eyes took in the smudge of flour on her face and her hands covered in a white film. "Is it something you're cooking?" he guessed, his voice exhibiting no elation at the thought of her "surprise" menu.

"Yes . . . why?" She was in no mood for his nasty remarks about her cooking.

"Can't you drop what you're doing and come in here and keep me company," he nearly whined.

She let out an exasperated sigh. "There's an old Monopoly game out on the shelf in the garage. Do you want to play that?" Her cookies would just have to wait. It was apparent he was going to bug her to death if she didn't find him something to do.

"I don't know how," he said unenthusiastically, "but I'll learn," he added as she shot him a blistering look.

"I'll get it then." Secretly, she couldn't have been more delighted. Monopoly had always been her game—as a child she used to win hands down when she played with her father. It would do her heart good to see Garrett go down in defeat when she slaughtered him on the game board.

Within minutes she came back with the rumpled, stained game and cleared off a space on the bed to set it up. "Now, all you have to do," she explained hurriedly, setting up the board

121

and giving him a pile of paper money, "is try to buy up all the real estate you can, then put houses"—her eyes grew real big—"or hotels on the property, if you can. Then, when I land on your territory you can collect rent money from me. Whoever runs out of money first, loses. I'm the banker."

"Wait a minute—hold on! Why are you the banker?" Garrett's blue eyes looked at her distrustfully.

"One of us has to be. Since you don't know how, then I'm the logical choice," she returned loftily. "Here—you're the iron, I'm the dog." She handed him a little metal iron to move around the board.

"I don't want to be an iron," he said frowning, "that's sissy!"

She let her breath out short. "Okay! I'll be the iron—you be the dog." She hastily traded pieces with him.

"Are you *sure* you don't know how to play any kind of cards?" he asked, dishearteningly studying the layout of the board.

"Positive. You throw the dice to see who goes first." She climbed up on the bed, crossed her legs, and got comfortable. This was going to be a snap.

"Now, let me get this straight—the object of the game is for one of us to monopolize the board and bankrupt the other," Garrett reviewed her sketchy instructions. "Is that right?"

"You got it. Now roll!" Her eyes roamed discreetly to Boardwalk and Park Place, as she chuckled deviously under her breath.

Within forty-five minutes, Garrett owned Boardwalk, Park Place, all four railroads, the electric company, the water works, numerous other board properties on which he had hastily erected hotels—and all of Chandra's money. She had been in jail three times, paid over six hundred dollars in income tax, and owned one house on Baltic Avenue and one house on Mediterranean Avenue.

"You want to play another one?" Garrett asked, gloating as he straightened his large pile of money.

"No, I don't," she said in a miffed tone. "How did you do

that?! I used to beat my father every time we played." She was astounded at how rapidly he had creamed her.

"He probably *let* you win," he shrugged, scooping his hotels back into the box.

"He certainly did not. And even if he did"—she bristled at the suggestion—"I think that he was a real gentleman for being that nice."

"What did you want me to do, cheat and let you win?" Garrett asked smugly, watching the way her eyes sparkled when she was mad.

"You're disgusting!" she snapped crossly, sliding off the bed.

"Come here, you little hellcat," he said gently, pushing aside the monopoly board. "I'm sorry I beat you at your specialty."

She didn't wait to be asked a second time. She went willingly into his outstretched arms, his mouth meeting hers in a lingering kiss of welcome. Closing her eyes she savored his familiar smell, his arms crushing her tightly against his chest. They kissed with a growing hunger as her arms wrapped themselves around his neck, her fingers slipping gently through the thickness of his hair.

"Hi," he whispered seductively as their mouths broke away reluctantly.

"Hi," she whispered back, her fingers reaching out to touch his cheek.

"I've been wanting to do that all day," he confessed as he gently nipped at her lips with his strong white teeth.

"I've wanted that too," she confessed as he buried his face in her fragrant hair.

They lay there for a moment, content just to be in each other's arms, willing the world and all its problems to go away.

"I should be going," she finally sighed, still lying in his arms. The thought of leaving him now was very disturbing. "I still have to finish your dinner and cookies before I call a cab."

Garrett was silent as he stroked her hair, his hands tightening possessively as she spoke. "I don't want you to go, Chandra," he said quietly.

She closed her eyes, tears welling up in them. "I have to, Garrett. If not tonight, then very soon. The Rhodeses will be leaving Saturday and my parents will be back from Europe anytime. I wish I could stay forever, but I can't." The tears slid silently down her face, dropping wetly against the front of his broad chest. His arms locked around her more tightly as he kissed the top of her head gently, unable to accept her words.

"Stay here with me, sweetheart. We'll work it out someway," his voice pleaded raggedly.

"It would never work for us, Garrett, you know that," she sobbed quietly. "I can't live the way you want, and you can't live the way I want. We would only end up despising one another. I couldn't stand that."

"Marriage isn't the answer to all of love's problems, Chandra, can't you see that?" he whispered coaxingly, his soft breath fanning her hair. "I watched my parents tear each other apart in a bad marriage, I watched my sister commit suicide over a bad marriage, I've watched my friends turn into drunks when their wives walked out the door taking their children with them"—his voice broke—"God help me, Chandra, I couldn't live through something like that." She felt his body shake.

She reached up and lovingly caressed his face, trying to ease the mental anguish he was battling. "But it doesn't always have to be that way, Garrett. For every bad marriage, there are thousands of good ones. Look at my parents. They've been married nearly thirty years and they've had their little spats, but they loved each other so they worked them out. I would be as committed to you, if I lived with you, as I would be if I married you. Don't you see, darling, you're always running the chance of being hurt if you love someone—whether there's a legal paper involved or not? If you're not willing to take the gamble on love and all its commitments, then you'll be a terribly lonely man."

"You make it all sound so simple, Chandra, but life isn't that simple. When you trust your very life to another person, and that person lets you down the way my mother did my father, then you form some pretty strong opinions about what you want out of life. You came from a happy home. You didn't have to watch your dad die by inches every day until he finally drank himself out of his misery. You didn't stand and look down at your baby sister's face in a casket, distorted almost beyond recognition from running her car over an embankment after finding her husband in bed with another woman. You live through that— then I'll listen to your theory of how life's problems are solved at the marriage altar."

Chandra's heart nearly broke as the bitter words poured out of Garrett, his large body trembling with emotion as he held her pressed roughly against him. She had no idea how unhappy his life had been. She ached to kiss away all the bitterness and pain, but the lonely prison he had locked himself into had no key.

"I didn't say marriage was the answer to all problems, I just said that if you loved someone, you trusted them. If they betray that trust, then of course, you'll be hurt—but if they return that trust and love . . ." She pulled his face down to where her eyes met his. "Oh, Garrett," she whispered, "if they return that love, then there's nothing more wonderful on earth than to love and be loved. Life makes no promises—two people who love one another have to make their own promises . . . and keep them. And it happens every day."

"I don't know, Chandra . . . I just don't know." He buried his face in her neck, her salty tears wetting the side of his cheek. "Please, sweetheart, don't cry like that. You know it drives me crazy." He kissed her eyes gently. "I think we need to talk about . . . Phillip."

It was Chandra who tensed this time. The sound of her fiancé's name made her react guiltily in Garrett's arms. She pulled away from him and rolled over on her back to stare at the ceiling. "What do you mean?"

Garrett lay beside her, his face devoid of all emotion now, one arm thrown up carelessly over his eyes. "Do you love him?" he asked in a dead tone of voice.

"I thought I did . . ." Chandra's voice faltered. "I really don't know, Garrett." Somehow, she couldn't bring herself to tell

125

Garrett that it was him she loved . . . would always love. But she couldn't take the chance of hearing him openly refuse that love, and now that he had told her why he felt as he did, she doubted that he would ever accept her terms in their relationship. And she couldn't accept his.

"I can't ask you not to marry him, Chandra. I don't have the right to do that. I have always respected other men's women—I've stayed clear of any involvement with them . . . up till now. All I'm asking is for you to think about it . . . be sure he can make you happy." He reached over and touched her hand. "I could make you very happy if you'd let me, you know that."

"I know you could," she returned calmly, her hand entwining with his, "but I feel very guilty about what I've done to Phillip. He's a very fine man. I wouldn't hurt him for the world. He's offering me marriage and love, Garrett. You're offering me . . . a short time in paradise. You can't imagine how I hate myself for betraying him the way I have."

Garrett turned over on his side, his gaze capturing hers. "That's what I've been trying to tell you about this thing called love and marriage. You're going to tear Phillip's guts out if he ever finds out what has transpired between us this last few days. Now"—he paused gazing at her intently—"tell me how marriage is going to change that," he finished grimly.

"But you forget," she said, meeting his gaze, "I haven't married him yet—I've made no promises—taken no vows as his wife. When I do promise a man my fidelity and love, he can rest assured he will be the only man in my life from that day on, unless he chooses otherwise."

"Are you going to tell Phillip about me?"

Chandra sighed. She had been thinking about that question for a long time. "Yes, I plan on telling him about . . . what's happened. I would never be able to live with myself if I didn't."

"What do you plan on telling him?" Garrett asked quietly.

"Why . . . the truth, of course. How I made a fool of myself—that I felt I owed it to you to rectify that mistake . . ."

"Is that all?" he questioned softly.

"No, I'll tell him how I moved in here with you and continued to pose as your wife."

"And," he persisted.

"And," she whispered in a small voice, "how I let you make love to me twice . . ."

"Wrong," he stopped her. "Not twice—three times."

"Yes, *twice* . . . you know that, Garrett. Don't you remember? There was once in your bed, then once in the showe—" Garrett's hand clamped over her mouth.

"And once after she damn near broke his back," he finished huskily as he reached out to draw her back in his arms. "You may have to do all the work, sweetheart, but if I'm going to lose you to another man, I'm going to have one more day with you in my arms." His mouth descended slowly to hers, the fires of passion burning brightly in his blue eyes. "There's no one else in the world right now, honey." His lips touched hers briefly. "Just you and me." The softness of their breaths mingled warmly as his lips touched hers again. A low moan began in his throat as he opened his mouth over hers, the floodgates of passion bursting open. She gave herself up, melting into his arms, her love for him blanking out all else. If these were to be their last hours together, she would hold back nothing from him. Today would only be a memory, one that would see her through many lonely years.

Garrett's hands reached out to unbutton her blouse, working her arms through the sleeves as his tongue joined hotly with hers. Nimble fingers unfastened her flimsy bra, and he impatiently freed her arms from that obstacle also. His large hand eagerly cupped her firm breast, his other arm pulling her on top of his lean muscled frame. "I'm sorry," he groaned between snatches of deep, searing kisses. "It's going to have to be like this. . . . my back . . ."

"Sorry? You've nothing to be sorry for," she gasped as he pressed against her intimately, letting her feel his need for her.

"Oh, Garrett, I don't want to hurt you. . . ." Her words were stopped by his mouth again, his tongue plunging deeply into the recesses of her warm, moist mouth. He moved against her suggestively as her desire built to new and frightening heights. His hands touched her body intimately, his breathing labored and heavy.

She buried her face in the hardness of his broad chest, the heavy mat of hair clutched tightly between her fingers as his mouth devoured every inch of her face, her neck, her breasts.

He broke away, panting in short spurts, his mouth capturing one of her breasts. His tongue made slow, lazy, wet circles around the nipple before he groaned painfully, his hands tangling roughly in her hair. "I've never met a woman like you," he breathed raggedly, burying his face in the softness of her hair again. "When I'm with you, I feel ten feet tall, able to face anything the world deals me—but when I'm away from you and I remember how I feel when I make love to you, it scares me to death. Why are you so different from all the other women I've known?" He brought his mouth back down on hers angrily. His kiss was violent and brutal as he fought the warring emotions racking his body.

Oh, Garrett, get it all out of your system, she willed silently, letting his mouth savagely bruise hers into willing submission. The anger slowly drained out of him as he became aware of the low groan of pain coming from her throat and he tasted the saltiness of the blood on her lip. Gentleness took over again as he murmured passionately, "I'm sorry, baby, I'm sorry. Love me, Chandra. I need you—right now more than I ever needed anyone in my whole life."

And Chandra did. She poured every ounce of her love for him into her body as she let him enter her in a frenzied act of desire. They moved together as perfectly as the sand and the ocean, blotting out all fears. With her hands she poured out her love, touching him, kissing him, caressing him. At that moment she would gladly have laid down her life for him, should he ask. But he didn't. He merely gave himself as freely to her as she did to him. Their bodies devoured each other in love, bringing unspeakable joy and pleasure. When they could no longer prolong the inevitable, they clutched each other tightly as violent tides of passion enveloped them, sending showers of tingling sensations rippling through fevered souls. Time held no meaning for them as they lay wrapped in a hazy world of sated passion, too exhausted even to murmur each other's name.

Her face was still buried deep in his shoulder, her breathing slowing to an even beat before she could finally manage to speak. "Are you all right . . . we didn't hurt you?" she asked in concern.

"I was too busy to notice," he moaned, running his hands over the satin smoothness of her bare buttocks. "If we did, it was worth every minute of it."

"Garrett, I was wondering . . . have you ever been in love before?" she whispered, softly touching his smooth, moist skin.

"I may have thought I was before, but I always managed to get over it," he said drowsily. "With you . . . it's going to be harder."

Chandra raised up on her elbow, her face glowing with love. "Are you saying that you're in love with me?"

"You know that I am," he whispered fervently. "I don't have to tell you that." His lips took hers again roughly.

"I love you too, Garrett. I'll always love you . . . no matter what tomorrow brings," she promised against the pressure of his mouth on hers.

"We both have a lot of soul searching to do. You have a fiancé . . . I have old memories that won't go away." He absently stroked the silkiness of one breast, his fingers gently teasing the budding tip.

"And we're no closer to an answer than when we first met," she added, bringing one of his hands up to kiss each long finger gently, sensuously.

"I told you, I wouldn't move in on another man's property— it's up to you to decide how you want to live."

"I won't live with you, Garrett, you know that."

"Then you're going to marry Phillip?" Garrett's hand closed over hers tightly, squeezing her small hand painfully.

129

"I don't know . . . I just don't know." She was suddenly very, very tired.

"He may not want you once he finds out we made love four times," Garrett cautioned, his need for her stirring against her bare stomach once again.

"Three, Garrett—just three times," she corrected sleepily.

His eyes locked with hers, his look disputing her words.

"Oh . . ." she grinned, her eyes coming alive with desire. "Why, I believe you're right," she corrected carefully. "It was four times. . . ."

"But who's counting." He grinned cockily as his mouth closed over hers once more.

The next three days were the happiest time of Chandra's life. They stayed locked away from the world, making love, spending hours talking with each other about their childhoods, making love, popping corn and roasting marshmallows before the fire, making love, talking for hours on end about what they wanted out of life, laughing together over silly jokes, and making love, and making love . . . and making love.

As with all things, it finally came to an end. The town was slowly coming alive once again as Chandra walked to the door with Garrett early Friday morning. They looked at each other for a moment, neither one of them saying a word. Garrett held out his arms, and Chandra went into them for what she knew would be the last time. Their kiss was long and sweet, their hunger for each other never more than barely concealed below the surface of their emotions. She held him in her arms tightly, hugging him one last time before he walked out the door for a meeting Mr. Rhodes had asked him to attend that day. Chandra stood in the doorway waving to him, he still waving to her as the cab sped down the street.

She hadn't told him she wouldn't be there when he returned that afternoon. The thought of saying good-bye to him was more than her fragile emotions could bear. No, it would be better if she was gone when he returned. He would be hurt, but he would get over it.

Finally she was able to shed the tears she had been holding back because they upset him so. She watched his cab turn the corner taking him out of sight and silently said good-bye, tears rolling down her cheeks, her eyes shining with love.

Good-bye, my darling Garrett, and may God fill your life with all the happiness you deserve. She walked back in and closed the door softly, a horrible bleakness overcoming her . . . it was over.

CHAPTER EIGHT

Tennyson once said, Chandra thought wistfully, " 'Tis better to have loved and lost, Than never to have loved at all." But for some reason that adage held no comfort for the slim, blond-headed woman lying bereft on the single bed, watching the rain trickle slowly down the windowpanes. It had rained or drizzled nearly every waking hour since Chandra had returned home four days ago.

Four days—four days without the sunshine of his smile, the sound of his deep, rumbling laughter, the feel of his mouth sending cold shivers up her body as he whispered love words to her when they lay together at night.

She could hear her mother rattling around downstairs in the kitchen, sounds she had heard since she was a small child—comforting sounds, yet Chandra was afraid she would never feel comforted again. One big, fat, puffy snowflake drifted by her window, the first of the season. This part of Oklahoma saw very little snow most winters, but this winter was starting out to be unusually wet and cold. That one large snowflake was joined by another, then another, until the heavens finally opened and millions of "cotton balls" danced and juggled merrily in the air.

She slid off the bed and walked over to the large window draped in rose-colored sheers and sat down at the window seat. With her nose pressed against the pane she watched the world outside begin changing before her eyes. The snow was sticking to the branches of the large cedar tree in front of her window, the fine, powdery substance reminding her of icing on a cake.

The neighborhood children began to pour out of their houses, shrieks of delight ringing out loud and clear in the cold afternoon air. Chandra watched them yelling and shuffling around in the snow, her eyes dull and lifeless. How she yearned for the days of childhood once again. Carefree days that knew very little unhappiness. Days of looking at her parents and wondering how they could always put a damper on things by worrying about what *might* happen. Days of Uncle John ruffling her crown of shining blond curls, saying, "Don't grow up too fast, Chadee. Enjoy your childhood. These are the best years of your life, little one—no problems, no worries. Someday you'll be grown with more worries than you'll need." *Well, Uncle John, that day's here. I'm all grown up with a problem too big for me to handle.*

The first tear slid out of her eye and dropped on the window pane along with the falling snow. She had not shed one tear since she had walked into her parents' house last Friday trying to keep a straight face. Her mother had looked up in surprise—her hands suspended in midair as she unpacked the large suitcase lying before her. "Chandra, darling! Why, I didn't expect you until Monday." Margo Loring paused, her eyes taking in her daughter's tear-smudged face. Without another word she had walked over and enfolded Chandra in her arms, tenderly stroking her hair. "It's all right, darling. Whatever is wrong, we'll work on it together." God in his infinite love gave some mothers the ability to know when to talk and when to just listen, and Chandra was one of the fortunate ones who possessed such a treasure. She had gone into her mother's arms, her body trembling, and had totally fallen apart. She couldn't speak past the pain of a tight, restricting knot in her throat. Her mother had helped her up the stairs into her old bedroom and sat her quietly down on the bed. She stayed with her, talking soothingly about her trip to Europe, the new flower bed she was planning in the spring, a new dress pattern she had seen in the store . . . anything to help her daughter still the cold trembling of her body. Finally, in exhaustion, Chandra drifted off into blessed oblivion, a warm, dark world where the pain wasn't so acute. She thought drowsily that she should pull herself together long enough to halfway explain to her mother what had happened. But she knew her mother would be there if and when she could bring herself to talk about it. For now, the world was too painful to exist in. For the next three days she had stayed in her room lying mutely on the bed, trying to piece her jumbled thoughts back together. Her mother had checked in on her periodically, bringing her meals to her on a tray. Chandra had managed to review sketchy details of her past week and a half, but it was still far too agonizing to talk about.

The tears were streaming down her face as the dam cracked and a slow healing process finally began. For thirty minutes Chandra sobbed away all the tension, frustration, and heartache —the bitterness and pain literally pouring out of her. At last, when there were simply no more tears left, she stood up, wiped her nose, went into the bathroom and splashed cold water on her face, then walked calmly down the stairs to join her mother. It was over—she had to go on living.

"Well," her mother said, turning off the small, electric hand mixer she was using. "Welcome back, darling."

"Thanks, Mom, I'm going to be okay now." She crossed the kitchen and sat down at the Early American kitchen table.

"Would you like a cup of hot tea?" Margo asked, resuming her work with the mixer, trying to ignore the swollen eyes and hiccupping sobs that escaped occasionally from her daughter.

"No, I'm not thirsty."

"You don't have to be thirsty to enjoy a cup of tea." Margo reached under the cabinet and extracted two round cake pans. She began to rub shortening in them, then dusted each with a fine coating of flour. "It would make you feel better," she encouraged lightly.

"It doesn't matter, Mom. If you want a cup, I'll drink one with you." Chandra blew her nose again, her fingers still trembling from the violent emotions she had just experienced.

"Good. As soon as I get this in the oven, I'll make us one." She poured the thick, creamy chocolate batter into the pans.

"I see you're making Dad's favorite cake again. How many of those things do you make a week?" Chandra asked, smiling weakly.

"You know your dad. He feels very deprived if I don't make him at least two a week." The pans slid into the hot oven and Margo set the timer for twenty-five minutes. Picking up the teakettle, she filled it with water and set it back on the burner

Chandra smiled tenderly as she watched her mother bustling happily around the kitchen. Margo and Daniel Loring had been married twenty-nine years last June, and she never remembered a single quarrel between them. Her mother had laughed when she had mentioned that fact to her on their last wedding anniversary. Margo had assured her there had been *many* quarrels in their marriage, but nothing that they hadn't been able to work out with a lot of patience and love. *Oh, Mom,* she thought sadly as she watched her mother work, *not all things can be worked out, no matter how bad a person wants them to.*

"It's really getting nasty out there. I hope your dad makes it home with no trouble," Margo worried, absently turning on the burner under the teakettle. "By the way, Darrell called. He said to tell you hi. Somehow he was under the impression you were staying with one of your girlfriends," she added thoughtfully, sitting down opposite Chandra at the table.

"I know. I left a message at his office telling him that's where I would be," Chandra replied softly.

Margo's motherly gaze caught Chandra's blank, downcast eyes. Reaching over, she took her hand and squeezed it reassuringly. "Do you feel like talking about it yet?" she asked gently. "You know I don't want to interfere in any way, but I must admit I'm totally baffled as to why you would have spent a week and a half with a man named Garrett when you were engaged to be married to a man named Phillip."

Just the mention of Garrett's name sent sharp pains riveting through her heart. He had not called or tried to contact her in any way since she had left. She had known he probably wouldn't, but still her heart had jumped every time the phone had rung.

135

Squeezing her Mother's hand back Chandra answered affectionately, "I guess it's about time you heard the whole story."

Over the next hour Chandra recited the bizarre, almost unbelievable story to her mother. Each time a stray tear welled up in her eyes she wiped it away angrily, then continued on with her story in a small, determined voice—ignoring the looks of disbelief, then outright astonishment, on her mother's face. Margo let her daughter talk, never once stopping her to ask the questions that kept popping up in her mind with every new segment Chandra entered into. Chandra was as honest as she could be with her mother without telling her just how far her and Garrett's relationship had really gone. She wasn't ready to talk about that yet, and she wanted to spare her mother the agony of knowing how deeply she was involved with this strange, wonderful man.

When her story was finished they both sat quietly in shared companionship, drinking their cups of cooling tea.

"I don't know what to say." Her mother finally broke the silence.

"There's nothing to say, Mom. Garrett doesn't want marriage. He had a very unhappy childhood with his parents and he thinks all marriages are doomed for failure."

"That's really sad. He sounds like a man who's afraid to love." Margo got up slowly and checked the progress of the cake in the oven.

"He's not afraid to love," Chandra whispered almost inaudibly, thinking of the last few days they had spent together. Garrett had told her over and over again that he loved her, but he couldn't offer her marriage. "He's just afraid to trust."

"I've known men like that," Margo agreed, replacing the hot pad on the kitchen counter. "They live their lives drawn into themselves, missing out on so much of life's pleasures because they're afraid of the pain that it might bring them."

"He's had a lot of pain and very little happiness in his life. I wish he would allow me to ease that pain," Chandra sighed wistfully, adding another teaspoon of sugar to her tea.

136

"Chandra! That's five teaspoons of sugar you've put in that tea," her mother scolded.

Chandra looked down blankly at the sugar in the bottom of her teacup. "I have?"

Making a clucking noise with her tongue Margo removed the cup of syrup and poured it down the sink.

"Oh, Mom, what am I going to do?" Chandra groaned hopelessly. "I love him so much."

Her mother turned to face her again, concern in her soft, brown eyes. "Is he able to offer you what you would be happy with in life?"

Chandra thought of what Garrett wanted—no ties, no commitments. He had simply offered companionship and one terrific love affair. That wasn't what she wanted. "No," she choked out bitterly. "He's able to, but he won't."

"He isn't married, is he . . ." Margo's voice trailed off sickly.

"No! No, nothing like that, Mom. I told you, he just doesn't want to get married."

"Well"—her brown eyes had grown even sterner now—"the next question I'm going to have to ask you is, what about Phillip?"

Chandra looked at her bleakly. "I don't know—I really don't know."

"He's a fine man, Chandra. He would make you a good, reliable husband, but if you don't love him . . ."

"I do love him . . . in a way," she protested. "He doesn't make me feel like Garrett does, but no one will ever make me feel as he did."

"Loving him 'in a way' isn't good enough, darling. The man you marry deserves all your love, not just what's left over from another man."

"I probably could grow to love him more," Chandra told her sincerely, knowing that she might if she really tried.

Margo turned and opened the oven door, the smell of chocolate cake permeating the room. "I suppose that happens, but is that what you really want to do?" She put the hot pans on a cooling rack, then turned to face Chandra once again. "Learn to love him?"

"I don't want to hurt him."

"You'll hurt him more by going into the marriage with this kind of feeling," Margo warned. "A man senses these things."

"I'm aware of that. I plan on being perfectly honest with him when he drives down for Christmas."

"Oh, my gosh!" Margo's hands flew up to her face. "I completely forgot. Phillip called while you were resting. He said to tell you he was coming down tomorrow night."

"Tomorrow night?" Chandra asked, puzzled. "Why's he coming so early?"

"I don't know, darling. He just said not to disturb you, but left the message he'd be here tomorrow. It had completely slipped my mind," she apologized.

I wonder why he's coming down so early? Chandra mused thoughtfully. Well, it might be for the best. She needed to see him again. Maybe when he walked through that door, all thoughts of Garrett would flee. That was about as likely as a dog laying eggs, but she could hope, couldn't she?

By the time her dad arrived home, the snow was blanketing the streets and housetops heavily. He came in the back door, stomping the snow off his shoes loudly. He kissed both his "girls," as he had always referred to them, soundly, demanding to know what smelled so good. Chandra began to feel almost human again, the pleasure of being with them crowding out all other thoughts. Everything would work out—it simply had to.

After dinner they put up a Christmas tree that Dan had brought home in the trunk of his car. They all three worked busily, stringing the lights and placing the colorful ornaments on the tree.

"Oh, I wish Darrell were here," Margo said, picking up a wooden toy soldier with his name written on it, caressing it lovingly. "That job of his always keeps him on the run."

"He'll be here Christmas, Margo." Dan laughed tolerantly,

tossing a dog-eared ornament of a babe lying in a manger toward Chandra. "Remember this one, Chadee?"

Chandra grinned, catching the tiny ornament in her hand. She looked at the miniature manger with baby Jesus lying in his cradle, the shepherds standing beside him and Mary looking on with adoration. She had made it when she was in the third grade, along with a finger-painted drawing of the scene for her parents.

"Do you remember when you brought it home and climbed up in my lap to show it to me?" her dad asked tenderly, placing the Star of David on the top of the tree.

"Yes." She grinned in embarrassment. "But I'm going to hear it again!"

"You climbed up in Daddy's lap and started pointing out the different characters you had drawn," her mother entered the conversation laughingly. "You pointed out the manger, the shepherds, the sheep, the star shining brightly in the East. . . ."

"And when I pointed to the slightly rotund stick figure you had standing up close to the cradle and asked you who it was, you looked at me with serious wide eyes and answered, 'Why that's Round John Virgin, Daddy!' "

Margo broke in on the story again, her voice bubbling with laughter. "I'll never forget the blank look your father had on his face when he looked up at me and mouthed the words, 'Who's Round John Virgin?' "

"Yes, and *I'll* never forget the look on both your faces when I piped up and answered disgustedly, 'You know, Daddy! Round John Virgin, Mother and Child,' quoting you my slightly off-key version of the words to 'Silent Night.' "

They all three burst out laughing as her father told them gleefully, "I still can't hear that song that I don't get tickled. You were sure a feisty kid!" His laughter slowly ground to a halt, his face turning serious. "Where have the years flown to, Chadee?" he asked wonderingly. "That seemed just like yesterday when you were a nine-year-old with gaps in your teeth. And now here you are, a beautiful young woman ready for motherhood yourself soon."

Chandra reached over and hugged her dad's neck tightly. "Oh, Dad, I want to thank you and Mom for all the wonderful years I've had growing up in this home." Chandra's eyes misted thinking of all the lonely, cold Christmases that Garrett had probably experienced in his life, growing up in a home sadly lacking in love. "I hope I can leave my children the same legacy of love that you will leave me."

After they all three wiped their eyes they stood back, their arms around each other as Dan threw the switch that lighted the large tree. The scotch pine came alive with strings of brightly blinking lights, their varied colors shimmering against the wispy strings of icicles that hung thick on the glowing tree.

"It's the best tree we've ever had. . . ." They all broke off laughing as the sound of their voices speaking in unison filled the room.

"That's what we say every year," Margo said happily, storing the empty ornament boxes in a larger cardboard one. "Any Christmas tree is beautiful when you're with the ones you love."

Dan and Margo tried not to notice the look that suddenly overtook Chandra's laughing face. Her laughter died, that haunting sad look that they had seen for days replacing the gaiety in her eyes. She walked over and lovingly touched the small, wooden toy soldier, a tear slipping silently down her face. Her finger ran tenderly around the little soldier's face. She wasn't thinking of her brother, Darrell, right now. Her mind was on another toy soldier—a stubborn, arrogant pill of a soldier. She wondered where he was tonight . . . and with whom.

Rather than have her parents see her dissolve in tears again she quickly left the room without a word and reached in the hall closet for her heavy coat and pair of boots. As the front door closed quietly, her parents exchanged a painful look with each other—a look that spoke volumes between them. Although they loved their daughter fiercely, she was locked in a world of misery that only she could escape from. With a heavy heart they turned out the lamp and arm in arm walked slowly up to their room.

* * *

Outside the air was cold and crisp, the snow still falling heavily as Chandra took a deep, cleansing breath, then sat down on the porch steps to pull her boots on. Accomplishing that she wrapped a heavy, knitted scarf around her neck, put her matching hat on, and stepped nimbly off the porch. Her spirits began to lift as she walked briskly down the snow-covered streets, playfully puffing her breath out in front of her in the frosty night air. She waved at the two teenage boys who couldn't wait for morning as they laughingly tried to build a nine-foot snowman out of the wet snow. They waved back, calling out with an invitation to help them. With a wave of her hand she declined their offer, trudging on down the street in the ever-deepening snow. She could feel the sharp bite of the night wind stinging her cheeks as she turned the corner walking on down Garner Avenue.

Experiencing the carefree world of her childhood days, she opened her mouth wide trying to catch the big, fat snowflakes as they fell. A few cars crept slowly by her, the drivers edged up on their seats trying to find the road with their strained eyes. Her feet carried her swiftly around another corner, the lights of the small park glowing dimly through the falling snow. Chandra had spent many hours of her childhood playing in this small neighborhood park. Walking faster, she turned into the small park and walked down a snow-covered path to the silent swings and merry-go-round sitting still and eerie in their frozen world. She remembered days of long ago when Darrell had brought her here and had swung her for hours. He would finally have to drag her off the swings bodily, then carry a screaming, wiggling sister home for Mom to do something with! She could hardly wait for the day she would be allowed to go to the park and swing alone. But when that big day arrived, the swings had lost their appeal and other, more important things had taken over. Such as trying to keep her defending title as champion home-run hitter with the boys in the neighborhood. By the time she was twelve, she could out-hit, out-pitch, out-catch, out-stare, and out-spit any boy on the block. Darrell used to come home in a fit of temper and demand his mother make her act like more of a lady after a particularly bad day at the ball park with his tomboyish sister.

Chandra walked over and sat down on a snow-covered bench, wiping off the seat with her mittened hands. Somewhere around fourteen she had discovered boys could do more than run bases and throw garden snakes at her to hear her scream. A boy by the name of Greg Loftis gave her her first kiss, and from that moment on Darrell had his wish granted. She put away her ball bat and glove, exchanging them for hose and makeup, and slowly developed into a lovely young woman. She never spat in public again, nor tried to out-cuss the neighborhood bully. For that Darrell was eternally grateful.

The years passed swiftly—she had graduated from high school, then taken a secretarial course. A close friend talked her into moving to Kansas City and sharing an apartment with her. She did, then promptly landed the job in Phillip's father's law firm. She had worked there a year before Phillip was discharged from the service and joined his father in the firm. They had enjoyed an easy, relaxed friendship from the day they met. After dating close to a year he asked her to marry him. Accepting the ring reluctantly she had agreed to the marriage, hoping that her feelings would grow stronger before the actual marriage took place. With each passing day the burden of her wedding grew heavier, until that day was fast approaching and she had returned back home.

They were planning to be married at the church she had been christened in as a baby. Her wedding dress was hanging in the closet, its beauty breathtaking. The cake was ordered, the invitations sent out, the wedding gifts unwrapped. All that was left was to speak her vows—but could she do it?

"Why didn't you at least leave a note?"

Chandra's daydreams tumbled to a halt as the soft, deep timbre of a man's voice broke the silence. In the dim light of the snowy night she could barely make out the tall form of a man standing in the shadows of an old oak tree. He was wearing a navy-blue pea coat, his dark brown hair covered with white flakes of snow. She didn't have to see his face to know who the voice belonged to. She heard it constantly in her dreams every night.

"The least you could have done was tell me you were leaving that day." He moved out of the shadows, stopping before her, his blue eyes hungrily caressing her face. "That's a hell of a thing to pull on a man," he said softly.

Her eyes turned up to his, her pulse behaving erratically at his nearness. Garrett stood facing her, his hands crammed tightly in the pockets of his coat. Chandra wished with all her heart she could stand up and touch him, but she had made a clean break and couldn't afford the pain of touching him again.

"I thought it was better that way," she managed to answer aloofly.

"Better for whom?" he asked tightly, his eyes never leaving her face.

"For both of us. We had said all there was to say to each other." Chandra rose to her feet, striving to break his powerful gaze. She walked over to a covered fountain and kept her back turned to him, feeling him more than hearing him follow her under the canopy. He kept a safe distance from her as he talked.

"Don't you think we have anything more to talk about?"

"Not really." She closed her eyes against the sharp pain that assaulted her, wishing he would go away before she dissolved in a pool of tears.

"I've missed you." Garrett's voice carried quietly through the air, his deep tone serious.

"Have you?" she laughed ironically. "I would have never known it. I've been gone four days now. . . ." Her voice died off before she could finish the sentence.

The sound of a match being struck filled the air as Garrett sat down on the concrete wall and lit one of the small cigars he smoked occasionally. "When I returned home . . . that day, you were gone. The damn house was like a tomb. I left the next morning for Arlington. I just drove into town an hour ago."

Tiredly he answered her unspoken question as to why he hadn't called her since she left.

"Did you get your clothes and car?" she asked for want of something to say, more than from any real interest on her part.

"Yes."

The silence hung in the air, neither one of them trying to ease the other's plight. Garrett sat smoking his cigar, the aromatic smoke curling around Chandra in the small enclosure.

"Come back to me, Chandra." Again, just his low voice touched her as he issued his husky plea.

She closed her eyes, fighting back the overwhelming desire to scream, Yes, yes, yes! Gathering her courage, she took a deep breath and replied calmly, "I can't do that, Garrett."

"Because of Phillip? Do you really love the guy that much?"

"No, not because of Phillip—because of Garrett. I won't live the way you're suggesting."

"Dammit, Chandra." He stood up and flipped the small cheroot out into the snow. The red tip flared brightly in the dark night. "I don't know why I fool with you. I know at least five women who would love to be given that invitation, and they sure as hell wouldn't demand marriage!"

Chandra turned around to face him coolly. "Then you better ask one of them, because I'm not interested."

"Lord, you're bull-headed!" He jammed his hands back into his coat pockets in severe agitation and turned to look out at the falling snow. As she stepped around him, moving out of the fountain area, he spoke again. "Six months, just give it a shot for six months. If I still feel the same way about you as I do now, we'll get married."

"That's mighty big of you," she taunted, walking steadily away from him. "You mean if I were real lucky you wouldn't tell me to 'hit the road' at the end of the six months?"

Garrett reached out and jerked her angrily to a halt. "You know damn good and well I wouldn't tell you . . . that, Chandra!" His voice faltered. "Dammit, I love you . . . you know that."

"That's not love, Garrett. What you're suggesting is lust! There's a big difference."

"Oh, lust my foot!" Garrett snorted in aggravation. "I don't feel just *lust*"—he dropped his voice dramatically as if she thought he was some dirty old man—"for you, and you darn well know it."

"Have you ever stopped to think what might happen if I turned up pregnant at the end of six months?" Chandra asked him in a reasonable tone of voice.

Garrett's face went blank for a moment. "I don't know. I never stopped to think about it." He stopped, a cocky grin breaking over his face. "I wouldn't mind devoting some extra time to it, but don't you think we could take precautions against that possibility?" he asked in the same reasonable tone.

"We sure haven't been!" she reminded curtly. "I suppose I could always explain to our baby, 'Sorry, little Garrett No-name, your daddy loved me, but the reason you have such a weird last name is because he didn't believe in the sanctity of marriage.' " Her voice dripped with sarcasm.

"That's not fair—" His voice broke off in exasperation. "How do I make you understand? I've never thought in terms of marriage—never even let it enter my mind . . . until lately." Garrett's eyes pleaded with her to understand his position. "Look, wouldn't you rather have . . . say, a trial marriage, get to really know each other before we take such a big step?" He had decided to rephrase his proposal more discreetly.

"No, I would not!" Chandra stared at him stormily. "If you really loved me, Garrett, you would trust me enough to know that I would never do anything to hurt you. At least with Phillip my future children will have a legal name!" She whirled and started to walk away furiously.

"You are *not* going to marry that jerk!" Garrett followed her hurriedly along the snow-covered path, trying to keep up with her short, angry strides. "If I have to come down there and personally break his damn neck on your wedding day," he ground out between clenched teeth.

Chandra stopped suddenly and spun around to face him, her patience clearly at an end. "Don't you dare threaten me," she warned ominously as she reached down for a wad of snow. "And I've warned you for the last time about that cussing!" She meticulously rounded the snow into a firm ball. As politely as a lady fresh out of finishing school, she reached up and very slowly ground the snowball into his stormy face.

A look of utter astonishment crossed his features as he sputtered disgustedly, "Well . . . damn, Chandra!" He reached up and wiped his face off crossly. "Now, that was a childish thing for you to do," he scolded heatedly. "We are two adults and should conduct—" His last words were cut off by another snowball hitting him squarely in the face.

All of a sudden the air was alive with flying snow missiles. Chandra scampered behind the large oak tree, her bombs hitting their target with amazing accuracy. She worked frantically to stockpile her arsenal as Garrett systematically bombarded her.

"You could at least give me a chance to get caught up on my ammunition," she yelled at him breathlessly, her hands flying.

"You think I'm crazy?" he shouted back through a heavy line of fire coming from her side. "I plan to show no mercy. Prepare to fight to the death."

"You're nothing but a big bully!" Standing up, she lobbed a gigantic ball of snow at him.

"And you're nothing but a spoiled brat who needs her fanny whipped!" Another barrage of snowballs came whizzing by his head. "You keep it up and I'll be just the man to do it!"

"Oh, yeah?" She stood up and put her hands on her hips arrogantly. "You and whose army?" Instantly she was knocked flat on her back by a hurling snow-packed projectile. "Garrett!" she groaned weakly. "Give me a chance!" Although he was definitely winning the war, she wasn't ready to haul down the flag.

"Nothing doing, lady. Do you want to give up?" His side of the fort was deceptively quiet at the moment.

Chandra frantically began to roll the snow in hard-packed

balls once again. "Yes, I surrender," she lied, snickering smugly under her breath, working even faster. There was still a disquieting silence from Garrett's end. Chandra kept her eyes peeled on the tree he was behind, her snowball pile gaining momentum. When he stepped out she was definitely going to lower the boom on him.

"Then I suppose you won't mind eating those snowballs you're rolling?"

Chandra froze as she hastily glanced behind her, her heart leaping to her throat. Garrett was towering above her, his hands on his hips in an angry stance. Chandra looked up at him and smiled sheepishly. Then with all the speed she had ever possessed she ran like the cold winds, streaking over the snow-covered park, dodging in and out of trees with Garrett in hot pursuit. The harder she ran the faster he gained on her. She developed a disgusting fit of the giggles, slowing her speed down to nil. Trying to run, looking behind her, and giggling uncontrollably at the same time was her downfall. With a violent lunge Garrett tackled her, coming down hard on top of her. They rolled over and over in the snow, Chandra's clear laughter ringing out into the cold night.

They finally stopped tumbling, Garrett coming to rest on top of her. "What's so damn funny?" he heaved, his breath coming in short gasps. "You'd better be cringing in terror. I plan on shoving those snowballs down your throat."

"Why?" she gasped innocently, a tremor of excitement running through her as he lay on top of her. His weight felt very familiar, very intimate, bringing a lot of unwanted memories to her mind.

"Why?" he mimicked nastily, his eyes fastening on her rosy lips.

Chandra's laughter died in her throat as she saw his eyes spring alive with unconcealed desire for her. With shaky hands she tried to push him off her, every fiber in her body calling out to him. Grabbing her hands he pinned her down on his broad chest. "Lie still," he grunted.

147

"No, Garrett," she pleaded, knowing her resistance would desert her if she lay there any longer with him.

Garrett jerked her up tighter against him, his voice low and miserable. "Yes, Chandra. I haven't had you in my arms for four long, lonely days. Now just stop your damn squirming and let me enjoy it. I'm not going to force myself on you." His hands held her in an ironclad embrace, his clean, warm breath fanning her face.

With a sigh of resignation she ceased her struggles, relaxing in his arms. The snow fell on the two figures clasped tightly together, their breath making frosty puffs in the frigid air. Garrett's eyes finally managed to capture her gaze once again as he pulled her face up to meet his. "Why are you so darn stubborn?"

"I'm not—it's you who's the stubborn one." Without thought she reached out and touched his face lovingly. "Why didn't you just let it be, Garrett? Why did you have to come looking for me?"

Garrett wasn't listening to her words, his eyes were watching the way her lips moved when she talked, desire for her surging hotly through his veins.

"Don't look at me that way," she moaned, her fingers gently tracing the outline of his lips now.

"I want to kiss you, Chandra," he said huskily. "I want to do a lot more than that, but I'll settle for just being able to kiss you right now."

Their eyes were locked, silently basking in each other's beloved faces. Chandra knew she could never let him touch her or she would end up going back home with him tonight. Her hands shook as she brokenheartedly brought his smooth cheek down next to hers, the closest gesture of love she would allow herself. "No, I don't want you to kiss me, please. You said you wouldn't do anything I didn't want you to," she pleaded, holding his face close to hers.

Garrett groaned, burying his face in her fragrant neck, breathing deeply of her scent. "Have I ever told you how good you always smell?" he breathed hoarsely, his hands tangling in her blond hair wet with snow.

"I . . . don't . . . know. . . ." She couldn't speak as wave after wave of desire washed over her while he seductively placed eager kisses along her ear. He began to work his way around her cheek, his mouth searching ardently for hers.

With one unexpected push she shoved him off her and jumped unsteadily to her feet, a strange weakness invading her body. "I have to go home now, Garrett. My parents will be worried about me."

Garrett rolled over in the snow, burying his face in his arms. He didn't answer her for several moments as she backed away from him hesitantly, her face a mask of torture.

"Wait a minute," he said resignedly as he rolled to his feet. "Walk back to the car with me, I have something for you."

They both walked to the street where his car was parked, neither of them speaking. Chandra was too locked in her grief to try to make idle conversation, and she couldn't tell what Garrett was thinking. He simply walked beside her, their bodies never touching as he guided her to a late model Trans Am parked at the curb. Reaching into the front seat he extracted a small bundle and placed it in her hand.

"What is it?" she asked as their hands touched briefly.

"Your dad's shirt I borrowed. I'm sorry I took so long to return it." He leaned forward, placing both arms on the top of the car, staring down at the ground.

"Thank you—you didn't need to bother. I had forgotten about that day," she spoke quietly.

"Did you? Funny . . . I've thought about that day a lot."

Chandra hurt inside as she heard the defeated tone of his voice.

"Well, I guess I'll be going home," she said, clutching the small bundle close to her heart, imagining that it was Garrett she was holding.

"Get in, I'll take you back." His arms dropped from the car and opened the door, then he went around to the driver's side.

Too tired and cold to argue, Chandra slipped into the passenger's side as he started the car's powerful engine. The trip home was made in a few short minutes, the sports car taking her right to her front door.

Garrett reached out and turned the ignition off, staring at the lighted dash for a moment before speaking.

"Are you sure this is what you want, Chandra?"

"Yes." She stared out the window, feeling cold and miserable.

"Couldn't you at least let me kiss you good-bye?" He lifted his head, bringing his agonized face up to meet hers.

"Garrett . . ." She could feel all the will power ebbing out of her now as his blue eyes pleaded mutely with her.

As he sensed her weakening resolve, he reached over and clasped her behind her head gently with one large hand. "I won't cuss right now, if you won't be stubborn," he whispered coaxingly.

"You're impossible," she whispered back hopelessly, her love for him shining in her eyes. Her mouth moved to meet his halfway.

Garrett's mouth touched hers lightly, teasing her with his lips enticingly. "I'm going to let you take this kiss where you want it to go," he said between agonizing brushes of his mouth against hers.

"What if it's gone as far as I want it to already?" she tantalized, bringing her tongue out to moistly trace the outline of his lips.

"I don't think it has," he reasoned, content to let her do the seducing now.

They sat in the dark car, their mouths teasing each other until they both were tense with desire. It was a rigid test of willpower between two strong spirits to see which one would break first.

Control seemed to snap for both of them simultaneously. With an agonizing groan, Garrett's mouth slipped over hers. He seared her mouth with hungry, penetrating kisses, pulling her closer and more intimately to him, letting her feel his growing need. Chandra couldn't get close enough to him to satisfy her.

She arched toward him, her mouth responding to his, eager for the touch and smell of him. She had known it would be wrong to let him touch her, and she had been right. He wanted her, she knew that without a doubt as her body strained hotly against his.

The front light clicked on as Dan Loring stepped out onto the porch. Chandra jumped when she saw her father eyeing the mounting drifts of snow.

"I have to go in," she whispered nervously, edging over to her side of the car.

Garrett looked at her, his breathing ragged and wanting. "Can I see you again?"

"No, Phillip will be here tomorrow. The wedding . . . is the thirty-first." She faltered, "I—I'll be married then."

"I believe you really mean that," he said coldly. "Don't keep pushing me on this, Chandra. I've made my last offer!"

Her hand went for the handle of the door. "Good-bye, Garrett."

He stared moodily ahead of him in the dark car as she got out and slammed the door. The roar of his motor echoed loudly in the dark night as he started the car and drove around the corner, the red taillights glowing eerily in the snow. "I will not cry—I will not cry," Chandra chanted over and over, walking past her father in a stony daze. "I've cried my last tears over Garrett Morganson."

Chandra was just coming down to breakfast the next morning when the doorbell chimed. Wondering who it could be this early in the morning, she flung open the door to come face to face with the same smiling delivery man from the florist, standing there in the cold light of morning. The snow had trickled off to a fine smattering of flakes in the air.

"Hi! Would you believe another four dozen roses?" he asked, extending a bouquet to her identical to the one that he had delivered two weeks ago to another address.

"He didn't!" she grumbled under her breath, signing the receipt and trying to balance the flowers in her arms.

Closing the door hurriedly she reached for the card in the middle, reading Garrett's bold scrawl. "If you won't consider six months, how about six weeks. I want to be fair about it . . . I love you. Garrett."

Chandra felt like stomping her foot in irritation. What was she going to do with this impossible—lovable—man!

"Who was at the door, dear?" her mother asked, walking into the living room with a cup of coffee. "Oh, my." Her eyes widened as they took in the four dozen roses in Chandra's arms.

"Just the florist, Mom. Here, these are for you." Chandra shifted the roses over into her mom's arms, taking her coffee cup from her.

"For me!" Margo shrieked in delight, searching hurriedly for a card. "For heaven's sake, who would be rich enough to send me this many roses?"

"I don't know, it didn't have a card in it," Chandra fibbed blatantly. "They're probably from Dad," she improvised.

Margo glared at Chandra irritably. "In a pig's eye! Are these your flowers, Chandra Lea?"

"Not now, Mom. I gave them to you," she said lightly as she ushered her mother into the kitchen. "You enjoy them—even if Dad didn't send them, he certainly should have."

"I'll bet your Garrett sent these," her mother guessed accurately as she filled a large crystal vase with water and set the beautiful floral offering into it. "He must *really* have it bad for you."

Chandra poured herself a cup of coffee, then walked to the window to look bleakly out at the drifting snow. "Not bad enough, Mom, not bad enough."

CHAPTER NINE

The day of Phillip's arrival had come sooner than Chandra hoped it would. It wasn't that she didn't want to see Phillip—she desperately *did*. It was that she dreaded what had to be done. After hours of tossing and turning the night before she had made up her mind that no matter what the outcome of their talk she would never be able to marry him. Her mother had been right. It would not be fair to marry one man when her love was given to another.

Phillip arrived late in the afternoon, his red Ferrari creeping slowly down the snow-packed streets. Chandra stepped out on the porch to welcome him, her eyes lingering on his tall handsomeness as he alighted from his car. Giving her a flashing smile he hurried up the sidewalk to her.

"It's really good to see you, honey," he greeted, taking her in his arms. He kissed her eagerly, holding her slim body next to his tightly. Chandra honestly tried to return the kiss, but it was like kissing a stranger. *Phillip's arms don't feel the same as Gar*—She checked her traitorous thoughts.

Phillip severed the kiss and leaned back to look at her assessingly. "I'd almost forgotten how beautiful you are—almost, but not quite." His mouth took hers again for one more welcoming kiss. Chandra stood like a piece of stone, unable to show any sort of enthusiasm for his greeting. It was she that broke the kiss this time, taking his hand to lead him into the house. After a warm greeting from her parents, they stood in the kitchen and made

153

small talk as Margo and Chandra put the final touches to the evening meal.

"Fried chicken and hot biscuits! I haven't had a meal like this in a long time," Phillip told Margo gratefully, taking a radish on the relish tray Chandra was carrying to the table. "Does your daughter cook as well as you do?"

Margo paused as she stirred the gravy, shooting Chandra's father a look of dismay.

"Hasn't she ever cooked anything for you, Phillip?" Dan asked casually, coming to his wife's rescue.

Phillip thought for a moment, then shook his head negatively. "Not that I can recall—have you, Chandra?"

Chandra kept her head down as she finished setting the table. "I don't think I have," she mumbled absently.

"Well," he smiled, "are you as good a cook as your mother?"

"Different . . . I'd say we cook differently from each other." She wasn't about to tell him what a lousy cook she was. Garrett had already insulted her enough!

"Yes, that's how I would describe it," Dan spoke again as he walked over and placed his arms on his daughter's shoulders and smiled at her teasingly. "Chandra has a style all her own."

"I've always let her have free rein in the kitchen," Margo said, defending her motherly obligations, hoping that Phillip would remember her words after her daughter fixed their first meal together.

"Well, anyone as pretty as Chandra shouldn't have to be a good cook," Phillip complimented, winking at her.

Fifteen minutes later they sat down to an outstanding meal, each one praising Margo's cooking with every bite. When she brought out the slices of hot apple pie, rich with cinnamon, sugar, and butter, Phillip groaned in disbelief. "I don't know where I'm going to put that, but I'm sure going to try."

After dinner Margo insisted that Phillip and Chandra let her and Dan clean the kitchen, urging them to take an after-dinner walk together.

The crisp, night air felt good to Chandra as they stepped out onto the porch, warmly bundled up for their walk. As they started down the street an unusually strained silence developed between them, each one waiting for the other to speak. *I know he's aware there's something wrong,* she fretted as they turned the corner and started down Garner Avenue at a brisk pace. *But where do I even begin?*

As if he could sense that she wanted to say something, Phillip turned to her at the same moment she turned to him, both speaking at the same time.

"Phillip, I need to talk . . ."

"Chandra, there's something I think you should . . ."

They suddenly stopped walking, surprise written on each face. Phillip began to chuckle, Chandra joining in readily. The strained tension of the past few minutes entirely evaporated.

"You first," Phillip said respectfully, his laughter crinkling the corner of his eyes.

"No, really—you go first," Chandra demurred quickly, wanting to delay the inevitable as long as possible.

Phillip took a deep breath, then reached for her hand to resume their walking. "I guess you're wondering why I've come down early," he began somberly.

"Yes, I wasn't really expecting you until later," she answered, keeping pace with his long strides, "but I'm happy to see you anyway," she added guiltily.

The pressure on her hand increased as he silently acknowledged her words. Chandra felt a rush of love for him as they walked on together in the snowy night. Certainly not the wild, crazy, exhilarating kind of love she felt when she was with . . . the other one, but a warm, sisterly kind of love. It was like taking a walk with Darrell—easy, compatible, a warm feeling that he really cared about her.

"I'm sorry I didn't keep in touch this last week, but with the trial case . . ." His voice was apologetic, almost too much so.

"That's all right," Chandra assured him. "I've been in and out . . . you probably wouldn't have caught me." Her conscience stabbed at her sharply, as memories of the man she had spent that time with assailed her. "Did you go alone this time?"

"No, I took Janet with me." Phillip increased his strides as the wind began to stir in the bare branches of the sycamore trees lining the residential street.

"Janet Rayburn?" Chandra responded thoughtfully, her mind conjuring up the tall, dark-haired woman who worked in the law office with them. Janet had always been a quiet, unassuming type of person, going about her work with enthusiasm. Personally, Chandra had always thought Janet would have made the perfect mate for Phillip. She loved all types of sports just as avidly as he did. He used to perch on her desk for hours, discussing certain plays that had been made by their favorite football team the Sunday before. Chandra had certainly never felt threatened by his attention to Janet. She paused in her thinking . . . her mind trying to visualize Garrett perched on that same desk. A stinging blaze of jealousy shot through her. Janet would have had her hair ripped out if Garrett had!

"Yes, Marcy was sick," he replied absently.

Marcy Simmons was a much older lady who worked in the office. She usually accompanied Phillip or his father on out-of-town trips. There were books of dictation to take since the trials usually ran for days.

They were walking along the crowded streets now, throngs of Christmas shoppers braving the cold and snow for last-minute bargains. Each window was lit with Christmas decorations, lending a festive air to the night. As they walked by the department store window that she and Garrett had stood looking at only the week before, her hand tensed in Phillip's. Her eyes watched the busy little elves building the toys while Santa sat smoking his pipe and rocking rhythmically in his chair before the fire. She could almost feel the touch of Garrett's lips on her neck as he had pulled her over to whisper suggestively what Santa would like to bring her for Christmas. Unconsciously she removed her glove, bringing her fingers up to touch the area below her ear.

The one spot he always went to first when he was trying to arouse her.

Mesmerized by the scene before her she finally admitted to herself that she was weakening. With an overpowering certainty she knew she would give in to his demands if she stayed very much longer in the same town with him. She was in love with him, and she wasn't sure she could face the future without him. Maybe it would be better to have part of him than not have him at all. Her heart ached at the thought that he might grow tired of her at the end of the six months—or weeks, whatever. No, it was best if she went home Christmas day and tried to put Garrett out of her mind.

"Are you cold, honey?" Phillip reached for the ungloved hand, rubbing it gently. "Let's get some coffee."

Phillip found a small bar off the crowded street and led her into it. They adjusted their eyes to the dim light, then walked to a secluded table in the corner.

"Do you want coffee or something to drink?" Phillip offered peeling off his heavy gloves and laying them on the table.

Feeling in the mood for something stronger than coffee, she answered hurriedly, "I'd like to have an apricot sour if they make them."

"If they don't, they'll learn how." Phillip reached over and took her hands in his. "I want to talk to you, Chandra."

Chandra looked up swiftly, his tone of voice grave. "All right, Phillip. I need to talk to you also."

A gum-chewing waitress came over to the table to take their order.

Phillip gave her their order curtly, then brought his attention back to Chandra. "I honestly don't know where to start, Chandra." His warm eyes were intent on her rosy face, the wind having kissed it to a pretty pink. "You know I mentioned that I took Janet Rayburn with me on my trip last week."

"Yes." Chandra watched his face intently. Phillip was disturbed about something.

"Chandra . . ." Phillip ran his fingers over his face impatiently, fighting to gain control of his thoughts. "Janet and I . . . well, you know we always enjoyed the same things. . . ." His voice trailed off.

"Yes, I know she loves sports the way you do . . . go ahead, Phillip," she urged, wondering why he was so upset.

"One night after a long day in court last week, I took her out to dinner. We had a few drinks . . . one thing led to another . . ." Phillip's eyes were tormented as he looked at Chandra helplessly. "There's just no way to say this without hurting you . . . I'd give anything not to hurt you, Chandra, but you have to know. Janet and I spent the night together. I don't know how it happened . . . or even why. . . . It just happened."

Chandra stared at Phillip's anguished face, his words rattling emptily around in her head. He was telling her he had slept with Janet Rayburn. Where was the pain, the anger, the sense of betrayal?

"I wouldn't blame you if you threw my ring back in my face," he told her truthfully, "but, if you'll still have me, the wedding will proceed as we planned."

"Do you care for Janet?" she asked calmly.

"I . . . we feel something for each other. I'm not sure what." Phillip dropped his head shamefully. "Maybe it's just that we enjoy the same things."

Chandra's heart began to lighten, a tiny smile creeping over her features as she reached out and took his large hands in hers. All of a sudden a fountain of bubbling laughter erupted from her, her clear, tinkling tones filling the small bar as the irony of the situation dawned on her.

Phillip glanced up in astonishment at her peals of laughter, his eyes filled with concern. "Honey . . . don't get hysterical on me. Maybe I shouldn't have told you . . . but I like you far too much to go into a marriage with this between us. I mean it, Chandra, the marriage is still on if that's what you want." He shifted around uneasily in the booth, completely at a loss as to what to do for her. The few people sitting at the bar swiveled around on their stools to stare in their direction. "Chandra . . . stop that laughing!" he ordered roughly, trying to snap her out of it.

"I'm sor-ry, Phil-lip," she chortled, "you just don't know how happy this makes me!"

"Happy?" Phillip looked blank. "What are you talking about, Chandra? Don't you understand what I just told you?"

"Oh, Phillip!" Her laughter was building again, elation filling her heart. She didn't have to hurt him! Thank God, she didn't have to hurt him! "You remember before, when I told you I needed to talk to you about something too?"

"Yes, I remember."

"Well, hold on to your seat, dear Phillip, because you're not going to believe what you are about to hear."

As the waitress set their drinks before them, Chandra began to pour her story out to him, sparing no details of what had occurred since she came home. Her emotions swung like a giant pendulum, going from tears to radiant smiles as she told him of her feelings for Garrett and the utter hopelessness of her situation. Phillip listened intently, stopping her occasionally to ask her for more details on certain parts of the story, squeezing her hand in comfort as she told of Garrett's proposition of love, but no marriage.

After the story was related in full, she leaned back in the booth tiredly, yet feeling like a tremendous weight had been lifted from her. "I didn't want to hurt you either, Phillip, but I knew that I couldn't marry you after I met Garrett."

Phillip's eyes were shining with love and admiration for her as he brought her fingers up to his lips, kissing them fondly. "You're one terrific woman, Chandra Loring. . . . My loss, I'm afraid." He grinned tenderly.

"I want you and Janet to find happiness together. I've always thought she would be the perfect woman for you," Chandra told him gently. "Tell her I think you're a super kind of a man. . . . *My* loss, I'm sure!"

"Thanks, I will tell her that. She's been worried sick over how you would take this news," he confessed happily. "I told her you'd wish us happiness."

"Now, wait a minute, Phillip," she grinned pertly. "What made you so *sure* I would take it this well?"

"Because I know you, babe! And I don't honestly think you were ever in love with me to begin with—now were you?"

Her sunny smile faded into a loving one as she looked deeply into his eyes, his friendship very important to her. "I don't think I ever really was either, not in the way you so richly deserve, Phillip. Forgive me?"

"Only if you and Garrett name the first boy after me," he teased solemnly.

"I wish I could promise you that, but I don't think it's going to work out for me and Garrett," she told him sadly.

"Maybe you should take the chance with him, Chandra. Who knows, it may all turn out fine," Phillip encouraged, hoping to ease the pain in her eyes.

"I don't think so. On top of all our other problems, I'm virtually a hex on him. He's had more accidents since he met me than in his entire lifetime," she confessed miserably.

Phillip's deep laughter rang out loudly as Chandra related some of Garrett's accidents in the last few weeks.

"It's not funny," Chandra scolded seriously. "He was in bed for a couple of days with that back injury." She had discreetly left out the events leading up to Garrett slipping on the soap—she didn't want to bore him.

"We're really something, aren't we?" he grinned engagingly. "Sitting here discussing our new love lives, when we should be depressed and angry with each other over these"—his grin widened—"shocking developments."

"Yes, we should be discussing important things, such as whether we know anyone that could use one five-tiered wedding cake, three hundred hand-decorated mints, and enough punch and champagne to float a battleship." A fit of laughter overtook her.

"If you happen to run across anyone like that, tell them I'll throw in reservations at the Hilton for forty people for a sit-down chateaubriand dinner. Plus"—he held up one finger temptingly —"I'll give them a hot tip on a men's apparel store that has five maroon-colored tuxedoes they'll rent out for a good price on the thirty-first of this month."

They were both having so much fun talking about their disastrous wedding plans they didn't see the tall, dark-headed man with a stunning redhead on his arm enter the small bar and seat themselves at a table not far from them.

"Are you going back to Kansas City in the morning, or are you going to help me call all the people we've sent invita—" Chandra's voice suddenly dropped off as she recognized the new occupants in the room.

"What's the matter?" Phillip asked, turning in his seat to get a better look. Her laughter and gaiety had died an instant death on seeing Garrett.

"It's him," she whispered desperately, her heart pounding in her throat as she surveyed the woman he was with.

"Who?" Phillip was straining to make out faces in the dim light.

"Garrett! He's right over there at that table by the jukebox." Chandra suddenly felt like crying. Garrett was talking in low tones to the girl beside him, his deep laugh reaching her painfully.

"No kidding." Phillip let out a low whistle. "Get a load of the dish he's got with him."

"Phillip!" she hissed angrily. "You don't need to point her out to me. I noticed her right off." Chandra was absolutely miserable now, wanting to slink out of the room unnoticed.

All hopes of that vanished as Garrett looked up, his eyes turning to cold slits as he spotted her and Phillip together at the table. Deliberately ignoring her presence his eyes dropped back to the redhead continuing on with their conversation.

"Let's go, Phillip," Chandra pleaded under her breath. She couldn't stand to sit here a moment longer.

"What's your hurry?" He pulled her back in the booth firmly.

"Don't you think it would be obvious if we jumped up and ran out the door right now? Just relax. Let's have another drink, then when the time's right we'll leave."

Chandra slid back into the booth and sat mutely as Phillip signaled to the waitress for two more drinks.

"Do you know the woman with him?" he asked conversationally, picking up one of her hands to study intently.

"No," she said in a miserable tone of voice. "I didn't know he knew anyone in town yet."

"Maybe it's just a friend," Phillip suggested, tracing the outline of her trembling fingers with one of his.

"Sure, that's probably it," she agreed dishearteningly. How gullible did he think she was?

After their drinks were set before them, someone put some money in the jukebox and a few couples stood up to dance.

"How about it?" Phillip held out his arms in invitation as he stood up.

"No, Phillip," she protested.

"Come on—what's it going to hurt?"

With a sigh of resignation, she slid out of the booth and walked to the dance floor. As she went into his arms she saw Garrett stand up and escort the redhead out onto the floor.

Chandra tried to relax and enjoy the music as Phillip pulled her close, dancing intimately with her to the slow love song that was playing. The words were sweet and haunting as they glided around the floor, dancing in perfect time together. Phillip kept edging her across the room little by little, until she felt them bump into another couple unexpectedly.

"Excuse us," Phillip apologized profusely. "I guess we were too engrossed in each other to look where we were going." He grinned at the couple engagingly.

"It's quite all right," she heard Garrett's deep voice answer curtly.

With a quick intake of breath Chandra turned her head to encounter the deep, blue eyes of the man standing practically on

162

top of them. She froze for a moment as his eyes bored into hers, her knees turning weak and watery.

"Chandra," he nodded briefly.

"Garrett," she acknowledged back softly.

"Hey! Do you two know each other?" Phillip's face lit up in smiles. Chandra had to force herself to keep from kicking him in the shins. What did he think he was doing?

"We've met," Garrett responded coolly.

"Well, hey . . . how about joining us for a drink? I'm Phillip Watson and you're Garrett . . ." He paused, waiting for a last name, his hand extended in friendship.

"Morganson."

"Garrett Morganson—and I didn't catch your date's name."

"I didn't throw it," Garrett said bluntly.

"A man with a sense of humor," Phillip laughed, completely ignoring Chandra's frantic punches with her elbow in his side. "Let's all sit down and have a drink."

The four approached the table in silence as Phillip stepped back and directed the redhead into the closest chair. Chandra's mouth dropped as he unconcernedly slid into the one next to her, talking a mile a minute. "So what *is* your name?" he asked sincerely.

"Jill Jenson." She glanced at Garrett questioningly.

Garrett and Chandra were still standing uncomfortably in front of the table, watching Phillip introduce himself to Jill.

Without a word Garrett took her arm and ushered her into the other chair, Chandra's stomach churning with butterflies as his familiar aftershave reached her. She wanted to scream, pull her hair, cry. All those emotions filtered through her mind as she sat trying to keep her leg from brushing against his at the small table. Phillip ordered a round of drinks once again, then settled back to get acquainted.

Chandra's nerves were at the breaking point as she sat and listened to Garrett and Phillip discuss everything from football to airplanes. Jill tried to make small conversation with Chandra,

163

but failed miserably when Chandra was unable to respond with anything more than one-syllable words.

She could feel the heat from Garrett's body as they were pressed tightly in the small area. She avoided making eye contact with him, afraid she would break out in tears if he blinked at her. It had been so long since she had seen him . . . only one day on the calendar, but to her it seemed a lifetime.

"Are you from here, Chandra?" Jill tried once again, completely unaware of the agony Chandra was suffering.

"Originally, but I've lived in Kansas City for the last three years."

As she spoke Garrett stared down at his drink, one long finger absently making lazy, wet circles on the outside of his glass. Her eyes were drawn immediately to the slow, easy motion. Watching the play of his hand reminded her of the times he had caressed her in sweet seduction, exploring her body with his hands, then how in a frenzied burst of desire his mouth would take their place. He had never hurried with her. He always made the union between them a sharing, loving experience. Chandra remembered the last night they had been together. Garrett had made love to her numerous times during the night, each time as thrilling and passionate as the time before. They had lain awake the last time until early morning, kissing and holding each other, whispering things lovers whisper to each other after a night of love.

"I love Kansas City," Jill said brightly. "I had a boyfriend who lived there once. Are you just home for the holidays?"

"Say, it looks as if everyone needs their glasses filled again," Phillip broke in, raising his hand for the waitress.

"Nothing for me," Chandra said hurriedly. "Don't you think we should be going now, Phillip?"

"Just one more drink. We're walking," he explained to the other two at the table.

"I'll have another bloody mary," Jill said, more than content to stay where she was.

"Make mine a cup of coffee," Garrett said blandly. "I'm driving."

"Would you mind too much if I asked Jill for a dance?" Phillip asked Garrett, after giving the order.

"It's fine with me," he said lightly.

Chandra looked at Phillip panic-stricken. He wouldn't get up and leave them sitting here alone, would he?

A few minutes later Chandra found herself alone with Garrett at the table, her heart fluttering wildly. Neither one of them spoke for a moment, the tension hanging in a heavy cloud over their heads.

"Did you want to dance?" Garrett's disinterested voice broke in the silence.

"No . . . no thank you," she said softly.

"What's the matter? Afraid you'll make your fiancé mad? It shouldn't. He seems to be enjoying himself."

Chandra watched as Phillip and Jill happily discoed to a fast record that was playing. She let Garrett's remark about Phillip being her fiancé pass without comment. She had no intention of telling him about her aborted plans. "He wouldn't mind—I just don't want to dance," she replied simply.

"Suit yourself." Garrett turned his attention to the dance floor, ignoring her completely.

"Where did you meet Jill?" Chandra could have bitten her tongue off. That was the last thing in the world she had planned on asking him. It seemed she just opened her mouth, and it popped right out.

Garrett turned back around to face her, his face a cool mask of indifference. "Does it matter?"

"Oh, no. . . . No, of course not. It's really none of my business," she added, flustered.

"That's what I was thinking," he returned snidely.

The waitress came over with Garrett's coffee and sat it down before him. She gave him an overly friendly grin in Chandra's estimation as she handed him his change. "Whistle if you need anything." Her big blue eyes spoke volumes.

"I didn't mean anything personal about Jill." Chandra couldn't seem to let it lie. "I just didn't realize you knew anyone here in town yet," she defended.

"I *didn't* know her until three hours ago. I picked her up in a bar over on Sixty-second Street," he stated casually, taking a drink of the hot coffee.

"You picked her up in a bar?" Chandra's voice sounded modestly shocked.

"What better way to meet a woman other than at a cocktail party?" he asked her dryly. "A fellow at the bar introduced us. He said she was fun to play . . . poker with." He sat his cup back down and looked at Chandra pointedly. "You got something against that?"

Chandra's lower lip jutted out, jealousy springing alive inside her. *Play poker, my foot.* "None whatsoever!" she spat out, turning back to stare into her empty glass.

"She's good-looking, isn't she?"

"Simply gorgeous." He wasn't going to trick her into losing her temper.

They sat in silence while Garrett drummed his fingers on the small table. "Did you happen to notice the way that dress she's wearing clings to her—" he began again.

Chandra had had enough. "Excuse me, Garrett," she said between tight lips. "I've suddenly developed a headache and want to go home." She angrily shoved the small table back as she started to stand up.

Garrett jumped back as his hot cup of coffee came tumbling down in his lap. With a choice, muttered expletive that Chandra hated he came to his feet immediately, sucking his breath in sharply between clenched teeth and mopping frantically at the hot coffee staining the front of his trousers.

"Oh, Garrett!" Chandra was instantly contrite, trying to help him sop up the dark, staining liquid.

Phillip was leading Jill back to the table when all the commotion broke out. "What in the world happened?" he asked, his eyes taking in the condition of Garrett's trousers.

"Ohhhh . . . I spilled hot coffee on him." Chandra grabbed another napkin and began to work harder at getting the stain out. She leaned over, intently scrubbing near his zipper, never once stopping to think of how it looked. A large hand grabbed hers, stopping it in midair. Raising her eyes slowly she encountered Garrett's lazy blue eyes staring at her in amusement, yet uneasily. "That's enough, Chandra."

Chandra glanced around sheepishly at Phillip and Jill, who stood gaping in fascination. Chandra blushed a bright red.

"Is there anything we can do for you, Garrett? That burn must hurt like the blue blazes," Phillip asked solicitously, pulling Chandra over beside him, seeing her acute embarrassment.

"No, I don't think it's too bad," Garrett refused concisely.

"Couldn't we get you something for the pain?" he insisted, escorting Garrett and Jill to the front door of the tavern.

"No, it's amazing how I'm getting used to pain," Garrett said resignedly. "I've lived with it constantly for the last two weeks now." His eyes looked at Chandra meaningfully. "I'll just go home and put some salve on it."

"I'm sorry, Garrett." Chandra hurt for him. Her churlishness was constantly getting her in trouble with him. She should have never let him goad her into losing her temper again at the table.

"Forget it." Garrett's voice held no anger as he watched the play of emotions scamper across her face. He reached out and gently tipped her face up to his. "It was an accident that I asked for."

"No, you didn't. I was being foolish . . . again," she answered back softly.

"Would you and Jill mind giving us a lift back to Chandra's parents? It's getting awfully cold to walk back tonight." Phillip's voice made them all too aware that they were not alone.

"No problem. I'll be happy to." Garrett turned and reached for his coat, helping Jill into hers. "It's getting late. We're ready if you are."

Garrett dropped them in front of Chandra's house, the Trans Am's engine purring quietly as they climbed out of the back seat.

Garrett didn't look Chandra's way as Phillip thanked him for the ride.

The sporty black car disappeared down the street, leaving Phillip and Chandra standing alone on the sidewalk. With a look of compassion, Phillip drew her to his side and walked slowly up the steps with her. She was grateful he hadn't spoken a word to her, just offered her his broad shoulder to cry on . . . and she accepted his offer.

"I hope you're not upset over my actions back at the bar," Phillip said as they walked up onto the old porch. "I just thought if Garrett saw you in my company . . ."

"Thank you, Phillip, but that wouldn't faze Garrett," she sighed. "He's very independent."

"I'll be glad to stay around and help pick up the pieces," he offered, taking her key to unlock the door.

"No, I'm a big girl now. I'll have to learn to live without him. I'll make it!" she told him. But would she?

The clock on her nightstand read ten minutes after two and still sleep eluded her. After an hour of tossing and turning she had gotten up and reached for a magazine to thumb through, trying to relax so she could go to sleep. Everyone in the house had been asleep hours ago. Her mind kept going back to Garrett. She couldn't help worrying if the burn had been a bad one. If she could just talk to him for a few minutes maybe that would relieve her mind. *Who are you kidding, Chandra,* a little voice interrupted. *What you really want to know is if he went home alone.* What if she called and interrupted something. . . . She shook her head, trying to clear that painful thought out of her mind. No, it wouldn't hurt if she just called and inquired about his injury. That's the least she could do for a . . . friend.

Creeping down the wide staircase she made it to the bottom, quickly sitting down on the carpeted stairs. Chandra couldn't count the hours she had spent sitting on this same stair talking to her girlfriends when she lived at home.

Quietly she picked up the phone from the small table it sat on and quickly dialed Garrett's number. The phone began to ring as she held her breath, willing him to be there . . . and alone.

A sleepy, slightly irritated voice came over the wire as she tucked the hem of her gown around her bare feet, protecting them from the cold floor.

"Hello?"

"Hi . . . did I disturb you?" she asked hurriedly, hoping he wouldn't be mad at her calling at this hour.

A brief pause met her question, then Garrett snapped grumpily, "Chandra, is that you?"

"Yes."

"Do you know what time it is?"

"Yes."

A long, resigned sigh came from the other end of the phone as Garrett apparently made himself more comfortable. Chandra could picture him lying in bed, his broad, hair-covered chest bare, his brown hair tousled from sleep. "Okay, what's the problem, Chandra?" he asked softly.

"No problem. . . . Are you alone?" Chandra chewed on her bottom lip nervously. *Please say you're alone.*

Another pregnant pause for a moment, then, "I'm alone."

"Well, I know it's none of my business . . . and that isn't why I called," she hastened to add. "I was just wondering how bad the burn was." She stared down at her toes and wiggled them experimentally as she talked.

"Not too bad," he said tiredly. "I'm clinging faintly to the small hope that if and when it heals, I'll still be able to father children."

"Oh." Chandra's face suddenly brightened as an exhilarating thought crossed her mind. "I guess it pretty well ruined your evening with that woman you picked up at the bar."

Garrett chuckled low. "I didn't pick her up at a bar, Chandra. I've known her and her parents for several years. She used to work in Arlington with me. She was visiting relatives in town, and I happened to run into her tonight. I'm sorry I misled you like I did. Jill is a nice person."

"That still wouldn't prevent her from being there," Chandra reminded curtly, a little put out with his deception.

"Honey, if I had a harem standing here, staring me in the face, the only thing I could do for them at the moment is whistle 'Dixie.'"

"I really am sorry about the coffee, Garrett, but it was pretty rotten of you to imply Jill was a—" Her voice broke off painfully.

"Would it really matter to you?" he cut her off in a tired, defeated voice.

"Yes, it would." Chandra couldn't lie to him. "I'm sorry, I know it's unreasonable, but I feel very jealous of her."

"Not fair, honey. I've offered you the position of being the only lady in my bed and you refused—several times," he reminded curtly.

"I know," she said, twisting the phone cord around her finger.

"All you have to do is say the word," Garrett offered again. "I'll be in my car in two minutes to come and get you."

"No, I love you and I want to say those words . . . but I can't," she whispered miserably.

"What did you say?"

"I said I want to, but I can't."

"No, you said something along with that," he pressed huskily.

"You mean the part about 'I love you.'"

"Yeah, that part. Say that again."

"I love you, I love you, I love you," she whispered tenderly into the phone, her eyes filling with tears.

"Sweetheart, I wish I could believe that. The only problem is, you love another man too. If you were only lying here beside me right now, I'd make you forget there ever was a man named Phillip," he whispered, his voice sexy and low.

Chandra was too overcome with emotion to speak for a moment. She closed her eyes, the tears dropping hotly down the front of her gown. She couldn't tell him she didn't love Phillip. He would expect her to come to him, and she was afraid that this time she wouldn't refuse.

"Are you crying again?" he asked in tender irritation. "I'm warning you—if you are, I'll start cussing."

She smiled through a veil of tears at his implied threat. Her tears drove him up a wall and his cussing upset her greatly. "You're a bully," she sobbed lovingly into the receiver.

"I know—a mean, cussin' bully." Garrett's voice clouded with desire. "Come to me tonight, Chandra. Let me hold you in my arms and show you how good it can be for us," he pleaded fervently.

"I thought you couldn't . . . be with a woman tonight," she sniffed, thrilled at the intensity of the words he had just spoken to her.

"Just having you here in my arms tonight would be enough for me, Chandra," he said earnestly. "Although I desire you more than any woman I've ever known, sometimes just having the right person with him is the most important thing to a man."

"If I'm really the right person, Garrett, why are we so far apart right now?" she asked tearfully, laying her head against the cold banister.

"Number one, there's a matter of Phillip; number two, there's a matter of your stubbornness. If you loved me, you'd break that engagement right now, call a cab, and come over here." His tone grew tense, the soft, sexy teasing gone now from his voice.

"And if you loved me, you'd ask me to be your wife, the mother of your children, the only woman you'd ever need," she told him crossly.

"I've asked you most of those things already," he snapped. "Why can't you be satisfied with that? You want me and Phillip both? Well, sorry, baby. I don't operate that way."

"That's not true, Garrett! I don't want any more than any other woman wants—a home, a husband, security."

"Dammit, Chandra . . . I'm not going to argue with you over this one more time. I'm going to lay it on the line once and for all. You give that damn ring back, cancel the wedding, then get yourself back over here where you belong! Then we'll talk about a marriage between us. If you don't," he warned grimly, "I'm going to put this house up for sale, find a small apartment, and try to regain some semblance of a sane orderly peaceful life—one I was used to living before I met you!"

"That's fine with me—go ahead! I will not buckle under your threats. I will not break the engagement and hang on to the bare thread of hope that you *might* ask me to marry you—and I will *not* come to your damn house!" Her voice was rising sharply now.

"Chandra Loring," Garrett's voice bellowed over the wire, "if I could get my hands on you right now, I'd give you that spanking that's twenty-five years overdue! And you better not let me hear another cuss word come out of that mouth of yours again—you understand?!"

She taunted him childishly with a string of curses, her temper boiling. "How do you like *that*, Mr. Morganson? That's what I've had to live with ever since I met you! And another thing," she was standing up, yelling into the receiver at him, "you're not going to have the opportunity to lay one hand on me because I'm going back to Kansas City first thing Christmas aft—" She caught herself, realizing what she had just said.

"Well, go ahead—finish your temper tantrum. You're going back to Kansas City—when?" Garrett simmered, his voice more alert than before.

"Never mind," she said hatefully.

"No, you said you were leaving Christmas afternoon, didn't you? Why?"

"Garrett . . . it was just a slip of the tongue," she hedged, angry she had let that piece of information slip.

"You're lying and that means only one thing. You're not getting married on the thirty-first, are you?" he demanded tensely.

"Either way it's not your problem anymore," she murmured, sickened at the way they always fought with each other. She had always been such a passive person until she'd met Garrett.

"Tell me the truth, Chandra," he ordered tightly. "Is Phillip out of your life for good?"

"Yes," she finally conceded. "I'm not going to marry him." It would be simple for Garrett to find out the truth—she might as well admit it to him. "But I'm *not* going to move in with you either," she warned heatedly lest he misunderstand the reason for the broken engagement. "I'm going back to my job and *my* sane, orderly life."

"Is that a fact?" he said airily, his whole mood changing now. "Well, don't be surprised if things don't work out your way." There was a pause then he added, "Phillip dumped you after he found out about us, huh?"

"He certainly *did not*," she bristled hotly. "I . . . we . . . it was a mutual agreement!" She wasn't about to reveal what actually happened.

"Then *you* broke the engagement, *not* Phillip," Garrett pressed intensely. "You're not in love with him any longer?"

"That's right! I broke it. I knew a long time ago I never was in love with hi—" She caught herself again. "I mean . . . not really in love with him."

"Well, well, well," Garrett breathed solemnly, "you don't know how happy I am to hear that." There was a small pause. "Get some sleep, you dippy broad. I'll talk to you later."

The abrupt click of his receiver sounded loudly in her ear. Chandra glared at her phone irritably, then slammed it back on the cradle heatedly. "Dippy broad!" she fumed on the way back to her bed.

He was undoubtedly the most nerve-wracking man she had ever encountered. Christmas Day couldn't get here fast enough for her. The sooner she got back to Kansas City, the better. Her nerves couldn't take much more of this.

CHAPTER TEN

Chandra's thoughts might have been brave, but in the cold light of morning she wasn't so sure she could live up to them. After seeing Phillip off she sat back down at the kitchen table with her second cup of coffee and a blackness descended over her. If it wasn't for the fact that she would disappoint her parents greatly by not being here for Christmas, she would pack her clothes and leave this very morning. Christmas had lost all its appeal for her right now. She just wanted to get it over and behind her as quickly as possible.

The final days crept slowly by as Chandra began the tedious task of canceling her wedding and trying to keep her mind off Garrett. He had called twice but she had refused to speak with him. With each passing hour the pain grew stronger. Each time a Christmas carol came over the radio she would get up and switch it off immediately. Tears were never far from the surface these days, and she tried to avoid anything remotely close to emotion. She had enough sadness to last her the rest of her life.

At last Christmas Eve arrived, and she had only one more day to endure before going back to her other life.

"I hate to see you so unhappy, dear." Margo was making a batch of peanut brittle late that afternoon as Chandra sat absently watching her mother measure the sugar, corn syrup, and water into the heavy pan. "You shouldn't be so stubborn. He's called twice, Chandra," she reminded gently.

Chandra watched as Margo sat the pan on the stove and turned on the burner, stirring the mixture as it heated. "I don't

174

want to talk to him, Mom. We have nothing to say to each other," she answered calmly.

"You'll excuse me if I disagree with that," Margo said skeptically. "It seems to me you haven't said enough to each other. Isn't there any way to settle this between the two of you?"

"Only one way, Mom, and I don't think you would be crazy about the idea," Chandra said wryly.

"I don't know, Chandra. I'm aware of what Garrett's terms are. I also know you've been raised to frown on the kind of relationship he's asking for, but I haven't lived forty-seven years without coming to the realization that love doesn't always follow the rules society has laid down for it so perfectly," she reasoned quietly.

"You're surely not suggesting that I *accept* his offer, are you Mom?" Chandra believed in miracles, but not in this situation, and certainly not from her old-fashioned, straitlaced mother!

"Of course not," Margo reproved mildly, watching the bubbling mixture in the pan before her intently. "I'm just saying love is a strange and wonderful occurrence. When two people find it—really find it—then they should fight to keep it. You have to hang on tight and fight for what is important in your life, Chandra."

"Even if it means taking the chance that in the end I would end up with nothing but bitterness and regrets?" Chandra asked softly.

"Sometimes a person has to take chances, darling. Trust between two people is very important. If you can't trust the one you love to not hurt you, who can you trust?" Margo laid the spoon down and walked over to take her daughter's hands in hers. "I can tell you the wisest thing to do, Chandra. I just can't tell you the right thing. All your father and I want is for you to be happy. We all strive to live a good, decent life, be God-fearing people, and do the best we can in life; but sadly, when it all comes down to it, we're only too human . . . weak in some areas, stronger in others. We all make mistakes—we're not perfect. If what you feel for Garrett is real, then go to him before you leave tomorrow and try to work it out. There will have to be compromises from both of you. There will be for the rest of your lives, but it's worth it if you love each other."

"Mom, you said if you couldn't trust the one you love, who can you trust? What if Garrett isn't worthy of that trust? I love him, but I don't know if he really loves me," Chandra said drearily.

"He's worthy, darling. If he wasn't, you wouldn't love him," she replied in motherly wisdom. "I know *my* daughter."

Chandra squeezed her mother's hands in affection, love filling her clear, hazel eyes. "How did you get so wise?" she teased mildly. "Or is it that I just have an exceptional mother who's always been able to make my problems seem smaller?"

"I'm neither wise, nor exceptional, I'm just experienced," Margo said, patting her hand. "Think about what I said, Chandra. Think long and hard, and it wouldn't hurt to ask for some help from above. Speaking of which," she added, "if you're going to make the early candlelight service at church, you'd better get busy. Dad and I have decided to go to the midnight one."

"Thanks, Mom . . . for everything," she smiled, reaching over to hug her mother tightly.

As she climbed the stairs to dress for church, Chandra mused that, although her problems were neither bigger nor smaller than before, it just seemed her burden was a little lighter to carry now.

The inside of the old church smelled of pine and holly. The strains of the pipe organ filled the air with Christmas carols as Chandra took a candle from the table in the foyer and lit it from a burning taper. With reverence she entered the chapel and took a seat, her eyes going to the altar covered in red poinsettias. The choir was singing Christmas hymns as the congregation filled the pews, only the flickering from each of their candles lighting the way.

Chandra sat peacefully, her mind going over what her mother had said to her earlier. Was it possible she was guilty of what she had so often accused Garrett of—too little trust? Should she take the chance on love, simply praying that it would turn out well in the end for her? The choir was telling of a perfect love now, and the thought filtered through her mind that even *that* love suffered its share of heartbreak. What gave her the right to think that she was any different from anyone else—that she deserved nothing less than peace, harmony, and security in her life? Garrett had known very little love in his lifetime, why should he trust her to give him something he'd never possessed?

The tiny white candle flickered brightly in her hands, the rich strains of "Silent Night" filling the old chapel. She was going to go to him tonight. She would accept his offer—his way—and hope that in the end love would win out. She had more than enough love for them both, and in the quiet sanctity of the church she resolved to give Garrett the love and devotion of a wife, whether she held the title or not. He was the center of her life, and if he were only here with her right now, her world would be complete.

A latecomer was pushing his way into the pew, mumbling low apologies as he edged between the tight pews, his large feet unconsciously stepping on the feet of the people sitting in her row. Chandra tried to concentrate on the deeply stirring solo in "O Holy Night" that one of the angelic choir boys was singing, ignoring the flurrying scuffle taking place in the pew.

A few seconds later a man squeezed in next to her, mumbling softly under his breath as he sat on her purse. Reaching over to move it, she glanced up while trying to pull the hem of her skirt out from beneath him. Her miffed eyes met with huffy blue ones.

"What are you doing here?" she hissed, startled by his sudden presence.

"I want to talk to you, Chandra," Garrett muttered tensely, cupping his hand to catch the wax dripping off his candle.

"Well, I don't want to talk to you," she shot back, all previous loving thoughts of him completely deserting her now.

"Help me do something with this blasted dripping candle," he ordered roughly. "I'm going to burn the church to the ground!"

The worshipers sitting around them were beginning to stare, several insistent "Shhh's!" coming from their lips. Gertrude Beason, one of her neighbors, had turned completely around in her pew to stare, her beady eyes boring into them pointedly.

"Where's the piece of paper that catches the drips?" Chandra sizzled tightly, her face turning bright red from embarrassment.

"What paper?" he gritted, disgruntled.

"The one lying next to the candles, you dolt!" She smiled sweetly and gave a tiny wave to Mrs. Beason, mouthing the words, "Merry Christmas!"

"I didn't see any. Let's get out of here. I want to talk to you," he ordered.

"I will not," she said between clenched teeth. "Go away—you're making a scene!"

Garrett grabbed for her hand sternly. "You're coming with me if I have to drag you out of here. This is no place for us to try to talk," he gritted out determinedly.

Chandra glared at him, then grabbed her purse and sprang to her feet. She made her way hurriedly out of the pew as Garrett followed, murmuring his apologies to the people whose feet he was trampling on the way out.

The large wooden doors closed quietly behind him as he ran into the small, dark foyer. Chandra was hurriedly donning her coat, trying her best to escape him. She ran for the front door of the church as Garrett jerked her to a sudden halt.

"Where have you been for the last couple of days?" he demanded belligerently, his blue eyes snapping fire. "I've been waiting for you to come around ever since you called the other night."

Chandra glowered at him sourly. "What are you talking about? I told you I wasn't coming over." She twisted around, trying to free her imprisoned wrists heatedly. "Let me go!"

"I know what you *said,* but I thought that you just *might* love me enough to at least come over and try to work out something," he grumbled irritably, stilling her squirming with one long, hard jerk. "Hold still—we're going to talk whether you like it or not."

"If I love you! You've got your nerve. It wasn't me that treated *you* like a . . . a . . . harlot!" she accused hostilely.

178

"A harlot! That's ridiculous!" His face was growing angrier by the minute. "You know I've never thought of you like that. We may have slept together, but you knew I loved you!" he fumed in a hoarse whisper.

"Shhhhh! People might hear you!" she whispered fiercely as she glanced uneasily at the wooden doors. "You don't love me enough to marry me. I'm nothing but a 'dippy broad' to you, Garrett Morganson." She fought the rising tears in her eyes. "Just go away. I don't want to hear anything you've got to say." She struggled ineffectually against his iron grip.

"Tough, because I'm going to say it anyway," he whispered angrily. "I know I hurt your pride when I asked you to just live with me. I'm sorry for that. That week you spent with me was the happiest week of my life—"

"Yes, Garrett, you hurt my pride," she hissed stormily, managing to break his grip with one vicious jerk. "But more than that, you've broken my heart!" She broke for the door in a hard run, tears blinding her eyes. As she bounded out the front door Garrett was right behind her in hot pursuit. Her flying feet hit the steps, making her nearly lose her balance for a moment on the thin coating of ice that clung to one of the steps. She grabbed for the rail to steady herself, then flew on down the steps.

"You'll never outrun me," Garrett predicted determinedly as he increased his large strides, gaining on her. "We're going to talk this thing out—like it or not. I'm trying to ask you a question, lady, and I'm not leaving until you give me an answer!" he bellowed, reaching the ice-covered step.

"You leave me alone, you big . . . bully! What jerk told you I was here, anyway?" she shouted, reaching the end of the steps, and looking around wildly for some means of escape.

"Your *mother* told me where you were," he panted.

"Oh, I'm sorry, Mother," she pleaded silently as she broke to the left around to the back of the church.

The running battle was immediately thwarted as Garrett let out a string of oaths, ending with a defeated, "Oh, Lord! Not again!"

Whirling around at the sound of his angry shouts, she saw him sitting on the bottom step of the church, a stunned glaze filming his eyes.

Skidding to a sudden halt, she backed up to peer more closely at him, trying to ascertain if it was a trick to buy him time to catch her, or if he was really hurt. She sauntered over closer, keeping a wary eye on him and curtly asked, "What's the matter now?" Her voice indicated she was getting fed up with his injuries.

"Nothing unusual. Just another of the periodic accidents I've had since I met you," he answered aloofly, reaching down to slip off one of his brown dress boots.

Chandra stepped closer, gazing down at his swelling ankle. "The ice on the steps?" she asked in interest as he pulled up his pant leg, revealing a hair-covered, muscular calf.

Garrett was busy examining the injury, his fingers probing the rising puffiness. "Well, this should lay me up for another damn four or five days," he grunted bleakly.

"It looks like it could be broken," she mused thoughtfully, leaning over in fascination to punch the puffiness with one of her fingers. "Does that hurt?"

Garrett jerked his foot back heatedly, wincing in severe pain. "Hell yes, that hurts! Leave it alone. Are you a sadist or something?"

"I'm sure it's broken," she announced in a tone of certainty. "I'll have to take you to the hospital. Where's your car?"

"I parked it about a block over," he answered, standing up slowly to test his weight on the injured foot, grimacing in pain.

"Give me the keys. I'll go get it," she said disgruntledly.

He dug into his front pocket and extracted a set of keys, flipping them at her arrogantly. "Try to get it here in one piece."

Chandra gave him a saccharine smile. "It isn't *me* who is accident-prone," she reminded him.

Five minutes later she gunned the Trans Am up in front of the church and waited while Garrett hobbled over to the passenger side and got in.

"I'll take you to the hospital but I don't intend to talk to you. Is that clear?" she instructed coolly, pulling away from the church.

"If you want to act like a two-year-old, I can't stop you," he told her, cringing when she hit the curb as she turned the tight corner onto Main Street.

"Don't you *dare* say anything," she threatened grimly. "I never drove a floor shift before!"

"Terrific," he gritted under his breath.

Chandra jerked and ground their way to the hospital in strained silence. Only an occasional muffled expletive escaped Garrett when she had trouble shifting, and the nerve-shattering grinding filled the car as she forced it into gear, her eyes *daring* him to comment. She could feel the tears welling up again as she drove down the crowded street berating herself for treating him the way she was. She didn't know what got into her when she was with him. The one person she loved the most she treated the worst. Only thirty minutes ago she had been planning on going to him and throwing herself on his mercy. Now they rode stonily together in his car, each one harboring ill thoughts of the other.

The car pulled up in front of the emergency exit, and a nurse reached for a wheelchair as she saw Garrett emerging from the car on one foot.

"I'll park the car," Chandra said as the nurse settled him comfortably in the wheelchair.

"Please do," he grunted, "while there's a piece of it left to park." He was grumbling under his breath as the nurse whisked him away through the wide set of emergency room doors.

Within minutes Chandra walked through the same doors, the antiseptic smell of the hospital assaulting her as she walked over to take a seat in the small waiting room.

It was thirty minutes before the nurse came back out, wheeling Garrett on a cart to X-ray, and another forty-five minutes before she returned with him, smiling at Chandra as she walked to her. An orderly pushed Garrett's cart back into the emergency room. "I'm afraid the ankle's broken," she said kindly. "The doctor is on his way to put a cast on it. There's no reason for Mr. Morganson to spend the night here. You can take him home after the doctor's finished."

"Thank you," Chandra said softly. "Is—is he okay?"

"He's experiencing some pain, but that's only to be expected. Can I get you some coffee?" she offered nicely.

"No, thank you. I'll just wait here until he can go home."

"He asked if you would see him now." She inserted her hands into her uniform pockets. "You're welcome to go in and be with him," she invited. "The doctor will be a while yet."

Chandra started for the door, the anger, childishness, and fight all draining out of her. She wanted to see him, tell him she loved him—she was tired of all the fighting and she only wanted to be with him now.

She entered the swinging doors and walked over to a cart Garrett was sitting on. A heavy-set, older nurse rolled up his sleeve and inserted a needle into his left arm as another nurse disappeared behind a screened partition.

He glanced up, his blue eyes meeting hers. A silent plea for a lasting truce exchanged between them as Chandra stood in the door drinking in his familiar features. A feeling of undeniable love surged through her. She walked over to him slowly and paused before him. "Hi," she said softly.

A tiny grin hovered at his mouth as he readily reached out and took one of her hands in his. "Hi," he returned gently.

She noticed his face was pale, the lines around his eyes tight from pain. "Are you all right? The nurse said you were having some pain." Chandra's knees were growing weak as she stood facing him, his hand grasping hers tightly. How could she ever have considered letting him go? He was the sun and moon for her, his very presence filled her with unspeakable joy.

"It's not bad—now that you're here," he answered, his eyes looking deeply into hers.

"I'll always be here, Garrett," she finally admitted, her love for him shining in her eyes. "I want you to know, I'll come and live with you. I can't go on any longer fighting you. I love you too much to deny what happiness we can bring each other. If the offer's still open, then I humbly accept. I want to be with you as long as you want me." Her voice was low, her eyes never leaving the depths of his.

"Do you know how many nights I've lain awake fantasizing that someday you would say those words to me, Chandra?" Garrett's look was returning her love a thousandfold in the quiet, antiseptic room. The two nurses slipped quietly out the door, leaving the couple alone.

"You've always known I loved you," she whispered shyly, aching for him to touch her, to feel the comfort of his arms once more.

"You've said the words to me, but you wore another man's ring."

"I didn't love Phillip . . . not in the way that I love you. You knew that, Garrett." Chandra moved closer to him, her arms creeping around his neck.

"I knew you had your doubts about the marriage, but I honestly didn't know if you would marry the man or not," he said sincerely, his arms going around her waist to gently urge her nearer. "I had to be sure you'd break the engagement before I gave my heart to you completely. I *had* to, Chandra!"

"I knew I wasn't going to marry Phillip from the first morning you left my house when Mr. Rhodes picked you up. I still forced myself to think I was, but in my heart I knew there would always be a blue-eyed test pilot somewhere in the world who had stolen my heart," she murmured truthfully, her fingers gently soothing his now.

"It tore me to pieces, Chandra, every time I thought about you in his arms. I never once allowed myself to really believe that you might be mine someday. I knew your loyalty to Phillip and your stubbornness combined would never let you come to me. I refused to even hope that what we had together would ever be permanent. The night I found out you had actually broken the engagement, I had to restrain myself from coming over to your parents' house and kidnapping you that evening. For the first time I really began to hope, Chandra—really began to believe that we had a future together."

"Garrett!" she exclaimed. "If you really felt that way, why didn't you come over? Why have you waited so long to try to see me?"

"You forget—I did try to see you. I called twice and you refused to talk to me either time. Then—well, hell! I got stubborn. I thought that if you loved me as much as I loved you, you would eventually break down and come to me. I knew I could give you until today to make the decision, before I took things in my own hands and came after you. There was *no way* I was going to let you go back to Kansas City."

Chandra smiled as her eyes glistened with unshed tears. She reached up to trace the outline of his lips with one finger, her love for him overflowing. "You tested me and I failed you. I've always told you I love you—that you could trust me not to hurt you—and I failed the first test miserably. I'm truly, truly sorry." She buried her face in his clean-smelling neck, the familiar scent of his aftershave tugging at her heartstrings.

"I'm more than willing to let you make it up to me," he whispered huskily, drawing her into a bone-crushing embrace. "In the future I'll let you know when I'm going to give a quiz on your love. That way you can bone up on ways to make me believe that you're mine . . . all mine." He moaned as his arms increased their pressure, nearly breaking Chandra in two with their intensity.

"Oh, Garrett," she murmured against his neck, her salty tears soaking the collar of his shirt. "There may be times when I'll fail you again in small ways, times I should tell you I love you and I don't say it, but I will never, never fail in my love *for* you. It will always be there strong and alive, whether I speak the words or not. I know you have had little reason to trust in any kind of love in your life, but I promise you you'll have mine for an eternity." She raised her face to his, tears of love and joy streaming down her cheeks. "And I would very much appreciate it if you would kiss me and help me get myself under control," she sobbed.

"With the greatest of pleasure, sweet lady. With the greatest of pleasure." Their lips met in a sweet reaffirmation of their love for one another, his mouth moving against hers, drinking deeply of her fountain of love. The feel of her had been denied him far too long, and he clasped her body intimately against his, hungering for her eager and willing body.

Chandra leaned into his solidness, her heart singing with ecstasy, her hands gently caressing the back of his neck, pressing his mouth deeply into hers. She knew without a doubt she had made the right decision. Her mom had been right, as she so often was. If two people really loved each other, it was worth whatever sacrifices she would have to pay. If he only gave her a month out of his life, she would take it and cherish the time spent with him forever.

"I think it's time you let me ask you what I've tried to all night," he murmured tenderly, kissing her eyes adoringly, trying to stop the flow of tears.

"I've just been up to Supply, Mr. Morganson, and you're lucky, there was one set of crutches left—oh, *excuse* me," a nurse said in embarrassment as she walked into the room.

"That's okay, nurse," Garrett replied calmly, his eyes gazing adoringly at Chandra. "This is the lady I told you about earlier."

"Oh, yes! I believe congratulations are in order," she smiled. "I understand you and Mr. Morganson are going to be married on New Year's Eve."

Chandra looked up in surprise at the nurse, noting that she was not one of the two who had been in earlier, then back to Garrett's smug face. "We are?"

"That's what I've been trying to tell you all night, sweetheart. If you weren't so hotheaded, you would have heard it hours ago."

"Tell me?" she bristled unconsciously. "Don't you mean *ask* me?" She was trembling almost violently, her pulse behaving erratically at the thought that he was asking her to marry him.

"No," he whispered softly, drawing her lips back down to his, "telling you. If I have to drag you to the altar, you'll marry me. You'll still have your marriage on the thirty-first, but this time instead of a nice, secure, hairless Phillip, there will be a tall, devastatingly handsome, mean, cussing, hairy bully of a test pilot standing next to you—whose life would not be the same without you." He kissed her long and convincingly, his lips reminding her that he was being flippant only because it was beyond his power to express the frightening depths of his love for her.

"I can't believe you're really asking me to marry you." Her arms hugged him tightly. "Is this what you really want, Garrett? I meant it earlier when I said I would live with you. No ties, no obligations—" His searching mouth cut hers off again.

"I hope you have a particularly . . . unique way you'll go about making me eat every bad word I've ever said about marriage," he whispered suggestively in her ear, his voice low because of the nurse standing across the room.

"I'll think of something while you're having your cast put on." She moistly touched his ear with her tongue. "Tell the doctor to hurry."

"Maybe they'll let me put it on myself," he moaned huskily, his hands seductively brushing one breast as she leaned weakly against him. "I'll tell them I have . . . pressing business to attend to."

"Oh, I love you, I love you, I love you," Chandra cried exuberantly, jerking her head up from his shoulder unexpectedly. It took Garrett by surprise as her mouth smashed against his roughly in her overzealous enthusiasm, her teeth biting into his lower lip. "Ohhhhh . . . darling! I'm sorry." Chandra stared at the bright spot of blood that appeared instantly on his bottom lip.

One large hand came down to wipe it away, stunned blue eyes staring resignedly at the amount of red on the back of his hand.

"I'm *sorry*, Garrett—I'm such a klutz!" Chandra stood beside him, wringing her hands. How much more could the poor guy be expected to take?

"No," Garrett held up one hand calmly, "don't think another thing about it. What's one more little cut? I'm too happy tonight to be upset if a diesel hit me in the parking lot."

Chandra and Garrett both looked up at the nurse and said in unison, "There're no trucks coming in here this time of night, are there?"

The nurse laughed. "Not that I know of."

Chandra turned back to Garrett, wiping at the small drops of blood trickling off his lip. "Oh, darling, when we get married, I promise I'll try to watch over you more carefully, and . . . I promise I'm going to learn to cook better," she vowed hurriedly.

"And I promise I'm going to watch my language when I'm around you, and I'm not going to get so upset with you over small things," Garrett promised her, sitting quietly as she dabbed insistently at his swelling lip.

"And I'm not going to cry as much—I know how much that upsets you—and I'll learn to control my temper. You won't be sorry you're asking me to marry you, Garrett," she assured him dutifully, listing all her weak points. "I'll even learn to play poker," she ended hastily.

"You don't have to learn to play poker," he grinned, catching her hand in his once again. "I don't want you changed in any way. As far as I'm concerned, as the song says, 'you're close enough to perfect for me.'" He lifted her hand, staring at it as he spoke. "Those are awfully small hands to hold my entire world in, Chandra, but I gladly give it to you. I trust you with all my future happiness. All I ever want out of you is your love." His blue eyes grew somber. "And I want it for the rest of our lives, Chandra. For me there will be only one woman in my life, and I've asked that woman to marry me. I haven't heard her answer yet."

"She answers yes, yes, a thousand times yes," she said, smiling radiantly.

"I really hate to break this up," the nurse said jovially, bustling over to the cart Garrett was sitting on. "We haven't had

187

this much excitement in here since the bus from the nudist colony turned over last summer, but—I'm afraid the doctor has arrived."

"You'll wait for me, won't you?" Garrett's eyes couldn't seem to leave hers as he held tight to her hand.

"Forever," she responded, kissing him again tenderly.

It seemed like hours before Garrett finally came through the emergency room doors again, but in actuality it wasn't that long at all. He hobbled through the doors on his crutches, a big, yellow balloon tied to one of them.

Chandra jumped up and walked over to take his arm, guiding him along the dim corridor of the hospital. The halls had hushed to a low murmur as the patients were being readied for the night, the entire building growing calm and peaceful.

"Where did you get your big balloon?" Chandra teased, tongue in cheek, as she held on to him tightly, his crutches tapping along the polished floor.

"That one damn nurse is as much of a clown as you are," he grunted, working his way painfully along the dim hall. "I guess with the prices these people charge, they want to send you out of here with something more than a pain in your"—he looked over and grinned at Chandra wryly—"git-along."

Chandra hugged his arm tightly. "Are you still in pain?"

"A little," he sighed heavily. "I don't know, Chandra—this rash of accidents has unnerved me. I've always prided myself on being careful, not taking too many unnecessary chances, but it's beyond me how I've managed to bust myself up like I have in the last three weeks," he fretted worriedly as they made their way slowly to the door.

"Oh, it's probably just one of those times in your life when weird things seem to happen to you," she soothed gently, gripping his arm tightly to steady him as his one good foot slipped on a puddle of melted snow at the entrance door. "Everyone has them. You'll probably go for years and not have another thing happen to you," she consoled reassuringly.

"I don't know," he said tiredly, clutching tighter to his crutches, regaining his balance shakily. "Maybe."

Chandra stopped and turned to face him, her arms going around his neck in loving admiration. "Whatever happens, I'll be here beside you. We'll both take care of each other. That's all that *really* matters, isn't it?"

He gave a weary grin and leaned forward to meet her ascending mouth. "Yeah, that's all that really counts . . . you sweet, dippy broad. Be careful of my lip!" he cautioned quickly as they met halfway in a kiss filled with promises of a brighter tomorrow.